the
'idiot spy'
(the series)
book five of ten

mechanized mayhem

c. benjamin lattimore

mechanized mayhem
Published: April 2021
Printed in the United States of America
ISBN: 978-1-7334945-4-0

DISCLAIMER: This is a work of fiction. Names, characters, businesses, places, events, and incidents are either the products of the author's imagination or used in a fictitious manner. Any resemblance to actual persons, living or dead, or actual events is purely coincidental.

a lattidreamer™ publication
© C. Benjamin Lattimore, 2021

To Marisa, my number 1 editor!
Thanks for your dedication to my passion.
I appreciate all that you do to help me with my projects!
Soon, I will get it right! (hahahaha)

ACKNOWLEDGEMENTS

To my children, Christopher, Monica, and Courtney, as well as my grandchildren, Isaiah, and Desmond for just being special. A unique and heartfelt expression of love to my sister, Mary E., and my brother, Darryl A. Again, venerate regards to Maurice Cheeks and Reggie Wilkes.

Special acknowledgements to Marisa, Dawn Marie, Nikki, and Jill.

Lots of love ethereally to my mom, Mary Alice, my dad, Walthro M., my little sister, Barbara Ann, and my big brother, Walter Eugene. Also, to my friends, Ernest Green, Gordon Gant, Joseph Bongiavanni III, Monique Gorham, Rahsaan Stevens and to my newest guardian angel, Mrs. Marjorie C. Cheeks.

CHAPTER ONE

In Russia, the testing program of the Carbon Factor had once again hit a snag because of a myriad of problems; poor assumptions, not adhering to the long standing principles of the periodic table, and impatiently trying to achieve efficacy at any price. After three failed attempts to develop the product, their efforts ended in the demise of additional scientists and engineers. Although some of those who accidentally stumbled across the formula were in various stages of investigation and intimidation, the bottom line was simple--the Russians needed the parts of the formula that inadvertently made its way to America and was under the control of an auspicious group of individuals.

The Russians' first attempt to create the Carbon Factor at a secret weapons testing plant was catastrophic, to say the least. The plant, the scientists, the formula, and other valuable information were destroyed in a blast that was felt around the globe. That blast placed the entire program in reverse, and as a result of trying to test concepts and not the actual formula, two additional catastrophic events would happen. Mother Russia was hell bent on being the first to produce the Carbon Factor and would stop at nothing to achieve her goal. After the previous expensive failures, the powers that be, suggested that the KGB get involved, find, and capture the American, at any cost, called the 'idiot spy'!

CHAPTER TWO

Everyone in the nearby vicinity rushed out of their homes after the massive ground shuddering explosion. As Courtney and the Sarge began to regain their senses, and as they looked back at the farmhouse, they were ecstatic to see that it was still standing. The duo began to clumsily make their way back to the farmhouse, to make sure that everyone was okay.

As members of the group exited the farmhouse and the guesthouse, almost all in a comatose state, they began asking, "what the hell just happened?"

Jong had the presence of mind to begin to take a head count. After three takes at doing it, he finally got it right and conveyed to the Sarge that all were present and accounted for. The Sarge instinctively yelled, "Form a perimeter! Everyone take cover!"

Ten minutes later, and without any apparent siege on the farm, the Sarge finally said, "I guess we're not the only persons of interest in this area."

Elsewhere, and in a secret bunker on the adjacent ex-senator's property, several cases of sweating C-4, nitroglycerin, and dynamite became interactive, and that collaboration concluded in an earth quivering episode. All's well that ends well!

CHAPTER THREE

It was as though Jong won the lottery when he randomly copied and erased sections of the data disks that the Carbon Factor formula was on. The remaining two parts of the formula contained the most critical aspects for a safe and controllable test of the Carbon Factor. Jong, in one million years of trying, would never be able to replicate his actions. He was unknowingly lucky but had the support of spirits far, far away when he cut parts of the formula that Helga and the developing scientist had deemed necessary in order to control the explosions. As long as the team controlled those final parts of the formula, they were almost certain to be safe from their government, but many others were also interested in the total formula. Walter, the group's nemesis, had 'left the reservation' and was seeking the team and their families to conclude their existence.

# # #

Despite the ever increasing threats to their lives, in middle America, members of the group were preparing to enter the institution of matrimony. Brown and Okema, along with John Lee and Somara, Jilkes and Yeshida, and Bernstein and Yvette, were all about to repeat the words "I do", to the officiating local preacher, who also went by the name of Clyde.

Clyde conducted the multiple wedding ceremony that was spectacular, and included words about helping each other, but always helping people to help themselves. It was a magnificent ritual. The feast that followed was larger than grand.

Ben Beckmire, aka the Sarge, had the privilege of walking each bride down the circular steps that led to the large veranda, where the nuptials took place. Although Okema's mother, typically kept a constant smile on her face, it was apparent she thought what was happening was a great thing. However, she continued to say to her daughter that she thought her husband was a little frail.

Later that night the sounds of love were abundant throughout the countryside. In some cases, the real reason for sex (creation) had already been accomplished. Okema, Somara and Yeshida were all pregnant, but only Brown was informed of his woman's condition. Although Somara and Yeshida had missed their cycles, it was a bit premature to fully ordain the notion that both women were mothers-to-be.

Ava, on the other hand, was wondering what was going on in the mind of Carlos. She wondered if Carlos was simply happy to have her as a lover or was there the possibility of a long-term relationship. Her uncertainty and insecurity were heightened because all around her people were getting married and/or preparing to have babies. Ever astute, Courtney noticed that Ava was withdrawn and delicately broached the issue with her. Ava finally admitted that she was becoming a victim of the nuptial atmosphere and Courtney tried to reassure her of Carlos's commitment.

#

Earlier, while the women fretted over affairs of the heart and hair, the men focused on concluding financial arrangements for Carlos and his men. Each man was given amounts between $3 and $4 million dollars, with the promise of another endowment in the coming months, to show the team's appreciation for the work of Carlos and his crew.

When the Sarge told Carlos of his plans, Carlos shared with the Sarge that if Ms. De Lombardo would have him, he would now ask her for her hand. His delay in proposing, as he explained to the Sarge, was that he felt as though they could finally, comfortably live on his money without him having to ask her for any. Carlos thanked the Sarge for the generous gift on behalf of himself and his men.

Almost everyone was happy and the mood was ever so festive, but the patriarch of the group, Ben Beckmire, was ever mindful of the fact that a cacodemon was looking for him and his crew. Therefore, he feigned his look of having a great time while simultaneously checking in with Clyde's people to make sure that all were accounted for and that they were remaining vigilant and watching over those who were having fun. He knew that in the morning, the entire group would be on their plane heading for their retreat in St. Thomas for ten days of rest and relaxation. He hoped he'd also be able to let his own guard down once they were safely in the Caribbean.

CHAPTER FOUR

In St. Thomas, the first thing on the group's agenda was to bask in the sun and feel the effects of it on their bodies. Carlos, who now felt that he had something to offer his lover and former employer, had secretly arranged with the resort's purveyor and their partner, Mr. Carter, to have a table set near the water. He had also arranged for musicians to provide soft and ambient sounds while he and Ms. Ava De Lombardo watched the sunset. This would be the perfect opportunity for him to prevail upon Ava to become his wife.

Carlos hitched a ride into town under the watchful eyes of Gladstone and Whitmore. Once in town, he went to Mr. Bassman's jewelry store. It was recommended to him by Mr. Carter. Mr. Carter also told Carlos to insist on at least a 10% discount on purchases up to $5 thousand and 15% for all deals over $10 thousand. Ever mindful of this information, Carlos walked into the store and began to look around at the merchandise and immediately became intrigued by a ring that was two full carats with small emeralds on each side. He decided upon the ring and told the owner that he was interested in that particular ring but needed him to consider discounting it by 15%. The owner asked him if he would like to know the price of the ring before asking for a discount and Carlos inelegantly stated that he did.

After settling on what was a fair price, Carlos handed him a credit card. Whitmore walked over and whispered in his ear,

"That card can be tracked. Why don't we lend you the cash and you can take care of us later?"

When the three men added up their cash, it became apparent that they didn't have enough funds on them to pay for the ring. The owner interrupted their conference and asked if they were familiar with Mr. Christopher Carter, and Gladstone replied, "That's our partner down here. Why do you ask?"

"If you fellows don't have enough cash to pay for this product right now, then the next time you're in town, pay me the balance."

Carlos responded, "The difference is going to be close to $5,000."

Mr. Bassman said, "I feel like I know you and I trust you guys because old man Carter didn't have a leg to stand on, and those people at that bank were going to stick him so deep that he wouldn't have a penny to get off the island. Everyone knows about what you guys did including your work with that adjacent property. Hell, if I can't trust honest people who help people and don't try to rip them off, then who in the hell, can I trust?"

Whitmore said, "We appreciate the confidence, but take my card and make an imprint in case we have to leave in a hurry, your money will be protected. My friend's card is from Spain and who knows how the hell, they do business over there. I'm just kidding, but my card is our corporate card. Hold it until someone either pays you or calls you and tells you to use the card. Is that okay with you?"

"Listen guys, keep your card and get back to me whenever you have the cash." Mr. Bassman insisted. He further stated, "You know when you pay with cash that's another 3% off the sticker price."

"Okay, then we will definitely be paying with cash. I will have someone deliver it to you this evening or first thing in the morning," Carlos announced.

The more Carlos held the ring, the more he knew it was perfect for Ava. "I can't leave this store without this ring and one of those temporary ring guards. I don't know the size of her finger," Carlos announced.

Mr. Bassman smiled, "Okay, let me wrap this up and you can pay me what you want now and pay the rest later."

"Sounds like a plan to me," Carlos said.

# # #

Gladstone was closely monitoring some activity outside of the store and called Whitmore over and requested, "Look at that guy near the fabric store. You see him?"

"He looks like one of our pilots," Whitmore replied.

"Exactly! Now, look over near that restaurant a block down," Gladstone suggested.

"What the hell! That looks like another one of our pilots," Whitmore responded.

"Okay, now look hard in the lotion and shampoo store," Gladstone requested.

"Oh shit, that looks like another one of our pilots," Whitmore instinctively touched his weapon.

"Let's just watch the interaction and see what happens. It appears to me that two of them are watching the guy near the fabric store. Oh wait, that's where the international phone is, I think," Gladstone announced. To confirm his hunch, Gladstone asked, "Mr. Bassman, is the international phone over by the fabric store?"

"Yes sir, that is exactly where it is."

Gladstone looked at Whitmore and said, "Let's just keep observing this charade and try to discern what the hell is going on."

As the three men watched the action, it was crystal clear that the person near the phone was extremely anxious. Carlos exclaimed, "I think I see and smell a rat! That guy is looking over his shoulder and is sweating like a pig! He's up to no good. We should intervene and find out what he's up to!"

Whitmore said, "No, let's see what the reactions of the other pilots are. I mean we must think about whether there is a coup of some kind going on. They seem to be watching him like a hawk and are trying to stay out of sight."

Gladstone said, "I agree; we don't do nothing, but observe. Whitmore, give Jong a call and see if he's aware of his people being in town."

The pilot nearest to the fabric store, walked to the phone and looked at his watch as if he had to be exact in his timing. After looking at his watch and surveying the environment, he retreated into an alcove. Two minutes later, he walked to the phone and again looked carefully at his watch as the other two pilots began to make their way directly to his position.

At exactly 1400 hours, he retrieved a piece of paper from his pocket and began to dial the number that was written on it. As he got halfway through the dialing process, he saw a fellow pilot moving his way with his hand under his shirt. He dropped the phone and attempted to run in the opposite direction. He then saw another fellow pilot with a weapon fully exposed. Gladstone and Carlos walked out onto the street from the jewelry store as Whitmore made his way around the back of the building and eventually onto a terribly busy street. It was apparent that all exits had been covered and that the pilot had a single option out of this dilemma, and that was to conclude his life or prepare his body for the new age torture and extraction procedure that John Lee would gladly provide.

Whitmore called Jong and told him he suspected that they had a rogue pilot who was selling information. Jong asked him how he knew that to be the case. Whitmore responded by saying, "I don't know for sure, but two of our other pilots have been following him and have him in their midst. We're probably going to need someone to extract him. Is John Lee available?"

"I have to take this issue to the Sarge and Mallory. Listen, I'm not going to second guess you guys, but get all of them back here and I will have the proper response ready to relate to the issue. You know I like for the Sarge and Mallory to make certain decisions. Secure him and bring him back to The Sanctuary."

One hour later and in a private room on their expansion property, the two loyal pilots, along with Gladstone, Carlos, and Whitmore entered with the pilot who was being watched. Gladstone said, "Guys, you know one of our faults is that we have not included you in our missions and have not asked you to be one of us. When my people get here and whether we find this pilot is innocent or corrupt, then we will have to develop a new kind of relationship. Now, the question is simple--is he reporting on you, or are you reporting on him? I don't know, but somewhere in this equation, someone is going to have to make a whole pie out of nothing more than a slice of bread. No one leaves this room and, for your own sake, do not talk at all about anything. No talking, whatsoever. If you speak, you will be summarily executed."

A few minutes later, Jong walked into the room and began to yell in his native tongue that no one understood. He finally calmed down and said in English, "Someone is going to have their nuts extracted from their body." He looked at Gladstone and said, "Call John Lee and Jilkes and tell them they have work to do."

Approximately ten minutes later, Jilkes and John Lee walked into the room. John Lee calmly said, "I want to try a new way of cutting nuts off." Jong took the liberty of reintroducing John Lee and Jilkes to the group and in detail, bragged about how he gutted Scottie from her vagina to her brain while she watched him, in a fear induced state, before he took a bite out of her heart.

Gladstone said to the two guys doing the apparent surveillance, "Me and my associates watched you two perform a cloak and dagger operation on this guy. Now, is the time for you to fully explain what that was all about." One of the pilots was about to speak when the other one said, "Let me do this."

"Mr. Jong gave us an incredible opportunity to provide a needed service for you people, in the form of being pilots and watching over your aircrafts. Our only female pilot took a liking to this guy but realized that there was something else at play with him. She deduced that he had alternative motives and they were not in the best interest of the group. She said at first, she just thought he was an aggressive flirt, but realized that someone else controlled his strings.

"On two occasions, in public, he was fully compromised by his reactions to a series of phone calls that made him look as though he was someone's bitch. At first, she said she ignored it, but then realized that he would leave the group and then rejoin them with a different attitude. She was thinking that he was married and was tracking his wife.

On a different evening, while at dinner, he went to the restroom and she noticed his phone buzzing with a request for his coordinates. She thought it was odd, but the second message was clear and more obvious, 'you must do this, or your family will pay the price'. At that point she decided to rethink her involvement and told me she suspected this guy was going to blow it for all of us. She thought he had a conflict of interest. It was at that point that I decided to watch him and try to figure out what was going on."

"Why didn't you mention it to me that you suspected that one of yours had a conflict of interest?" Jong inquired.

"Mr. Jong, you and your people treat us extremely well and pay us even better. We like what we do and wanted to handle this situation in our own manner to avoid involving you and your group until we had something significant to report. Our goal was to find out what he was up to and then present it to you guys. All we had was conjecture, but that created enough suspicion for us to want to resolve this before he was in control of another plane with you guys on it. Other than what we have assumed about this guy, the rest of us are loyal and love what we do for you guys."

The pilot in question looked at John Lee and said, "Listen, I have heard what you do to people to make them talk. Let me start by saying, I will tell you everything you want to know, and you won't have to cut me or decapitate any aspect of my body."

Jilkes said, "That seems fair enough. However, we have corroborating information that confirms that someone is in control of your life. You care to tell us who it is? Just be mindful of the fact that your left arm will be cut off at your elbow if you lie. If it is an egregious distortion, then you will watch as my skillful friend cuts your leg off at the knee. Now, let me remind you, this will all be done without the use of pain killers or sedatives, and, therefore, the pain will be enormous."

The pilot pleaded, "Those people have my wife and children under their watchful eyes. Thus, they have engaged me to spy on this group and make periodic reports about your whereabouts."

"How on earth did they capture your essence? How were you exposed?"

"They knew all about your new plane and apparently I was the weak link, in that I had the most to lose. What they didn't know is that I played both sides of the street. I reconfigured my phone and programmed it to show options that were not a part of what was visibly shown to them in my reports. Listen, I was trying to find a way to keep my family from harm, and yet, not expose you guys to any danger."

John Lee asked, "Where be your family at this time?"

"They're in DC, and the people who are forcing me to track you guys sends me pictures of my children inside of my house, as well as photos of my wife bathing. They clearly have my family under surveillance."

Jilkes said, "Show me how you double deal and protect us from these people."

"I simply installed a pre-programmed Sim card into my phone that sends pictures and provides false coordinates. They can never break my code because I created it myself and I know it's good."

"When they be sending you threats, do you be knowing where they be coming from?" John Lee asked.

"I do and they're usually never near where my family is which makes me wonder about how they are tracking me and my phone."

Jilkes asked John Lee, and Jong, to huddle with him. Once alone, he said, "I half-ass kind of believe what this dude is saying. Now, my question is simple--do you guys have any faith in what he says?"

John Lee replied, "I really believe him, but I need to bleed him to verify what I be hearing him say. I just need to cut him lightly and see his reaction. I mean, I know when people be scared to death, they react differently."

The men broke their huddle and walked over to the pilots. Jilkes told Jong to call the Sarge and Mallory and invite them down for a castration. The pilot in the chair screamed, "I told you the truth and everything that I know. Where is your honor?"

Jilkes unsheathed his blade and said, "My honor is in trusting people to trust us and reporting to us when they have been compromised. You clearly have been compromised and now you have placed us all in jeopardy based upon some bullshit program that you think provides false GPS monitoring!" Jilkes exclaimed.

"Sir, I don't have to think about what my program does because I know what it provides and how it manipulates incoming calls to disorient their systems."

John Lee walked over to the pilot, also pulled out his knife and said, "That sounds like a bunch of pigshit to me and I'm going to bleed you out." He then ran the knife across the left leg of the pilot to let him see the blood ooze out of his leg. The pilot screamed, "Stop, stop, I beg you. I'm a hemophiliac. I will bleed to death unless I'm treated."

John Lee paused and remembered hearing those words before, and said, "I once knew a guy who was one of those and we thought he was joking so he bled to death right in the bar from a simple cut on his hand. You be one of those kinds of people who bleeds really fast?"

"I am the poster child. I will need medical attention shortly or I will be the second person you will watch bleed out."

Jilkes looked at him and said, "I am the only one who trusts you. I am going to get you to the hospital, but if you're not telling the truth, you will watch me authorize a $3 million dollar hit on your entire family including your children. If you're fucking lying to me then you will have the unfortunate memory of watching your children butchered in front of you. Do you understand what I'm saying?"

"I understand clearly what you are saying and I'm saying that I have not betrayed anyone. I just tried to handle the situation by myself."

Jilkes continued, his interrogation, "If you are so worried about your family, why on earth were you trying to pursue a relationship with our only female pilot?"

"Unless you're blind, she is absolutely gorgeous and one sexy woman. I need to get to the hospital or I'm going to die right before your eyes," the pilot indicated.

John Lee gave Jilkes the nod and Jong seconded it and told their pilots that what they did was in their best interest but what was needed were decisions that were in the best interest of the entire group. Jong called the Sarge and told him that he needed Courtney's expert advice.

A few minutes later when Courtney arrived on the scene with the Sarge, she asked, "What's up guys? Isn't he one of our pilots?"

"He is, and he claims to be a hemophiliac or something like that," Jilkes stated.

"That is nothing to play with. That cut is significant to a bleeder and we need to get this guy to a hospital in a hurry or wait for him to bleed out."

"You heard the lady, move people. Why don't you pilots escort him to the hospital. In the meantime, interrogate him, figure out what is fact and what is fiction, and whether we have to pull a rescue mission for his family. Jong, if you're not busy, why don't you and Whitmore accompany them? I mean if we can't trust the guys or lady flying our planes, then we have another fucking problem that we have to address," the Sarge indicated.

After the group left the hotel, the Sarge said, "I have the number to a detective in Hollywood, Florida, who uses a bunch of drugs and a lie detector test to determine the truth. I will call him and suggest that he make his way down here tomorrow and we can put each one of them through the test. Any thoughts about that?"

Jilkes said, "Hell, it's bad enough we have to worry about mechanical issues. Now, if we can't trust our pilots then we're shit out of luck."

"I be agreeing with my man," John Lee stated, "We give them a chance to tell us all the bad shit that they be done did and then we check it against that there lies detecting shit. I like that plan. I'm glad I thought of it."

## CHAPTER FIVE

The Sarge called Allen and generally inquired about what was going on, how he was holding up, and whether he needed more cash. Allen told the Sarge that the news about Walter had dried up and he thought that was not a good sign. He indicated to the Sarge that there was not even a rumor on the streets about any clandestine activities and/or groups being recruited. The Sarge also thought that it was too quiet for comfort and asked Allen to keep his ears extra close to the ground and to inform him of the slightest intel that may impact his group.

# # #

That evening, romantic music was being pumped from the new intercom system and it filled the air with smiles. Courtney asked Mr. Carter if they could look forward to music every evening and he responded, "Your wish is my command. You must admit, it does kind of make you smile and make you just want to cozy up to someone special and have a nice cocktail."

"Great touch! Now, only if I could find my husband," Courtney stated.

#

Carlos called Ava and asked her if she would like to take a walk on the beach and she told him that she had a headache. He advised her that it was a beautiful evening and it would truly please him if she would walk with him along the beach. Prior to asking Ava to take a walk, he asked John Lee, Jilkes, Somara, and Yeshida to lounge around the table on the beach and act as if it was for them.

Ava reluctantly came down to the lobby and emphasized, "Carlos, I really have a headache and I am tired."

"Mi amante, please stroll with me because I feel inferior to the people in this group and I need to talk with you or I'm going to head back home in the morning." That statement caught Ava by surprise, and she started to cry. Carlos, naively asked, "Why are you crying? I'm the one who should be crying because I have nothing to offer you except my eternal love. I mean, people all around us are getting married even though it seems they barely know each other, and I have known you for a great deal of time but unfortunately, it was as an employee. This transition has caused me a tremendous amount of stress, and I feel that I needed time to consider mine as well as your possibilities, as I see them."

As they walked on the beach, Ava saw Jilkes and John Lee, along with Somara and Yeshida and she continued to cry. Carlos caressed her and said, "Ava De Lombardo, I love you with all of my heart and soul, but I cannot keep you appointed in the lifestyle that you are accustomed to and maintain my dignity as a man in the interim. I am no soldier of fortune, nor am I a gigolo. I am a man with strong Catholic principles and a love for a woman that the world has never known before."

"Carlos, I love you, but it makes me sad that the country bumpkin and his boyfriend can arrange to have an oceanside table with romantic music playing for them and their loved ones. I don't think that would have cost a tremendous amount of money. I just need to be loved and honored. I don't give a shit about money or your ego. I just happen to have a ton of money, and you are the man that I want to spend every damn penny of it on. Yes, I'm going to go there!

"I have never loved another man since Ben Beckmire and circumstances have us all together once again, but on a helluva mental rush. I don't need much. What you need to do is simple--pick a rose from the garden, embellish a stone with our initials painted or carved on it, take a selfie of the two us doing stupid, but most importantly, love me like I mean something to you and let it never be about money. I detest that notion and that is why I love what this group does with their money—they give it to great causes. We can do the same thing. Zanthius, I can tell you, does not want a ton of money. All he wants, is that woman who will hurt you bad if you look at her man in the wrong way."

On the beach, Carlos and Ava shared extremely passionate kisses. John Lee said, "Hell, I bet you $1 they don't make it to this here setup."

"I'll bet you $1,000 they do and within the next ten minutes," Jilkes said.

Three minutes later, Carlos and Ava walked near the table, hand in hand and he asked, "Are you guys going to exclusively use this table or can we join in the festivities?"

"This here table is for all of us who love someone deeply. I love Somara; I love Yeshida; I love you too, Ms. Ava and I love you, Carlos. Most of all, I love Jilkes. Now, that be a lot of love, but that be the way I be feeling. Why don't we let them have our favorite table for a minute and we go inside and get some of them there drinks with the umbrellas inside of them."

As Carlos held the chair for Ava, the entire team and hotel staff appeared on the beach to watch Carlos drop to his knees, pull out the engagement ring from his pocket, and ask Ava De Lombardo to marry him. Ava cried hysterically, but mustered the ability to shout, "Yes!"

Courtney said, "Okay, too much water going out and not enough going in. Okay, people, back to the bar until I get our next bride hydrated and under control."

"Did you know about this?" Ava asked Courtney.

"No, but if I did, I wouldn't have spoiled the occasion. Listen, shut up, drink the water, and enjoy the night. That is a fabulous ring. Did you pick that out by yourself, Carlos?"

"I did! When I saw it, it had my fiancée's name all over it." Ava and Carlos embraced again.

The Sarge had started his retreat to the hotel bar when he said to himself, "I am a much better human being than this." He turned around and walked back towards the group with everyone watching him. Courtney saw her man coming towards her and decided to let him be who he is--a wonderful human being who loves a lot of people.

Beckmire said, "Listen, I know there are moments when things are a little awkward and, perhaps, even a little uncomfortable. I just want to say that I'm comfortable, and I appreciate the way that you two have blended in with our team and have provided protection for all of us. Carlos, she is one hell of a woman; but keep an eye on her. She has a habit of disappearing. I still love Ava, but I'm in love with this beauty next to me. I wish you both the best and I wouldn't change a damn thing if I controlled time. Love to all!"

CHAPTER SIX

Jong called Mary Alice to meet him for a drink and swim. Since she did not answer the phone, he decided to go to her room. He knocked on the door, called her name, but there was no answer. He saw one of the hotel staff in the hallway and asked her to open the door because he suspected there was a medical emergency. She placed her key into the slot, but the deadbolt was on. Jong started screaming, and John Lee walked out into the hallway and asked what was going on. After a brief explanation, John Lee looked at the door and slammed his foot into it sending parts of the door flying into the room. As Jong and John Lee entered the room, it became apparent that Mary Alice was in a drug induced state. John Lee called the Sarge and told him to send Dr. Courtney to Room 323 because Mary Alice was comatose. When Courtney arrived at the room, she found Mary Alice unconscious and told the guys to get ready to transport her to the hospital. Mary Alice had overdosed on her insulin shot.

#

Much, much later, at the local hospital, the doctors conferred and deduced that the newly prescribed medicine was the wrong dosage and that the injection pen she used was faulty. When she came to and saw Courtney and Jong she said, "I feel totally naked and embarrassed. I should have, at some point in time, told you that I require insulin shots."

"I'm not concerned about what you use, but how you feel right now. Are you okay?" Courtney inquired.

She started to cry and Jong, uncharacteristically, embraced her and told her that he was happy that she was okay. He also said, "I need to pay closer attention to you. You, my dear, must get over those ghosts in your life. When you get out of here, you will move in with me and we will discuss our next steps as a couple, and not as friends. Now, that is of course, if you're on the same page, but it will be your call."

"I was beginning to think that you found me unattractive or something. You kiss me on the cheek when I want you to kiss my lips, and you hug me like a friend when I need you to hug me like your lover. My ghosts will disappear in time with the proper help from someone who sees me as a lover and not as a friend."

Courtney said, "Well, Mr. Amazing, it sounds as though someone is asking for a different Jong to show-up. It also sounds like you need to get busy with the personal side of this equation and the other things will take care of themselves."

# # #

Once rehydrated, Ava was the queen of the ball. Mr. Carter's staff prepared a fabulous meal for her and Carlos and the wine kept flowing and well-wishers passed by and congratulated the two on their engagement. Carlos said to Ava, "You know Mr. Beckmire and his team thanked me and the guys for our support and the dependability that we provide them. Their team endowed us with approximately $3 to $4 million for each man. I now feel that those funds are a good beginning for us and that I also have something to contribute, ergo the engagement ring. As a man, I cannot sit back and live off your funds. At least now, I can come to the table with something to offer and not be looked at as your gigolo."

"Carlos, the money is inconsequential. When it comes to the way I feel about you, if you like, we can give it all away and just exist off your money. Do you like that idea?"

"Ava, that is the dumbest thing I have ever heard you say. I don't want you to give your fortune away. I just want to be able to take my soon-to-be wife to dinner without asking her to leave the tip."

"Honey, I'm done with the conversation about money. Is there anything else on your mind that we should talk about, such as, when the hell we are going to get married?"

"Ava, I just want to share in our costs. Now, insofar as my love is concerned, that is another matter. But really, I need to feel needed financially even though I know you need me in other ways that are equally as important as money. I will love and honor you, cherish the sand you walk on, always end and begin our days with a hug and kiss, pull your chair out, open doors for you, and love you for all eternity."

"Carlos, you are the light I kept in the dark for protection, who has become the man I plan on marrying and loving until death do us part. Under my nose for most of my life but dissuaded to pursue by a grumpy old man. You were finally there in my moment of need. I love you so and I'm sure you know that Zanthius is happy with our union as well. My son is so lucky to have two mothers and two fathers who all love him unequivocally. I was once your employer, then your mistress, now your lover, and soon, your wife. Each of these stages have shown me the man that you are, and I will forever love you through infinity."

## CHAPTER SEVEN

Allen gave Beckmire a courtesy call and relayed to him the chatter on the street, as well as some critical information from Mike, Walter's former protégé. He told Beckmire that a group of thirty strong had been hired in Japan. Beckmire asked him how he knew that, and Allen told him about the number of visas that had been applied for, their point of demarcation, and that they were all due there in one week. He also told Beckmire that according to Mike, on the local level an equal number of people had been recruited, mostly ex-military, Desert Storm era, a few from the Vietnam timetable, and one from Korea. Beckmire thanked him, told him to stay low and to create a disappearing act for him and his people because he may need to hide several woman and children.

#

The night ended with Beckmire saying to the group, "Tomorrow, we will get back into shape. It appears that a fleet of dragons are coming from across the water and one is being resurrected on this side of the water to present a final solution to us. Gentlemen and ladies, my cousin has hired premium groups of people, from near and far, to conclude our existence. I want to make sure that we are capable of handling them as well. People, they apparently are the best of this genre. They think they're Ninja, and that we're old and near dead. Tomorrow, we shall at a minimum pace run and walk ten miles. We have received the suppression devices and I think once we get back to Virginia, the time will be right to test our ODS."

Whitmore asked, "Sarge, what the hell, is the ODS?"

"Whit, I'm glad you asked. My son, Zanthius, and Mr. Amazing had his infamous cousin install machine pistols all around the farm that are controlled by our iPhones. To me, it sounds like mechanized mayhem. We didn't have the ability to test the system because we didn't have the suppression devices to affix to the weapons to reduce the noise levels. When Jong gets comfortable with his new relationship, and gets her over her misuse of her drug, I will engage him to teach us how to target a sector and eliminate all intruders by simply hitting a button. In the meantime, I need all of you people to love and love hard as if there were no tomorrow."

John Lee inquired, "That there tone be misleading. Are you expecting a problem and, if so, how do we get it under control?"

"We get domination of them by being prepared like we were in the jungle. There are going to be at least sixty-five or more people coming for us to terminate our existence and, more importantly, that of the children in our group. I think we have at least five days to sharpen our skills, as well as recognize the fact, that our women are not going to leave our sides. Perhaps we should ease them into the inevitable and mentally disturbing notion of eradicating another human being. If, in fact, we can't depend on them to pull the trigger, then we all will be moments away from a horrifying death."

#

The next day, people were lined up in front of the hotel in their jogging outfits. Ava said to Courtney, "Now, that is a very bright outfit. Are you trying to be seen by people on Mars?"

"No, girl. I just wanted to upstage that grey mess you're wearing."

"Now, that sounds like a slight, but I started it, so I'll let that round go to you. Okay, no fooling, where did you get it?"

"You stood next to me in Target, where the yellow brick road is. I guess you must have had that devil of a man on your mind. I guess you feel a lot better since he gave you that eye blinding ring."

"I guess I just didn't want to be the only one in the group who wasn't getting it on with someone that they loved."

"You're happy about this matter, right?"

"Sometimes I am, and sometimes I'm not," Ava confessed. "I mean I have strong feelings for Carlos, but he just doesn't get the work done that I need in the bedroom, if you know what I mean."

"Honey, you need to bring that conversation up at your next meeting. If there are unmet expectations on either side of the fence, then that will lead to a disastrous relationship and, in your case, potential divorce before marriage. Don't waste any time. Have that talk and be descriptive, so he doesn't have to guess what you want, what you need, how you need it, and where you want it. You also might inquire about what he likes, in the process."

"You're really one crazy woman. I can't imagine having a detailed conversation with him about that."

"Well then, I suggest you give him back the ring and move on because these things called marriages require a shit load of constant work plus a boat load of give and take. I think, in your case, you have always been the queen and, as such, have had your way. In a meaningful relationship, there is no king or queen! Just two people trying to make sure they are healthy, happy and horny (HHH)."

"The Sarge interrupted by yelling, "Saddle up, people. We need to run some of those drinks with umbrellas in them, out of us. This is going to be at a slow pace, and we want to cover a distance of ten miles. Now, more importantly, I need you people to pair up with someone and no matter what happens, do not leave that person or let them out of your sight."

Ava whispered to Courtney, "Can we have drinks later? I need your advice on how to train my dragon."

"It would be my pleasure because, girl, I had to break down Mr. Ben and then reconstruct his notion of satisfying me. I think it will be fun, but I hope Carlos does not see us and figure out it's me who is putting vile ideas in your head."

# # #

During the walk/run, the Sarge would occasionally gather his troops and say, especially to the women, "If you are assigned to guard a door and a hostile attempts to break in, what would be your response?" He called on Marisa because he knew that she and Ava had already participated in the taking of a life.

Marisa responded, "I would have to do what I did at the farm, and that was not to hesitate, but immediately aim my weapon and fire at the intended target."

"How did you feel after taking someone's life?"

"Very little, since he was not there to invite me to a party."

The group walked/ran a few more miles and the Sarge huddled with them again and asked, "Monica, a man is approaching you with a knife in his hand with the intent to kill you. What would be your response?"

"First, I hope that doesn't happen, but if it does, I will aim as my husband taught me and I would fire my weapon without turning my head and make sure that I have at least disabled my potential attacker. Sarge, once we get back to wherever we're going, I will be on the firing range and I will be accurate and conclusive."

"What on earth does that mean?"

"No one hurts my husband, my friends, and my true friends who are on this beach with me this morning. Therefore, ole fearless leader, my aim will be precise."

At the eight-mile mark, the Sarge said, "Rashida, you have been awful quiet. Will you be participating in target practice when we get back?"

"Sarge, they placed a suicide vest on my baby. It was at that moment that I swore to never leave my or any child that I know vulnerable. Therefore, I, too, will be firing until I am as precise as Monica."

The Sarge said, "The key to our continued survival is based upon what we each will do beyond our comfort zones. To take another human being's life is not an easy task. However, if that human being is determined to take your life or the lives of any member of this group, then it is important for you to have our six. Each person here must be willing to pull that trigger and reload their weapon and pull that trigger again and again."

The Sarge continued, "Historically, this thing has been handled by me, my boys, Carlos, and his men, and I want to publicly, state that they are not only some of the finest fighters that I have run across, but they are also our friends. Lately, we have been helped by our new lady friends from across the pond. So, people, I'm looking for the day when I can call you guys on the phone and have a thirty-minute call and hear babies hollering in the background without having to watch our six. I want this to end so we all can go back to civilization, that place that includes others who are not trying to hurt us.

"Okay, going back is going to be two moderately paced walks/runs--one slow as a turtle walk, one almost fast run, and then you're on your own. Tomorrow, is for the diehards—a five miler with a clock. Be there or be square."

Courtney was watching as one of Carlos's guys was staring stupidly at Rashida. Finally, he walked over to Rashida and said, "I am an expert shot and I would like to show you how to use your choice of weapons."

Rashida smiled and asked, "Why do you want to show me? Some of the other ladies don't know much about guns either."

"They are not as cunning and as beautiful as you are. They are also interested in other people. I have noticed that you are not attached and that you mainly keep an eye on the children--a thing that I admire," the guy stated.

"Do you have children back in Spain?" Rashida slyly asked to draw this guy off base.

"Oh, no. I was once in love with a woman in Spain. After being gone so long, she found someone else. I guess our love wasn't meant to last the test of time. She is now parading around with one of my ex-friends and I hear that she has joined the ranks along with his other admirers. I guess for me it is probably the best outcome since I'm such a romanticist. As young and beautiful as you are, why are you not attached?"

"You seem to have a lot of compliments today. I've seen you, but you never said a single word to me. Why is that?" Rashida asked.

"I have been practicing this speech for over four months. I am not the most forward person, but eventually, I make myself accountable."

"And just how do you make yourself accountable? And what is your name?"

"I am so sorry, Ms. Rashida. My name is Carlos Juan Montaego. You may call me Juan if you like."

"How do you know my name?"

"I have only been watching you since you showed up at the farm."

"Why are you suddenly having so much to say to me, Juan?"

"I'm not sure you are aware, but we suddenly had a significant payday and I now feel as though I am able to come to you with some semblance of status. If your wish is that I first approach Mr. Beckmire and let him know of my intent, then I will do that. However, I must admit, whenever I'm around him, he scares the shit out of me. I saw him hold Jong in the air with one hand and no one should be able to do that to another human being. Jong is not a feather."

"Wait, Juan, I might be just a little slow, but what are we talking about here?"

"Ms. Rashida, I am willing, if you are willing, to explore and entertain the notion of a strong union between the two of us. I have watched you and have also admired you. The first time I saw you I told *mi amigos,* that I thought I was in love. It was after the incident in the Midwest when the children had those vests placed on them that I felt useless and unable to protect you. My heart flutters whenever I see you. I will speak with Mr. Beckmire and ask him if he would allow me to have brunch with you, of course, in front of other women to protect your honor."

Rashida said, "Juan, before you speak to anyone it might be best to speak to me and ask me how I feel. The Sarge is my father--he is not my owner. Although, I will admit, if someone were to hurt me, then he would probably break their back or something crazy like that. So, before you start thinking about who it is, I am, you had better decide to ask me if I'm interested in exploring a conversation with you about anything. You got that? And where the hell did you learn to speak English like you do?"

"Ms. Rashida, the last thing on earth I wanted to do was offend you. I am not accustomed to the ways of your men, but I thought it was in my best interest to ask Mr. Beckmire if I could at least have tea with you in front of the group to make sure that there was no opportunity for gossip."

"Dude hold up. I am no child bride. I have a child. I am a fully constituted woman and again, if you want to speak and have tea with me, then you had better ask me and not Mr. Beckmire. I am in charge of this temple. Mr. Beckmire just happens to be my overlord."

"Ms. Rashida, I feel as though I have shot myself in the foot. The approach I bring to you was suggested by *mi amigos,* because we truly don't understand how things work in your country. If you think about it, I have been preoccupied with providing protection for the group and ending lives of your enemies, a task that I'm not so proud of."

Rashida exclaimed, "Juan, here is the deal. Me and my child will be swimming in the ocean in thirty minutes. If you want to join us and have some fun, as well as meet my child, then you are more than welcome. Discard the formality and remember to respect me at all times and we just might have a chance to begin a long-term conversation!"

"Done! I must go and buy swimming trunks. Should I at least mention to Mr. Beckmire that we are going to go swimming?"

"Juan, if you do, then you will be swimming by yourself. Do you understand what I'm saying?" Juan bowed his head and walked off.

Courtney said to Ava, "Well, I'll be damn, that guy that works for you is making a play for my daughter."

"Is that a problem?" Ava inquired.

"Let's get those drinks first and then we'll talk because sometimes your arrogance or your 1%-er comes out," Courtney stated.

"Courtney, what the hell are you talking about?" Ava asked.

"Oh, there's Monica, let's invite her to have a drink with us. She'll probably order ginger ale or some lame drink like that, but she's fun."

As Monica walked over, she asked, "Are you guys having soda or real drinks?"

Courtney replied, "I don't know about Ava, but this drink is a pina colada maximus."

"That's what I want," Monica announced.

Courtney interjected, "When did you start drinking?"

"Courtney, I drink frequently. I just can't hang with you, that's all," Monica amplified.

Courtney yelled to the bartender and he knew exactly what she was ordering. Ava said, "So, Monica, you look a little bit out of sorts after our ten mile hike, walk, and run."

"And it's not about the walk, hike, and run. No girl, as John Lee would say, that be about that crazy-ass white boy I married," Monica replied.

Courtney said, "Oh my, you too?"

"What's that, 'you too shit', Courtney?"

"Well, Ms. Ava De Lombardo got engaged on that very same beach that we're looking at and now doesn't want to be a member of that party."

"No! Ava, did you have an epiphany or something?" Monica asked.

"No, he has this bedroom antic that I don't like, and he thinks that I'm a vessel for his enjoyment," Ava announced.

"Take him to church and tell him that shit don't work." Monica replied. "Listen, my husband wants to continuously protect me, even when he fucking can't. He thinks that I'm too much of a lady to handle a fucking gun. I told him that I'm not going back home without him and, therefore, every adventure he goes on, I go the fuck on. Then he asked, 'why do you use the word fuck so much'? I smiled and replied, 'because sweetheart, you apparently ain't using it enough, so catch my drift and get on board'," Monica amplified.

Courtney said, "You know I have known you a long time and we were in that restaurant when Malik came in with the intention of blowing your head off." She took a swig of her drink and said, "For your edification Ava, Monica and Rashida shared the same vile human being—Malik, not together but nevertheless, the same sick motherfucker. Mallory is a wonderful human being and he thinks that you are soft, but what's wrong with being soft and feminine? Listen, these guys are happier than a guy who likes guys when they are in jail. My friend Tommie told me that he was not getting it enough and, therefore, he was going to rob a bank. He knew they would put him away for a long time. I told him that he is a doctor and he said, 'Forget that shit! I ain't happy and, therefore, I need to be in an environment where there are plenty of people who need to get that thang off—jail, baby, jail."

"Ah, Courtney, what the hell does that have to do with me or Ava?"

"How the hell would I know? I am just drinking and telling a story. Why, I don't have a damn clue, but it was a good story, right?"

"How many of these things have you had already?" Monica asked.

Courtney began to cry and said, "I have never been this happy." Between sighs, she said, "I have my man who I would kill for, as she looked at Ava, my children who I love to death, my old friends, and new ones like Ava, who had the pleasure of pleasuring my man. However, I'm an adult, but I worry that he finds you more attractive than me."

"Are you that drunk? Are you second guessing your man and putting me in the middle of it? Are you fucking crazy or just stupid and drunk?"

"Oh please, *brujas*. I'm crying because I see my daughter having a conversation with a real man. That other shit was just shit. Look in the water. Juan is trying to teach her child how to swim. That is what makes me cry because he may have penetrated her shield and opened her mind and heart to at least a conversation. She needs much more penetrated and I think they make a decent couple. What say you witches?"

# # #

Later in the afternoon, the pilots requested a meeting with the leadership to discuss their current problem. Jong said, "Give me thirty minutes and we will meet in the bar and go from there."

When Jong arrived at the bar with Mallory, Monica was in a heated discussion with the pilot who had been operating suspiciously. Mallory burst onto the scene and yelled, "Whoa! Back the fuck up or get broke up. You work for her, and that is not how you treat your employer."

The guy said, "Her cell phone has been bugged and that is how those people know where you guys are."

"Get the hell out of here. She barely knows how to use the phone."

The pilot said, "Watch what happens when I engage my app that provides a false signal to those trying to monitor me." He tapped his screen and within two minutes, he had the coordinates of another phone and it was exactly where Monica was standing. The pilot's phone beeped, buzzed, and hummed that her phone was bugged.

He said to Mallory, "Your wife's phone is bugged and is the sole reason they can find us whenever they want. Those people are going to figure out that I have been deceiving them, and they are going to hurt my family."

Mallory looked at him and his phone, as well as Monica and her phone, and told Jong to get the Sarge immediately."

# # #

When the Sarge arrived in the bar, he asked, "What's the urgency?"

Mallory began to give him the details and told him that somewhere along the way, Monica's phone had been bugged and was probably the reason why recently Walter always knew where they were. The Sarge asked, "How do we know that it's Monica's phone?"

Mallory answered, "Our pilots are very trustworthy people. We must get a plane in the air and extract this guy's wife and children."

The Sarge asked, "How many people do we have to send with them?"

Jong chimed in and replied, "None! The other pilots can meet them and provide the extraction. I have made it a point to not leave our aircraft at any one location over a forty-eight-hour period. Therefore, we have two jets in Miami and those pilots can be on point in a matter of an hour or so. Anyway, we will have two pilots here with us and the other six will attend to this matter."

"That sounds a little risky, doesn't it? I mean, we are not a part of this scenario, yet we have to believe in the very people who fly our planes," the Sarge stated.

"I know where you're coming from Sarge, but they must handle their business or we must look for new pilots--it's a simple matter. Protect and secure your own or look for a new job," Mallory replied.

"Damn, I'm glad you're not my boss," the Sarge responded.

As the Sarge began to walk away, Jong heard him say, 'slap your employer and humiliate him', referring to Jong slapping the Sarge.

"Although enjoyable, the purpose was clear—bring you back or leave you in tunnels and dark places that you can't handle."

"Jong, do your thing. I'm done with the other. Do your thing."

#

Mr. Amazing purchased a simulation program that instructed people how to shoot various weapons. When he came upon Courtney, Ava, and Monica, he said, "I think you ladies should go rest and not practice today. I will give you instructions tomorrow. I think you had too many pina coladas."

Courtney said, "This would be a perfect time to try to understand the mechanics of guns and shooting them, while we're intoxicated. There are hazards involved in the handling of guns, Jong. Better while we're here in the islands, less than sober, as opposed to being, in the actual line of fire and fired up. What say you, ladies?"

## CHAPTER EIGHT

The flight to their base in Maryland was uneventful. The soccer moms' vans were waiting to transport them to Asiram's farm in Virginia.

Once on the farm, Rashida and Juan began to demonstrate to the children the things they should do if they heard the words, "Positions—now."

As for her personal business, Rashida told everyone that horses don't talk and until they heard it from her, nothing was going on but people gossiping. She told her mother that Juan was nice but wasn't what she was looking for in a man. She indicated that he was funny and attentive, but they only talked about things in general, nothing specific such as dating or any nonsense like that.

Courtney had iterated to Ava that she'd better watch Juan because if he made the wrong move on Rashida, he would come up missing permanently.

Rashida and Marisa were charged with providing educational services to the children. Juan suggested that they should include Spanish and he could teach the course. The two women thought it was a great idea and asked him for a curriculum. Juan stumbled around that notion but understood what they were requesting after Rashida showed him the mathematics curriculum.

# # #

Jong's cousins finally installed the suppression devices on the fifteen machine pistols that were a part of the ODS. Jong called for everyone to come in the house, but asked Rashida and Marisa to take the children downstairs.

Jong said, "Each of you should know how to use this system in case something happens to me and you're near the control panel. There are fifteen machine pistols in the field, and each are capable of firing 120 rounds of ammunition. The positioning of these weapons are all towards the ground so that each round has a limited path to travel. First, I'm going to turn on this monitor and go to Channel 111."

"Suppose them there guys cut the power to the house?" John Lee astutely asked.

"That no matter because there are three back-up systems to this unit. Each system operates on its own power source and has three 8-D batteries supporting it that have a continuous charger mounted to them. As I was saying, tune to Channel 111 and this is what you'll get once you put in your password."

"You want us to put in a password during a firefight?" McArthur inquired.

"It's four digits so that each of you morons can remember it; it's the last four digits of your social security number. This is a simple system because you are simple people." There was a loud growl as Jong continued, "As I was saying, there are three and only three steps. Step 1—arm the system by saying or typing in the last four digits of your SS numbers. That will arm the system. Step 2—hit the word target or say target. Step 3—hit the word engage or say engage and that's it.

"Now, of course you want to make sure there are no friendlies around, so you hit scan and it will tell you where body heat is. Now, once you say engage, this is what will happen. I have had my low life cousin reduce the load factor to 20 rounds for each weapon. Now, these weapons are on the east side of the farm and can cover our eastern, northern, and southern sides, of the property within approximately, 200 feet of the farmhouse and guesthouse. That means, if intruders come with that range, they become active targets. On the west side of the farm her property borders with someone else who we are in negotiations with to extend her property line by 1.5 miles."

Jong looked around the room and paused. He was trying to discern if everyone comprehended the instructions. He said, "Also, this thing can fire a single burst or lay 1800 spent shells on the ground at one time. My low life cousin also has programmed an attack scenario with a large force entering from the road and another from north of the barn and onto the ex-senator's property. This is an exaggeration of course, but for the hell of it, I took the liberty to use an attack force of 150 well-armed individuals entering the property from the south and another 150 entering from the north. This is my first time using this system and if it doesn't work, I know of a low life family member who will be on a boat back home. Okay, let's try it out. Who wants to be the first to use the system?"

Mallory replied, "I think it should be your royal highness, Sergeant Beckmire."

Everyone concurred and he said, "I need my glasses." Everyone laughed. The Sarge looked at the control panel, and mumbled, "mechanized mayhem".

Jong asked, "What did you just say?"

"I didn't say anything, Mr. Amazing," the Sarge replied.

"Then, Mr. Sergeant Beckmire, where did I hear the term 'mechanized mayhem'?"

"Any way, Step 1—arm system. I have to put in the last four digits of my social." He typed in the first two numbers, paused, then he looked at the guys and said, "I worry about identity theft.   Step 2—I'm hitting the button that says engage."

"Wrong. Can I slap you again?"

The Sarge's head tilted downwards and then up and he said, "Not if you want to see tomorrow, brother."

"I thought you would say something like that. Anyway, Step 2—is hit the word target or say the word target."

"Step 2—target."

"Okay, before you say engage, look at the lights illuminated on the screen. They represent the enemy. Now, Sarge, complete Step 3."

The Sarge said, "Step 3—engage."

The group watched the machine pistols target individuals from the north and south and then methodically begin to eliminate the red dots.   In less than two minutes, 300 individuals had been wounded or terminated. The Sarge said, "Oh my, God! Is your cousin related to the anti-Christ? That's some sick shit if that is an accurate indication of what we could do to real people.   That is complete, unadulterated and mechanized mayhem."

"Those were not real bullets fired out there and each weapon fired 20 blanks. For safety reasons, and not knowing who if any of our group was out in the bushes, I decided to use blanks. Each weapon has a capacity of firing 120 rounds," Jong said.

"I don't know if I like that system. All we need to do is sit back and watch people get shot like it's a video game. That is some sick shit and by the way, thinking of your cousin, is he in any way a liability? And before you scream at me, let me say since we had the problem with the pilot everyone outside our immediate unit becomes suspect. We survived in the Nam because we depended on each other and now we are depending on a bunch of people that we don't know."

Jong said, "Sarge, my cousin and those who work with him, are my relations. I support them, near and far, meaning that we have family members in universities and colleges and our families no longer must search through the garbage for a meal. They are as loyal to me as I am to you. They would die an honorable death rather than expose or compromise us. The vans, the cars in DC, the weapons, the intel, and this new mass-killing system, is for our protection. I vouch for them as I would vouch for you."

The Sarge asked, "Wasn't it you who said that I am the Supreme Ruler?"

"I never said no shit like that, but I did say that I would follow you to hell and take two hits from a 'BB' gun, for you."

"Anyway, it's what you said and how you brought the pilot issue to me that got me to thinking about where our vulnerabilities are, including Monica's phone being bugged. Okay, think about it. We now have Yeshida, Somara, Yvette, Okema, Mary Alice, Ava, Carlos and his people, and Lord knows who else as an integral part of our defense and offense. We have arms, a weapons system developed by your cousin, and food being catered by your new girlfriend. Yet, we do some badass things to people who are trying to hurt us because the 'idiot spy' kissed and swallowed. I need everyone to engage in due diligence with their mates and make sure we don't have any loose ends or unknown, unintentional connections."

"Now, Sarge, I be trying to figure out how to illustrate how my woman might be a spy or something like that," John Lee exclaimed.

"John Lee, your woman is a fucking spy, so is Brown's and Jilkes's. Unless I missed something, what the hell are you talking about?" The Sarge asked.

"I be trying to figure out if she be spying on us or in love with me?"

Jilkes answered, "El stupido, she loves you and you might get a surprise tonight, but don't let on to it. Swear to me, no matter what she says when you get some critical information, just be damn surprised."

"Now, boy, what the hell did you just say to me? You sound like that Scottie woman and I didn't understand a word she be saying. Her dumbass told me that she was going to tell me everything I wanted to know. I told her that I don't want to know shit other than why you be doing my woman like you did."

Jong said, "I fully understand what the Sarge is saying. Listen, over there it was just us and we knew each other's farts, smells, coughs, sneezes, and everything else. I see exactly where the brains of this organization is going with this here shit. I get it, Sarge, and I'm going to put the fear of God in my family, as well as give them a great bonus, for this awesome Outfield Defense System."

"I don't know what you're proposing but confer with me because that was some brutal shit I just saw. That saves wear and tear on our old ass bodies. Don't worry about the Sarge, you know he would rather save a life even if they are pointing a gun at his head, than kill someone," Mallory articulated.

"No, Mallory, he's correct. We have a shit load of people that we don't know, who don't know us, we have to protect them and can't depend on them to cover our six. He's right as usual, and we need to make sure that we do some screening of the people in our fold. That thing with the pilots could have been disastrous for us. Suppose that guy was mentally defective and pulled that shit that the nut overseas pulled and dove the plane into the mountains with people who trusted him and had no beef with him whatsoever?" Jong stated.

"Listen, Jong, we are in a modern era where people are independent, rely on their iPhones and other technologies and just forget about the notion of human interaction. Our people are strong, and I don't suspect any treachery," Mallory professed.

"Would you bet Monica's life on that?" Jong asked.

# # #

The farm was overly active with people focusing on trying to operate weapons and fire them accurately without a single round hitting the targets. Jong and Whitmore, along with Gladstone, walked people through the paces of firing a weapon. Surprisingly, the doctor, the person who was charged with saving lives, was the most prolific of the women. Ava was okay when the target was straight-on but would turn her head before firing her weapon. Whitmore said, "Get Carlos in here. Let's see if he can fix this issue."

When Carlos walked in, Ava asked, "Oh, you have time for me?"

Carlos looked at her and replied, "*Mi amante, que pasa*?"

Ava, lit into him in their native language and after a few minutes of listening to her rant Carlos asked, "Ms. De Lombardo, would you like to have a private conversation with me without a gun in your hand?"

Ava placed the weapon on the table and as she was about to leave, Whitmore said, "Ms. De Lombardo, I need you to finish this session before you leave. Carlos you can help her."

Ava blasted back, "I don't feel like finishing this shit right now."

Whitmore asked, "When are you leaving the compound?"

Carlos said, "Whit, give me a minute, please, before this moves further up the chain."

Carlos and Ava began to walk towards the center of the field, and he asked, "What's happening to us? I thought you were happy with my proposal as well as my token of commitment to you. It seems as though I am not the person or of the status that you're accustomed to or want. If you're not into me, then that's okay. I love you Ava, but since we had that magnificent evening on the beach, you have apparently been looking for an opportunity to tell me something and I guess I have been trying to avoid hearing it."

"What do you mean?" Ava slyly inquired.

"I mean that I don't think I measure up to your standards and, therefore, you want to conclude this relationship."

"Is that why you have been coming in at night half-drunk and tired, or signing up for night watch duty?"

"Listen, woman, I love you very much and I know that we are from two different stations. I also know that I have known you for a long time. If my station in life is the thing that matters most to you, then I am prepared to go back to my role of protecting you, if you will have me in that role. I have a feeling that you have not gotten over the wonderful Mr. Beckmire."

"Carlos, leave Ben out of this. I thought you were avoiding me because you didn't want to be with me anymore and that you had used me for your purpose and that was it."

"How can you say that mi amor? Mi amante, how can you say such a thing? I love you more than God intended for a man to love a woman. You are my life, my love, my sunshine, my sadness, and my tomorrow. I can't meet your standards and, therefore, I have taken this route to try to end our relationship."

Ava looked at him as she cried and said, "I can't believe after all we have been through you think that status is what's on my mind? I thought you didn't want me anymore and that was more hurtful than you can imagine."

"Ava, you are my heartbeat and without you, there is no me. Love me or leave me, but hopefully, love me. This can work, just give it a try and if there are things that I haven't accomplished in the bedroom, give me time for I will make it a perfect place we both cherish. It's new, and I have historically been subservient to you. Loving you is a chore that I want to perfect."

"Let's defer this conversation until later. I need to apologize to Whitmore and finish my lessons. Will you help me?"

"Of course, I will. Not only will I help you, but I'll also show you how to hit the smallest of targets at a distance with a pistol. Let's go back and begin anew."

Ava walked directly to Whitmore and whispered in his ear, "If you dime on me, I will kick your butt. Please, keep my meltdown to yourself."

"Now, that you have threatened me, do I have a choice? Anyway, let me tell you a secret. The purpose of this is to make sure we all have a chance to survive whatever is thrown at us. If my back is to you and you see someone about to shoot me, I hope you shoot them first. We have to protect each other."

"I'm sorry for being a little brat. Let's start from the beginning and I want to do this until I get a better score than Monica and Courtney."

## CHAPTER NINE

Allen talked to Mike and received an update on the force that Walter was amassing. Walter had also upped the ante on Mike's and Allen's heads. He called Beckmire and said, "I am so sorry to have given you imperfect information, but the numbers I gave you before were totally inaccurate. As a matter of fact, I asked Mike, in the future, to verify them before giving me information. Oh, and by the way, Mike is destitute and in need of some funds. I could use a few thousand myself."

"Okay, first things first. Where does he want the money delivered and where do you want me to send yours?"

"I think a couple of prepaid cards will do us both good. I forwarded all the funds you sent me last time to my wife, whose new man took every penny. I can't afford to get involved with her poor decision making, but my daughters have confirmed that he has struck her before."

"I can handle that for you if you like. Just let me know what you need done. Now, what was the other reason you called me--because you gave me some bad intel?"

"Mr. Beckmire, I feel bad about what I'm about to tell you and I have decided if need be, I will hitch a ride to where you are and join forces against the person that wants us both dead. Mike has indicated that he would help you out as well."

"Allen, you are asking for money and apologizing at the same time. In my book, that's not a good sign. What in the hell is going on?"

"Mr. Beckmire, I told you that Walter had put together a team of about sixty-five people to handle that problem he has with you. In addition, he has gone against the senator who vehemently told him to stand-down in his pursuit of your group. He reminded her that he has a significant contract on her and for her to mind her fucking business or it will be instituted. He also assured her that he has an additional source who knows the balance of the formula and, therefore, you people are auditioning for roles in the *Walking Dead*. I don't know what your relationship with the senator is, but I would be extremely cautious about contacting her and asking for whatever or agreeing to anything."

"Allen, I appreciate the intel, but what is the misinformation you provided me with?"

There was a long pause on the line. Beckmire asked, "Allen, are you there?"

"Yes, I'm here. I told you that your dear cousin had put together a team of about sixty-five people to complete his relationship with you. I presented you with information that had been confirmed by several sources and finally Mike. That number is significantly under-reported. It is estimated that your cousin has garnered a force, north of two hundred and fifty individuals with an attack date of four days and if they say four, you can bet it's going to happen in three days."

"Damn! He has hired in excess of 250 people to kill us?"

"Mr. Beckmire, Mike and I can be of assistance because we both owe you."

"Allen, you don't owe me anything. If I had to make a bet, it is that we owe you and we forgive you for trying to kill us."

"Hell, I'm glad I didn't succeed."

"Yeah, me too. We have been on this phone for a long time. Call me back in a couple of hours and then dump that phone and hit me with a new number. How much do you want me to put on those prepaid cards?"

"Any more than a couple of thousand will create suspicion. Mr. Beckmire, you had the chance to do some bad shit to me and you took a major chance on what decency I had left. I am dirty and so is Mike. We know the farm and we like wallowing in the mud and we can help you against these superior odds. You give me the word and he and I will be there to drive the devil back to hell. He has made my life, as well as others, a living hell."

"Hit me back in a couple of hours and we will let you know what our needs are. Allen, thanks for looking out for me and mine. Catch you later."

The Sarge walked towards the barn where he saw Rajz, the horse that Walter spent time talking to. As he got closer to the barn, Rajz walked slowly towards the barn as well. Beckmire said to himself, "That damn horse had better not give me any bad intel or I'm going to shoot his ass." Rajz was no dummy--he knew when he saw humans walking towards the damn barn it was treat time!

The Sarge had never provided a treat to a horse and was reluctant to have the big teeth of the horse bite into his hand and possibly bite his damn fingers off. He saw a protective glove and decided to try to give Rajz a treat. He placed a treat in his hand and said aloud, "I have to have my hand flat or you'll bite my damn fingers off." He looked at the horse and then its mouth and decided to forgo any notion of feeding it. As he turned to walk away, the horse made a helluva horse sound--'neigh'--and clawed its hoofs in the ground. The Sarge said, "Okay, if you bite me, I'm going to blow your damn head off."

A soft voice said, "You're about to get your fingers bitten off. Let me show you how to do this." It was Ava who was with Carlos.

Carlos said, "You know what, I think you two need a moment together to put closure on some history and satisfy any old concerns. Ava, I think it is more on you, then Ben. I'll give you two some privacy to conclude a relationship that never ended properly but produced a great young man, Zanthius Beckmire De Lombardo. Take a few minutes and complete this thing or others will continuously hurt, knowing that what you once shared was more than magic, but a fantastic journey. Take this opportunity to make your choices, I have made mine and, Sarge, I assume and hope, you have made yours. Ava, perhaps you need to get all of that dust off your chest and move on."

Carlos walked around the barn slowly, picking up rocks and throwing them innocently into the woods. On his second time around the barn, he picked up a rock and threw it deep into the field and was momentarily blinded by a reflection from afar. On his third time around the barn, he saw Courtney approaching and waited patiently for her. He said, "Courtney, I need you to do me a big favor and not go into that barn."

"Carlos, is my husband in there with your fiancée?"

"I don't play that shit either, but my fiancée abandoned your husband years ago and I am allowing them an opportunity to finish their history so that I can move forward with Ava. Your husband is solid as a rock, but she left him and disappeared. I know because I was there with her and helped raise Zanthius. Now, more importantly, I need you to do something for the good of the order. I have been walking around the barn throwing stones. On the west side of the barn, I threw a stone and noticed a reflection in the field. I am thinking someone is watching us from the woods. I need you to play as if we are flirting or something and look at approximately 10 o'clock and see if you see anything moving."

"Carlos, where the hell is 10 o'clock, while I'm walking?"

"Oh, sorry. Let's just say we are standing at 6 o'clock. After that comes 7, then 8, 9, and then 10. Just treat where we are as if it were a clock and if you look straight ahead, that would be 12 o'clock."

"Gotcha! Okay, let's do this."

As Carlos walked backwards and Courtney walked in front of him, she saw the sunlight hit at least three different objects. She said, "Carlos, I saw three separate flashes."

"Don't look back. Shake your head as if we're playing a game or something."

When they entered the barn, Carlos and Courtney saw Beckmire and Ava embracing. Courtney asked, "So, Ben, do we need to talk?"

Beckmire said, "Honey, we can talk about anything you want because you are my wife. Ava and I never concluded our relationship and Carlos thought it was time for us to have a moment alone and think about what we did, why we did it, and the product that resulted from it, Zanthius Beckmire De Lombardo."

Carlos asked, "Are we good and is all good between all involved?"

Ava said, "I told him that I will always love him and that he's the father of our son. I also told him that I respect Courtney and that she is a wonderful *amiga*. Courtney, when we met, I had planned to try to express my concerns, but as you will recall, someone tried to kill us in the restaurant."

"Ava, Ben Beckmire would rather sleep with one hundred rattle snakes, than pull some dumb shit on me. Listen, we have a bigger problem. Carlos and I saw what he considered people watching us at 10'oclock."

Carlos said, "That clock only counts from the position you were in at that point in time. It is now a different clock time."

The Sarge asked, "Carlos, do you think we're in danger?"

"Sarge, I saw one reflection and your wonderful wife saw three. I don't want to make this call because my focus on our safety was distracted."

"A needless action because all we talked about was you two. We never officially resolved a thing other than the fact that I love Courtney, and Ava so much wants to be your wife. Let me call John Lee and Jilkes and see if they smell anything."

# # #

Later, John Lee told the Sarge that he and Jilkes saw those reflections and had checked it out and it turned out to be a busted scope and a pair of binoculars. The Sarge asked Jilkes to contact Mallory and have him to pull together the core team for an important meeting, including the three Asian ladies and Larry. The Sarge indicated that this was important and was to happen ASAP.

Approximately one hour later, after the core group was assembled in the barn, Jong said, "You have the timing of a damn blind doctor doing a colonoscopy."

The Sarge asked, "What the hell are you talking about?"

"I think Mary Alice likes me, and she was about to take a shower with me when you called."

"Mr. Amazing, what were you going to do after that?"

"I was going to call you for instructions," Jong retorted.

"Thanks for joining me in the barn. I had a conversation with that horse, and he told me that a bad wind is about to blow our way."

John Lee asked, "Is that problem with the horse peculiar to your family?"

"Naw, not really. I spoke with Allen and he first told me that approximately sixty-five people had been recruited to take us on. However, after further digging, he indicated to me that the number is north of 250 people."

John Lee pointed out, "Damn, Sarge, that's a helluva difference, but more importantly, what are we going to do? We ain't going to run, so we must prepare for a long fight. Now, if we get them coming at us from the north, south and east, then them there machine pistols can reduce that number to a few peanuts. I wonder if Jong's cousin can come up with something in a hurry to help on the west side?"

Jong said, "The west side is precarious because any force would shoot downhill from that area and that would place us in harm's way as well. But I will call him and tell him that his performance is subpar, and I might have to ship his lowly ass back home."

"Why do you threaten him all of the time?" Mallory asked.

"Because I can," Jong flatly stated.

The Sarge exclaimed, "If we can stay with the issues! Two hundred and fifty people coming at us with who knows what, is an awesome task--even for us. If we add all our people in this equation, we are probably looking at nine aggressors per person, that is a lot of sleepless nights for anyone. If we can get any kind of mechanized help on the western quadrant, then I think we might stand a chance. Jong, please call your cousin now and see what he says. Actually, tell him to get his ass out here in a hurry."

The Sarge continued, "We need to get everyone together and let them know what potentially is coming our way. By the way, Jong, how did the ladies do on the simulator?"

Jong said, "I hate to say, but the doctor scored a perfect six out of six. Ava was next with five out of six, and Monica and Marisa each scored four out of six each. I know you think those shots were close-ups, but they weren't. Those are scores from sixty-five to eighty-five yards out, with pistols. Also, they handle the weapons well. I mean no closing of eyes, just straight out shooting."

Mallory said, "Damn, that is good shooting except it is computer generated. Let's set some targets up right now and see what they can do with live ammunition."

"Mallory, get some paper and set up the targets and let them fire live ammunition. We still have shotguns for close-up work, right?" the Sarge asked.

"We do and they each have learned to operate and load the shotgun as well. I have attempted to show them how to fire from their sides, thus minimizing the recoil from the blast. I think each one can mentally handle close up work and we could probably prevent intruders from estimating our strength based upon the number of positions that weapons are being fired from," Mallory stated.

"Damn, good thinking, Corporal. If we can get any kind of mechanized support for the west side, along with random shots being fired from our support team, then I think they will think there are more of us than might have been reported."

Jong walked back into the room and said that his cousin was on the way. He didn't ask him to bring anything specific because he works best under pressure and without any preconceived notions. Jong indicated that his cousin would arrive in about 45 minute.

Zanthius asked, "Has anyone actually ventured into the tunnels to check upon the efficacy of using them for our escape?"

The Sarge asked, "Son, why don't you and Larry handle that aspect?"

Larry replied, "Rashida and Juan had exercises with the children to check out the tunnels. Perhaps we all should take a moment to look at our escape options should this place get overrun with vermin."

"Mallory, set the targets up and tell the women we're going to use live ammunition in the field. Larry, I think everyone should know how to access the tunnels and where the hell they lead to. After we meet with Jong's cousin and have a shooting drill for the ladies, then we will have a meeting and explain to everyone what is coming our way and what each person will be required to do to defend our family. Speaking of Rashida, did she participate in the simulation drills, Jong?"

"She did not. I don't even know if anyone asked her since she is so busy with the children. Did you ask her, Sarge?"

"I did not and that is probably my fault and oversight. Larry, will you work with her later?"

"Pops, she knows how to handle a weapon but does not like to."

"Larry, I think we all feel that way."

"Touché, Pops. Touché."

## CHAPTER TEN

Jong's cousin showed up and without being prompted said, "You have all those things on this side of the farm. You no have shit on that side. You humble me so much you never let me do my work. You need protection on that side. If you spend less time threatening your only family here, and started paying them better wages for great work, then you could have more time to see the wisdom of collaboration instead of humiliation."

"Get your ass to work on that side or I swear, I will pay to have your enemies flown into this country and cut your head off."

"Please forgive me, Cousin. My wife she makes fool of me in front of other members of family. I have many ideas and many resources Cousin, but you must direct me because I am a low life person who needs direction to make things happen. Please forgive my arrogance and in trying to tell you, as smart as you are, where you should set up defenses. Please forgive me, oh great relative."

"If you speak without my consent in the future, I will have your tongue cut out and hung around your neck."

"A thousand apologies, my Cousin. Please tell me. Why you have summoned such a low-life to be in your presence."

"I need a quick and reliable solution to the west side of the farm. Do you have any ideas as to how I can secure that area with a mechanized system, yet not have bullets raining down on us in the low part of the farm?"

"Oh, mighty cousin, may I speak freely to ask myself questions and answer them to further my thoughts?"

"You may but be quiet and quick."

Jong's cousin used his soliloquy to cuss his cousin from one side of the ocean to the other. He described Jong as a dog without paws, and a man without a woman. He screamed his name in the foulest of sounds and then relented when he remembered that it was his gracious cousin who contracted him with work that provides enough money to have useless daughters at MIT and Harvard, a son at Penn and his favorite son working alongside him.

He knew Jong was a good man, but tradition and protocol were important. Finally, he said, "I have somehow come across a wonderful weapon, it fires many rounds that follow their own minds. I can have a crew meet me and place the same kind of equipment on the other side, minus the ability to target individuals by the iPhone. I can place many large caliber automatic weapons throughout the field so you, my lord, can target and execute your enemy. I can give you some protection, but the west side of this farm is on a hill and that means bullets coming too close to the house. I can make the machine pistols target in a range of forty to seventy yards and make the long guns target, say, one hundred plus yards. Beyond that the target will be running downhill towards you and that shot might be suicidal."

Jong emphatically added, "I need this configuration in place tonight by only members of our clan. No nasty foreigners."

"May I speak?" His cousin asked.

"Speak, dog, but make it quick. Also, more importantly, why didn't you use larger capacity drums to hold 240 rounds of ammunition."

"My Lord, I fired 200 rounds of ammo out of those machine pistols and some of the barrels exploded. I also fired 175 and 150 rounds and there was no problem. I want to make sure that you are safe and, therefore, I believe the maximum canisters should not exceed 120 rounds."

"Can you do that tonight?"

"I do not want to be sent back across the waters, for there are those who seek my lowly form to end my existence. I will have other members of our clan bring the necessary equipment and we will have it operational by morning."

# # #

In the middle of the field, the ladies were practicing their shooting. The Sarge suggested that the ladies be outfitted with Smith & Wesson .9mm because they had a safety click on them.

He saw Rashida and inquired, "I guess we haven't had time to play our video games, have we?"

"All's good. I know we're under attack and that your focus is on keeping us alive."

"Sweetheart, you're an enigma. You help the kids but keep mainly to yourself. Do we need to talk?"

"Dad, you know that I don't get in your way when you have stuff going on. I disappear until you send out 'the all' clear sign, that I haven't seen for a while." Rashida, looked away, then at her dad and said, "Perhaps it's you who needs to talk to me about somethings. Are we okay?"

"Baby Girl, we will never be okay until we end this thing and on our terms. I know you don't like guns, but I'm afraid I'm going to have to ask you to watch my back and that may mean blowing a hole in another human being."

"Dad, I never said I didn't like guns, everyone just assumed that I didn't. I always thought no one had faith in me pulling the trigger if I or the children were in danger. I have never shot a human being, but I am certain if they are going to try to strap another vest on any of the children then I would have to eliminate them."

"Will you walk with me to where Courtney and the others are practicing?"

"Sure, but I need you to call Carlos and ask him if Juan can watch the children."

"Speaking of Juan, what's going on with that? I mean do you like him?"

"Dad, if that fool ain't been to you and asked you if he can have dinner with me then, ain't nothing happening."

"Oh, I see. You're my girl and always will be. He must be mentally challenged or stupid, then again, he may be making sure this is the direction he wants to go."

"Dad, I'm not sure I even like his crazy ass, but he has added Spanish to the curriculum and the children absolutely adore him. I must admit, Dad, he's good with the children and come to think about it, he's good and kind to me. You know I hadn't thought about it, but I haven't been with another man since that jerk. Do you think it's time for me to begin to live a little?"

"Rashida, come here and give me a hug. You know I love you and there are certain things that men and women should do that is a part of the natural order of things, and that includes love and sex, Girl. Now, you know if I'm saying this to you, then it's time for my baby to get back into the game. I love you and I'm not suggesting that you go to the barn and wrestle with Juan, but you need to live, my love. You have been existing, and I must admit, you had a good reason because your baby's daddy was vermin. He's gone and you know that Courtney, Larry, and I love you and the baby. However, there may come a time when you need a different kind of love, my angel."

#

From the middle of the field, Jong asked, "Oh, Rashida, are you going to try to hit the target?"

"Jong, I don't like guns, but if I must use one, I want to assure everyone that I can do this. Have you seen Larry?"

"Larry can't do this for you, Rashida."

"You're right, but I need to ask him a question."

Five minutes later, while Rashida was watching people shoot, Larry showed up. She asked him to walk with her away from listening ears and asked, "Did you tell them that I beat you a thousand times in our games?"

"Rashida, this is no game. You are about to fire live rounds."

Rashida looked at Larry and then walked back to Jong and said, "Unlike the other ladies, I don't have my own weapon. Do you have something that you would like me to try out?"

Jong picked up a .32 from the table and said, "Try this."

Rashida looked at the weapon, smiled and then asked Jong, "Do you play with dolls? I don't do dolls and I like that big gun."

Jong said, "Rashida, I don't recommend that weapon. It's a dragon slayer."

"Jong, is this weapon ready to fire?" Rashida asked.

Jong said, "Sarge, I need your intervention here. She wants to fire the .44!"

The Sarge asked, "Rashida, is that the weapon you want to fire?"

"Dad, this is the one. Is it safe to fire towards those targets?"

Jong announced, "Okay, fire when ready."

Rashida opened the cylinder and noticed that there were no rounds in the weapon. She looked at Jong and said, "It's a good thing you're not the target." She saw a box labeled .44 and retrieved six rounds and chambered them in the weapon.

Jong said, "Fire, when ready."

Rashida said, "Wow, this thing is heavy." She began to carelessly flirt with the weapon until Jong grabbed her hand and the weapon and said, "You're not ready to handle this."

Larry yelled, "Jong, step aside."

Rashida placed the weapon on the table. She then put sound suppression earmuffs on her head and fired off six shots from the cannon. She hit six out of six bullseyes.

Jong exclaimed, "Get the shit out of here!"

The Sarge said, "Oh my, you have always been full of surprises. When on earth did you learn to shoot like that?"

"Dad ask Larry. Those video games are like simulators, you learn how to react and fire."

Jong said, "We aren't playing games here."

"You come near my child or any of the children and you will have your head blown off. I know the difference between a game and what has been happening to us for a long time."

"Sorry, Rashida. Is that the weapon you want to carry?"

"No! I don't want to be saddled with that big thing. I like those S&M's .9's. If you could find one of those for me, then I would be happy."

The Sarge, shaking his head but full of pride, said, "My children. Damn, I love my children!"

Larry said, "Sarge, you should see her throw a knife. Now, that's some crazy shit to watch when she unsheathes a knife and hits the center of a bullseye from twenty feet. Absolutely amazing to watch your daughter throw a knife at a target. I have no doubt that my sister will send an aggressor to hell, without blinking an eye."

## CHAPTER ELEVEN

Whitmore and Gladstone along with Montomie and Chakes decided to run around the perimeter of the farm for exercise. On the western flank, Gladstone saw the binoculars and scope but essentially discounted them because they were pointing west towards the mountain and hidden from the view of the ranch.

The Sarge asked Mallory to assemble the entire tribe. In the family room of the ranch, the Sarge asked, "Asiram, it won't be long now, will it?"

She responded by saying, "Are you talking about me having my baby or killing your son for impregnating me?"

The Sarge said, "I'm not going to address that, but please don't kill my son, I just met him. Anyway, people it's great to see you all and realize that we have been through hell and have come back. This next test will certainly let us know how strong our faith in the Lord is. I had initially received information that there would be sixty-five angry people coming to end our existence. I hate to have to report this, but it appears that there will be 250 plus people. I can't confirm either report, but as you can discern, that is a huge discrepancy. Now, I want to propose a strategy that allows us a modicum of survivability."

Courtney stood up and said, "Sarge, you need to move on from that notion because the women here aren't going anywhere, and we have all become proficient at shooting people. So, move on to the essence of our situation. Thank you, dear."

"As I was saying before I was interrupted by my wonderful wife, we are in for the fight of our lives. Now, before you start to wonder why we're feeling just a little cocky, we have fortified Asiram's farmhouse and have added some escape options as well. I am going to assign Rashida, my amazing daughter, to handle the tunnels. She and Juan have ventured into them to figure out how they can benefit our survival. I hope that's the reason they were in them." Beckmire paused as the room laughed while Rashida blushed slightly.

The Sarge continued, "Immediately after this meeting, we are all going to go down and figure out how to escape just in case those guys bring tanks and rocket launchers with them. Now, some of you don't know this, but we have some mechanized pistols we can target from our phones as well as our command center. We owe our thanks to Jong and his family for that." The Sarge looked around the room and saw how troubled people looked, and said, "People, we can beat these odds, but we have to be there for each other."

"I'm going to let some of you in on a secret. Those guys who came to protect us are some incredibly special people. We survived because we watched each other's six, or backs, and that is exactly what I'm hoping that you, our extended family, can do for all of us. This is an undeclared war, but the stakes are high, final, and we need you to make sure that you're willing to pull that trigger to end another human being's life, if necessary."

Courtney stood up and said, "My husband just issued a call to arms. If you are not willing to die on this farm for our friends and family, then I suggest you let us know now, so arrangements can be made for you to leave. I am a doctor sworn to save lives, but I have had to take a life to save my husband and me. I will do it again because I believe we are on a righteous mission. There is no shame in following your mind."

Asiram said, "These have been the most rewarding times of my life. I have a husband who loves me, a father-in-law who has destroyed three of my homes, two mothers-in-laws, and a boat load of new friends who have our six. Now, I may not be mobile, but I can sure as hell hit a target from close to a mile out with my long gun. If I'm going to die here on this farm, then me and my child will be at peace because we died with a group of people who loved us and cherished the moments we shared together."

"Okay, enough about dying. I don't plan on forfeiting my life to a bunch of people, half who will be traveling from across the sea and the other half so distracted by a dollar amount that they will never see," the Sarge iterated.

Whitmore said, "So, Sarge, on our run around the perimeter we ran across what looked like a broken scope and a pair of binoculars."

Carlos said, "Courtney and I saw those things reflecting the sun."

"No way, they could reflect the sun because they were behind some bushes and both items were facing west."

"I'm sorry, Whitmore, but we both saw the reflection. I saw a single image and Mrs. Beckmire saw three distinct flashes. Am I correct, Mrs. Beckmire?"

"Whitmore, he's correct. That is exactly what we saw."

Whitmore said, "Let's take a ride out there and make sure. John Lee and Jilkes will you join us because you two scoped out the area as well."

"Whitmore, what are you suggesting exactly?" The Sarge asked.

"There are two interpretations of the positioning of that gear. Perhaps we are being watched from afar and, therefore, I want John Lee and Jilkes to have a look at the area again, but with a different focus."

"Good point. But approach it from different angles and get back to us. I will hold off the tunnel tour until you guys get back," the Sarge cautioned.

# # #

The area of concern was directly northwest of the farmhouse. Jilkes and John Lee rode in one of the mules and dead reckoned where the materials were. Whitmore, Courtney, and Carlos drove the other mule due north to the end of the property line and then made a left turn and headed towards the site. After reaching the site, Courtney said, "There is no way we could have seen this from the barn, Carlos."

Carlos laid down on the ground, attempted to look through the glasses and realized that they would have to be raised three feet to get a view of the barn. He said, "Someone has altered the position of these glasses because you can't see any parts of the barn from this present location."

John Lee motioned to an area west of the paraphernalia, and said, "Someone be smoking cigarettes over in that corner. Maybe this here be one of those ruses. They done leave this stuff here and take their real stuff knowing that we will check this area and see old stuff lying around. They be smart, but they be smoking over near that tree and burying the butts in the ground. Looks like they do this here spying on us in two shifts. I wonder if they be seeing that demonstration with them there machine pistols?"

# # #

Later back at the farmhouse, John Lee and the others gave a report on what they saw and the questions they raised. He told the Sarge his main concern was whether the intruders heard or saw the demonstration with the machine pistols. The Sarge told him that they would circle back to that conversation once they understood how the tunnels worked and when everyone was back together again.

Jilkes said, "You know, Big Country, I could see the barn and the house, but I couldn't see where the guns were."

"Lets you and I ride back up there and see what we can see. Sarge, me and my colored neighbor are going to ride back to that spot and take one more look. Give us ten minutes."

"Take Larry with you, and I know you people have pistols, right?"

"Hey Larry, can you find a pair of binoculars?" John Lee asked.

"John Lee, what are those things in the window?"

"Oh, I see. I guess I didn't see them earlier."

# # #

Once the men returned to the area in question, certain things became obvious. From the vantage point of where the scope and field glasses were laying, it was obvious that the only things visible were the barn and the farmhouse. The woods located to the southeast of the farmhouse was where the artillery was located, and because of the direction the wind was blowing, this group of intruders probably didn't hear the suppressed sounds of the weapons. As the three were preparing to return to their mule, Larry turned around and placed his finger over his mouth indicating that someone was near. John Lee heard sounds as well and he sent Jilkes to the left while he went to the right. Larry, who didn't know their protocol slowly dropped to his knees.

The conversation of those arriving was curiously loud which made Larry wonder if they were just locals out hunting. As the two men walked past the tree where Larry was kneeling, he admonished, "Don't move a muscle and don't turn around. What are you people doing out here on my aunt's property with those military style weapons?"

Jilkes saw one give the other a signal and advised, "Don't be stupid."

John Lee said, "I have you in my sight, so gently place them there weapons on the ground in front of you and step back five paces. Get down on your knees with your hands locked behind your head." The two men complied without saying a word.

Jilkes said, "My young friend asked you a question or two. Now might be a wonderful time to explain to him why you're on this property with those military style weapons!" There was extreme silence and Jilkes asked, "Did you people hear me ask you a question?" There was still no response.

John Lee said, "That there was the easy part of this here press conference. Now, you get to meet our extractioner, and the fact you showed up for this here interview with him, is an automatic decapitation of a finger or toe or an ear." The men were secured and thrown into the back of the mule.

When they arrived at the barn, the smell of bleach was strong. John Lee said, "Oh, don't mind that smell, we be trying to clean up body parts and shit like that." The two men looked as if they were made of stone. John Lee tapped on the boot of one of the guys and said, "Hell, this here ain't no steel-toe boot." He unsheathed his knife and surprisingly, plunged it into the foot of the guy who immediately passed out.

John Lee said, "Your friend be giving up a lot of blood ain't he? Is your boot steel-toe?" John Lee tapped on his boot and said, "Shit man, this here ain't no steel-toe boot." He then slammed his knife into the man's foot.

The guy screamed as loud as he could and John Lee said, "Jilkes, put some damn tape over that guy's mouth. He be making me deaf and dumb. Now, here is your bleed-out time. See that there wound is now contaminated with all kinds of shit. You have twenty minutes before you bleed out and three minutes to answer my friends' questions. Why you be on this here property and why you be carrying military style rifles?"

Jilkes said, "I don't think he's going to cooperate."

"Hell yes, he is. Give me my blowtorch and his ass will tell me anything I want to know." Jilkes handed John Lee the blowtorch and watched as he lit it. John Lee turned to Larry and asked him if he could fetch the Sarge and Mallory.

John Lee torqued the blowtorch and placed the blue flame on the guy's friend foot, who had passed out. He then turned his attention to the other guy who spat and said, "You're a sick human being and I promise you I will see you in hell."

John Lee sarcastically replied, "I don't be understanding how you gonna see me in hell when you can see me here and right now. All I need from you is information. If youse is believable then I might just let you get to the hospital before I do more damage to you. Your choice--you feel like answering questions now?"

There was a significant pause that was breached when the guy said, "We were on a recon mission and got caught by an old ass cracker and his slaves."

John Lee shook his head. Waving the blowtorch angrily, he said, "Now, that's going to cost you because them there people be my absolute best friends on this here earth and you call them slaves. I have to take part of your hand off for that one." John Lee slammed his knife into the guy's hand and literally split it open to the wrist. The guy screamed and coughed up blood that filled his mouth. John Lee said, "Now, to help you keep infection out of that there wound, I got to give it a blast of fire. If you be smart, you will apologize to my friends and ask one of them to put some duct tape around that wound. Give me solid information and I'll even call an Uber to pick your ass up and take you to the hospital."

"Who hired you and are there others spying on us?" John Lee asked.

The man gasped for air, but couldn't see the extent of the damage and said, "You expect me to answer you when you just split my hand wide open?"

"No, I guess not, but I do expect you to answer me when I slam my blade into your dick. You want to try me out on that one?"

"Listen, I'm a contractor." The man cried, "We never know who actually pays the bills, we just know that the middleman has the money."

"Okay, who is the middleman and where can I find his ass?"

"If I give him up what will you guarantee me?"

"I'll get you fixed up and let you disappear. You can't go back to your master because he'll kill your ass for being stupid. Are there others spying on us, and who is the middleman?"

"That is the man in the middle and he is in direct contact with the man who pays the bills."

"Okay, now don't test my resolve. I have gutted people in here before, for lying to me. Don't you dare fucking lie to me. If this here guy ain't the guy, then by morning you'll be wearing panties," John Lee said.

The man pleaded, "I swear to you, he's the person giving orders and making payments. He came out today to size up, the ah, competition, so he can give a first-hand report to his handler. He's the man's, man."

"How many other people are watching us from the woods and tell me why you think me and him look like a couple of modern-day slaves?" Jilkes asked.

"I was just trying to be a tough guy and didn't realize how crazy and determined your friend is. I need a damn doctor. Your friend is crazy. I'm in a lot of pain. Listen, this guy has hired every kind of radical son-of-a-bitch that you can imagine. He played the race card and that is the key to getting this job. He hasn't told them shit about you guys except that your activity boarders on the illegal, and when successful, he will pay $100k in cash and will provide lawyers to the loyal who are silent. Mister, please, I need a doctor. I'm in a lot of pain."

The Sarge and Mallory, having turned the corner and hearing parts of the guys admissions, the Sarge asked, "What on earth could he say about a bunch of old people?"

"He told everyone that you people are like a new Black Panther group, and that you are killing innocent white people and raping white women in Virginia."

"What the shit are you talking about?" The Sarge demanded.

"Sir, I don't know who you are, but I need a doctor."

"But you came here to make sure that we needed a doctor. You came here to spy on us and to make sure we are murdered. Are you in contact with Walter?"

"Who the hell is Walter? My contact's name is Allen."

"You're telling me that the person you work for, is named Allen?"

"That is the name he told us. Why? Is there someone else named Allen who is involved in this project?"

"Describe your Allen to me."

"He is a person you'll never forget. He has tats all over his body, he is big, and strong. He is at least 6 feet 7 inches tall and a beast. He loves to fight and picks on guys he knows he can beat without a problem. He is your classic bully." The man became more frantic as he begged, "I am getting dizzy, I need a doctor, please, I have been responsive. Can't you at least be honorable?"

Beckmire, ignored his pleas and demanded, "Where did you leave your vehicle? Is it where my people ran across you?"

"Yes, it is. Then I guess they are your crew? I hope you have a lot more of them because this guy is coming for you with an incredible number of people."

"I think you be stalling about something. My partner asked you a question and you haven't answered it yet," John Lee stated.

"Listen, I'm losing a lot of blood. Can someone help me? What was the question?"

"He done asked you twice. Are there other people watching the ranch like you and your friend were doing?"

The man spoke through desperate gasps, "I don't make the assignments, but if I had to guess, that guy lying on the floor kept saying you people were old, stupid and lucky and that his forces were going to clean your clock. Therefore, I guess he and I were the only one's out here. Insofar as how many people will be coming your way, I'm guessing there could be up to 250 or more. The strategy may be changed as a result of you capturing his eyes and ears on the ground. But they are going to flank you from the north, south, east, and west, an equal amount of people coming at you from all sides and everyone firing weapons at the same time. He was forecasting a blitzkrieg!"

"Is there anything else you can provide us with?"

"You ask the questions and I will answer, but I need to get to a doctor."

The Sarge directed, "John Lee, you and Jilkes drop him off where you found him, let him fend for himself and find his way out of here. He can't go back because they will execute him on arrival. Oh, and when you come back, I need you two, along with Carlos and his people, to watch our six while the rest of us try to spelunker."

"What that there word spelunker mean, Sarge?" John Lee asked.

"It means cave diving, my friend."

The intruder turned around as he was limping out of the barn and warned, "I'm a dead man regardless. If I were you, I would prepare to fight tonight or leave this place in a hurry. When his man doesn't report in, he's going to figure you people tortured him and me and we spilled the beans. Also, that area where your people stumbled upon me and my associate, that was the designated area of entry. They probably realize that it should be cancelled. I would look at other aspects of the farm and see where your vulnerabilities are and then fortify those areas or get the hell out of dodge. They don't plan on taking any prisoners except one, and you can count on that."

## CHAPTER TWELVE

The tunnels were well camouflaged and protected by two-foot thick steel hydraulic doors. As the group entered the first tunnel, Rashida said, "Juan and I, along with the children, have followed each tunnel to its conclusion. If you take any of these tunnels, they will lead you to rooms that have lots of guns, water, bandages, food supplies, communications equipment, and other stuff. One of the tunnels is a little more treacherous to reach, because there are wires dangling and lights flickering. I'm not sure if it was completed according to specifications, but it is the better of the three if you ask me for my opinion, because it provides the entire group with additional opportunities and exit strategies."

The Sarge walked over to Rashida, gave her a big hug and said, "You are my breath of fresh air and I love you so much. We all thank you for doing what we didn't take time to do. Thanks a million, Girlfriend." That exchange brought tears to Courtney's eyes because she knew that Rashida was still battling her demons of yesteryear.

In the tunnel that led to where the ex-senator resided, everyone saw exactly what Rashida meant. Gladstone said, "This tunnel has more options for defending ourselves. The others were straight shots and this one has turns and alcoves and weapons wrapped and ready. This is the one we should focus on, if needed we can defend ourselves as well as close it off with explosions."

A smiling Zanthius announced, "This tunnel is named 'Asiram' after my beautiful wife. In designing this one, I considered how my relationship/marriage has progressed and this tunnel defines where we are. At the end of this tunnel, Rashida, there is another tunnel that clearly gives us the ability to outflank those chasing us and allows us to seal, contain, and conclude our suitors."

"This is a beautiful thing, and how familiar are the children with these tunnels?" the Sarge asked.

Rashida replied, "Daddy, they know each tunnel and know what dictates which one they use."

"How did they learn to do that?"

"Juan taught them the system of retreat depending upon where you are if the house is over-run."

"Well, I'm glad they won't have to use them, but it's good to know our options. Rashida, will you give Jilkes, John Lee, and the others a tour of the tunnels and explain to them the differences?" the Sarge asked.

# # #

On the other side of the farm, Jong's cousin was cursing everyone who was not from his village as well as some who were. He was a genius at designing automated weapons systems. He felt that if he could secure it, then he could control it from afar by using the iPhone. This would be his greatest work because he felt this may be his last effort for his overbearing cousin.

He strategically placed solar powered motherboards in the trees that could target and fire a weapon independent of anyone pulling the trigger once a code was entered. This action would allow two sets of long guns to target those from the west. The machine pistols covered the north, south, and east--a perfect plan as plans go.

In the live round firing sequence, the ladies did exceptionally well. Rashida once again walked into the area and sang, "This is how you do it!"

Courtney said, "I hope I don't have to put you over my lap and whip your ass, young lady!"

"No Mom, I'm just fooling around."

"Are you fooling around with that shadow of yours?"

"What on earth are you talking about, Mom?"

"I'm talking about a person named Juan. Give me the 411 on him and tell me where you are in this equation. You know I don't like surprises and I have had too many for my tender age."

"Mom, I must admit, I like him, but I'm not into that touching and sex. He's attentive to the children and is teaching everyone Spanish. I don't like where I have come from and I can't go back there. Malik killed my soul and my desire, Mom. I can't get over that. Juan is a male friend and only that."

"Honey, I'm here for you, but you do what you feel you have to do. I just hope you get a chance to experience love without abuse and pain."

"Mom, I know. You, Dad, Larry, and of course LaGina, are the real people in my life. Now that I have met all of dad's friends, plus a few others, they are as well. I'm a little cranky because I want to be in school. I don't want to be a nurse any longer; I want to be a pediatrician."

"Oh, my goodness. Now, I'm one happy camper. I love that decision on your part. Have you told your father?"

"I have not. I wanted to make sure you supported me on this one first."

"Girl, let's get this done."

# # #

Jong and Gladstone got in a mule and drove to where his cousin was setting up. Jong asked, "How am I supposed to defend this area with this system?"

His cousin answered, "I'm working on a great design, but I haven't perfected it. If you give me two more hours, I think we will be able to program a simple game and transform it into your operating system for the long guns we have placed into operation by using a simple motherboard. I have to concentrate, and I need you, my royal overseer, to give me time and space to test my work."

"I will be back here in exactly two hours and you will be ready to demonstrate how this works. Am I clear?"

"It will be done, my master. It will be completed."

As the two men headed back to the farmhouse, Gladstone asked, "Why do you play that game with him? I know he's senior and you're his dung."

"He has several children in college at major universities and I support him and them. Consequently, he allows me to be important. Keen of you to understand that aspect of my culture," Jong acknowledged.

"How does he know so much about weapons, technology, and cars?" Gladstone asked.

Jong replied, "In my village, he was considered a genius because he could fix or make almost anything. He was a natural at boosting the horsepower in cars. He used a new product to make our cars bulletproof and he loves increasing the capacity of machine pistols. He has a drum that will expend 500 rounds of ammunition. He is just a smart person who sees a problem and develops a fix for it. He's like a father to me."

# # #

Allen called Beckmire to check in and see if he could be of any help. The Sarge told him what he needed from him and Mike was a way to find his cousin so he could gut him from his penis to his brain. He told them to spare no expense, but to also be discreet in their inquiries. Allen told the Sarge that Mike had mentioned a young lady that Walter liked, and he had stationed a few of his buddies to watch her place. Allen in summation, told the Sarge there was an evil wind blowing his way and that if he needed some additional firepower, then he and Mike would come and lend a helping hand. The Sarge thanked him and reiterated his need--find his cousin.

# # #

Insofar as preparations were concerned, the farm was as ready as it would ever be. Everyone was aware of how the tunnels worked, where they led, and how to access them from the different rooms in the house. There were weapons placed strategically out of sight all around the house and throughout the tunnels. It was obvious that each adult was now holstering a pistol and the automatic weapons were stored in secure locked spaces throughout the house that opened once the ODS was fully activated.

Jilkes said to the Sarge, "I think we should start surveillance duty as soon as this evening. What's your take on that?"

"I was thinking about that. Based upon what Jong showed us, we can watch the entire northern, southern, and eastern flanks of the farm as far as 2.5 miles out in each direction. I am worried about the western flank because that terrain is uphill and we're downhill. His cousins are over there now hooking up something to give us some coverage. Oh, there he is with Gladstone. Call him in and let's see what's going on."

Jong walked in and said, "Before you start to scream at me, have a Milky Way. Whatever the problem is, I did not do it."

"Mr. Amazing, can you give us an idea as to what your family is doing over there on the western flank?"

"I can do one better than that. In exactly ten minutes, his time will have expired and I can ask him any question I want about what the hell he's doing. All I know at this point is that he is hooking up long-guns to handle some of our problems."

"Well, why don't we all head over there in ten and see what he has cooked up. Gladstone, can you alert Larry, Mallory, and Zanthius for me? Thanks."

When Gladstone made the call to Zanthius, Asiram answered the phone. Gladstone told her that the Sarge wanted Zanthius to consult with him on some defensive issues. Asiram told Gladstone that she and her man would be there in a few.

A few minutes later, Gladstone reported to the Sarge, "I called your son's room."

"Say no more. When will they be here?"

"She indicated they would be here in a few. Larry is on his way and I must tell you something, I saw Rashida and she had a .9mm and two clips on her belt," Gladstone announced.

"She is the best shooter out of all of the women, with Courtney coming in second. Don't know how she learned, but she is a helluva shot," Jong said.

"Yeah, that other son of mine probably taught her and now that she knows that everyone is going to have to help defend us, she will not hesitate to pull that trigger. I can guarantee you that."

Asiram wallowed into the room and the Sarge said, "My, my. You look, I mean you look, ah, wonderful."

"Daddy-in-Law, you are a terrible liar. I am fat and swollen like one of John Lee's pigs and you say I look wonderful? Okay, let me make this mess known, I'm going to hurt your son first and then I'm going to come for you. He did this to me, and he to swears I look beautiful. Anyway, what's going on?"

Beckmire kissed Asiram's head before saying, "Honey, we're going to ride over to the western flank to evaluate our defenses."

Zanthius added, "You know one of the tunnels leads to the highest point on that hill. I'm just saying this because if we have a significant rush of mercs from that area, a few of us with machine pistols could do a lot of damage from there. If we used grenades that would do more damage. Just saying."

"Larry, will you find your sister and Juan, and ask Courtney or Ava if they can watch the children for a few? Zanthius, who dug those damn tunnels and are they trustworthy?"

"Pops, the people who dug those holes were brought here in vans without windows and each man was scanned before he entered the van and when he left the van. It is doubtful they knew where they were other than when they entered the van and then they made circles and counter-circles before entering and leaving the property. The other thing is, they were from Spain and were still in service to my, ah grandfather. They also consider my mother the daughter of the devil, so they are not interested in trying to do stupid."

Rashida showed up with Juan not too far behind her. The Sarge asked, "Dude, are you trying to date my only daughter?"

Rashida exclaimed, "Dad, not fair!" She looked at Juan and said, "The man asked you a question. Do you have a response?"

Juan choked up and uttered something unintelligible. The Sarge said, "Mister, I didn't hear that." He looked at Jong and said, "Mr. Amazing, did you hear his response?"

"I did not Sarge. Is this someone we have to watch?"

Juan, in the meantime, changed colors and began to profusely sweat. The Sarge said, "Okay, Juan, you and I will talk later, right now I need to know while you were learning to spelunker with my only daughter, did you happen to go to the end of the tunnels and perhaps exit them?"

Juan momentarily regained his composure and replied, "Mr. Sarge, I am most interested in speaking to you about Rashida, but she doesn't even know I exist. She talks to me because she thinks I am smart, not handsome, or sexy, just smart. On the matter of that other question, yes, we have been to the end of each tunnel with the children and have only opened the one's in the north and east. Those two are not armed. The tunnels in the west and south are on a different circuit breaker and I did not know where that one was, so we bypassed those two."

The Sarge asked, "Rashida, what is that on your hip?"

"Hey Dad, all the women are carrying these. We decided that you and the rest of the guys are fighting for us and we should be able to fight for you in return."

"Honey, the thing you want to say to your daughter is that you love her. You don't want her to have to wear a weapon in front of you. I love you and everyone in this compound and if it hadn't been for my son, who didn't know how to kiss without swallowing, we all would be back in our homes getting fat," the Sarge announced.

Asiram gently slapped Zanthius upside the head, looked at the Sarge, and asked, "Are you calling me fat? Are you the same guy that caused three of my homes to be destroyed? Even so, I love you and respect all that you do to keep us all safe, Sarge."

Juan said, "Rashida and I were going to check out those two tunnels to figure out why they weren't armed. So, would you people like to walk with us or ride those mules to the top of the hill over there?"

"Hey, you cowboys, go for a hike. Me and my man are going to ride this mechanized mule. Whistle when you get there," Asiram stated.

As Rashida and Juan led the group in the tunnel, Rashida said, "We should be at the end of this in a few minutes or so. On your right, there are handles. Each one from this point forward will have a different set of notches on its back. This handle has three notches which means that we should be nearing our exit in about nine minutes. It's our contention that everything is multiplied by three.

Rashida continued, "When we get to the next handle, that will be on the left, you will find that there are two notches, and so on. Oh, and by the way, between each handle there are sliding wall panels approximately nine inches from the handle where you should find a loaded weapon. I mean this is intricate and sophisticated. A bumbling fool would not pay attention to those details, but my ah." Rashida paused and looked at Juan and then said, "Sorry, my friend and I figured it out, but did not have time to check to see why this tunnel and the southern one were not wired."

At the end of the tunnel, Juan grabbed the handle on the left and said, "At the top of those steps there should be a blinking red light. If it's green, then the tunnel has been discovered and is compromised."

Jilkes inquired, "How on earth could you know that from here?"

"There are more cameras around here than I can recall. Every aspect of the farm is covered, and there are killing zones in some of the areas. A lot of them depend on solar, but some of them are powered by windmills that are hidden on each quadrant of the farm."

"How the hell do you know that?" Zanthius asked.

"Because Rashida and I have been investigating the security of the farm and we both have keen eyes. Listen, this is not a stand-a-lone tunnel. This place was developed with a mindset to survive, and air is critical to survival. We've been all over this place pointing out weak spots and noting them on our phones."

"How did you do that?"

"GPS, my brother. You ought to know that since this is all probably your design. Is that correct?"

Zanthius looked at him and answered, "Yes, you are correct. I, purposefully, told them not to connect this section and the southern one because I figure those would be the easiest escape venues. The other two don't provide much cover for moving large numbers of people. Also, I have a way of destroying the farm once again, if necessary." Zanthius looked at Asiram and said, "Honey, the reason those two tunnels are not on the security grid is because I can send false signals and images moving through the other tunnels. The two that are off the grid are in case the deal goes south, and it is destruction time. These two tunnels can withstand any blast that would once again, blow the house to smithereens. I didn't want to tell you that I had a plan to blow our home up again."

Asiram sauntered over to Zanthius and whispered in his ear, "You are my 'idiot spy' and I like the way you plan. We have enough money to rebuild this place many times over. I just like the idea that you take our security so seriously."

The Sarge said, "The rest of us would like to know what the hell is going on!"

"Just telling my husband, if you blow up another place of mine, I am going to make Courtney my enemy. I was also sanctioning his actions for annihilation of the property, if necessary, to secure our escape and ultimate revenge."

"What a family! Damn, Son, when were you going to tell me about this?" The Sarge asked.

"Pops, I was afraid to tell you because I didn't think that you and the guys would agree with my views. I had full information about the tunneling as well as the skulls and bones from the Civil War that were buried here in mass graves. Those two tunnels, for some odd reason, unearthed an awful lot of skeletons. I felt those bones required acknowledgment—regardless of which side they were fighting for. There were hundreds of bones discovered while the tunnels were being dug."

"Son, you must learn to trust us."

"I made these decisions on my phone Pops, while we were all over the place trying to bring an end to this madness. I hope I haven't compromised anything."

Rashida said, "My brother, it is a good thing that we are covered by the same cloth—Ben Beckmire. He taught me and Larry to think outside of the box and into outer space. No limits!"

Zanthius walked over to Rashida and said, "I think this is the only time that we have really spoken to one another." He proceeded to hug her, and she began to cry. Zanthius with tears in his eyes confessed, "I wanted to take you for a walk so that we could talk, but it seems like we were always under attack or on the offensive. You are like the quiet reality that says nothing. We all need each other, and I need you to tell me about my dad. Larry is so tight lipped."

Asiram asked, "Is there any chance that a shorted wire, errant bullet, or someone other than one of us could set off this explosion?"

"That would be highly unlikely," Zanthius replied. "Everything is coded except the handles. If the handles are pulled out and turned to inverse, then there is no going back. Rashida and Juan were correct, three is the magic number. The handles are the failsafe when all else has been exhausted. Once they have been altered, there is a six minute window before the explosion rips through the house and the other tunnels."

"Damn, Son, did they do mind experiments on you, over there in Europe?"

"Naw, Dad, I just know how these people play and they have no rules."

# # #

Rashida asked Juan to walk with her for a minute because she had something, she wanted to ask him. As the two ventured towards the center of the field, Rashida grabbed his hand and said, "Juan, you know I just realized that you are always around me. What is it you're trying to do? Are you trying to seduce me or something?"

"I have watched you since this thing started, and while in Australia, I was hoping you had the same dreams I did. I realized months later that you didn't. Listen, Rashida, I like you a lot, and I can't figure out why you don't know this. I eat with you and your child, I play with her and you, but you just seemingly don't notice me in a romantic way."

"When I was speaking to them about the tunnel, I realized that we do a lot and we're always together. My mom asked me if you were trying to connect with me and I essentially told her that we are just friends. But today, I saw you explain in detail to my dad our observations and I realized that perhaps I must be a little blind. Now, I'm not trying to seduce you or anything like that, but I am interested in getting to know you on another level. I mean we communicate extremely well, and I wonder if romance would nullify that after a while."

"Rashida, you are a complex woman. You are also unbelievably detailed in everything you do. I'm going to let you in on a little secret, my heart tells me that you are the woman of my dreams. My heart also told me not to rush you into anything because you would certainly reject me. I don't know what happened in your past, but I am now an official suitor with the highest possible outcome as my objective. Do you think we could have dinner to discuss our feelings and immediate expectations?"

"I think Mary Alice will setup for dinner around five or so. Let's shoot for six and reserve the back porch," Rashida confidently announced.

Courtney told the Sarge to take a nap, and he told her that he wasn't tired. She said, "Ben Beckmire, close your eyes and rest for a few minutes. I won't let you miss anything."

The Sarge sat on the bed and, before he knew it, he was snoring his head off. Courtney covered him and said, "My man is a machine."

Two hours later, the Sarge woke up and said, "I'm hungry. Let's get something to eat." As he stretched and yawned, his phone that was dedicated only to Allen, rang.

Allen said, "I know you have a lot on your plate, but this is some scary shit I have to pass on to you. One of my comrades who is on the run from Russian intelligence, gave me a call and told me that his government is not having any success with the Carbon Factor formula. He also told me the powers that be, suggested that the KGB get involved and secure the 'idiot spy'."

The Sarge snapped back and asked, "What does secure the 'idiot spy', mean?"

"Exactly what it states. They want to interrogate the 'idiot spy' and see if he has certain aspects of the formula tucked away for safety's sake."

"Allen, you can't be serious."

"Mr. Beckmire, I wish the hell this was just across the water noise. It was confirmed by an agent who has been assigned to investigate the feasibility of the situation. He reached out to me with a bunch of 'BS'. I asked him what I owed this call to and he said, "I need you to get me to the 'idiot spy'." I told him good luck with that, and he said, 'it is not a matter of luck, but a priority for his agency to secure and break the 'idiot spy'." I explained to him how many hundreds of people you and your team have killed in the last few years, but that didn't seem to disturb him. I will watch his moves and forecast them to you once they are translated."

"Perhaps we need to get a message out that the 'idiot spy' was simply a vessel and he has no strategic knowledge or understanding of the science involved in the development of the Carbon Factor. Do you think that's a possibility?"

"Mr. Beckmire, I will send a strong message along those lines. I hope they aren't vengeful for having their agent turn over state secrets to an American."

"Allen, keep me posted. Have you heard anything else about our impending threat?"

"It appears they have put the lid on this one. No chatter anywhere about a large number of people congregating."

"Thanks, Allen. As soon as you hear something, give me a call."

The Sarge drifted into deep thought and began to ask himself the obvious question. How could that many people go unnoticed? He thought that someone, somewhere must have seen or heard rumors of a large strike force meeting up.

## CHAPTER THIRTEEN

Walter realized that something was amiss when his henchmen did not report in. He appointed another one of his trusted crew to study the maps of the place and to target it from all four sides. Walter told him that the north and south aspects were critical because they led to a newly acquired property by the group that mirrored most of their existing land. Walter also indicated that in the east and west, those aspects butted up against neighbors' land and, therefore, were probably not considered viable avenues to escape. He instructed his henchman to make sure that the pictures of Zanthius, Beckmire, and Asiram were circulated and that extreme caution should be used if they were encountered. He vehemently stated to his man, "Make sure no harm comes to those three, if possible, especially, Beckmire! His other son and his wife can be killed on the scene, but I want the fetus extracted from Asiram and recorded. The kid, well, just decapitate him and take pictures so I can verify."

On the other side of the evil, Rashida was trying to find something to wear and appeared to be in a frenzy. Marisa, Larry's wife said, "Girl, if you don't have any suitable country clothes to wear, then make sure your hair, eyes and the rest of you are looking good. There is nothing wrong with having dinner with someone you never noticed for years. You can wear jeans but dress that hair and face up."

Marisa called Courtney and told her what was happening, and Courtney indicated she would be right there. She turned to the Sarge and asked, "Did something happen with Rashida and Juan today?"

"Not that I'm aware of. Why?"

"Marisa called and said she was a wreck trying to find something to wear to dinner."

"Something to wear to dinner. I am going down there with you."

"Ben Beckmire, you're not going anywhere with me. If she is finally breaking out of her shell, I don't want you scaring her back into it. I'm just going to give her some girl talk; you know, like don't trip him up and beat him to the floor-- amazingly simple things like that."

"You are such a nut. Trip him up and beat him to the floor. Wow!"

A few minutes later, Courtney knocked on the door and Rashida opened it and said, "Marisa, I'm going to kick your ass. Why did you call mom?"

"Because she knows how to settle you down. So, deal with it."

"I am so happy you're having a date. Wait, who the hell are you going out with? You told me that you didn't see Juan in your plans."

"When we met today in the tunnels, I took a good look at him and watched him interact with the Sarge, a thing that can be terribly intimidating. Anyway, I looked at him and said to myself, I must be slightly blind. He is a gorgeous man and quite smart. Mom, I looked at him and it hit me, I like this guy, but we're just having an exploratory dinner. This is basically to see if we want to move to another level."

"You look beautiful, girl. You're smart and you know how to handle yourself. I just came down here to tell you that I'm proud of you and happy you're at least smelling the roses."

Jong, on the other hand, was trying to convince Mary Alice that he was a keeper regardless of the fact that he was currently married. He told her that he was in the process of concluding his marriage. When Mary Alice saw Rashida, she went over to her and said, "Hi, my name is Mary Alice and I cater most of the food here. What's your name?"

Rashida looked at her and said, "Mary Alice, cut the crap."

"Rashida? Rashida, that's you? Oh my, who on earth are you meeting and are you having dinner here?"

"I was planning on having it here, but if you keep drawing attention to me then I might just have to have it in the field."

Juan showed up out of breath with a single long-stem red rose. He had his best shirt on and his work jeans. He walked over to Rashida and said, "You are the most beautiful woman I have ever seen. Will you have dinner with me?"

Mary Alice passed Jong and said, "Maybe you should study them and see what a woman needs and likes. We need romance, Mr. Jong, not modern technologies--romance. We need walks and hugs, kisses, and smiles, touching and yearning, but most importantly, honesty and love. Perhaps when you get my drift, we can have a wonderful dinner with roses, candlelight, music, and atmosphere. Ah yes, those things lead to romance, Mr. Jong, not conversation all of the time."

A rejected Jong left the area and headed out to where his cousin was way past his deadline. When Jong showed up, he said, "Cousin, I love a woman, but she wants flowers, romance, atmosphere, candlelight and music. What is wrong with these women? They must know that Japanese men have to be the master."

"Son, you are not home, the women here are not obedient, and are mostly disrespectful. Have you ever heard the saying, 'when in Rome, do as the Romans do'? Or this stupid one, 'catch more flies with honey than vinegar'? Every stupid person knows that. But you are in America and they are all pretty stupid. Look at this election and those people who listened to a guy with no plans say, 'I'm going to make it beautiful. Or 'it's going to be great'. This country is stupid, but their women love to be loved. Forget your ego and beg her to give you another chance. Tell her you want her to teach you how to love her."

"Enough of this madness. Where are we on this project?" Jong demanded.

"This project will provide you with 360 degree targeting. There are eight long guns with fifteen shot magazines, positioned approximately, 50 yards a part. They can only be controlled by an iPad or small computer. The spread between the weapons and the controller is as much as I could do with the antiquated materials that I'm forced to work with. You have slightly less than a half mile of gun clusters, but the capability of hitting moving targets at a maximum of 1500 yards which is 260 yards short of a mile. Next time, my wise and stupid relative give me more time and I can let you people eat popcorn and shoot everything that moves from your bedrooms." He started to say something else and his eyes watered up.

"Why are you about to lay a river of tears at my feet?" Jong asked.

"Your niece made a bad choice in meeting people and her boyfriend beats her. I'm afraid to consider what else he has done to her."

"Get me address immediately. I will have people on site tomorrow. Why didn't you tell me this?"

"I didn't want to embarrass our family."

"Get me details and it will be handled at my people's discretion."

"What does that mean? I don't want her involved with the law."

"He will disappear and be fed to the fish or burned into fertilizer."

"You can do such a thing?"

"Cousin, my people can miniaturize your head and put a bone through your nose."

"I will get you address. I also need to test this system tomorrow, is that going to be a problem? However, in case you need to use it tonight, this is how it works."

After ten minutes of conversation and dry demonstrations, his cousin said, "Goodbye, Cousin."

"Don't waste important time on dumb things like guns. Go make girl happy with flower, rap music, and food."

"One last thing Cousin, are those weapons hot?"

"Each has the first round chambered and are set for single shots."

# # #

John Lee, Jilkes, Yeshida, and Somara were entertaining Okema when Jilkes casually looked at his cell phone and said, "Hell, look at all that movement near the road." He yelled, "ALERT!"

Jong who was sitting with Mary Alice pulled out his phone, saw the movement, and placed the weapons system on standby. He studied the movement closely and realized that it was a herd of deer. As he zoomed in on the camera system, he could see clearly that the intrusion was caused by animals. He yelled, "Stand-down. The deer are on the move." He walked over to Jilkes and said, "Good catch, my brother. We need to have someone monitoring that system 24/7. Have you seen the Sarge?"

Jilkes said, "He and Mallory are checking the area where the property was extended. They are trying to figure out which tunnel gives us the best option for survival." He turned to John Lee and said, "Suppose those weren't deer. We would have been massacred."

"I feel you, brother, and we need to move to another level. Where is Chakes and Montomie, perhaps we can put them on first alert? You, being senior and all, I think you need to make the call," Jong stated.

Jilkes saw Gladstone and Whitmore and clearly stated that he wanted them to monitor the outfield defense system. Whitmore asked, "Where are the Sarge and Mallory?"

"I have no clue and, therefore, I need you guys to give me four-hours of monitoring. Is there a problem with this request?"

"Not at all, my brother. My question was merely seeking information and did not broach questioning the request. You know how we roll."

"Thanks. When I see the Sarge and Mallory, they may want to approach it differently, but as for now, I need you two guys in front of those monitors."

Jong said, "You guys be sure to keep those iPads charged and ready to roll. If we are overrun, then the goal is to destroy that closet where the equipment is. Those wires are a façade; the entire system is Cloud based."

# # #

When the Sarge and Mallory returned, they witnessed Gladstone carrying an assault weapon. Mallory asked, "Why are you parading around with that thing?"

"We had a breach of the property by a herd of deer. Jilkes thought it best that he assign someone to monitor the system. Along with that responsibility is to be ready and armed. I'm just following protocol."

Mallory said, "Good man. Jilkes is correct. We act as though this is our world and we control it. We have been lax and act as if we're still on holiday."

The Sarge looked around the property and realized just how vulnerable they were. He said to Gladstone, "What's your take on his actions?"

"He's senior and I follow orders. If I were senior at the time, I would have ordered the same protocol. He and Jong agreed to move to a heightened state of alert and ordered everyone to arm themselves with at least pistols."

"Where are they?" Mallory asked.

"Check the kitchen," Gladstone suggested.

The Sarge and Mallory walked into the kitchen and found John Lee, Jilkes, and Jong looking out of the window in the southern most direction. The Sarge asked, "What's going on?"

Jilkes replied, "Didn't know where you were and during that period, we had a herd of deer breach the property in the south. I had movement on my phone, and I called an 'alert'. Jong focused in on the intrusion and realized that it was animals and not men. I felt that we were exposed and I assigned Gladstone and Whitmore to monitor the sensing devices. I also ordered everyone to be armed and our guys to have assault weapons on them."

"Good call." Beckmire agreed. "As I look out of this window, I see a vast amount of land and realize that there are only a few of us compared to the numbers that are probably going to show up here. I worry about the western aspect of the ranch."

Jong said, "My cousin installed a few automatic weapons on that side with a range that is slightly short of a mile. We haven't tested it yet, but tomorrow he is coming back with suppression devices and we will test it out. However, they are armed, and I can control the firing sequences."

"You know you people are the absolute best friends a man could have. I have disrupted your lives and it's been way over two years since we have been back together. Everyone in this place can exercise command without hesitation. You know something else, that was one of the reasons we survived in the Nam. We made independent decisions that impacted us all but kept us safe. Now, that is brotherhood at its finest. What a group of friends!"

#

As the evening began to roll into night, Juan asked Rashida, "Do you think that I'm just out to jump your bones?"

"Perhaps! And perhaps, that's exactly what I need."

"Rashida, I would love to just jump your bones and passionately work you back into the world. I know I like you a lot. I can't imagine what it would be like after being intimate with you. My problem is that I have had intimacy, and it's not where I want to be in this situation."

"Juan, you were supposed to jump on that statement and make me turn you down vehemently."

"Oh, I see. I would like to talk seriously for a minute. Why are you talking to me now when you have had months to realize that I was scoping you?"

"Oh, that's what you were doing? I mean scoping me and what on earth does that mean? Were you stalking me? Were you spying on me? Just what does one do when they scope?" Rashida adamantly inquired.

"Sweetheart."

"Wait, I'm now your sweetheart? When did this all happen?"

Juan hesitated for a moment and said, "You seem to be in attack mode tonight. Why don't we try this another time?"

"Juan, I'm not attacking you. I'm attacking myself because I need a friend first, a lover second, and a mate third. I'm not trying to settle for any of those independent of each other, but it just ain't working for me. I know I like you and I know that we're friends, but I had a bad experience when I was young, and I swore to never venture down that road again."

"Rashida let's try to enjoy dinner and talk later. I felt as though you suddenly just jumped me without reason. Perhaps internally, there are some things you need to reconcile before we can move off this spot we seem to be stuck on?"

# # #

John Lee, Jilkes, and their companions were sharing a bottle of wine, when Okema walked in and said, "It is official! Mr. Brown has impregnated me."

Somara said, "Congratulations and good luck." She and the group followed up with hugs and well wishes.

Yeshida also congratulated her. Somara said, "That Mr. John Lee has impregnated me as well."

Yeshida and Okema congratulated Somara. Brown walked into the barn and congratulated John Lee on his impending role as a father.

Jilkes looked at Yeshida and said, "Go on. Tell them your news." She lowered her head and said, "I, too, think that I'm pregnant by that beast I call my husband."

John Lee said, "I be done known that."

"And just how would you know that Mr. John Lee?" Yeshida asked.

"My friend has been worrying me to crazy land asking me how to tell if you be done started that baby making process. I told him to look in your eyes and watch your habits change."

"You are so full of it, Mr. John Lee."

The group toasted each other, and John Lee said, "I be wanting to say something. I am one happy camper and I know that my mates are too. I be wanting to thank my lucky stars for that night in the bar when I met my new wife, and I just want to say that I love her more than I love Jilkes." Everyone laughed and John Lee walked over to Jilkes and murmured,

"You know that ain't no woman going to keep us apart. Love you, dude!"

"You know we have a lot of pregnant women floating around this place. We need to figure out how to deploy them or put them on a plane before this problem starts all over again," Brown said.

"Yeah, I been talking to my hardheaded woman and she refuses to leave. I told her the other women were leaving and she said, "they no love their man like I love my man. I no go nowhere." She talks funny and all, but I just love me some Somara," John Lee stated.

"So, none of them are leaving. I have an idea. Let me get Jong up here," Jilkes announced.

Minutes later, Jong waltzed into the barn holding Mary Alice's hand and asked, "What's up?"

Jilkes replied, "We have some really hardheaded pregnant wives who will not board a plane and seek safety. I was wondering, since we can't force them on a plane, can you instruct them how to fire the mechanized weapons on the north, south and east sides? Also, did your cousin finish the installation on the west side? Can you also teach them to handle those weapons?"

"Unfortunately, you guys have wives who are less than obedient. My woman will not be anywhere near this area when the shit hits the fan."

"I beg your pardon. Is there someone else on this farm parading as your woman or am I that same person?"

"Honey, can we talk about it later?"

"No, Mr. Jong, we talk now or there will be no later. I am not going to stand by and do nothing while everyone here is apparently at risk. Make me an offer I can't refuse, or I'm off in the morning to visit my family abroad and I will not return to this country for a long time."

Jilkes knew this was an awkward moment for Jong and asked if he and the guys could have a caucus. The men walked out of the barn and Mary Alice said, "I want to congratulate you, Somara, on being pregnant." A silence grew over the barn until Somara announced, "All of us are pregnant."

Mary Alice said, "Damn! And he hasn't even tried to seduce me. How sad. What should I do? I'm not leaving the compound until this guy sleeps with me. Am I that ugly?"

Jong walked in and asked, "Who is ugly?" Mary Alice ran out of the barn and Jong went racing behind her. When he finally caught up with her, he said, "Okay, let's do business first. You can no longer provide the food service because it compromises us. Secondly, I want you to be with me. Things happen fast with this group and we don't always have time to pack a bag. I want you to experience the family and love that these people have for each other and hopefully, you will share that same love for me one day."

"Why can't you see that I already love you and why won't you even attempt to corrupt my soul? We sleep in the same bed, but not together and never as one. I must be that ugly duckling that they spoke of when I was a child."

"I'm from a different culture than you and it takes time for me to figure things out, but I promise you I will change my approach."

"Are you out of your fucking mind? You're in America where the most contentious presidential race is underway with allegations of pay for play and child rape are at the center of the universe. You speak to me of a different culture. Have you completely lost all of your marbles?"

Jong bowed his head and replied, "I see that I have offended you. How can I make this go away and improve on my culturalization? Listen, my wife back home is a pig and is currently sleeping with a dog. I have had such hate for women, and it is only since you, that I realize that I am not whole and I'm in need of a mate, a friend and someone to trust. I need you because my nights and days are consumed with thoughts and desires of you. I can't tell you how much I ache for you. In my culture, we aren't told to express such emotions lest we be perceived as weak and undesirable. Today, I say to you with my heart and soul, that I want you and if you will have me, then I will have you."

"Why must there be conditions? My love is not based upon whether you love me and will have me or not. It is based upon my loving you and hoping, to hell, that you want to love me."

# # #

Courtney asked her husband, "Ben, when this is over, are we going back to our house or are we moving away?"

"What on earth brought this on?"

"Everyone is talking about building houses and I wouldn't mind relocating to a slower paced place like where John Lee lives. I think there are too many bad memories for me at our current home. Not many women can say that they killed an intruder in their home. I took an oath to save lives, not to destroy them."

Beckmire looked at his wife, realized that she was on the verge of crying and said to her, "Honey, you have been a real trooper and a great companion in this mess. I will move anywhere you want. You never complain and you attempt to be the rock for the rest of the women. I love you for that and I say, with conviction, you name the place. If we both agree, then we move."

"Ben Beckmire, you are so slick. First you say, wherever I want to move is okay with you, then you say, 'if we both agree upon the location' then we move. You speak with a forked tongue, Ben Beckmire." Courtney slid up next to her man and whispered, "Now, might be a good time to get some play time in, big boy." As they kissed, the passion began to flow, and Courtney fell back on the bed. As Ben laid beside her, his phone rang. It was Juan who said, "It is imperative that I speak with you."

"Juan, I'm in the middle of something. Can I call you back in half-an-hour?"

"Yes, sir, that would be perfect."

As Ben returned to the point he left off, he started caressing Courtney and the phone rang again. Mallory said, "Sarge we need to talk about the western defense system as soon as possible."

"Mallory, can I get back to you? I'm in the middle of something at this moment. Can you give me half-an-hour?"

"Sure, Sarge, take your time."

As he refocused on Courtney, Monica called Courtney and said, "Listen, Juan is so upset about how Rashida is treating him. We need to intervene before he flies the coup."

"Monica, can I get back to you in a few minutes?"

"Okay, give me a call."

Ben Beckmire exclaimed, "Damn! I guess no one thinks we need alone time." As the two lay there in each other arms, Courtney's phone rang again. It was Rashida who said, "Mom, I need to talk to you. I can't get rid of my past."

"I'll meet you on the back porch and we'll take a little walk." Courtney was about to speak to Ben when his phone rang. It was Allen who told him that he had heard that a group of foreign mercs were going to take them on tonight. The Sarge asked for clarification and Allen said, "I don't have full intel on this one, but it's from a reliable source—Mike."

"Let me call you back and set some things in motion here."

The Sarge called Mallory and asked him to meet him in the kitchen. He also called Jilkes, who called Brown, who called Montomie, who called Gladstone.

When the group arrived in the kitchen, the Sarge said, "Oh, I forgot to call Mr. Amazing. Has anyone seen him?"

Brown replied, "I saw him near the corral feeding the horses."

Five minutes later, Jong walked in and asked, "What's up, my people? I have a date tonight."

The Sarge said, "I received a call from Allen who told me that Mike indicated to him that a bunch of people are planning to breach the property tonight. I don't know where they are from or if the threat is credible, but those guys have been looking out for us in the deepest parts of the sewers. We need to go on alert. Mr. Amazing, what systems work and what systems need testing?"

"Everything here works. Bernstein and Yvette are monitoring the system now."

"Yvette?" the Sarge inquired.

"Yes, Yvette. She is extremely technology savvy and has pointed out some minor issues with the system. They basically are doing a stress test on them to discern any technical glitches."

"Mallory, we have to make assignments, Allen could be correct."

"Sarge, we do not need assignments in the field. We can monitor and engage from the command center. Our forces should be focused on and around the house. We have coverage in the outfield," Mallory stated.

"I know we have coverage, but is it as reliable as when we're protecting each other?"

"Sarge, the purpose of these systems is to eliminate the stress on our people, who without it would be spread thin around the farm. Perhaps this way, we can scare people off before they get close to us."

"Okay, Mallory, I don't have a clue about the size of the force or where they are from, but we need to protect the center. Make the assignments."

# # #

John Lee asked Jilkes, "Do you think we will ever be able to go home?"

Jilkes intently looked at him, paused and said, "Dude, this is the greatest time of my life. I'm with you, the rest of the guys, and we have married these two lovely women, who speak ill of us sometimes. So, no, I don't want to go home without settling this thing one way or the other. I'm hesitant to tell you this, but I love the adrenalin rush that I get by keeping a weapon near me."

"I don't want to sound like a 'me to echo', but this here stuff is great for me as well. I mean, me and you are in lockstep together and we have some great looking backup. My woman be done told me a hundred times that she is happy I selected her and not one of those women who color their hair blond. What she be meaning by that?"

"John Lee, you've heard the blonde jokes. Your woman is happy she is not blond and/or perceived as dumb. 'Dumb blonde', I know you have heard that before."

# # #

As the notion of an impending strike against them increased, the Sarge called everyone to arms. Mallory made the assignments, and everyone was on full alert.

Jong said to Mary Alice, "It's probably not safe for you to leave the compound anytime soon. The Sarge received word that a strike is imminent. I would hate to have people see you leave this place and then use you as a potential bargaining chip."

"Jong, why would they assume I'm with you guys?"

"Listen, it's your choice, but I would like to make the decision for you because you have no idea of the resolve of the people who are coming here, have. No one is safe, including the children. Just for your edification, at Asiram's ranch in the Midwest, they placed suicide vests on the children and blew the ranch to pieces. We escaped because there were tunnels the perpetrators did not know about."

"You're really beginning to scare me."

"My intent is not to scare you, but to convince you to stay here with me. I love you, Mary Alice." He reached over and gave her a sloppy kiss and she said, "Oh my, now that's what I'm talking about. Give me another one of those and a weapon."

#

Courtney caught up with Rashida and asked Juan if he would excuse himself for a minute while she talked to her daughter. Once the two women were alone, Courtney asked, "Baby, what's wrong? Don't you like him? For over three months now, the two of you have been inseparable. What's the problem?"

"Mom, I don't know what to do. I'm afraid to express my feelings and emotions, I don't even know how to approach the conversation. I like him a lot and he is kind to me and LaGina and the other children. He's attentive and honest, but I don't know how to show my affection."

"When he comes back in here, tell him about what happened to you and why you are so apprehensive about moving forward with any kind of relationship. Give him the full details, so you won't have to have the conversation again. Hold his hands and let it flow. If he loves you, you will feel it, and he will show it. Don't let him walk away from you because you are unable to respond on any level. Talk to him and not at him, as I have heard you do. That guy worships the earth you walk on, but he might be reaching his limit."

#

Jong walked in and stated, "I have to assume operational authority of the systems. Rashida, I asked the Sarge if you and Juan could be my backup. The primary question is simple. Are you willing to take another's life to preserve your life and that of your child?"

Rashida looked at Juan and said, "First, Juan, will you help me get through this? Second, Jong, we got this!"

She turned to Juan who said, "I am here for you for as long as you will have me as a friend."

"Juan, I'm looking for more than a friend. Is that the limit of your intent?"

"You know what Rashida? You talk entirely too much." Juan made a move on her that was so smooth and fast, she didn't have time to think about or analyze it. Instead, she fell into his arms and he gave her a sloppy kiss which was a ten, on a scale of one to ten. Rashida looked into his eyes and knew this guy was the real deal and asked, "Dude, what took you so long?"

"Oh, I just wanted to make sure you could survive one of my kisses because they are packed with love, emotion, commitment, and security. That was a kiss of love, my dear."

"Damn, I feel dizzy. I have never felt like this before. Juan, kiss me again and again until I pass out."

Jong returned to the control center with Mary Alice and interrupted the kissing session between Rashida and Juan. He said, "You no can watch monitor with lust on your mind. I need you to focus on our security. Can you do this?"

Juan started to say something, but Rashida knew that Jong would be less likely to give her hell, so she said, "Jong, please don't tell my father you caught me kissing this guy. Can you imagine what he would do to him?"

"Oh, I see what you mean. I slapped him twice and he tried to kill me. You kiss his daughter and I know he will kill you. You had better go and tell him that you kissed his daughter before he comes looking for you with daggers in his eyes."

## CHAPTER FOURTEEN

At exactly 1500 hours, Jilkes who was acting erratic and talking to himself finally said to John Lee, "If I didn't care about casualties, I would send a small number of our people to test our defenses. What say you?"

John Lee thought about the question, pondered several answers, and blurted out, "Damn, minority fellow, you be done hit something on the head. If I have 250 people who are going to attack a place, why not first send fifteen or twenty of them out there so they can show me their defenses?"

Jilkes called the Sarge and said, "We need to stand down on the weapons systems and place some of our people in the fields. I think your cousin is going to test our defenses. I submit I have no strong data, but that first wave will probably be trackers with cameras on them that will indicate whether they were in a firefight or were cut down by a damn Gatlin gun."

The Sarge huddled with Mallory and Jong and they discussed the information. The Sarge said, "We are alive because those two unlikely members of our group always considered alternatives and could smell or detect problem areas. I trust them and will always trust them."

"I'm with you, Sarge. I trust their judgement. I will have Rashida and Juan stand down on the field defense."

"Rashida is handling the mechanized weapons?" the Sarge inquired.

Jong answered, "She and Juan are the most proficient on the system. I think Larry might be better, but he has not shown an interest in doing it."

"You're saying my daughter and Juan are the most efficient at using the system?"

"Sarge, she is better than he is. And now they are an item."

"What the hell are you talking about? What does an 'item' mean in your world?"

"I think sooner than later, you will have more grandbabies." The Sarge gave him a look that would scare a bear and her cubs. Jong turned to walk away and the Sarge said, "Thank you for assigning her to that task alongside Juan. My child was heading straight to hell and I think he has restored her humanity."

Meanwhile, Mallory said to the Sarge, "I sent Jilkes and John Lee into the field with their women. I have Brown, Okema, Bernstein, and Yevette on the roof."

"Damn my niece is operative as well?"

"Sarge, you should watch more of the action rather than develop the strategy. Each person on the farm is now carrying a weapon and is proficient in the use of it. The question is-- will they exercise the right to defend themselves and us against intruders?"

At 1530 hours, the Sarge gave the command to stand down from use of the ODS. He knew that Jilkes, John Lee, Yeshida, and Somara were scattered throughout the southern part of the farm. Mallory assigned Gladstone, Whitmore, Montomie, and Chakes to the western side of the farm. Larry, Jong, Mary Alice, and McArthur were covering the barn area, along with the Sarge and Mallory. Asiram, Zanthius, Courtney, Ava, and Marisa provided protection for the farmhouse. Carlos and his guys were assigned to the eastern aspect of the ranch.

At 2103 hours, Rashida issued an alert. She reported, "There are seven dots on my screen heading towards the farmhouse from the south."

Juan yelled, "I have five dots coming from the west and on my other screen, I have four breaching the compound from the east."

"I also have four coming from north of the barn on my screen," Rashida stated.

In a low methodical voice, the Sarge explained, "This is an exploratory group. I need a few of them alive. I want to grant quarters, but they're here to hurt us. People, this is terminal."

As the intruding forces reached a certain point, they reversed their tracks and quickly retreated. John Lee said, "I be thinking them there fellows just marked their shooting positions and they might be using more than bullets to attack us. I mean maybe they would use something like a rocket propelled grenades out here!"

Jilkes said, "I'm with you. That seems like a mark position incursion. No one fired a shot which makes me think they might believe they can just run up on us the next time. Perhaps we need to talk to the Sarge and give him our take."

# # #

Strategically, the Sarge had his people maintain their positions. He walked into the room where Rashida was and asked, "Baby Girl, you got my back?"

"I have my hand on the trigger; I will exercise it, Dad. You can count on me."

"Love you, Baby Girl."

In a caucus, Mallory said, "Those guys just ran a certain distance and then retreated. What's up with that? I mean if I didn't know any better, I would say that they just marked off an artillery strike." He smiled, paused, and then said, "Kiss my ass. We have been measured. I suggest that we measure them as well."

The Sarge asked, "What does that mean?"

"Why can't we use those tunnels to get behind our enemies?"

There was a silence in the room and John Lee said, "I'll be damned. I think we done figured a way to hurt them and contain them, like herding damn pigs."

"Oh, yes, I see where you're going with this one. However, we don't need to get behind them, we can attack them as soon as they breach our perimeters. They saw how easy it was to run up on us without firing a shot or being shot at. Our ODS would desecrate their forces in a hurry. If they attack from the west, then the long guns will target them as well as those on top of the roof. Our only foreseeable problem is if their entire force entered from the west. We might kill a third of them with our automatic weapons, but the other two-thirds would be on our butts in a matter of minutes," Jong stated.

The Sarge inquired, "Do you have faith in that weapons system?"

"No, not entirely. I have faith in my cousin because he knows if anything happened to me, he wouldn't be able to afford those college tuitions that I sponsor. If you would like to send a detail out, I could show you precisely how they will appear on the screen as dots and which bank of machine pistols will respond. Or Rashida can show you while six of us ride up the road and begin to make our way back to the farmhouse," Jong said.

"It's far too dangerous to do night maneuvers, especially, after having people run up on us and mark their territory. I think it's safe to assume they will be monitoring us from afar and we should act as calm as possible. I don't think we have the luxury of running any more weapons tests. I wish your cousin could bring those suppression devices out here tonight or first thing in the morning," the Sarge suggested.

"Sarge, I don't think we'll have to worry about an assault for the next two days because it's going to rain. He's planning on bringing them tomorrow and we can detect if there are bodies hanging around. Remember, we have scanners, cameras, sound equipment, and metal detectors all over the place. What I like to suggest is that Zanthius and I make a run out to the end of the property line, along with Jilkes and John Lee, and scout the area. It wouldn't hurt if you had Whitmore, Gladstone, and McArthur on long guns watching our perimeters," Jong announced.

Zanthius walked into the room and asked, "What's going on?"

"Son, I will inform you of our decisions as soon as we finish our meeting. How is Asiram?"

"She's finally eating for two people and has somewhat forgiven me for impregnating her. She mumbles about how actresses deliver babies, and the next month, they are on television showing off their after-birth bodies. Her favorite person to hate is that big butt girl from that reality TV family."

"Son, exactly how does the sound and metal detectors work out there in the field?"

"Pops, I showed Rashida and Juan how to control the system and listen for sounds and discern the difference between animals and humans. For instance, the animals are going to set off sensors. If they're carrying an AK-47 then the metal detectors will engage at some point, but the animals are going to set off motion only sensors only."

"Okay, now I understand. Well, I'll be, here's my newest daughter-in-law. How are you feeling? You look absolutely fantastic. Just to bring you both up to speed, we had some intruders from all four quadrants of the farm, run up on us and then retreat without firing a single shot."

"Did you capture any of them?" Asiram asked.

"No, we didn't. My people think that they were an exploratory team sent out to assess our defenses. As it was, we monitored them and know exactly where they stopped. What I must share with you is something that we saw over in the Nam. The enemy would send people out and mark their progress and then fire mortar shells. I'm kind of thinking that they might come with RPG's."

"Oh shit! That's some serious stuff. Honey, can the house survive a direct hit?"

"Our most vulnerable point is the roof. We can probably withstand, two hits on each side of the house before the integrity of the outer shields fail. Now, that is all dependent upon what kind of missile they fire at us. My guess is that we want to make sure that no one gets an opportunity to fire that kind of weapon at us."

"Daddy-in-Law, have you seen Rashida? I left LaGina with Courtney and Ava, the two new best friends. You might not want to say anything incorrect in the near future, because I think they have been discussing the mighty Ben Beckmire— ooooh."

"I know you have every reason to dislike me. Three houses later, but two have been rebuilt and fortified and I, I'm sorry we, are still in the business of protecting you and the guy who kissed and swallowed."

"Ah, Pops. Really?" Zanthius saw that Asiram was unknowingly losing this battle so he jumped in and said, "You're going to be a mother soon. I need you to stay away from the negative so your delivery will be without any issues. You are going to be a grandfather again and I need you to be kind to my wife and your daughter-in-law."

"Well played, Son. Asiram, my problem is that I think about all that has happened, and it saddens me. Hell yeah, I would be hating me some Ben Beckmire too. Three houses later! I never wanted none of this to happen, but at least we didn't lose a single life. My guys came to help us, and while we all have enriched ourselves, I still find it hard to relate to you. You are my daughter-in-law and the mother-to-be of my newest grandchild. I know I'm tired and probably in need of rest, but I must admit, I can't sleep at night because of the pain I have caused you. I just think that my son deserves more of the blame than I do. Okay, I'm just kidding, but I feel the sting when we are together. You know, one day soon, you and I are going to go for a long walk and talk. I mean just talk about nothing and everything."

Asiram walked over to Ben Beckmire and said, "I need that, because I trust you, and couldn't trust my own father to do right by me."

"You will always have me here to kick butts for you, Asiram. You are my family and I admire you for helping us out."

As Rashida was reading her daughter a bedtime story, LaGina asked, "Mommy, why are there glow-sticks in the field?"

"Honey, what are you talking about?"

"Look in the field. Can't you see those glow-sticks?"

"Honey, I can't see a thing from here. I will check it out in the morning."

# # #

In the morning, McArthur, Whitmore, Chakes, Montomie, and Carlos's team, minus Juan, scanned the western perimeter of the farm. John Lee, Jilkes, Yeshida and Somara investigated where the intruders were. Jong and his cousin were cautiously installing suppression devices on the long guns.

In the area McArthur and Whitmore scanned, there appeared to be a lot of boot prints. Whitmore radioed the Sarge that he might need the hound-dogs to figure out where they came from and where they went. The Sarge told him when Jilkes and John Lee finished their site inspection, he would send them to him. Chakes hearing the transmissions chimed in and informed the Sarge where he, Montomie, and Carlos were, there seemed to be a lot of footprints as well.

Cigarette butts and cigar remnants were prevalent in the places they checked, as was plastic water bottles and coffee cups. When John Lee and Jilkes caught up with McArthur and Whitmore, they took a long look at the site, and decided the area was used less than two hours ago.

After having a strong cup of coffee, Rashida met up with Juan and he gently grabbed her and kissed her lightly. She said, "This adds a new dimension to how my day begins. I like it. Keep up the good work, dude."

"Rashida, would it be too much to ask you to call me Juan instead of 'dude'?"

Rashida was about to say something flippant but decided against it. Instead, she said, "Juan if I offended you, I apologize. It is a dear term for me when I think of you, that's all. Oh, last night, LaGina asked me if I saw glow-sticks in the field. You see anything like that last night?"

"I did not," Juan said.

Later, Rashida and Juan entered the room to monitor the systems and relieve Bernstein and Brown. Brown said, "When you see Jong, tell him that something is interfering with the signal. Tell him it actually blanks out for minutes at a time."

Juan said, "I'm going to fix myself another cup of coffee, would you like one?"

"No, not really, maybe a bottle of water. Wow! Did you see that?"

"See what?"

"The screen went completely blank for a second or two. We had better let Jong know about this. I think his cousin is here and maybe he needs to tweak something? I'm going to call him."

Rashida informed Jong of the problem and repeated what had been told to her by Brown and Bernstein. Jong called his cousin and asked him what would cause the screen to go blank in the monitoring room. His cousin told him that there were no spikes in power and that the systems were good, and that he would check it out after he installed the last suppression device.

When they entered the room, Jong's cousin ran a scan and realized there was a signal being broadcasted somewhere in the field. He asked Jong if anyone had installed different sensors than the ones he used and was told no. Rashida said, "My daughter asked me if I saw glowsticks in the field last night, but I didn't."

Jong's cousin said, "If in line, they break signal and ease a worm into the program. Someone has installed signal blocking devices in the field that are used to block communications, that are interfering with our systems. This problem did not exist yesterday, my cousin. Perhaps you had visitors during the night?"

Jong said, "We did indeed have visitors who came onto the property last night. They reached a certain point and then retreated. If they placed some things in the field, then if we change or terminate them, they might change their strategy. What are your thoughts and how can we get around this issue?"

"Cousin, the thing they use is childlike. You can keep it as is and let them think they have penetrated your system. That mess is only good for twenty-four to thirty-six hours. When you want to kill it, simply switch channels. Give your people a series of operating channels. No worm can get into my systems, no hacker. You switch channels and all is fixed." He looked at Rashida and said, "Young miss, you stay detailed and all will be okay."

"It is a good thing you just didn't let that go?" Juan asked.

"Juan, I need to find my dad and Mallory."

"I saw them walking out by the barn. I'll monitor the system?" Juan said.

"Okay. I'll be right back." Rashida walked out of the room and noticed a flashing battery light. She saw Zanthius and asked, "Brother, why is that battery light flashing in the closet?"

"I don't know, but I'll check it out."

Near the barn, she saw Mallory and her dad talking. She excused herself and said, "Can you guys walk with me back to the house? I have something to show you."

"Can it wait?" the Sarge asked.

"Dad, no, it can't. This is critical to our existence."

A few minutes later, the Sarge, Mallory, and Rashida, entered a room.

Zanthius was talking to Jong and his cousin about the flashing battery light. Rashida inquired, "Really, Brother? You don't know what that battery is for?"

"Frankly, I don't Rashida."

"Rashida, you brought us here to discuss a battery," the Sarge asked.

Rashida yelled, "Disconnect the damn thing and see what happens! Sorry Dad, but last night LaGina could see glow-sticks in the field, I didn't. This morning, Jong's cousin informed us that there are communications blockers out there. Those people who came up on us last night placed them strategically in the field. The product they planted, also interfered with the ODS. Okay, we have the solution to that, but what strikes me as critical is that Jong's cousin said the product is only good for twenty-four to thirty-six hours. If I were to guess, I would think that we are going to get hit tonight."

The Sarge looked at her and asked, "You put that scenario together, Rashida?"

"I did, and I know you make the decisions relative to preparation."

"Okay, Lady General, we're going on full alert." As soon as the Sarge said that, Zanthius pulled the blinking battery out of its container. The entire defense system shut down.

Jong's cousin said, "That's a 12 volt and I think I have a new one in my truck. But before I do that, I want to rewire that battery and make it the backup rather then the primary and place a kick switch to engage if the generator is activated. Does that makes sense to you people?"

Zanthius said, "That's truly a design flaw. Your prescription, is it a temporary or permanent fix?"

"I no need medicine. I fix problem without medicine."

"I'm sorry. When you fix the problem will it be temporary or permanent?"

"I only fix permanent problems. He fixes temporary," as he pointed to Jong.

"Baby Girl, I'm so glad to have you on board. Look at the things you are paying attention to that we just ignored."

Jong whispered to his cousin, "You try to make me smell bad in front of my friends?"

"No, Cousin, I just state the facts. I usually don't talk to them devils, but you live with them, so I tried to make them understand. That big guy offers me medicine. I no need no damn medicine."

"You know what, Cousin? Whatever! Fix the shit and try to get out of here before dark. Tonight, I think it's going to be the blood-moon!"

"Oh, when I get the new battery, I want you to look at new scope I fix for rifle and for night. It is crazy but I can magnify an image clearly 1.5 miles out. I see pimple on face at 1.5 mile. You look, see, and let me know if you want to use. It is big, but it is something I started to work on for you."

"Thank you, Cousin."

"Our family can help you if you want. We know how to fight and we're good. You think about it and let me know and I will get ten members here and place them on the outskirts."

"I thank you for your concern. I will let you know if we decide we need help. Thank you."

# # #

An hour or so later, after fixing the battery and rewiring it to a back-up unit, Jong's cousin showed him the scope. It had the circumference of a red wine glass. John Lee said, "I could see that from a mile away."

"Suppose this allowed you to see 1.5 miles away including a close-up that shows pimples on the face?"

"No damn way. Only telescopes have refractors that strong."

Jong's cousin picked a target that was closer to two miles away and said, "I need you to relax and close your eyes for ten seconds or more. When that time is up, I want you to only open the eye looking through the scope."

John Lee followed instructions and when he opened his right eye, he jumped and exclaimed, "What the fuck! How can this be? Just because you can see that far doesn't mean you can hit a target that far away."

Jong's cousin said, "I make a bullet like a missile. You lock on target with scope and fire bullet, then bullet find locked on target."

"Jong, your cousin is full of shit!"

"No, John Lee, he is an admirable man and has proven his worth to us repeatedly. Cousin, can you demonstrate?"

Jong's cousin answered, "Okay, I only have one box of these bullets that I made so far. This rifle is a modified M1. I replace barrel, grip, stock, chamber, and everything. I want you to scope something as far as you think you can see and then press 1st trigger position."

John Lee targeted a huge oak tree. Jong's cousin placed a huge odd-shaped round into the chamber and told John Lee to deviate from the target by 45 degrees. He told John Lee to brace himself and fire the weapon at the deviated target. John Lee fired the round and it sounded like a cannon. After the recoil, he refocused on the original target. He witnessed the round hit the tree. John Lee said, "Well, kiss my favorite hog's ass. That there be some crazy shit." Upon hearing the noise, everyone who was off-duty, grabbed their weapons and began to scour the area. Jong gave the all clear signal and people returned to what they were doing.

"I be apologizing to you, sir. That there be the craziest thing I ever did. That there recoil is mighty beasty, but hell, that damn bullet had a mind of its own. I apologize, sir; incredible. John Lee then said, "Can't you see that there big ass scope reflecting?"

"Nope! You no see it. I no put filter on it."

## CHAPTER FIFTEEN

Jong said to Mary Alice, "I have a feeling that we're going to be attacked tonight. I can get you off the farm if you like. I love you, Mary Alice, but this is going to be a very bloody night. People are coming here to kill us and anyone who is on this farm, including the children. Let me get you to safety."

"Jong, I am as safe as I have been for a long time. On this farm I feel serenity. I know you love me, and I love you and, therefore, if I'm going to die, then what better place than here, now, and with you?"

Jong held her hand and found her waiting lips. They kissed gently at first and the passion moved them to the next level, and then the love making consummated their relationship. Jong jumped her body like a thirsty man in the desert after finding water. He moaned, thrusted, and she moaned and double-thrusted, and they thrusted until they both collapsed on the floor. He said, "I have never been so adventurous or aggressive. You bring out the wolf in me."

"And you bring out the woman in me. I have never made love before. I was doped and raped, but I now know the difference. Oh, my goodness! I'm going to work this magic everyday with you. I sure hope you have the stamina!"

After a brief rest, Mary Alice began to kiss the man of her choice on his chest and then worked her way to his nipples. An overexcited Jong couldn't handle the sensations and began to laugh. Mary Alice knew at that point she had her man. Jong attempted to provide the same sensations, but it was noted that he needed help in that area. What he didn't need help with was becoming aroused again and taking control of Mary Alice's body. He remembered watching porn in the Nam and pulled a very satisfying act on her. She moaned and held his head in place while experiencing a massive orgasm. Completely spent, she laid in his arms and said, "To die feeling like this is not a problem for me. How about you?"

# # #

Elsewhere, it was time for Rashida and Juan's break. Juan asked, "Do you want to get LaGina and go swimming?"

"I want to go swimming, but I don't want to have to watch LaGina right now. I need some time alone with you. Okay, I'll catch you back here in ten minutes."

Six minutes later at the pool, Juan exclaimed, "Oh, my God! You look fabulous, darling."

"Thanks." She dove into the water and swam to where he was and said, "Oh, my goodness, the water feels fantastic." Juan took the opportunity to touch Rashida low on her side. She jerked away and asked, "What the hell was that?"

"I meant no harm by that gesture. I wanted to send you a message that I want to make love to you. I'm guilty of a lot of things, but with you, I just can't get it right." She swam over to him and said, "You can't just feel me up like I'm for sale or something."

"I never equated you with a for sale sign. Stop being so predictable. I knew that was going to piss you off and that's why I did it. You don't want to discuss your past, but you want to let it dictate your future. Somewhere there's a disconnect. Do you follow what I'm saying? I'm hoping that you gain control over that part of your life that scarred you, and allow me to enter, repair, and love you. I need a little trust and then I think I can clear the cobwebs and proceed to plant a newer and longer lasting picture of us in your head."

Rashida swam to the other end of the pool and back. She looked at Juan and said, "I think you just need to get laid."

"How dare you speak so casually about something that should be sacred. I don't need to be laid! I need to be loved and I have saved that honor for you."

Rashida once again swam to the other end of the pool and back, but this time when she came up for air, she gave Juan a sloppy 10 kiss and placed her body close to his to arouse some vital organs, for each party. She purposefully moved from side to side and his little brain did exactly what she predicted—rose to the occasion.

Rashida said, "Please don't talk. Just try to enjoy the feeling. I'm not sure I want to go further than this right now, but I want you to at least experience my sensitivity. Please, don't think I don't want to make passionate love to you. My suffering is deep and painful. I am the only one who can get me beyond it. I must admit, the feeling of your private part near and on mine, excites me to make an irrational decision. I need passion and I know it is only you who can provide that for me. But you must know, I have a lot of baggage and if you jilt me, I will fucking kill you."

"If your father doesn't do the honor first. Can we dispense with the threats and focus more on the love and passion? It seems to be the more desirable path that leads us both to places that are permanent. I want to be young and in love, middle age and still admiring you, and old age and still trying to figure out how to get some late at night. Those are my thoughts. Stop trying to kill me for attempting to seduce you and love you."

Rashida rested her left elbow on Juan's right shoulder and kissed him like no other woman had ever kissed him before. She placed her right hand on his already excited and about to explode member. As she did so, that is exactly what happened. Juan prematurely ejaculated into the pool. Rashida knew what was happening and made sure to give him the pleasure that he was seeking.

An embarrassed Juan said, "I'm humiliated, but satisfied. I'm ashamed but relieved. I do not know what to say. I so much wanted to share that with you on another level, but apparently, it was for all to see." He lowered his head under water and swam to the other end of the pool. He stepped out of the pool and never looked back.

Rashida called to him to no avail. She admired the way in which he departed from her with dignity. She thought to herself, "He left passion for me in the pool. I so much wanted that to be a part of my body. Damn, I love that guy and don't know how to show him!"

Rashida went to her room and showered. After exiting the shower, she heard a faint knock on her door and thought that it was LaGina. When she opened the door with just a towel on, Juan said, "I love you and I need to try to show you how much." Without resistance, he removed Rashida's towel and once again admired her beauty. He kissed her lips and moved methodically to her neck. He used his free hand to caress her love zone. Rashida began to moan as Juan physically backed off and began to fondle her breast with one hand and kiss the other. Juan looked at Rashida and said, "I love you so much." He then proceeded to kiss Rashida in places she had never experienced. His demonstration of certain love-making techniques caused her to abandon control and to submit herself freely and fully to him. It was magical.

It caused Rashida to have one thunderous convulsion after another. Weakened and shaking, Rashida murmured, "Please stop, I feel faint."

CHAPTER SIXTEEN

The farm was on full alert and everyone had a station. Instead of having people in the field, camped out, and cold, the team was now relying on unproven technology. The gun stations were armed and ready with an all clear signal registered at the command center. Jong, McArthur, Brown, and Okema had first watch. Mary Alice sat quietly in a corner reading a book and attending to her man. The Sarge did not remove the sensors that the intruders placed on the property. Instead, Jong's cousin reprogrammed them with weapons directly pointing at each sensor.

There was hot food, cold drinks, and plenty of ammunition for each station. Asiram and Zanthius, along with Ava, camped out in Asiram's boudoir. There were hidden gun-ports throughout her room, as well as the entire house. Marisa, Larry, Courtney, Monica, Bernstein, and Yvette had sole responsibility for protection of the first floor and the basement.

The children were in the western tunnel watching television with headsets on. John Lee, Jilkes, Yeshida, and Somara were planted on the roof and had lowered a slide to be able to quickly evacuate the roof, if necessary. John Lee was in control of the super-scope and bullets that were designed by Jong's cousin. Juan and Rashida were in the tunnel reading to the children in Spanish and had been assigned the second watch of the command center.

Whitmore, Montomie, Gladstone, Chakes, and Carlos and his guys had eyes on the barn. The Sarge and Mallory had eyes on everyone and everything. Mallory said, "For some odd reason, I think this feels like what George Armstrong Custer must have felt when he knew the entire Indian nation was about to come and pay him a visit. We don't know the strength of the group, but if everything works, then a lot of dead and wounded people will be out there. Do you think we should speak with Asiram and put the cleaning people on alert?"

"That's a good idea. We can't have a bunch of dead people strewn all over the property. Let's go upstairs and see what's happening with them."

The door to her bedroom was open. The Sarge knocked on the wall and said, "Hello. Is there anyone home?"

"Hey Daddy-in-Law, just me, your son and my mother-in-law. Just one happy, big-ass scared family."

"Baby Girl don't worry. Zanthius, if this thing looks bad, take Asiram and your mother and head for the tunnel. Use the west tunnel because that's where the kids are. Once you shut that door, don't open it for anyone. Me and my guys will do this thing to the end."

"No, Daddy-in-Law, that's not why we did all we have done. It will be all of us or none of us!" Asiram exclaimed.

Ava said, "I agree with my daughter-in-law. All or none."

"Damn, you women complicate things. Me and my guys know how to do this. You people are a bunch of greenhorns. Please follow my instructions. If things get bad, go to the western tunnel and seal that damn door."

"I am so sorry you don't understand me sometimes, Daddy-in-Law. Let me try it once again. The shit you're talking about--ain't happening. It is all of us or none of us. Right, honey?"

Zanthius looked at his father and lowered his head and said, "Sorry, Dad. We already talked about this moment. Everyone in this house is going to give you the same answer. Save your breath. It is as my voluptuous wife says, 'all of us or none of us'."

John Lee inquired of Somara, "If I ask you to leave this place, would you do that for me?"

"Mr. John Lee, you know the answer to that retarded question. It has no relevance and, therefore, I think that it comes from a brainless caterpillar. My man should know that I will not leave his side—ever."

"I just be thinking that we give you and the baby a chance to survive. This is going to get nasty and I would at least like to know that my woman be safe and all," John Lee muttered.

"Mr. John Lee, please focus your attention on the environment. I will not listen to such childish talk."

Jong's voice came over the radio and said, "People, I need everyone to switch to channel 44. That is the new operative channel and I will change it again if necessary. I need all stations to check in with my assistant by station numbers and in order." Everyone knew that channel 44 was a ruse and that the real channel was 52.

The Sarge and Mallory descended into the basement where he was met by his wonderful wife and mate. He said, "Baby, if this thing gets bad, take the kids and hideout in the tunnel."

"Ben Beckmire, have you lost your damn mind? I am not hiding while you're being attacked. This thing you ask, is not going to happen. You're my husband and we will all survive, or we will all die. However, it's been one helluva ride. I mean the mayhem and excitement, the uncharacteristic love that is demonstrated, and the new lovers. This stuff is what dreams are made of. Save yourself some energy and let it go, because I'm not going anywhere, and neither is anyone else from the way I see it."

On another part of the farm, Mallory whispered to Monica, "Last night was immaculate. I thought we went to the moon and back! I left the room this morning feeling invincible. Why was it so different?"

"Honey, I don't know, but you can rest assured that I want to try that again. That was over the top and beyond. Oh, I'm a little embarrassed, but I love that new thing you taught me last night. While you were reaching for the stars, they came to me as well. Now, that was incredible. I mean, can you imagine how your pleasure, translated into my pleasure and then into our pleasure. That was some crazy muddle, but I so look forward to trying that again."

Jong issued a radio silence command. He summoned the Sarge and Mallory to the command center. Mallory kissed Monica and said, "Honey, I have to go. If all else fails, try to save the children and anyone else. Don't come looking for me. I will see you again in the afterlife."

"Mallory, after last night, Dude, you either had better tell Ben Beckmire you quit, or find a way to get your ass back to me. I have more things to experiment with. Stop this fatalistic mess. You and the guys survived the Nam, I'm confident you can figure out how to handle this mess. Give me a kiss and go do what you do."

As the Sarge and Mallory started up the steps, Mallory said, "My wife told me to essentially stop whining and go do what I do. That woman has never encouraged me to go and kick butt. You know what, Sarge, fuck this shit, if they come on the property, we wipe their asses out. No quarters. Please tell Jong to issue that order, if in fact, that's how you feel."

When the two men entered the command room, the Sarge looked at Mallory and then Jong and directed, "Send out this statement. No quarters are to be given. It's a terminal affair."

Jong said, "Here is the value of those sensors we have posted around the property. This is a perspective from the south--now look in the upper left-hand corner of the screen. That could be a herd of deer or a group of armed individuals. Now, look at the right side of the screen and you will see that it is the same kind of configuration. Now, that is the northern aspect of the farm. Okay, look at the bottom left side of the screen, that is the western portion and, of course, the right side of the screen is the eastern view. Now, there is a sizeable amount of people at all four quadrants. My question is simple, how close do you want them to get to the farmhouse?"

"I need you to send out the 'red alert signal'! I'm not sure what those sensors mean, so therefore, I want to start terminating at one hundred yards from the house which is approximately where they had set up their devices."

Jong programmed the systems to target a couple of fields and the die was cast. At 2200 hours, the blimps on the screens were stationary, waiting on what one would surmise, were instructions. The Sarge said to Jong, "What if those are some kind of anomalies; you know, like ghosts on your screen?"

Rashida and Juan walked in and the Sarge vehemently said, "I hope your intentions are honorable, young man!"

Rashida asked, "Dad, what are you doing? Do you and I need to have a conversation, right now?"

"No, Baby Girl. Just trying to make sure he understands that I don't take prisoners when it comes to my baby."

Rashida screamed, "Dad!" Please focus on the immediate threat. I will talk to you as soon as we have a moment."

She looked at Jong and said, "Juan and I are here to relieve you. You can stand behind me, but they are advancing. Those sensors they laid out weren't about sound. They throw a false hiccup and pulse that is not accurate. Look at the tail of the lines—they are 400 yards from us on all sides and in range of the ODS."

Jong exclaimed, "Impossible! They are firmly placed at the point of the pulses on the screen—roughly 500 to 600 yards out."

"Mr. Jong, you and your cousin missed the virtual reality tour. That is what those sensors are providing, large scale. They are now at 400 yards and holding."

The Sarge's phone rang and it was the senator who said, "I want to give you a heads-up! Your cousin, Walter, is planning an attack on your farmhouse tonight, as we speak. Is there any way you can have the 'idiot spy' send me the last section of the formula?"

"Senator, it looks like your bid for the highest office is not going to work out for you. Your people underestimated the other immigrants who are from all over the world and who came specifically out to vote for your opponent. Most people were distracted by the pipeline smoke screen and a few other issues while your opponent worked those elderly, toothless, unemployed, and poor supporters of a particular persuasion. He's probably going to beat you in the election. On another note, if you have any control over my cousin, I plead with you to ask him to stand down or face our true wrath."

"Sergeant Beckmire, your people must be a part of my opponent's camp. We will end your existence, and all who are there."

"Senator! The Sarge exclaimed. Did you just threaten the life of the children that are here?"

"Mr. Beckmire, I didn't threaten anyone. You have thirty minutes to transmit the final piece, or I will no longer be available to you for conversation."

"Senator hold on a minute." The Sarge then yelled to Zanthius and said, "Son, the senator wants the final piece of the Carbon Factor formula, or she is going to release her attack dogs on us. Do you want to give it to her?"

"Dad, tell the senator that we will see her in hell and give it to her there."

"Senator looks like you'll spend countless years and expense, trying to figure out the key parts to the puzzle. Goodbye."

The Sarge turned to his two main tactical operatives and said, "I bought you two plus minutes. Did you figure out where they are?".

Jong called John Lee and asked, "Can you see any movement with that super scope?"

"I have who I think is their leader in my scope. They are holding about 400 yards out. If the Sarge gives me the order, I can take that there guy out who be directing the group on the western side of the farm."

"Standby, John Lee. Beckmire cautioned, "We're trying to figure out if that group is 500 or 600 yards out or what."

"That there Rashida be right--they are 400 yards out and there be a shit load of them. I be thinking they may have between fifty to sixty people over on the west side. Can you make out how many they be having on the other sides?"

"Rashida is saying there are probably fifty to sixty dots on all quadrants of the ODS screen," Jong said.

The Sarge said, "John Lee, I want your group to target the leader on the western flank and then God have mercy on us all. We're going to see if this ODS thing works."

"Attention all units! This is the Sarge and I'm in the command center. We are soon going to be under attack! I will give the engage signal, John Lee will fire the first shot, and from that point on, we all need to protect our vectors! Good luck and stay safe! No risk taking. Let them come to us."

The Sarge nudged Jong and pointed to Rashida. Jong said, "Rashida, let me get there."

"We got this, Jong."

Juan said, "Rashida, this might require some adjustments to the system. Let Jong do this. We need to protect that back door; it is vulnerable."

Rashida looked at the Sarge and asked, "Why won't you let me do this?"

"Baby Girl, I'm not about to let my only daughter pull the trigger and perhaps slay or wound over 200 people. That's not the kind of thing a father places on the shoulders of his daughter, unless it is the only option. I don't even want Jong to do it, but he knows how to compartmentalize what we do. Baby, we hurt people and terminate lives. We have done so much of it that I'm embarrassed to have to apologize to you for what we did for our country and for our own survival. I can't let you play a video game that's real. I need you to understand that when you hit that button marked 'engage' a lot of people are going to die, if the system works at all. If it were just you and I, then my resolve might be a little different. I have seasoned soldiers who have killed people and still have nightmares. To end a life, is not an easy matter to process. And, in this case we're talking about hundreds at a time."

"Dad, for you, I would do it and shoulder the burden. I understand your reluctance and I guess I'm kind glad that you didn't ask me to go through with this."

John Lee reported, "It be looking like them there fellows are going to make a move. They be checking the weapons and I guess they be making them hot."

"Roger that. John Lee, you have the first shot on my command," the Sarge said.

"Roger that. Them there fellows are beginning to move," John Lee warned.

"Roger that. On my command, I will give you the go-ahead. Make it a nasty shot and scare some of them out of here."

"Roger that. They be approaching the 300 mark in about thirty seconds."

The Sarge tapped Jong on the shoulder and said, "Make the ODS hot."

"On-line in 5-4-3-2-1. ODS is hot," Jong confirmed.

"John Lee, what's the approximate range?" the Sarge asked.

"They be around 250 yards and slowly making their way here," The Sarge raised his hand to his chin, rub it twice and methodically stated, "John Lee, on my mark, 5-4-3-2-1, mark!"

A loud blast echoed into the night and the individual leading the western flank received a huge hole in his head and three others who were lined up behind him fell to the ground. All of the groups hit the dirt.

The Sarge looked at Jong, turned around as if he were going to walk out of the room, turned back around and softly and hesitantly said, "On my mark, 5-4-3-2-1, mark."

"Sarge are you sure about this?" Jong inquired.

"Jong, please hit 'engage'."

Jong hit the engage button and all hell broke loose. The ODS sprayed the areas as if it were a lawn service man spraying weeds. On the northern, southern, and eastern flanks of the farm, the intruders were decimated. The automatic weapons paused and would fire a single burst if there was movement. On the western flank of the farm, the long guns disoriented the intruders and picked them off one by one, from afar without them ever seeing their enemy. Jong, Beckmire, and Mallory watched the mayhem, but no one said a word. The intruders were checking their retreat options, but none were available. Many of the intruding forces were hit by as many as five large caliber rounds. If there was movement in the field the ODS would fire a single burst to terminate the threat. On the western flank, those who were hit were victims of high-powered rounds and the likelihood of survival was nil.

The Sarge ordered, "Disengage the ODS."

Jong reported, "The threat is not over, and if I do that then we endanger all who we are trying to protect."

Mallory said, "Delay that order." He walked the Sarge out of the command center and asked, "Them or us? What's your preference? They came here to kill you, me, plus your grandbabies, and wife. Them or us?"

"Mallory, they never saw what hit them. We slaughtered those people."

"Once again--Jong, me, Jilkes, McArthur, Brown, Bernstein, John Lee, Montomie, Chakes, Gladstone, Whitmore, and finally you, had to be protected. What is your preferred outcome from this?"

The Sarge looked at him and replied, "That's an easy choice. Mr. Amazing, job well done. Call Asiram and Zanthius. I need them to have the cleaners make a precarious extraction at first light."

Jilkes called in and said, "There are a lot of bodies in the field and woods. We just slaughtered 200 plus men and women, and they never saw our faces. Damn, this is incredible."

Mallory asked, "I wonder what they would've done to us and the children and the women. Do you think they would have put more suicide vests on them, and made sure they killed our very essence?"

"Mallory, I'm a part of this group. You don't need to preach to me about the pros and cons of this situation. I was there in middle America when they blew that ranch to hell. I have no fucking compassion for anyone in that field. However, they are still humans and deserve some modicum of respect. After all, that is the job they chose, and we are doing what we do to make sure we are all safe and protected."

Jong said, "I'm the one who pushed the button. I will not be able to sleep for many moons."

The Sarge admonished Jong before his mood became contagious. "Cut the crap. Stay focused. I need everyone monitoring their positions and staying vigilant. My cousin would sacrifice 1,000 souls, just to be able to ease a catastrophic device in our midst. Stay focused."

John Lee interrupted the Sarge and reported, "I have significant movement on the southwestern flank."

The Sarge ordered, "Jong, make ODS hot again."

As the ODS came back on-line, there was another contingency of intruders approaching from the west. Two-thirds of the weapons rounds had been expended, but John Lee, Jilkes, Brown, Somara, Yeshida and Okema, would fill the void. Jilkes yelled out, "I think they have a big gun."

John Lee exclaimed, "Jong, if those long guns have any juice left, then now be the time to deploy them!"

The Sarge gave Jong the signal. He targeted the intruders and hit the engage button. The eight-long guns gave no quarters. They tore through each person's alleged bullet proof vest, and subsequently their bodies. Over the sound of gunfire, Yeshida yelled, "There is movement on the northwestern flank of the ranch."

Jong announced, "We have no coverage there with the ODS. Earn your pay, people."

Jilkes said, "Honey, after you fire, rotate three times."

John Lee yelled, "What you be talking about? She best rotate five times. We all then fire again and then hit that damn slide to get off the roof and into the house because them there fellows are going to pour a shit load of lead at us. We got to go and get dirty with these people. But I need you women to cover our retreat."

Somara quietly whispered, "You go, I go. We cover each other."

Jilkes said, "I count about twelve. Let's hit six, take the slide, hit the streets, and finish these guys off."

Suddenly, there was a significant number of rounds being fired from the rear of the house. Jilkes said, "On my mark, 3-2-1- mark. They all fired simultaneously hitting their targets and then they safely made their way to the escape slide. As they hit the second-floor landing via the slide, the Sarge said, "I need more fire power at the rear of the house."

Asiram, Zanthius, Ava, and Courtney were in a shoot-out. Ava and Courtney randomly fired their weapons in a sweeping format while Zanthius and Asiram targeted intruders from their port holes.

Jilkes yelled, "Cease firing, unless you have a clear target. We are going to get up-close and personal with those fellows. If it gets to be too much, I will hit you on the radio and you can provide retreating fire for us. Courtney and Ava, please load for Asiram and Zanthius. Please don't take a shot unless you're absolutely sure of the target and the shot. We beg you!"

As the six members of the team hit the first-floor landing, the Sarge said, "Ladies, I need you three at those portals over there. Mallory and I are going into the field with you guys."

Larry came up from the basement and hearing the rear end of the conversation, said, "Sarge, we need you and Mallory at the control panel, not playing backup. I will go with them if these guys trust me."

Somara was about to say something when the Sarge said in an extremely compelling voice, "Move, ladies! This is not a negotiation. This is a command."

The four men slithered out of the front door and made their way towards the back. Larry asked, "What's the plan?"

Jilkes said, "We have a few termites trying to get close to the house. I think they may have explosive packages or an RPG and are trying to figure out the weak side of the farmhouse."

Jilkes then radioed the Sarge and said, "We need Zanthius or Asiram to engage that Star-Wars shield."

The Sarge asked, "What the hell are you talking about?"

"Sarge, tell your son or Asiram to raise the secondary defense system, now."

Asiram had her earpiece in but believed in protocol and waited for the Sarge to instruct her to engage the system. The Sarge said, "Asiram, come in."

"I'm here," she replied.

"What is the secondary defense system?"

"No time to discuss, but it's going up in two seconds." Asiram hit the remote-control switch on the wall in her bedroom and a permeable shield rose thirty feet into the air on all four sides of the house. She said, "Daddy-in-Law, I couldn't wait for your command. I think everyone needs to brace themselves. I think they have an RPG and they are going to fire it."

A large explosion could be heard, probably all the way to Washington, DC. As Jilkes, John Lee, Brown, and Larry came up from an intermediate tunnel that was beyond the shield, Larry asked, "What the hell was that boom?"

"That there be those fellows firing RPGs at us." John Lee answered, "I think Zanthius reported our shield can withstand two to three direct hits. We got to get to them there fellows before we watch the farm get blown to bits."

Larry said, "I saw their resolve in middle America. You guys flank, I'm going straight at them full speed. I'll give you twenty seconds once we clear this tunnel to get in position."

"That's not how we do our work, mister. You will wait until one of us tells you what to do. Is that fucking understood?" Jilkes adamantly stated.

"I'm sorry, I was having a flashback of you guys being blown to hell, in middle America," Larry recalled.

After that comment, there was a moment of reflection. Jilkes looked at Larry and said, "Give us thirty seconds. We will try to protect you."

"Listen, first, they are going to be surprised that someone is running full speed and shooting at them. Second, your flanking fire is going to be critical to my success and survival," Larry said.

Jilkes looked at John Lee and asked, "You don't have any input about this impending disaster?"

John Lee paused before answering, "I don't like the surprise, but maybe that's the key to us whipping their asses. I mean he's willing to be a target, but it's up to us to stop them. I like his gumption. I think he be crazy as all hell, but this here be his design."

"No more talk. They're probably trying to figure out why the fucking house is still standing. Now or never gentlemen." Larry opened the hatch to the tunnel and disappeared. Jilkes and Brown rolled right, and John Lee rolled left.

As they were positioning themselves, Larry found himself in the midst of the intruders. After firing his two weapons, he hit six people immediately, leaving two, hopefully, to the skilled marksmanship of Jilkes, Brown, and John Lee. The men fired their weapons and Larry captured their position but, more importantly, he acquired their communications systems. As the three men approached the area, Larry placed a finger to his lips and pointed to a radio broadcasting the live inquiry of a wounded intruder. He suggested that the three men secure the area and make sure there were no other threats. The voice on the other end of the radio was yelling, "What are you talking about? Did you hit the target? I say again, did you hit the target?"

Larry picked up the radio and saw that the guy who had it was Asian. Then in an attempt to mislead the voice on the other end, replied, "I prepare shot number two. I think first shot, bad rocket. It no get near house."

"Damn. How the hell did you miss a big ass building? From my position I can still see a standing house."

"They have counter measures. They make missile miss big ass house. I try again. I load weapon myself."

"Hold off. I'll do it myself. Watch your six. I'll be there in two minutes or so."

Larry summoned Jilkes, Brown, and John Lee, and told them someone who gave orders was on his way there. The men flanked the area and waited patiently. Two men making a lot of noise, came storming through the woods. As they approached the scene, Larry yelled, "You're surrounded! Drop your weapons! Don't try to be a hero. Place your hands behind your head and lock your fingers!"

The men complied and Larry and his three friends circled them. John Lee asked, "Which one of you be the person in charge?"

Neither guy replied. John Lee asked again, "I need to know who be in charge."

# # #

Later, in the barn, the Sarge, Mallory, Jilkes, Brown, John Lee, and Larry began interrogating the two men. Jilkes placed tape over their mouths. He said to the Sarge, "We have a ton of bodies in the field. We need to get the cleaning people out here in a hurry. I'm sure those explosions and that loud rapid firing is going to draw curious eyes."

The Sarge called the house and Zanthius answered the phone. He asked, "Can we stand down?"

"Not yet, Son. I have no idea about the status of those people in the field. I need Asiram to call the cleaners."

"Pops, you two think so much alike. She called him and told him there may be live garments in the field and there could be as many as 200 to 250."

The conversation was interrupted by Mallory who yelled, "I need to see you."

"Son, let me call you back." As Beckmire walked back into the barn, he asked, "What's up?"

Mallory whispered, "Look at the loops on his belt. Do they look familiar?"

"I'll be damn. Don't tell me we done hit the jackpot again? John Lee, I need you and Jilkes to handle the extraction. Is that a problem?"

"We were trying to retire from gutting people and cutting off feet and hands, but if you insist, we'll handle this job for you," Jilkes stated.

As the two men sharpened knives, the guy with the loops on his belt mumbled something. The two men ignored him. A minute or so later, John Lee donned a rubber apron and asked, "Who wants to go first?"

The guy with the loops on his belt kept trying to get their attention. Jilkes removed the tape from his mouth and he said, "You don't have to do anything to me or him. Ask me whatever you want, and I will tell you the truth as I know it to be."

Jilkes yelled, "Sarge, do you want to have a conversation with this guy before we cut him into little pieces?"

Moments later, the Sarge walked in and inquired, "Is he a hard ass who won't talk?"

"No, sir, I'm willing to answer any questions I can," the man pleaded.

"Were you in charge of this group?"

"I am the operations person. My main job is to make sure the job was completed before people were paid."

"How many people breached our property?"

"There were 204 mercs on the ground."

"Are you telling me that there are 202 dead or wounded people lying around this property?"

"I'm afraid so."

"What are those loops and keys to on your belt?"

"They are to the cash boxes that hold each man's payment who signed on for this mission."

"What was your mission?"

"My mission? My mission was to pay each man $100,000 once all of you were confirmed dead."

"And who is the orchestrator of this mission?"

"I'm surprised you ask. I assume you're Ben Beckmire, the Sarge. It's your cousin, Walter."

"Where is he right now and where is the money?"

"I have no idea where Walter is. The payment money is in a rigged SUV that has a phone he controls with a ring tone that changes randomly. He said you people have enriched yourselves at his cost, and he didn't want to subsidize your adventures against him any longer if this mission failed."

"Who is this fellow besides you?"

"He's the accountant, Mr. Alsher."

"Does he always carry a weapon?"

"We both have weapons to look the part. Mine doesn't have any bullets in it. As I said, I'm the operations person. I don't execute the plan. I'm as good as dead and so is Mr. Alsher."

"How much money is in that truck and where is it?"

"It's on the road with two security people who don't know it's rigged. There is a total of $20 million dollars in that truck. The accountant and I withdrew more than we needed to cover our airline expenses, food, women, booze, drugs, strip-club fees, chauffeurs, and other costs, if this event failed."

"You don't play fair, do you? Where did you withdraw that kind of money?" the Sarge asked.

"I play to win, but I knew I had to get out of dodge on this one. I like to do my homework, and after what I learned about you people, and what was rumored to happen to Scottie, well I bought me and the accountant an escape route. Listen, we're dead, dead, and dead.   I told Walter during a phone conversation that you people either were waiting to die or were extremely confident that there would be no attempts on you here. Especially the way you people just meandered around without a care in the world, as it was reported to us by our scouts. Insofar as the money is concerned, we went to his private bank and took the requisite number of cases of money and left the place."

"Hold on a second. Jilkes, call Mr. Amazing down here, and remove the tape from that guy's mouth. Let's show a little decency here. Now, sir, I guess you know that Walter is going to execute a contract on you. Do you have any idea how to thwart the ring tones so that perhaps I can give you and Mr. Alsher some getaway funds?"

"I personally don't have a clue."

Mr. Alsher replied, "There is a way to counter the ring tone systems by copying the randomly used tones. When I saw his man installing it, I told him that I wasn't about to help him knowing if, in the universe of ring tones, one was activated that matched his and that I would be blown to bits.

He told me in the universe of tones, he selected only twenty and they're in a loop. Also, there is one thing that the operations guy doesn't know."

The Sarge asked, "And what might that be?"

"In his haste to follow exact instructions, we miscounted the number of cases that were loaded. There isn't $20 million in the truck, it's more like $30 million."

The operations man looked at him with astonishment. His associate said, "Hey, I'm a damn accountant. Sometimes I make mistakes."

Mallory said, "Suppose we offered you your lives, a sizeable amount of money and the telephone number to a person who can provide you with a new identity overnight? Your cost would be to figure out the code and use those keys to open the boxes."

"How did you know about the keys?"

"Some details are often overlooked when planning an event. We try not to ever miss the minutia. By the way, what is your name?"

"My name is, Mr. Ernest Green."

"Mr. Alsher looked at Mr. Green and said, "It's child's play."

Mr. Green asked the accountant, "If you disappear, what's going to happen to your young wife?"

"Hopefully, her young boyfriend will keep screwing her and she won't miss me at all!"

"I see. I'm not as fortunate as you are. I happen to love my lady, but she loves, now dig this shit, the fucking postman."

"Guys, sorry about your issues, but we're trying to figure out a way to not kill you even though you came here to kill us. You need to focus," Mallory mandated.

Jong walked in with McArthur and they both were packing heavy. The Sarge said, "I need you to work with this guy and figure out how to breach the random ring tone system. Walter has booby trapped the van that's carrying the money for all of those dead souls."

McArthur said, "We're now working with the enemy?"

Mallory replied, "We're trying to figure out how to enrich ourselves by $20 or so million. You got a problem with that?"

"Hell no. I like working with the enemy to reach amicable and mutually beneficial results."

After answering additional questions, the Sarge instructed Jong, Mallory, and McArthur to go and secure the contents of the truck. The Sarge asked the operations guy, "Are the cases booby trapped as well?"

"No. He and I loaded cash from the pallets on the floor, into the cases that we pulled from the back of the building."

Mallory instinctively asked, "Back of what building?"

Mr. Green said, "We rendezvoused with two of his associates. They blindfolded us and drove us to a building where the cash was housed. No landmarks were gathered from our trip. We discussed it later but couldn't come up with any recognizable environmental sounds or smells that were prevalent.

# # #

When the group reached the truck, the guards were ordered to lower their weapons, and they complied. Jong listened to the ring tones through the headset and determined they were indeed in a loop. McArthur investigated the cases and recognized that they were magnetically sealed. The units seemed to be self-contained, and he beckoned Mallory to join him and give him a second opinion. In the meantime, Jong and Mr. Alsher realized that the ringtone was a ruse, and that no matter what tone rang of the recorded twenty, none of them would activate anything. Mallory on the other hand said, "This shit is live and is seemingly compression based. This is a scale. How were you supposed to pay people after the job?"

"From the back of the truck, each man was to turn in his weapon and receive his payment in a brown canvas bag. Mr. Alsher and I were told to pay them simultaneously. Meaning two weapons, twenty stacks of money or $100,000."

"What a cunning son-of-a-bitch. Jong, can you get under here and figure this shit out?"

"Okay, Mac, can you come and keep an eye on our guests?"

Jong went under the truck from the front, not from the side. As he was making his way down to where Mallory was, and said, "Oh shit, there is a flashing light up here. Let me clip these wires, and we will see if its rigged."

"And just how will we know that?"

"We be no more, dude. Boom!" Jong animated.

"Wait a minute, let's think about this and make sure we're doing the right thing."

"Too late, I've already cut wires. Are the packages beeping or anything?"

"Jong, you are out of your mind. What should I do with the packages?"

"Take them out and hand them to the Alsher fellow."

Jong examined the cases and used the portable scanner that his cousin had given him. Mallory called the Sarge and said, "We think that crazy ass Jong has defused the packages, but I think we should open them up here rather than endangering our people. What say you?"

"I say you have operational control. Exercise it," the Sarge instructed.

"Roger that." Mallory looked at Alsher and Green and said, "This is where you earn your money and your freedom. Extract each case and open it."

Alsher said, "I'm not opening those things."

McArthur pulled out his side arm said, "Okay. I'm just going to blow your head off."

"Wait! No need for that. I trust your man did his due diligence." He and Green pulled the first case out and opened it without hesitation. There was no explosion.

Jong handed them extra strength trash bags and told them to place the contents into the bags. Eight, double lined, industrial size trash bags later, the group made their way back to the barn. The Sarge exclaimed, "So happy no one was injured, and what do we have in these bags?"

Mr. Alsher replied, "Approximately $30 million, give or take a thousand or two."

The Sarge said, "Count out $5 million and place it in front of me." Alsher and Green pulled stacks of $10,000 each out of the bags and precisely reached the $5 million mark. The Sarge said, "If there is a single dollar over $5 million, then we will end your life."

The two men checked the stacks and Mr. Alsher said, "I don't trust his math therefore, I am going to count each stack and make sure that the math is accurate."

"Don't bother. Divide the money into two stacks and disappear. Take your funds and go. The two guys who drove that truck deserve some money. Take four additional stacks and give it to them. Don't cheat them. Here is a number for a person who can get you far away from here. Don't go back and don't call your employer. As a matter of fact, I will give you each another $2 million if you can give me any information about where I can find my cousin."

"If I knew where he was, I would give you the information for free in hopes that you terminate his ass before he finds me," Mr. Alsher said.

"Mac, you and Chakes escort these two guys up the road. Montomie and Gladstone, follow them and provide coverage. Remember people, there are a shit load of deceased or wounded individuals out there in the fields. Take one of the vans that have that extra shit on them," the Sarge said.

At the end of the road, McArthur said, "You got your lives back, so disappear and never show up in this area again."

The two men entered the truck and said to the two security men, "We worked a deal out for you. We are going to give you $5,000 for your work." Mr. Alsher whispered to Mr. Green, "It's supposed to be $20,000 each."

Green whispered back, "Don't know if you know it, but disappearing is an expensive project. You are going to need every nickel you can find, trust me."

# # #

One of the security guards driving the vehicle asked, "What the heck was that all about? We're approaching the Post Office. You guys have a safe trip back."

The two men got out of the truck and entered a mangled vehicle and began to count their pay. Three minutes later, a bright light lit the night sky and a loud boom could be heard in places far away. The truck that Messrs. Alsher and Green were traveling in, exploded. The obvious placement of ordinances under the truck was a ruse, but under the hood of the car, were two sticks of C-4 that blew the two men beyond recognition.

# # #

Mallory gave Jong a verbal tongue lashing about the vehicle that exploded carrying Alsher and Green. Jong fell to his knees and wailed, "I could have gotten us killed or injured, with my cockiness. I need to rest. I am no good to this group in this state of mind."

Mallory waltzed over to him and said, "You can't even tell that was a truck. Take my advice, go to your woman, and try to seduce her. Stop messing around and go straight for the zone."

# # #

It was clear that Jong was crying and unsettled because he realized his haste could have cost injury or death to his comrades. When he entered his room, Mary Alice was lying in wait in a sheer, decadent garment. Dumbshit bowed and asked, "What's the occasion?"

"If this picture doesn't give you a clue, then I have truly wasted my time on you, Hyshime Jong."

"I was just kidding around."

"I'm not."

Jong developed a sense of bravado and became the new Don Juan of the group. He told Mary Alice how much he admired her outfit and that it was the kind of look he would like to see each day for the rest of his life. He told her it was only fitting that given the cultural differences between them that he demonstrate to her the old ways of doing things. He lit candles, paused for a few seconds, and said, "Oh well, we're here and the old ways are just what they are--old." He kissed her passionately and the seduction process began yet again, within this group. People were meeting, falling in love, becoming impregnated, and getting married. That was the nature of the relationships that had been fostered by the members of the group.

## CHAPTER SEVENTEEN

When the cleaning company arrived, McArthur asked them to open the trucks up so he could inspect them. After clearing the vehicles, he called ahead and told the Sarge the cleaning company was on site with six dogs and twelve men. The Sarge told him to hold them in place until he could get John Lee and Jilkes up there to inspect the undercarriage of the vehicles.

When the two men arrived, John Lee said to the lead cleaner, "I got to get up under your truck, and my friend is going to inspect your engine, so pop your hood."

John Lee instructed McArthur and Montomie to check around the wheel wells and all other places where explosives could be hidden. The lead cleaner said, "I know you have to do this, but every person here is family, including the dogs."

"You see that there explosion on Route 211? Well that there vehicle was supposed to have us in it. We just be tightening security a little more. Move this truck down the road fifty yards and have the second truck come on to me," John Lee instructed.

The lead cleaner said, "Not sure if this has any relevance, but a van turned off the road about a mile back. It looked like one of those vehicles that moves people. We can start our work on the west side of the property, but we will not come east until someone has neutralized that van or at least gained intel on who's in it."

John Lee called the Sarge and gave him the information that he had just received. The Sarge saw Juan and beckoned to him. He told Juan to pass the word that they were still on high alert and that everyone should be well armed.

When Juan saw Mallory and Monica, he told them what the Sarge had told him and acted as though he was the Sarge's new best friend. Mallory looked at Monica and saw that she was unarmed, and for that matter, he was as well. He immediately directed her to a closet where they both retrieved weapons and vests. When they finally reached the Sarge, Mallory asked, "What's going on?"

"Apparently, a van carrying people pulled off the road about a mile back and the cleaning company thinks that they may be eventually working their way here."

"Where are John Lee and Jilkes? And where are Gladstone and Montomie? We need to shut down the cleaning and have them get the hell off the property now. We need to have those four guys move in from the south and head due east for a mile or so."

The Sarge ordered, "Get Jong's ass down here to monitor the cameras."

Juan walked in the room and said, "Mr. Beckmire, your daughter and I can do this. She is on her way here. We know how to operate the ODS."

The Sarge called Jilkes and said, "Tell the cleaners to vacate the property and find refuge near Georgetown, and we will call them in two hours. Have them leave now and make sure everyone with you is fully loaded."

Jilkes told the lead cleaner to vacate the property and that he would receive a call when all was clear. He called John Lee, Montomie, Chakes, Gladstone, and McArthur for a sidebar. He looked at each man and asked, "How much ammo are you guys carrying?"

After receiving various reports on provisions, he realized that they would be at extreme risk because they didn't have enough ammunition to venture into a fight. He looked at the cleaner and said, "You wouldn't happen to have any extra ammo laying, around would you?"

"We don't have any extra ammo, but we can provide a friend with twelve clips, if that will help."

"Damn. You guys are fantastic."

The six men collected additional ammo and headed out towards the east. John Lee radioed the Sarge and asked if they should move quickly. The Sarge told him that haste makes waste, especially, when you aren't sure of where you're heading and what you may encounter. Jilkes said, "I don't like this. We don't know who or how many people we might have to engage. Let's not form a group. Let's spread out and provide flanking eyes from twenty-five to forty yards out."

He looked at his pedometer and threw his fist up in the air. John Lee sprung into an immediate panic. He motioned for the team to retreat. Each man practiced what he had learned in the Nam and slowly retraced his tracks. After retreating for a quarter of a mile, John Lee called for a huddle and said, "They be having people in the damn trees looking like branches."

"What the hell's the matter with you? What are you talking about?" Jilkes asked.

John Lee said, "I saw a limb move twice and form a different shape like that Ninja shit."

Jilkes called the Sarge and told him what John Lee had said. The Sarge called Jong over and told him what John Lee had reported. Jong told him they should evacuate the area because John Lee was right, those were the people that his cousin had spoken about. He told the Sarge if they could lure them back in the range of the ODS, they might stand a chance of annihilating them before they could try their chicanery on them.

"Are you telling me you believe in those ninja fairy tales?" The Sarge inquired.

"It no matter what I believe in. You must act with haste, so we can contain their fast and deadly movements," Jong replied.

The Sarge radioed Jilkes and told him to make haste back to the road. Jilkes communicated the statement to the group and John Lee indicated that a slow retreat was their best defense. He suggested that if the group started to run in the dark not knowing where they be running to, it would spell a problem. "I be knowing which branches on that there tree moved, and I suggest that three of you spray in a ninety-degree pattern,' John Lee instructed.

Jilkes said, "We don't fire a single shot unless compromised. We get the hell out of here and support the farmhouse from afar."

John Lee looked around and said, "We should leave now. Backtrack slowly and place each foot before planting it. Those tree limbs are moving again fast. We might have to run like hell. Mac, you, and the guys best be heading out due west in a hurry. Jilkes and I are going to spray this area for bugs. Y'all be needing to go now."

Everyone looked at Jilkes and he shouted, "You heard the man. Get the hell out of here."

John Lee said, "I don't be knowing why your blind asses can't see that there tree moving. On my mark, we spray and get the hell out of here like the devil himself be trying to screw us."

John Lee didn't bother to count down, he yelled, "Mark!"

The two men sprayed in a ninety-degree pattern and then took off. They caught up with the others and literally passed them.

When they hit the road, Jong was in a mini-van waiting on them along with Mary Alice, who was driving. The group loaded up and headed towards the farmhouse. Without notice or permission, Rashida armed the ODS. When Juan turned around and saw that the system was armed, he yelled, "What the hell are you doing?"

"They may be Ninjas and all that other shit, but they're not invisible." She hit the engage button and twenty highly experienced combatants were laid to rest. The Sarge entered the room and demanded, "Who gave the order to engage?"

"Dad, no one because no one saw what I saw. By the time I would have summoned you and you looked at what I was seeing, they would have been at the front door."

"Baby Girl, it turned out alright this time, but we follow a chain of command. Without one we would all be operating independently without a common acknowledgement, which would cause chaos. Not a good thing to have when my brother is my keeper. You saved us, but you must never operate without a command from those in charge; you performed a coup on us!"

"Dad stop it. I saw them and no one else did. I didn't have time to request authorization."

"Rashida, there is a chain of command that must be followed. Ask any of my people why, and they will give you a thousand reasons. What you did could have signaled to the enemy what our defenses are and, therefore, they could develop alternative approaches. Those souls out there could have been paper targets or an imposing force. In this business, you must have complete intel or you're subject to place the entire compound at risk. More importantly, I had six of my people in that area. You could have hurt or killed them."

Rashida looked at him and ran out of the house. The Sarge called to her but didn't expect her to respond. He looked at Juan and said, "Well, don't just sit there, get your ass up and see to your woman."

Jilkes walked into the ranch house and said, "That was some timely engagement. Those guys were on our asses and, I want to give a kiss to whoever pulled the trigger."

The Sarge looked at him and said, "It was my daughter and she did it without my consent."

"Oh shit, we have a command system, and that is why we have it. Listen, we knew that all protocols were off once we used civilians to sure up our defenses. We need to have a meeting and explain to civilians the problems that independent actions can have. I mean she saved our asses, but at the same time, she could have targeted us, and that would present another kind of problem. I have said this before--I don't like working with civilians to protect us. What's your take, John Lee?"

John Lee nodded before speaking, "I be thinking like you. I don't like it, but we be needing it. So far Carlos and his people have been solid, and the women have shown they will empty a clip in your ass. Rashida had the balls to engage that system and watch those poor bastards get cut to pieces. I don't like it, but in this situation, we be in, I be thinking we need all the help we can get. We just have to add controls on what they can do when we be in the field."

## CHAPTER EIGHTEEN

Allen called the Sarge and reported, "Your actions are attracting a lot of attention. Your neighbors are calling the local police and telling them they're witnessing a lot of flashes that resemble gun fire. Also, a police helicopter will be dispatched at 0900 hours to look at the farm. Get that damn cleaners there in a hurry and clean up that mess, or you will have another problem to deal with. I don't mean to sound so commanding, but I need you to survive because if you fall, then I'm a dead duck."

The Sarge asked, "Do you have any good news to offer this morning?"

"Sarge, this is no joke. Keep the locals out of your business, have everyone acting normal like playing in the field, riding those horses, and swimming in the pool. Have a cookout or something as well. Just have a lot of regular action because if the locals keep telling the Feds that something isn't right, then you're going to have a full scale assault against you. By the way, are the cleaning people still accountable to you?"

"How about you call me back in ten so that I can get this place in order in the fashion that you demand. Give me ten minutes, Allen, and then call me back."

The Sarge went upstairs and knocked on Asiram's door and asked, "Daughter-in-Law, are you in there?"

"Come on in, Daddy-in-Law. We were just watching the action from the south and were commending Jong's cousin on the ingenious defense system."

"Each time I see you, you look absolutely fabulous. We have less than three weeks, if my math is correct, before you deliver me another grandchild. I'm excited and can't wait. By the way, you need to call the cleaning people and get them here in a hurry. It looked like the 4th of July at the Monument Grounds. I mean it wasn't that loud, but it was extremely bright."

After he left Asiram's room, the Sarge called Mallory and asked him about the funds that had been gathered from Alsher and Green. He was told it was close to $30 million and that perhaps $5 million was destroyed in the explosion.

The Sarge walked out the front door with an automatic weapon and said, "I'm going to look for my child who doesn't understand how we roll and how we have survived because of a basic principle."

Mallory pointed to Jilkes and John Lee and gave them the assignment to accompany the Sarge. Yeshida and Somara put their vests on and followed their men from a distance.

The Sarge saw Juan and Rashida sitting in the field with a flashlight on and vehemently and incredulously asked, "Okay, are you people stupid? We're under assault and you guys are sitting in the middle of the field holding a fucking flashlight. What's wrong with this picture, Juan? You of all people should know better. You people are illuminated targets waiting for someone to end your lives. Back to the house where we can discuss this matter safely." The Sarge then looked sternly at his daughter before gently touching her shoulder, and said, "I'm surprised by your earlier reaction, Rashida. Do we have a problem?"

"Dad, no. I thought I was doing something to show you that I'm not useless and that I can contribute to this effort."

"Where on earth did you get the notion that you are useless? I would never say such a thing and I know your mother wouldn't either. Where's this coming from?"

Rashida hesitated for a few moments and replied, "I heard one of your guys say that if we didn't carry a weapon then we were useless."

John Lee spoke up and said, "I be the one saying that, but I be talking about everybody, not just you. That was some time ago when I made that statement and since then you done took shooting lessons and, in your case, you done killed a shit load of people. That don't speak about someone who is useless, now does it. Come here and give me a hug. It be a misunderstanding. I wasn't talking about you."

Jilkes said, "I told you about running that mouth of yours before you engage that bird brain. See what happens when you say stuff and don't consider the environment?"

"Now, who be talking too much?" John Lee asked.

The Sarge gave Rashida a look that she knew. She walked over to him and he said, "Baby Girl, do you trust me?"

Rashida emphatically answered, "Absolutely.   You, Mom, and LaGina are all that I have in this world."

"What about Larry?"

"Yes, and I did mean to mention Larry, Zanthius, and everybody else, for that matter."

"We have a code that has kept us safe. It is what we believe in. I am my brother's keeper, meaning that we have each placed our lives in the others' hands. When you engaged the ODS, you could not discern who you were targeting."

"I see where you're going with this, Sarge. What makes me sad is that I realize that I screwed up. I could have killed John Lee and Jilkes and the rest of their squad. I understand the nature of that command stuff you spoke of. I was trying to impress my father and show you that I had your six and I screwed up. I'm sad and confused."

"Baby Girl, that is all I want you to be cognizant of. I had my people in the field and you made them vulnerable because you acted without input from the team, and the team is what we depend on."

"Dad, it won't happen again. I promise you."

"And where were you Juan when this happened?"

"Mr. Beckmire, I turned around and saw her about to hit the engage button and yelled for her to stop. However, I was too late. However, I'm glad she did it, but sad that she didn't follow the protocol that has saved us on many occasions. I will never let her out of my sight again, Sir."

#

In another part of the farmhouse, Mallory walked into a room where the Sarge was, and said, "I need to have a word with you." He looked at Asiram and said, "I, haven't seen you or Boy Wonder lately. Hope all is going well with the pregnancy."

"Thanks for asking, Mallory. We've been hunkering down and watching the action from afar with long guns near us. I'm not as mobile as I used to be and, therefore, he keeps me away from the action. I must admit, Monica is a real jewel and you're lucky to have her as a mate."

"I often wonder what she sees in me. Anyway, I have the cleaning people and their dogs on the property and wanted to make sure that no one engaged the ODS. Sarge, I need to have a word with you when you finish here. Zanthius, if you like you can listen in as well."

As the three men huddled, Jong yelled, "We have a new problem coming at us from the south and the ODS is out of munitions. As the men scrambled into the command center, Jong said, "Oh shit, that's a herd of deer, but behind them are people."

The Sarge said, "The cleaning people and their dogs are out there."

"I think it's time we relocated and regrouped. Too much is going on here," Jong said.

Mallory looked at him and said, "That's a great idea, but Asiram is so close to delivering her baby, it wouldn't be smart to put her on a plane at this stage."

Zanthius said, "Why don't I ask her and also get Courtney's opinion? You know, she does not like it when people arbitrarily make decisions for her."

"I agree. I believe this place is closing in on us once again. We could take the plane and head west, but that is a long flight. We can't go to the island because I'm sure she would want to deliver her baby here. But you're right, we need a break. Everyone knows exactly where we are right now and they are going to keep coming and coming until we surrender or they kill us all," the Sarge said.

Zanthius looked at his father and asked, "Are you feeling okay? You sound as though you're considering throwing in the towel. Are you weary?"

"Son, sometimes I scare myself. I am not giving up, but my guys have been saddled with me and probably need a break."

"Horseshit!" Mallory exclaimed. "This murderous affair has been taxing, but also stimulating and financially rewarding. These guys are troopers. I know we're tired of people trying to kill us, but we end up killing them--that is the nature of this event. Maybe it's time you called for a meeting of the guys first and then open it up to the public. Everyone has a stake in this adventure. It's time for a pow wow."

"Right now, we are still on alert. Once the cleaning people have left, we can schedule a time. Jong, where is Mary Alice?"

"She is guarding the basement with Marisa and Yvette. Don't go down there without yelling you're a friendly."

"Do you think she can figure a way to get us provisions for a healthy meal? I mean I need to eat a couple of medium rare filets with a plateful of potatoes and broccoli on the side. I need to feed this beast," the Sarge announced.

Everyone shared the vision the Sarge had just described. Jong said "The neighbor has cows and lots of them. I don't think he would miss one, do you?"

"We don't steal food, anymore. Those days are over," Mallory reminded him.

"I will go and ask her if she can accomplish this mission," Jong said.

"Listen, why don't we take two of our vans and hit Wegmans? We call ahead and tell them that in an hour, we want to pick up fifty filets, ready for cooking, a sack of Idaho potatoes, broccoli, spinach, onions, garlic, biscuits and whatever else we need. We have grills here so let's just have a barbeque right here this evening. Jong, can you get your cousin to restock the ODS?" the Sarge asked.

"He's on his way, cursing you, me, and everyone else."

"Why is he cursing us?" the Sarge inquired.

"It is a sign of reverence when he can curse those who pay him and do not complain about his work. So, he is happy he gets paid, and he is happy we do not complain and that makes him curse us because he thinks only, he can provide us what we need."

"Strange custom, but who am I to talk, with all kinds of strange things emanating from Australia. Okay, who is on food duty, Mallory?"

Jong raised his hand and announced, "Mary Alice and I volunteer."

The Sarge said, "Mary Alice didn't volunteer for squat. If you want to keep that woman, you must not be so domineering and speaking for her. You must ask her if she would indulge you in this event. You can't just volunteer her unless you want to rid yourself of her. Is that what you want to do?"

"I keep making tactical mistakes, and I love my brothers who correct me before I make an ass of myself. However, I can say I want John Lee, Somara, Yeshida, and Jilkes as my backup. Now, I know I can command them people," Jong boasted.

"However, I would be extremely cautious about thinking that way with those four. They are in love. You ought to know yourself, when that bug bites, you don't have time for anyone or anything else. Think about it brother and once again, I would ask them to accompany you and Mary Alice--if in fact she wants to go with you," the Sarge said.

"So, my culture is causing me new problems, right? What must I do to not run this woman away?"

"First, if all she is to you is 'this woman' then perhaps you might want to look for another." The Sarge admonished, "If she is the love of your life, then refer to her as such."

CHAPTER NINETEEN

The lead cleaning person drove to within fifty yards of the house and summoned Asiram. He was unaware of her pregnancy and was eventually joined by Zanthius and Mallory. Zanthius said, "My wife is indisposed and, therefore, I'm handling this matter along with Mr. Mallory. We know that we have made you extremely rich and in return you have made some strategical errors that could have caused injury to our people. We recognize the gravity of this current affair, as well as the magnitude of the work, that you had to do. Unlike my wife, I count past deeds and efforts into the equation, and then attempt to reach an accord on the final pricing."

Mallory looked at Zanthius and said to himself, 'That apple didn't fall too far from the tree'.

The cleaner said, "We have made some major errors in the past, and we are thankful that you continue to place trust in our ability to do this specialized kind of work. If you consider the enormity of our efforts this morning, you will hopefully find this number acceptable." He handed Zanthius a piece of paper with a number written. Zanthius cocked his head and immediately handed it to Mallory who said, "Seems fair, boss. We'll be back in a few with the payment. Thank you and stay tuned."

"I'm not sure you realize how many garments were tattered and needed to be destroyed. We included that service at no additional cost," the lead cleaner stated.

Mallory said, "We sincerely appreciate your due diligence in this matter. However, I must ask a question. This amount is significantly lower than what you charged for half that number of garments. What's the reason?"

"We had a leak in our organization that we had to clean, and, therefore, we feel we owe you because of your allegiance. I only use seasoned family members. I must tell you, working with you guys has made us happy taxpayers. We believe in our democracy, and we also know that it cost money to run our screwed-up government and to support our military and police. We don't need to screw you in this process because you have been loyal, although you have had every reason to fire us."

# # #

The Sarge met with his guys and they literally shouted him down, yelling, "When is our next mission?" As Mallory gained control over the group, he said, "This meeting is officially called to order. Our esteemed leader launched into his issues without calling the meeting to order, therefore, you people took that opportunity to challenge his horseshit."

The Sarge looked at Mallory and said, "Horseshit? Are you people out of your mind? I call a meeting and you shout me down because I didn't do protocol? I guess I need to bypass this aspect of the meeting and invite the rest of the group to take part in it?"

McArthur yelled, "That is what a prudent man would do in this situation."

Mallory got the nod from the Sarge and summoned the rest of the group into the room. As Mallory was instructing people to notify other people, the Sarge's phone rang. It was

Allen who reported, "You got a huge problem heading your way."

"What the hell are you talking about?"

"I told you that each attempt by the Russians to test the Carbon Factor formula has led to destruction and death. The KGB is under the assumption that the 'idiot spy' is in possession of the controlling factors. They have their people in transit as we speak."

"Allen, what does in transit mean?"

"They have mobilized their teams in America to converge on New York. That is their staging ground because the environment is dysfunctional and gives them easy maneuverability."

"What's the timetable?"

"Sarge, I don't have that window, but Mike is the one who gave this info to me. One of his old contacts reached out to him and told him that the sadist Dimitri Knosnoviac is leading the team."

"And who the hell is Dimitri Knosnoviac?"

"He reminds me of you. He has killed and tortured a lot of people much like you and your people. You remember that Russian diplomat who wanted to defect to the West? You know, the one who they found butchered along with his wife and two daughters with apples stuck in their mouths?"

"Allen, I do not remember any such tragedy. We are sort of stuck here because Asiram is due to have her baby any day now. So, travel is rather questionable. Do you have any contacts with local law enforcement in Virginia? More importantly, where is that chickenshit cousin of mine?"

"I don't have any contacts, but perhaps Mike does. Speaking of Mike, he's in need of some financial assistance. Any chance of you helping him out?"

"I can have Jong place some money in that new account we created for you, and you can get it to him. Since we're talking about money, how about you? Do you need me to hit you up as well?"

"I'm good for about another two weeks or so. My wife's lover essentially robbed her. He took her jewelry and her debit card plus $20k in cash. I'm waiting for the request."

"How can you wait on a request? Have you spoken to her or the children?"

"I have not. I just know she was robbed."

"Damn, Allen, did you set this thing up to get revenge?"

"Can you tell me another way to measure true loyalty? Her boyfriend owed me $100k and I put her in touch with him knowing he was going to screw her because he's a real dog."

"How about a little faith in the woman you married? Have you ever tried that path?"

"Sarge, I was in the spy business. That should tell you a lot about my paranoia."

"Wow. Let me know what you need. Are Mike's needs immediate?"

"Sarge, if we ask, then it's immediate."

"Just thought you might want to know, we picked up $25 million the other night. I figure you and Mike have earned at least $1.5 million each. Is that fair for the services you guys provide us?"

There was a silence on the other end of the phone and the Sarge asked, "Allen, are you there?"

Between sniffles, Allen replied, "I'm here and thank you."

"Seems like you're having a hard time adjusting to your new way of living. We can make room for you and Mike. Lord knows we could use a couple more shooters."

"Actually, Sarge this new way of life has taught me a thing or two. I tried to kill you and every fucking body on that farm. You hear me, Man? My job was to bury you people, and now you're providing care packages to me. My soul has not paid a fair price yet. Once we get Walter, hopefully me or Mike are instrumental in that happening, then I will want to break bread with you and your group. I haven't earned the right to be at or even near your table yet. I must say that Mike has been honorable, helpful, and dedicated to your cause. He's a good man, and Sarge, if we can get him off the streets and back into a job, then that would make me happy."

"None of what you said can happen until we meet Diablo and destroy him," the Sarge replied.

"I know and we will keep you abreast of Dimitri. He's another mean son-of-a-bitch and probably makes Walter look like a choir boy. Catch you soon. But Sarge, you have got to get rid of that Carbon Factor formula. I know you realize that they're going to keep coming at you, and one of these times, God forbid, they might get lucky."

"Allen, if we get rid of it then who's to say it will stop there?"

"Catch 22, Sarge! Any chance you have any friends in the incoming administration?"

"Jesus, we voted for the senator and she has unleashed her fury on us. She can't control Walter and he's hell-bent on killing all of us. If I went after his family, I would be going after my own kin, therefore, I'm limited in my means for drawing him out."

"Damn, Sarge, you just gave me an idea. I know some people who can find a spotted cockroach. It might cost you a few dollars, but this might work. I mean we've used all the conventional means of locating him. We need to resort to the unconventional and seek him in places where he's probably operating—in the fucking gutter. We are looking for him in high places like the 'W'. We need to look for him in low places like Russian strip joints. Catch you later. I'm calling Mike to get his take on this. Will hit you back."

The Sarge went back into the house and said, "I would like to call this meeting to order. As you all know, for a long time, people have been trying to dispose of us from this life. I personally do not want to think about the number of souls that are roaming around Hades because of us. I don't feel sorry for them because they signed on for a task that was daunting--to kill us. We are not your normal targets, and my guys have proven themselves repeatedly. Now, we also have some newcomers, former spies, converts, and an extractionist. We have an old foe, Allen who once had the job to kill us. We have a comrade, Mike who is feeding us critical information about what the sewers are saying and proposing. We can also thank Mr. Amazing's cousin, who has placed some serious artillery in the field to support our survival, known by me as 'mechanized mayhem'. Yeshida, Somara, Okema, and Yvette have proven their loyalty as well.

"My son, Larry, and daughter, Rashida, have proven to be extremely helpful in a variety of different venues. My daughter-in-law, Marisa, has proven herself when people attempted to hurt my grandbabies. Ava, Carlos, and their people have been invaluable to our security as well. We also have Asiram, the most gracious hostess, who watched as three of her places were blown to pieces. However, we made good on our promise and rebuilt each place with the notion of security as the preamble. You know sometimes events can change even the mildest of people. Monica, our lawyer, is now proudly walking around the farm totting a .9 millimeter on her hip. My wife, the doctor, has had to give up her Hippocratic oath and conclude lives instead of saving them. Finally, we have the guy who swallowed and created this event, my son, Zanthius Beckmire De Lombardo. It is because of him that we are all caught up in this mindless display of survival of the fittest."

As the Sarge was about to continue his sermon, his phone rang, it was Allen who told him the KGB thing was real and that the senator had issued a hit order on Walter. The Sarge thanked him and asked him to keep him informed.

The Sarge apologized to the team for the call and said, "I know each of you have asked yourselves the question, when will this end?" The Sarge paused for a few seconds and announced, "As long as we are in control of the final piece of the formula for the Carbon Factor, we will have problems. If we turn the final piece of the formula over to known devious individuals, such as the senator who is linked to my cousin, then they will find a way to do a Mayor Good on our asses."

John Lee cocked his head to the left, interrupted the Sarge, and asked, "What be that Mayor Good thing?"

Jilkes looked at him and whispered, "Drop a bomb on us."

John Lee turned to him and said, "I asked the Sarge, I know you know everything, but sometimes I like to get my information from one of them there other news stations."

"Alright you two, settle down. In Philadelphia, the police and mayor's office had an issue with a radical but peaceful group called MOVE. When the City couldn't dispatch them from their house by legal and ordinary means, they dropped a bomb on their residence that eventually burned downed an entire community; Google it. Just so everyone understands what is going on—we, people, are like the MOVE group. However, our enemies are international, national, and local.

For example, if any of you wanted to strike out on your own and say, 'screw you people I'm out of here' it wouldn't be long before they would find you and use you to the disadvantage of the group. In other words, you would be in a hostage situation and probably their first move would be to send some recognizable body part to us as a sign they have you and that they are serious about doing business. I know, damn well, this is hard living, but it's good living. We seemingly knock each other over at times, but it's safe. I did not ask for this mission. My people did not ask for this mission, and none of you openly requested to be shot at and strapped in suicide vests. This is a mess and we must hold fast, or splinters will finish all of us."

John Lee raised his hand and was recognized by the Sarge.

"Sarge, I be confused. Is Jilkes trying to skip out on us?"

"John Lee, this is serious."

"I be serious, too. Is there someone who thinks they live with us and we should be living without them?"

"No, that's not the reason for this sermon. I haven't received any requests or notices that people are abandoning our quest."

John Lee looked at his fingers and began to silently count them. He then said, "If'n nobody be leaving, then why you be preaching?"

The room broke into hysterics except the Sarge who, knowing the gravity of the situation yelled, "Because the fucking Russians now want my boy and they can't have him."

A deathly silence came over the room and Ava began to cry. The Sarge screamed, "If you got a strategy for us to employ, then let me hear it. This is no joke! People, this is real!"

Jilkes stood up and said, "Sarge, sometimes laughter is good for what ails you. We all heard your message. No one is leaving and from what I've seen, we are all prepared to conclude our existence here on this farm. I'm sorry, but we are with you. My pregnant wife reminds me of the burden of leadership. I must now remind you--I think we all need some sun and sand."

There was a huge reaction to his statements, but Courtney stood up and said, "My new daughter-in-law is pregnant as well as a few other *conjeos'*. I would like to take all the expecting mothers to the hospital and have the doctors do prenatal stuff. Once I can see the reports from their visits, then I might sanction such a trip, but I would also take one of the smaller planes along just in case."

Mallory stood up and said, "I know Asiram had a problem at our hotel, but I employed, along with Mr. Amazing, a new local security force. When we had the place rebuilt with around the clock contractors, it gave me the idea to hire the locals to secure the entire island on an around-the-clock basis. We give everyone a chance to work and earn a living. Until we rebuild confidence that people are safe there, we are fighting an uphill battle. The entire world heard about a pregnant woman being dragged from the beach by a couple of thugs. No one is going there until we improve the image. Therefore, we have an island wide approach to crime, and so far, it's working."

Asiram stood up and said, "I love the fact that everyone speaks for me without my consent. I yield to my mother-in-law and passionately believe that her wisdom is all that matters here. I'm not listening to no man. And by the way, I hate my husband."

Zanthius looked to the floor and said, "Her arrogance has provided me with a secure existence. If she wants to go and Courtney is willing to handle the unexpected delivery of our baby at 30,000 feet in the air, then I'm good with it. My wife is my wife and I love her dearly. She is a demanding and difficult person, but she has provided me and you guys with places to, at least, consider home while the rest of the world hunts us."

"Son, you are correct. Listen, I don't want to turn this into a thank you session. What I want to do is try to get a feel for the status of our community. This has been hard on us all and I worry about the mindset of the children."

"Sarge, I need to ask you a question. Is your commitment to the issue waning?" McArthur asked.

"Mac, my commitment will never wane as long as you guys are supporting my efforts, but you haven't been back home since this thing started."

"Sarge, I can speak for a few of us; Chakes, Whitmore, Montomie, Gladstone, and me; we weren't doing so well, at that thing you call home and, therefore, we are not interested in returning anytime soon. Now, Brown, Bernstein, Jong, Jilkes, and John Lee have secured themselves in relationships. We are diligent, but not stupid. This is a group thing, and, on each occasion, we have needed the extra resources to watch our six.

"Yeshida, Somara, Okema and the rest are critical to our survival. I know you may not like it, but with Rashida and Juan on that trigger, we're okay with that too. Let's allow Courtney to make the decision about travel. Also, cutting through the chase, we met a bunch of sorority sisters from the Dominican Republic on holiday in St. Thomas. We want to get back there in a hurry and send our plane to the DR to fetch people we like."

Mallory yelled, "Why the hell didn't you say so? Those are your planes controlled and scheduled by Mr. Amazing.

We are a family here and we could have had your friends flown here, or anywhere, for that matter to hook up with you guys, if in fact, that is what you wanted."

"Mallory, it was the moral aspect of the event that prevented us from requesting use of the planes."

"They're your fucking planes and you're adults who have needs. You don't have to ask for permission. They're your planes, guys."

The Sarge heard the interaction and said, "I think that this misunderstanding is my fault. Damn, Mallory is correct. You don't have to ask about utilizing the planes. There is a protocol, scheduling, safety, destination, and timing. Other than that, talk to Jong and do your thing, but let me know because I will need to sure up security in your absence."

"Sarge, when we leave the compounds we leave together. We send for them we don't go to them. That's our plan of action."

"Damn. You see what a little bit of conversation does. I think John Lee started this and I appreciate the dialogue. We are not in Vietnam, people. Speak your peace or forever hold it. Mallory, make the security assignments."

## CHAPTER TWENTY

Jong's cousin rearmed the ODS. He also developed medallions that the ODS could identify. When confronted by Jong he said, "I brought you these medallions, so when your people are in the field the ODS can identify them and not shoot them up."

"How reliable are these toys?"

"Honorable cousin, you can take one and place it around your neck and we will see if the system shoots you?"

"Why don't I put one on your low ass and send you running around the field?"

"Cousin, I would not bring such a thing to you unless I had at least 95% confidence in it. Each medallion has its own signal and can be assigned to specific people. You could get medallion number 1."

# # #

Later, Jong explained the medallions to Mallory who said, "We don't pay that guy enough. He is always trying to keep us alive and all you do is treat him like a piece of dung."

"Mallory don't let him hear you give me shit about money and good work. That little cockroach will double his fee. He's a snake, and never deal with him one-on-one, or you will end up rewriting all arrangements I have with him."

Jong proceeded to assign the medallions to every person on the property, including the children. As the Sarge walked up to the two men, his phone rang and it was the senator who said, "I just happen to be in the neighborhood and would like to stop by and have a word with you and your people. Is that possible?"

The Sarge hesitated and considered the request but decided to defiantly state, "Senator, people don't just happen to be in this area unless they have a specific destination and purpose in mind. What kind of vehicle are you driving and how many people are with you?"

"I'm traveling in a Black Chrysler Sedan with three associates."

"Tell you what, Senator, I will meet you at the top of the road and save you a very bumpy ride down the hill. It is under repair and is basically unpassable. I'll be riding in a mule with a few of my people. I will be at the top in fifteen minutes."

The Sarge sounded the alarm and told John Lee and Jilkes that he needed them on the east side of the road in five minutes. He told Chakes and Montomie to be on the west side of the road in five minutes. He ordered Jong and Mallory to accompany him with light fire power visible, but ammo and automatic rifles in the bed of the mule.

Jilkes asked, "Who are we hunting or eyeing?"

"The senator is paying us a visit with some of her people and I don't want them down here at the ranch. I just need eyes on us to make sure we're safe."

"Roger that. You heard him people, let's roll."

Yeshida said, "I'm going with you and so is Somara."

Jilkes said, "Get one of the vans and cover the road about .25 miles from the entrance, okay?"

"We will be there in seven," Somara said.

As Jilkes and John Lee entered one van, John Lee asked, "Do you mind all of the attention and demands to never be out of her sight?"

"Brother, I love the fact this woman is concerned about me and wants to make sure that I'm okay. Do you have a problem with Somara doing the same thing?"

"I wasn't sure at first but hearing how excited you be about having your woman always near when possible, made me think. I love that woman like heaven, but I don't be wanting to get her hurt trying to protect me. I got you to do that, but it puts more pressure on me when I now got to worry about my pregnant woman watching my back."

At the top of the road, Chakes and Montomie headed to the right and John Lee and Jilkes headed to the left. Once in position, Jilkes said, "Perhaps we need to take our women for a walk and tell them how we watch each other's back out here and that when they are trying to help us, they only confuse us and make us think about their safety. Why don't we try having that conversation if this thing doesn't escalate into a larger issue?"

"Now, that be what I'm talking about. You got my six and I got your six and that is the way we be rolling. When we add them there women into the equation, it gets us confused. Is that about, right?"

"That's about right Old Country. We'll take a walk and have a talk with them once we get back."

On his way to the entrance to the farm, off the main road, the Sarge saw the two vehicles on the side of the road and asked Mallory, "Why did they bring two vehicles?"

Mallory answered, "If I had to guess, the guys took one and their ladies took the other and they're probably in it guarding the road."

"Interesting addition because I don't trust this witch. She has tried to screw us at every turn. I hope this time will be different."

# # #

Jong's cousin had shut down the ODS and there was no one watching it. He was in the western part of the ranch rearming the long guns. When Juan and Rashida attempted to find a place to share their passion, they entered the command center and began to kiss wildly, as if they were trying to find each other's esophagus. As Juan backed her up and reached for her blouse, she accidently engaged the monitoring system. As she looked at the systems that were engaged, she pushed Juan away and asked, "What the hell is going on? The Sarge would never send two teams on the same side of the road to watch his back." As she zoomed in, they both saw the ground move in three places. She told Juan to get Larry in there now.

John Lee and Jilkes assumed their position with a view of the road and John Lee said, "Damn, this here thing don't feel right. I be smelling cologne from way over there. I be thinking somebody just went this way. Can you smell that shit?"

"I don't smell shit, but this area seems like it's been stirred up. That's our old lookout tree over there and this is where we have the best view of the road, but this shit doesn't feel right to me either. Let's call the Sarge and tell him to back off until we can calm down and figure out what's going on."

Jilkes called the Sarge and said, "I need you to freeze for five minutes until we check out some things. Shit ain't right where we are."

Larry ran into the command center and asked, "What's up?"

Rashida said, look at these two points in the woods. As she enlarged them, there was slight movement. Larry said, "Oh shit. Did you see the ground move?"

Rashida targeted the two positions with the ODS. Larry said, "Juan, I hope you're in shape, we're going to cover the area in record time. Get a vest and an automatic weapon and clips from the rack at the front door. Ten seconds. Juan let's roll."

Larry, who was without a vest, was in front of Juan. He did, however, have two .45s with suppression devices on them and two additional clips. He was in constant contact with Rashida ,who said to him, "Larry, slow down and join the sounds of nature. You're .33 miles from where the earth is moving."

As Larry began to enter the woods from the road, he saw the Sarge and placed a finger over his lips.

John Lee said, "We need to get the hell up out of here. This here shit is compromised."

What the team didn't know but would learn later is that the senator had enlisted the services of Special Forces members who had the opportunity, unknowingly, to bury themselves in the most advantageous lookout positions facing the road while the ODS was being replenished. As John Lee began to stir, the ground around him stirred more. Suddenly, Jilkes and John Lee were covered with lasers from weapons on all aspects of their upper body. The two men were captured by the senator's team.

Jilkes and John Lee were stripped of their weapons. John Lee stoically looked at Jilkes and said, "Well, I be damned! I sure didn't see this coming."

The Special Forces people taped John Lee and Jilkes' mouths and locked their hands in plastic cuffs. Jilkes knew he could get out of the cuffs but had to wait for the opportune moment to apply his trade. The three intruders never said a word but motioned as to the coming events with hand signals.

Rashida called the Sarge and urged, "Dad, I need you to back down the road now! Jilkes and John Lee have been captured by three individuals. I need you to back down the road. Don't give me lip and don't mention protocol."

The Sarge exclaimed, "You guys heard her! Do as she said!"

As the group was backing up the extremely loud mules, Yeshida and Somara saw the action and knew their men were in trouble. As they were about to leave the vehicle, the Sarge waved his finger in the air from east to west. The Sarge also got a call from the senator who said, "I'm waiting on you. Where are you?"

"I'll be right there. Sorry to be late," the Sarge said.

On the other side of the road, Chakes and Montomie didn't have a clue what was about to rain down on them. As they heard sounds from their rear, they were surprised by the gun barrels pointing directly at them from their front.

Larry said, "Juan, there are four on your side. Let me disable these guys and then I will come and assist you."

"Larry, I see four and I can take them. My question is, will you need my help?"

"I'm going to sting my three in ten seconds. Don't be a hero and get our guys hurt or killed because the Sarge will kill you personally."

Juan called Rashida and said, "I hope you have my back as well as your brother's, my love!"

"I have pasted targets on seven frames and the ODS is hot. If they screw with my brother, I will cut them in half. If they fuck with the man I love, I will blow them away."

"Larry, you heard your sister. It's now or never."

Larry said, "On my mark. 5-4-3-2-1- mark." The muted sounds from the suppression devices on the weapons, hit their targets with less than fatal shots. Larry took a knee, reached in his boot, grabbed a knife, and cut the cuffs off John Lee. Jilkes had already freed himself of his restraints, pulled the tape off him mouth and said, "Damn, I'm glad to see you, Larry. We have people on the other side of the road as well."

"Juan, come in. What's your status?" Larry sked.

"I have two fatalities and two slightly wounded. I didn't want to put double shots in them, but two of them tried to return fire. I didn't have a choice."

"Did you free our people?"

"Roger that!"

Larry said, "Sarge, you should go and meet the senator, and invite her down to the barn."

"I'm sure they have signals and she is smart enough not to come to the barn. I'm going to call her back and tell her that she has incurred a few fatalities and that some of her underground people need medical attention," the Sarge stated.

The Sarge dialed the senator and growled, "You just got a couple of people killed and others wounded. You're the most untrustworthy person I have ever encountered. I have fought with enemies who have stated that they didn't have any ammo. Since we didn't have any either, we called a truce, and went our separate ways. But never have I faced an enemy as diabolical as you. You're the biggest snake in the field, and it is no wonder that the bully won the election.

You have one recourse remaining, insofar as we're concerned, give me my cousin and I will give you the final route to the Carbon Factor. I want nothing else from you and

I don't want to hear from you except when you have the place and time for the delivery of Diablo--your damn son."

The Sarge continued, "Get the fuck off the property and away from the entrance. Send a car with a single driver and we will get your dead and your wounded to you without conflict. Don't test my resolve, Senator. We have your car targeted with an illicit weapon that we stumbled across. Oh, if you think that by switching cars, you're safe--forget about it. We have your entire caravan targeted with precise strike points. Let me tell you another story. We have Gatlin guns targeting your armada at three points before you hit Route 211." Then the Sarge uncharacteristically said in Spanish, *'no me joda'*, or with people who have agreed they're already dead because we find ways to take the living to hell with us."

# # #

As the group reconvened at the farmhouse, the Sarge called all the people together and said, "We were blatantly screwed by the enemy today. They not only dug holes to hide in, but they knew exactly where we would be. How the hell could that have happened, people? Let me tell you how it happened. We have gotten fat and complacent. Ain't no way in hell the two best trackers and situation men in the world could be caught off guard and then rescued by my daughter, her whatever, and my son, Larry. People, John Lee and Jilkes were caught with their thumbs up each other's ass."

"Dad, may I speak?"

"If you have something relevant to add to this commentary, then yes."

"Jong's family members shut down the ODS to rearm it. I think those people accidently fell in line with his mission.

John Lee and Jilkes knew they had been compromised when John Lee spoke of cologne in the air. The senator being in the area was luck. They caught us lunching and took advantage of the deal. John Lee and Jilkes were backing out when the earth around them came to life."

"Daughter, I know the details, or I can imagine them. What you civilians don't realize is, that is not how we roll. You're putting too much pressure on us to do our jobs effectively by assuming we always got things covered. I'll bet you $100 bucks; our guys had other things on their minds before assuming their positions. One hundred bucks. Anyone willing to take the bet?"

John Lee said, "Sergeant Beckmire, Sir, permission to speak freely."

"Granted, my friend."

"When you be doing things, long as we be doing things, then you be learning everything about the guy next to you. I love my woman and she loves me, thankfully. My partner, the colored guy, he, and I had a conversation about our pregnant women watching our six. We be done said, 'I got him to watch my back and he got me to watch his back. That's the way we be doing this here stuff for years. And now when our women are trying to watch our six, we misplace focus'. Mr. Sarge, we done screwed up. We smelt them there guys, but when we done finished talking about our women, we were thinking about them being in the field trying to protect us. We be the culprits, we be the cause, we be taking a walk with our women and explaining how we do our work effectively."

Jilkes stood up and began to clap his hands. He said, "John Lee, the language you used was right at the threshold of being an articulate American. That was a wonderful speech, my brother. I love you and that was the exact truth without shame. Those guys caught all of us taking a nap."

Chakes stood up and said, "Sarge, I need to have a moment." He then looked behind him and yelled, "Juan, stand the hell up." After Juan stood up, Chakes said, "We were in the field with our asses bare. He, and he alone, saved our asses. I mean this guy rode in without a horse and bang, bang, bang, and bang and then another bang and bang. He was decisive about his approach, and conclusive with those who tried to react to his advance. We too were off target and were surprised by the moving earth."

Juan said, "Larry and I followed Rashida's orders. She noticed that the ground moved while the system was rebooting and called me in for confirmation. Without her actions, all of the advance team would have been captured."

Courtney stood up, looked at Rashida, and asked, "Is this true or is he trying to gain favor from you?"

"Mom, it's true and the only favor he wants from me is for me to marry him."

Courtney struck the pose as if she had won the jackpot, marathon, Powerball, Mega-Millions, and every other game in the world.

## CHAPTER TWENTY-ONE

Jong's cousin placed several cameras at the entrance to the farm. When confronted by Jong, he said, "Perhaps you need an intermediary to discuss needs with worthless cousin."

"What the hell is an intermediary?"

"It is a person who arbitrates between stupid and what's right," his cousin said.

"Are you calling me stupid?"

Jong's cousin fell to his knees and swore allegiance to him and swore that he would never insult the supreme member of his family.

Jong said, "You seem to have challenged my role in this family. Do not do it again or I will test your system with your low ass running through the grass. Is that clear?"

"I thank Buddha for my time to serve you, my masterful family member."

Mallory walked into the command center and asked, "Is there any way to keep a visual system in place while the weapons are being serviced?"

Jong's cousin looked at him and remained silent until given a nod by Jong. Subsequent to the nod his cousin said, "If my supreme cousin wants such a thing, then his wish will be my command."

# # #

The Sarge asked Courtney to join him in a talk with Rashida. She agreed, and, on their way to speak with Rashida, they found her and Jong's cousin having a heated discussion about the efficacy of the ODS. Rashida asked him adamantly to give her access to the coding protocols so that she could tweak the system when needed. Jong's cousin was about to respond in a condescending manner to this female thing talking to him, but saw he was within earshot of Jong, the Sarge, and Courtney. Rashida said, "I need to understand the programming protocols to modify the system when he's not here. Can you explain that to him?"

Jong looked at his cousin and his cousin said, "I was about to give her the codes when you showed up Cousin. Is there anything else I can do before I go?"

Jong walked away and his cousin said to Rashida, "If you know your ABCs then you know the codes to the system. Analysis, Base and Configuration. Know your ABCs and you will know how to change the schematics. If you do so, please indicate to my cousin that you changed the codes so, he will not have me shipped back to the east. I trust you with my life and my destiny, little lady."

Rashida bowed politely and low. She impressed and acquired a new mentor by the simple gesture. Jong's cousin said, "The spirit in which you showed respect supersedes any that I have ever encountered in this land. You are truly a virtuous person and I bow to you in total respect. Here is my card. If you have any problems with the system after exploring and taking ODS to its basic nomenclature, do not hesitate to call me, my Daughter. In all my years in this country, never a more gifted warrior have I encountered. Keep my cousin and his beloved friends safe from harm. Remember, dreams are to be analyzed and forgotten. Your path is on the right road, and the right road will keep you and all who matter to you safe, including my low ass cousin."

"I thank you for trusting me with the information. I know I can figure it out, but I will reach out to you when I have success and confirm the schematics. Thank you, once again. Your great work has been discussed by my father and the rest of the group. Without your craftsmanship, we would no longer exist, as we know it."

# # #

As the Sarge prepared to entertain Courtney his phone rang, it was Allen who said, "You're not going to believe this shit, but in less than two hours, forty bad motherfuckers are going to storm you from the north."

"Man, what are you saying?" the Sarge asked, "Where're you getting this mess from?"

"Mike called me and said that a buddy of his was hired to do some wet work in Virginia and to be the mouthpiece of a certain senator."

"Allen, she is not that dumb to advertise her moves and make it common knowledge amongst the infantry. She would only divulge that kind of knowledge to brass, not low-life infantry."

"Sarge, Mike's friend is brass and the leader of the pack."

"Does that bitch know how many souls are roaming around in Hades because of their attempts to neutralize us? Has she lost her fucking mind?"

"Sarge, she is going to keep throwing souls at you until you break and give her the key ingredients to the Carbon

Factor. Mike told his friend that he was going on a one-way trip and that you people have probably slaughtered over a thousand people. He also told him to goggle you, your people, and your antics in Vietnam. I said to myself, no slight intended, that you people were breast fed on the devil's nipple and that your group is formidable and evil. Mike told him to tell his family that he loved them because he wouldn't be returning from this mission. You know what he said?"

"I can't imagine."

"He said no humans are that good, especially a group of people who should be in retirement homes, in rocking chairs, and wondering why they just walked up a flight of stairs."

"Damn, what a slight! I hope he heeds the warning and runs away from this mess. Our entire strategy is being transformed by a technology oriented mean bunch of young people, including my daughter and two sons, who are hell bent on 'mechanized mayhem', as a way to kill intruders. Tell your friend that the rain will pour down on him and his comrades and that their bodies and souls will end up in a bowl of chemicals. A sad way for your friend to end a journey that should be promising. We will not give any quarters, Allen. If Mike values this person, then he has to persuade him to find a new career."

"Sarge, that large contingency of people that perished in that last battle, well they were guinea pigs. They have decided that your weak point is on the north side and that is where they are going to hit you with some unconventional weapons for an urban area. According to Mike, they are going to blast you out of your rat hole."

"Allen, hopefully, I will live to speak with you another day. I thank you for your allegiance and hope that we survive this new onslaught. Thank Mike, and I sent a little extra money to that fictitious account. Pray for us, brother."

"Damn it man. Mike and I can help protect you. Give me the word and we will find our way to you."

"Allen, as long, as Walter is looking for me, he will be looking for you and Mike. I say that if we are not together, hopefully, one of us will get to kill that son-of-a-bitch. I need you guys just where you are. On the outside keeping us aware of the shit in the sewers. Thanks dude, hit you later."

The Sarge went into the kitchen and hit the dinner bell. Every living soul on the farm quickly entered the family room. The Sarge announced, "I just received a call from Allen who informed me that we will be invaded by a group of forty plus mercs from the north side. He told me that our last incursion was a test of our defensive systems. From the north side, we will have to provide mano a mano intervention. Mallory, I need you to make assignments, and as of this moment, people, we are on full alert."

As the Sarge turned his back on the group and prepared to walk away, Rashida said, "Dad, there are two possible solutions to responding to this threat."

The Sarge smiled and said, "Sweetheart, my guys will take care of this."

Rashida said, "My way allows them to take care of this matter from afar. I can reprogram the long guns to hit targets on the north side. Suppose the notion of an attack from the north is a ruse and they come at us from the east and west? I can give them a huge blast and limit our guys' exposure to a gun battle. Dad, I can do this."

The Sarge paused, looked at Rashida, and asked, "Will you take a walk with me? Mallory, delay that order. I need to understand this new strategy my daughter is proposing. Actually, Mallory, I need you to join us."

"Rashida, what's going on in that head of yours? You never liked video games, shows, or movies that depicted wholesale death, but yet, you're willing to hit the engage button on the ODS. What's come over you?"

"Dad, really? I'll give you the short of it and then you decide. That guy, your cousin, placed a suicide vest on my child, and I swore I would do everything possible to protect my family. I just can't sit around and watch a door when I can be doing so much more. Jong's cousin gave me the codes to the ODS and all of the information I'll need to redirect the firing positions, but I need to get to it before we have more unwanted guests."

Mallory said, "We would rather take this time to sort things out than to have to get you psychological help later. Killing a person is something that never goes away. We have thousands of souls looking for us in Hades--another adventure that I personally don't relish. When you hit that button, there is no taking the action back."

"They didn't seem to hesitate when they put those vests on the children, did they? They acted as if they were helping them get dressed for school or church."

"Rashida, you have to tell your mother about your new sought-after responsibility and what it truly means. You seem hell bent on doing this thing and, if she approves or not, you would have at least informed her about your new tasks. I can't and will not fight that battle for you. You know exactly how she is and I'm not getting in the middle of this one."

#

Juan was searching for Rashida when he walked around to the front of the house and saw her, the Sarge, and Mallory. He tried to retreat, but the Sarge saw him and said, "Mister, I need to speak to you."

Rashida said, "Dad, you're going to scare the man I love away."

"No, I'm going to ascertain his intentions, and then decide whether to break him in half or shoot him."

"Dad, please be nice to him. He is so sweet and loving."

The Sarge instructed Mallory to make temporary assignments. As the Sarge and Juan began their walk, Juan asked, "May I ask you a question, Sir?"

"Make it a relevant one, because I don't do interviews."

"Would you have hurt Jong when you had him dangling in the air with one hand?"

"Son, that situation was foreign to me. I didn't know what was going on. In a conflicted state, anything is possible. Which leads me to ask a simple question-- what are your intentions towards my daughter? She is a fragile soul and I will dismember any man who attempts to take advantage of her without a lasting purpose."

"Sarge, you are an intimidating figure and I still don't believe what my eyes saw when you dangled Jong in midair. I know all that happened to Rashida and the nagging memories of Malik. I'm no Malik because my love is good and not derived from anger. My family was once dirt poor but are now earning a salary and living comfortably outside of Barcelona. Rashida wants to become a pediatrician and I want to become a businessman. We both want to go back to school, but in the interim we also want to have more children. Due to the generous payments from Ms. De Lombardo, and our unexpected bonus from you, we can afford a modest home for LaGina and can also enter school at the same time. She is ahead of me in terms of academics, but I'm sure I will finish school and support my family. I love Rashida. I have had affairs and sex, but I have never felt love and passion like I do for her. If you allow me, I will become a wonderful husband to your daughter and father to your granddaughter."

"Are you in any way, shape, or form, related to Ms. De Lombardo?"

"I don't understand the question."

"Juan, if you are related to her, and Zanthius is my son, then somehow you might be a distant cousin which complicates a natural bond between you and Rashida. On another note, I know you will do well by my daughter or I will personally and quietly kill you. Nice to speak with you and this conversation remains private and between us. Is that clear and do we have an accord?"

# # #

Mallory summoned the Sarge from the field and told him that Allen was calling on the house phone. The Sarge got the phone, walked outside and said, "What's going on? You're calling me on the house phone?"

"I was mugged, and everything was taken from me. I might need medical assistance. I think they broke my nose."

"It's time for you guys to get out of the pits."

"No Sarge, a few good friends took care of their asses, but they did get away with my phone and my stash."

"Did they take your shoes?"

"No, I got them."

"Then go to any ATM and get what you need because you have a very lucrative card between the sole and the lining. You have got to be more careful. If something happens to you then we're shit out of luck and we would be blind. I know that sounds selfish, but I'm trying to protect the entire world plus old enemies from one dangerous son-of-a-bitch."

# # #

When the Sarge walked back into the house, he saw Juan hovering over Rashida. Rashida said, "A perfect defense would be to watch the intruders stage their forces, once they make their move, we use the tunnels to come up from behind them and catch them in a crossfire with at least three thrown grenades, assault weapons spraying them from behind and long guns pinpointing them as well."

"Why don't you suggest that strategy to your father? Maybe he will listen to you."

"Why do you say it like that?" Rashida asked defensively.

Juan explained, "I'm just saying. He has developed a different level of respect for you and is thankful that you have shown an interest in defending us all. Just suggest it and see what he says."

The Sarge was standing in the foyer having a conversation with Zanthius when Rashida walked up, excused herself, and asked, "Dad, can I show you, Mallory, and my brother, since he's here, something on the computer?"

As they walked in the room, Juan was at the helm and Rashida instructed, "Juan, show them."

"It's your idea and a good one at that. You show them," Juan stated.

Rashida proceeded to explain that if the attack came from the north, then there were two options available to inflict injury and death on their enemies, within the limits of a safe outcome. She focused on two trees on the northside and said, "Those two trees are within range of the long guns that are stationed in the west. To further minimize the risks to our team, we can have two or three people open up the hatch, right about 10 degrees north of those trees, spray the area with machine pistol fire, and throw a couple of those grenades that were captured. The long guns would complete the attack."

Zanthius said, "That would certainly confuse them as well as inflict significant damage on their group, all while our people are underground and protected. Those stairs leading to the outside from the tunnel are designed so three people can escape at a time. The hatch to all the tunnels are fully automatic, which means that once rounds have been fired and those grenades have been launched, we can slide down the stairs as one of our guys hits the button slamming the hatch as tight as a witch's ass. I like it, Sis. You're becoming quite a tactician. Pops, what are your thoughts?"

"I want my little girl playing with dolls and not trying to figure out how to destroy people. But we no longer live in those times," the Sarge sighed.

Rashida's posture shifted and the Sarge said, "Smart ass idea. Not bad. Not bad at all. Is this really your idea or was there input from your man-friend?"

Juan was about to say something, when the Sarge looked sternly at him. Rashida replied, "I ran it by him, and he thought it was worthy of consideration by you."

The Sarge nodded, "Did he now? I like it, but I would like to make a small modification to it. Why can't we use the tunnel and have a small contingency of our people to attack them from that position? Is it because you wouldn't know who you were targeting from the west?"

"Not at all. Jong's cousin gave him medallions that are quickly identified by the ODS. We also have cameras in the area." Rashida hit a series of buttons and the area was illuminated on the screen.

The Sarge asked, "Where is the hatch to the tunnel?"

Rashida zoomed in on it with one of the cameras and it showed the general location of the tunnel.

"How many people can ease out of that tunnel and provide flanking fire, but if need be, get out of there in a hurry?"

"That's the problem--getting in and out quickly and safely, I wouldn't want to have more than three people exposed in that area. Remember, we want to flank them, fire on them from the west, cover their disclosure to the east, and have our people disappear into the tunnels. No long-term spotlight at all."

Zanthius said, "Pops, your little girl has figured this mess out. On another subject, Courtney believes that Asiram can fly. If you agree, we will make special arrangements with the hospital on the island, if we survive this mess. You need to talk with Asiram and Courtney to make the call. She thinks the island is slightly remote and backwards when it comes to health care and delivering babies. I have tried to convince her that they have some of the finest doctors in the world there, plus, Courtney will be there.

As day began to turn into night, from the balcony of her bedroom, Asiram said to Zanthius, "You know I hate you, right? You have ruined my figure, placed a lifetime responsibility on my shoulders, married me, and made me the happiest woman in the world. This has been crazy. I mean despite all the shooting and blowing up of things, I wouldn't have it any other way. Your mom, dad, sister, brother, your dad's friends are some incredible people. I have never met a more orderly group than Mr. Beckmire's. I used to think they were too old to be playing war, but damn I'm glad they're on our side. I mean 'formidable' doesn't come close to how they work. And for you, big boy, I love you more than life. You have become an amazing partner, friend, and lover. But I am still not going to forget that Helga shit. Not in a million years." Asiram smiled and began to kiss her husband.

"Sweetheart, Helga, RIP, was a little more decisive about what she wanted than you were. After I figured out the sordid details of my employer, you, and Helga, I was just lucky to get my ass off that mountain and back home. I didn't know I would need to enlist the support of a father that I didn't know existed. But all is good, and I only think of Helga, now and then," Zanthius teased. Asiram lightly punched her husband.

Zanthius, after looking at the limited amount of ammo they had in the bedroom, told Asiram that he was going to get some additional munitions. She told him she didn't think they would need it because unbeknownst to the enemy, they had just awakened another Beckmire.

Zanthius asked, "What do you mean?"

"The worst thing anyone could have done was to put a suicide vest on Rashida's child. Have you not noticed her focus and determination? I stood by the door and watched her and Jong's cousin have a discussion. She belittled him, and then honored him to the point that he gave her his codes to the program that operate the ODS. I assure you this is going to be like a video game with her. I don't care where they come from, she is going to kick ass. Just wait and see."

Zanthius said, "Well, just in case she has a hiccup, I'm going to get more ammo and perhaps a couple of the .380s."

"Honey, we need to decide on a name for our child. We don't know if it's a boy or a girl yet, but I would like to name a girl Marisa, the reverse of Asiram. If it's a boy, I would like to name him Zanthius Beckmire De Lombardo the II. What are your thoughts?" Asiram asked.

"I would like to name a son, Benjamin Beckmire De Lombardo. It is strong and full of character. Say it to yourself, Benjamin Beckmire De Lombardo. The girls are going to want to bid on him when he's three years old," Zanthius noted.

"You are such a character. How about if it's a girl, I get to name her without any input from you and if it's a boy, the honor is all yours!"

"I think we have an accord. Shall we have a minimum notion of love making to seal the deal?" Zanthius slyly inquired.

"Come to momma, but no banging, Daddy," Asiram amplified.

CHAPTER TWENTY-TWO

Later, the entire ranch was on alert. The Sarge made his rounds, along with Zanthius, to make sure that everyone was in place and had significant firepower. Larry said to Marisa, "This has been an unsettling adventure, dear. I wish I could have sent you and the twins to a safer place while we dealt with this thing!"

"Larry, really? I'm getting a chance to shoot people and you want to deny me that? You put a suicide vest on my children, I will kill anyone. This entire chaotic scene has made me strong and has produced some incredible and steamy nights for us, a thing that we lost after the twins arrived. No sir, we will all survive this, or we will all be a blur in the memory of those who don't have a clue as to what we stood for. By the way, what the hell do we stand for?"

Larry laughed and said, "I'm standing for more nights of powerful sexual explosions. I just usually do what my dad asks. He's my hero and I trust him with our lives. He is an incredible human being. Rashida and I owe him and Courtney an awful lot. They are legends and Gods to us. They picked us up and helped us become grounded and never asked for a thing in return, other than that we help other people help themselves. They invested a boat load of money in our education and have never, I mean never, asked for a single thing in return. They are gladiators and saints. I used to think there was an ultimate task I would be asked to perform, but that notion never occurred. I was so used to the fact that nothing is done without a price. Yet, they just loved us as human beings, even though we had a history."

"Come here, baby. I need a long kiss from you."

"You mean you want a quickie?"

"Damn dude. You're getting my flow. Quietly, lets slip in the bathroom and try to make it happen."

# # #

At 2100 hours, the house phone rang, and everyone froze. Asiram picked up the phone and Allen asked, "Did you have the baby yet?"

"Who's inquiring?"

"This is Allen. I used to want to see to your demise."

"Hold on. Let me get the Sarge."

"Wait, wait a minute. Listen, you of all people know the business we're in. I was turned by a good man who spared my life and who has supported me and my friends in the sewer as well as my family. Ben Beckmire is a compassionate human being and I regret the day that I drew arms against him and his old ass band of friends. I say that to say, I am most sorry for the attempts I placed on the lives of the people on your property. My rebirth is that I now provide you guys with what I hope is important intel from the sewers. Please forgive me for trying to kill you, but we all have control buttons."

"Allen, thank you for that. As with space travel, you must go and hope you get back. In the spy business, it is always acknowledged as a one-way trip. Let me get the Sarge for you. Nice to have words of peace with you."

Once he gained the phone, the Sarge asked, "What's going on?"

"I spoke with Mike and he and I have joined forces and are at this very moment watching people enter your property from the east, moving north to circle the wagons on the west and south sides. I misquoted the number, Sarge, there are another 100 people who think that they are truly ninjas."

"What are you doing near this place? You can't be here."

"Sarge, Mike and I have already eliminated fifteen of their people by having a few of our sewer friends force them off the road. When the cops showed up, they were arrested because of the number of weapons they possessed. They may not know it, but we saved their lives."

"Allen, this is not the way we do business. You, of all people, know better than to show up near me without prior notification."

"Sarge, you may not know it, but Virginia is a free state. We just happen to be driving by. We tried to call, but the phone line is dead and that is the only way we can contact you. We met at Regan National Airport and asked a few friends of ours to accompany us in stolen vehicles. We were going to assault those who are planning to breach your farm. Listen, Mike and I are as lost without you as you are without us. Your cousin wants us all dead. Do you want us to come on the property or drive west and watch from afar?"

"Allen, I would recommend that you watch from afar. My daughter is ever mindful of the fact that someone placed a suicide vest on her child, and she has automated the art of war beyond anything that I could describe. I would prefer that she played with dolls, but damn, she is lethal and absolute. No quarters given and no chance to ask for a parlay."

"Sarge, we are here and can help, all you need to do is let us into your space."

"Allen, this thing has reached beyond the jungle fighting strategy. This place is armed to the teeth. Stay put and come only if you see a huge fireball in the sky. All who belong here are wearing medallions that are recognized by our defense system. If you enter the property without one, you will be shot until your body ceases to move. This thing, this 'mechanized mayhem', that she controls, is devious and unfair. If you can find a safe place to perch and have a pair of binoculars, then I suggest you sit and watch what a slaughter looks like."

"Sarge, we're here to help. Use us if you need to. Take care and God Bless."

# # #

At 1100 hours, the screens in front of Jong, Rashida, and Juan began to pinpoint moving objects. Jong saw Zanthius and told him to get his dad and Mallory in there in a hurry. Tell them the place is being infested with roaches.

Zanthius saw Mallory and told him the screens were showing signs of intrusion and that Jong wanted his father there in a hurry. Mallory asked, "Is Rashida and Juan in there?"

Zanthius replied, "They are. Why do you ask?"

"They are the only people who really understand the ODS. Jong knows a little about it, but those two, I put my money on them," Mallory replied.

"That is great to hear because I was under the impression that Rashida is a little trigger happy, if I can use that analogy," Zanthius noted.

Mallory paused, stared at Zanthius and inquired, "Have you noticed that people don't call you in to conduct the initial interrogation of suspects. I guess you do know why. On the other hand, Rashida and Juan are just what the doctor ordered. She didn't really put our people in jeopardy as your father thought, she saw two sets of lines and guessed the right one to fire upon and it was the one that was not retreating. I would have done the same damn thing. Do you know how to operate the system?"

"Frankly, I don't. I, like the fact that you have faith in them," Zanthius admitted.

When the Sarge arrived Mallory said, "Your daughter and her suitor need to see you. Jong is in control, but they're calling the shots."

"How the hell can that be? Then he is not in control if they're calling the shots."

"Sarge, we are about to be attacked, check out the options they are proposing," Mallory said.

The Sarge entered the control room and Jong said, "You need Chinese beads to count with. That is more than forty dots on our screens."

"I know. I just got a call from Allen who said it is more like a hundred."

"Dad, sorry, but it is more like 150 people staging in all four areas of the farm."

"How can you be certain about that?"

"Dad, all of us have this thing around our necks and it acts like a radio collar. This screen shows all of the radio collars and they are all accounted for, right, Hyshime?"

"Why you call me Hyshime?"

"That is your name, isn't it?" Rashida inquired.

"Yes, all of our collars are numbered and accounted for and can be viewed on this screen. Those other dots are from uninvited sources. Rashida is correct, there are at least 150 people about to move on us," Jong replied.

"No, they aren't about to move on us, they are moving on us in clusters and from the different quadrants of the farm. Okay, watch this sector that represents the west. In sixty seconds from, 5-4-3-2-1- mark, they're going to move," Rashida announced. She continued, "The next dots to move would be the east, then north and then the south."

The Sarge asked, "How did you know that they were going to do that?"

"We went back to their arrival, watched their movements and put them on the grid that calculated the distance and time in which they moved. One other thing, they are communicating with some new equipment that does not register on our system. Awhile back, Asiram placed that box in the center of the field to amplify our communications and to make sure that we were always in contact. You remember that? Well, these guys are communicating, but I don't know how."

"Rashida, you figured this all out by yourself?"

"Dad, in some sense of the word, this is a video game, not that dissimilar from those that Larry and I played years ago. When Jong's cousin gave me the codes, he suggested that I embrace them and use them in any way necessary to protect the family. When those words finally hit home, he was telling me to protect the base, home plate, the goal posts, the basket, and everything else. Can't you see it? Protect your base. So, dad from here, I have targeted every dot on my screen with a series of alternate firing schemes and this is all from those damn video games. Can you get Larry down here quickly?"

A few minutes later when Larry arrived, Rashida said to him, "Larry, look at this screen. What does it remind you of?"

Larry looked at the screen and then requested the previous screen and the one before that and said, "This is a base game.

Protect your base and use alternate firing schemes to accomplish it. Pops, that means, shooting off buildings or ricocheting shots off platforms to hit your target. Okay, you look confused. I know, you like the game of pool and more importantly playing 'one pocket'. Just think of banking a shot from the side rail and into the corner pocket. Same difference, except in this game, you use bullets and dispose of your opponents through a series of incredible shots that earn you points—it's a video game."

Juan reported, "Rashida, all four quadrants moved at the same time."

Rashida responded, "As expected and they should make four more simultaneous moves. On their fifth joint movement if there is no assault from us, they will begin to converge on us like locust and Dad, that is when I will hit the engage button. Oh, and by the way, my thoughts are that from this video game there is a high probability of success without breach. I personally would still deploy people in strategic places and send the children and Asiram into a tunnel. My assumption is that they will come at us in approximately twenty minutes."

"My dear daughter, are you telling me that you are not sure what time they will show up?"

"Dad, I'm telling you that in twenty minutes they are going to feel so cocky, oh sorry, they're going to think that we have gone to sleep, and the farm is theirs for the taking."

The Sarge looked at her, Juan, and then at Jong and said, "Jong and Mallory, huddle with me outside of this room."

"When the three men were away from the control room, Jong snickered and said, "I guess the pear don't fall too far from the farm."

Mallory looked at him and said, "You are really retarded at times. The saying is, 'the apple didn't fall too far from the tree'."

The Sarge said, "I don't give a shit about none of that. Can you believe how they've mapped this shit out? They use a video game to play a game to kill a shit load of people. How damn insane is that?"

"Sarge, we barely understand the damn cell phone, and this is another one of those occasions when you have to say, they're smart with video games and cell phones."

The Sarge asked Mallory, "Who did you assign to the roof, and who do we have on tunnel duty, and where are the rest of the people?"

The two men quickly went over the details of the placement of individuals when the Sarge said, "I don't have a good feeling about this shit. Get all of the women and children in the west tunnel where we have vehicles stashed and ready to go if this shit goes bad."

Mallory hesitated, looked at Jong, and said to the Sarge, "That will send a helluva message to our women."

"I would rather see my wife, yours, as well as all the other women safely away from this place, if we should fall."

Rashida yelled, "Dad, get in here."

When the three men entered the room, Rashida said, "I think you should send non-essentials to the tunnels, but don't send them west. There's too many woods and unknowns. Send them south towards the road where we have vehicles stashed. But I'm telling you, get them in the tunnel now. I got this one or I'm going to die trying to kill every person who would dress my child, or any child, with a suicide vest."

Zanthius walked in and grabbed his father by the arm and said, "I need to have a word with you now."

"What's up, Son?"

"I have taken the liberty of sending the women and children into the tunnel that leads to the south. I need you to believe in your daughter and her mate and remember the things we saw when we were in the outback."

The Sarge made a monstrous sound and yelled, "Baby Girl, you got our six?"

"Dad, we are on it. I just need you or Jong to okay my final firing scenario and then the die will be cast."

"Mr. Amazing, you're in command of the control center. Those civilians work for you. Use them and abuse them to our advantage."

As Jong studied the screens and flip flopped between them, he said, "We need to become the aggressors."

Rashida announced, "That's the last thing we need to do. They have cautiously moved in tandem because they are not sure how we can overcome superior odds with just a few people. And besides, just give them another ten minutes or so, and they will probably come at us in a synchronized fashion—blasting their firepower at the same time at the structure assigned to them. Please, wait ten minutes and see what happens."

In the meantime, Asiram yelled at Zanthius, "I ain't going in no damn tunnel unless your ass is in there with me. I have plenty of ammo and my aim is still good. My movement might be a little slow, but I can still shoot a damn weapon."

Marisa said to Larry, "Hey honey, grow up and be a man. You keep the children for a change, and I'll go and kick some butts. I'm not going into that tunnel until the very last moment. I'm going to put the kids in one of the lockers and let them watch TV, but I'm going to be a part of our defense.

So, honey, put me in a place where I can just fire the damn weapon without looking at what I'm shooting."

The Sarge walked up to Courtney and said, "Please talk to these women. We don't need any additional distractions. There are over 150 people waiting on something before they come at us with a vengeance. Can you talk some sense into them?"

"Oh my, God! Ben Beckmire, do you have a headache? Do you still have a sense of smell? How about a fever? Do you have one? What about coughing? Do you have a dry cough? Anyway, everyone feels like this could be out last hurrah and you want us to go and hang in a tunnel and hide like rats until its daylight? Listen, my husband, that ain't going to happen. I am a doctor sworn to save lives. Tonight, I am Mrs. Ben Beckmire whose husband is under siege and she and the other women folk here are going to give up their lives to save their men, their families, and their friends. You need to give us assignments and get over the bullshit, we ain't going into no tunnels until we all go."

Beckmire looked at his wife and asked, "Honey, do you even know how to fire that thing?"

"Ben, I'm a damn doctor. I know the intricacies of the human body, and what goes where, and how to fix it. This is a simple machine that man made to destroy the body." Courtney clicked the safety off the assault weapon and asked, "Would you like to see me accurately hit a target at fifty yards?"

"Honey, please put the safety on the weapon." He looked at Mallory and then at Monica. Monica said, "I don't know why you're looking at him. He and I have already had this disagreement. Plus, I've been free for years and subject to make my own decisions."

The Sarge looked at Mallory and said, "Make the assignments. Who is going to watch my grandbabies and the other children?"

"Why don't you try doing that, Ben Beckmire. It's really special to spend time with them and watch their development."

Rashida yelled, "They simultaneously moved ten paces forward. Did you see that Jong? I bet you in three minutes they're going to give us all they have. Dad, can you come in here a moment? I want you to see this firsthand."

"Mallory, please handle our dissidents. Give them front line duty, so that they can get a sense of what we do and how it's critical to defend that part of the land given to you."

The Sarge walked into the control room and Jong said, "Sarge, leave this thing to them. Their eyes are faster than mine and they know this game better than me. Get Larry back down here and substitute someone in his position. She and Juan saw movement that I didn't."

The Sarge looked at him and said, "This is a part of their revolution. The civilians are not following orders, they are all attempting a coup of our dictatorial leadership. When this is over, we should appoint a civilian council to govern us."

When Larry came down the steps the Sarge said, "I'm leaving the ODS to you and your sister. Is that a problem for you?"

"Dad, you taught us well. If it's a game they want to employ, then we will surely show them how we play to win."

"Son, those are human beings out there."

"Oh, I see! And I thought we were humans as well? Rashida, what side of this thing do you want me to play?"

"You take the north, Juan. Larry, you take the east and I have the south and west. We don't want to engage them until they're fifty yards in, and then God be with us all."

Rashida and Larry watched the screens and saw that another group of individuals were amassing on the southwestern front. Rashida yelled, "Dad, I need you in here now."

The Sarge ran into the control room and asked, "What's wrong?"

Rashida said, "Look at the dots forming in the southwestern quadrant of the farm." The Sarge looked and said, "I don't understand these different dots. Quick analysis."

"In essence, there are at least thirty or more individuals preparing to launch an assault."

"Are they the same group?"

Rashida looked at her father and then replied, "Dad, hold on a minute. Let

me run out there and ask them! How would we know that?"

Mallory laughed and then asked, "How many people do we have on the roof?"

"We have ten. And they all have long guns."

"Tell Jilkes I want those on the roof to focus on that area."

"Dad, they are moving on all fronts. Do I have your permission to engage?"

The Sarge paused and realized that dots were converging on the farmhouse. He asked, "Are you sure about this?"

"Sergeant Beckmire, that is the enemy converging on us. Can we engage?" Rashida paused, changed her demeanor, and yelled, "Can we engage, Sergeant Sir?"

The Sarge looked to the heavens and finally yelled to the top of his lungs, "Engage, engage, engage!"

Rashida said, "On my mark. 5-4-3-2-1-mark."

The Sarge and everyone else in the control center watched as the computer methodically took control of the weapons and preprogrammed the targets and began to decimate everything that moved in each quadrant. The puffing sounds from the suppression devices attempted to minimize the sounds of the weapons being fired. It was obvious from the moans and smacking noises of bullets hitting their targets, that the ODS would become the new reality for the team! Once the ODS had been engaged, the streaks from the automatic weapons filled the night with bright flashes. It took less than two minutes to conclude or incapacitate the lives of 150 mercs. It was as though time slowed down and the rounds from each of the 15 machine pistols and long guns meticulously hit their victims, vividly demonstrating their wounds, catching the look of horror and pain on their faces, before the subjects hit the ground. It was surreal, devastating, emotional, and conclusive. Those impacted by the ODS, never saw their aggressors, and did not have the opportunity to discharge their weapons.

It was similar to picking apples off a tree--the ten people positioned on the roof, purged another forty mercs from the southwest part of the farm.

The Sarge said, "I don't know how much more of this I can fathom mentally. Our ODS is insatiable and will, and can, conclude another 150 souls. We need to abandon this place and forever leave it as a memory."

"Dad why is it bad for us to defend ourselves? They knew we were not going to surrender and hold our hands in the air and be massacred. They do this for a living and for money. We do this to protect those we love. We, as well as they, had options. We need to find your cousin and give that white witch that final piece of the puzzle," Rashida announced.

"Honey how do you know about the final piece, and who are you calling the white witch?"

214 c. benjamin lattimore

"Dad, I don't know about you and your guys, but the rest of us talk all day long and gossip about things in the middle. That other person I referred to is that senator lady who ran for President and got beat bad by that arrogant, lying, self-aggrandizing person of little character."

"Wow, I guess we talk a little loud!"

Mallory walked in and said, "We had a friendly to sustain a minor wound. Your wife is looking after him now."

"Who got shot and how bad?"

"One of the horses, Sarge. The bullet must have ricocheted off a rock or something and grazed his big ass. I haven't told your daughter-in-law and I reserved that right for you, Master."

"Oh my, here I go again. That child is going to hate me forever.

Can Courtney fix him?"

"She's a doctor, right? Then I suspect she will be able to keep him alive. It's just a flesh wound."

CHAPTER TWENTY-THREE

Allen called the Sarge and said, "You people are crazy. Mike and I saw what you did to those people. Were you hiding in the woods as usual? That was an insane kill. Gunfire from all over the place. Did you hire mercs to assist you?"

"When I see you, I will explain everything to you. It's not safe for you guys to show up here tonight, go west about twenty miles on the main road and you will see a couple of hotels. Take your pick. Before you go, I want you to look around for the vehicles that transported those people," the Sarge requested.

"Sarge, I was going to tell you that we are eyeing two of them right now. The code of mercs is that payment is made immediately after the work is completed. Mike and I believe that there is a shit load of money in them and only three guys watching them," Allen said.

"Why didn't you and Mike just purloin those damn trucks and drive away?" the Sarge asked.

"We discussed that option, and it didn't pan out too well for us, in the long run," Allen replied.

"What the hell does that mean? There is probably $20 million in one of those trucks and you tell me it didn't pan out well for you two. What does that mean?" the Sarge obstinately inquired.

"Sarge, we think there is more like $30 million in cash in those vehicles. Our problem is the same one you have. No matter the money, Walter is still out there looking for you, for

Mike, and me. We figured we would protect it for you but take whatever our needs, minus commission, but the money is best cared for in your delicate hands."

"Okay, enough with the bullshit. Why didn't you take the trucks and disappear?"

"Because I'm looking for salvation and Mike is trying to stay alive. That is the real conversation we had when we figured out that the trucks were full of money. We never once got greedy and besides, if you can kill that many people, then he and I wouldn't be a problem. We don't need money. You keep us supplied with money, and you have a bank for both of us. The one thing we both realize is that you are the most honorable man we have ever met, and your word is your bond and your bond is your word. I don't know of any other human being that I can say that about."

"Are you done blowing smoke up my ass?"

"For now, master, for now!"

"Let me forewarn you, the contents of those trucks are probably wired and full of some pretty nasty shit. We picked off one and it was loaded with a suspicious white powder. Once it was analyzed, it had remnants of Mr. Anthrax. We have someone who analyzes these matters for us and cleans the product with some sophisticated equipment. I'm just surprised, and happy, that you guys didn't run off with the contents without offering us a share."

"Sarge, we have the same common enemy. And remember I told you that I could be obsequious to you if you didn't kill or maim me. I've been true to my word, and poor Mike, is on the run for not following orders from the mad man."

"I'm going to have someone call the cleaners to get these bodies off the property, but I need you and Mike to secure those trucks. I would prefer you not injure those who are watching the vehicles unless they present a danger to you guys. Secure them and once my man gets there, he will scan the product. I will instruct him to give those guys $50k each. If all goes well, I will give you and Mike a 20% finder's fee and credit that amount to those secret accounts. Or you can take your chances and try to clean it yourselves. I really don't want to deal with any more illicit money, and I hope you and Mike run the hell off with it."

"Sarge, we made a deal. You're holding a significant amount of paper for us as it is. However, another $3 million, or so, makes him and I both, smile. You did the work and all we did was secure the money trucks. Oh Sarge, I have an important call coming in. Let me hit you back."

"Before you go, don't mess with those trucks. I have people on their way to examine them and the contents."

Allen answered the other call and it was Walter. He said to Allen, "I never would have thought that the people behind trying to do me in, would be you and Mike. I loved you guys like brothers."

"Walter, I never would have thought that you would put a hit on me and my family. Poor Mike is still wondering what the hell he did to you that would have you turn street goons on him? Anyway, I know you didn't call me to talk about old times so, what's on your mind?"

"That's my Allen, cut right to the chase. I need to have a sit-down with my cousin and with the senator as mediator. There is the matter of the Carbon Factor, and personally, a significant amount of my money that has been taken from me."

"Walter, why are you calling me? You should call Ben Beckmire and attempt to settle your differences. I don't have any leverage over him, so why are you calling me?"

"Listen, you little snake, if you want me to drop a certain action against you, then you should act a little less obnoxious and a little more beholden. I know exactly where you and Mike hang out, in the sewers and trashy places like that. If you can broker the meeting, and regardless of the outcome, I might buy that paper back that is circulating with your picture on it.

"Listen, I don't know how to reach my cousin, so if you can do this for me, it might make things better for all of us. Have him give the senator a call, let her and him set up the meeting time and place. I don't believe there are any mercs left in the world. This senseless slaughter and attempted slaughter must come to an end. I really want to work this thing out, shake hands, and part ways. Insofar, as the Carbon Factor is concerned, I think that's a deal to be made with the she devil."

Allen looked at his phone and hung it up. He called Walter back on Mike's phone and apologized. He then said, "Walter, I will try to reach him and give him your message. One more thing, I'm no snake and your idle threats don't cause any panic in my system. From what I've seen, you might want to find a huge rock and hide under it. I believe your cousin is determined to gut you from your penis to your brains. Have a nice day."

Mike asked Allen, "Was that really Walter?"

"The one and only. I have to call Beckmire and relay a message."

Allen in the interim, called Beckmire and said, "That last call was from your cousin. He wants to have a sit down with you, and have the senator mediate. You should call her office and have her set it up. There are several issues that need to be discussed; one is the Carbon Factor, and the other is a significant amount of money that he believes you have taken from him. He said nothing about his attempts to kill you and everyone else. Those are the two issues. Oh, he did say that if Mike and I can arrange this meeting he would buy back some paper floating around with our pictures on it. I told him that he should find a huge rock and climb under it because someone that I know wanted to gut him from his penis to his brains."

"Did you really tell him that?"

"I kid you not. He keeps threatening me and I'm a little sick of it. Screw him."

"I can't forgive his actions, and I find it difficult to consider meeting with the very same people who have been trying to kill us for some time. I don't trust her, and you know I don't trust his ass. He has suffered significantly with his attacks and has betrayed us on every turn. It ain't going to happen. I show up for a meeting and those people will arrest me or shoot my ass on sight. I don't feel like committing suicide anytime soon."

"I don't disagree with you at all. Perhaps a phone conversation would be better. I agree with you, they have been trying to end your happy life for a while. You show up and bam. Then they could easily use the National Guard to finish the work, including bombing the ranch. I don't trust her, and I don't trust him. Can I call you back? I need to attend to some business," Allen stated.

# # #

Mallory walked up to the Sarge and said, "The cleaning company told him that a number of the garments needed further attention and that his people performed the service for free. I think they are ready to make a final sweep of the entire area again before they give an all clear signal."

"Okay, get with Jong and figure out the payment. Also, I spoke with Allen who said that Walter and the senator want to have a sit down with me."

"I know you're not considering it. Those people are as trustworthy as the new guy coming into office. They'll probably assassinate you," Mallory concluded.

"I'm not considering meeting with Diablo and his mother. I will speak with them on the phone, but insofar as he's concerned, I never want to see or hear from him again until I'm ready to gut his ass from his mid-section to his brain. I need to find Courtney and see if we can get to the airport and leave this place in the next hour or two."

"Damn, that would be wonderful if we could pull that off. Courtney and the ladies are in the basement telling tales."

"Is Asiram down there as well?"

Mallory replied, "I'm not really sure."

# # #

The Sarge entered the house and headed for the basement. As he turned the corner, all the ladies were coming upstairs. He stepped back and said, "So sorry to be in your way. Where is Asiram?"

Monica answered, "She went to her room with her husband in tow."

"Is everything okay? I mean is she feeling ill?"

"No, I don't think so. She seemed fine when we were in the basement."

"I'll go knock on her door and check on her," the Sarge stated.

The Sarge walked up the steps and knocked on the door. Asiram said, "Come in."

"Hi Baby Girl, is everything okay? I came to have a little chat with you. Hey son, we survived another one."

"Yes, we did, Pops. How long can we bat a thousand without a single casualty? We need a new strategy and it's probably time to disappear for a while."

"That's the purpose of my visit. Asiram, are you fit for traveling? I didn't ask Courtney because she can only guess and assume what may happen. I need you to tell me if you can fly comfortably?"

"Daddy-in-Law, I'm fine and I don't expect to have a baby for another two to three weeks. If you want to go to the islands, then let's get this show on the road."

"Okay, but it depends on what Courtney has to say about your ability to travel."

# # #

Twenty minutes later, the Sarge caught up with Courtney and asked, "Honey, in your opinion, is Asiram okay to travel?"

"She is able and willing to fly. I will obtain a few things for the trip, but other than that, she's good to go."

"Quietly pass the word, we are out of here in two hours. I'll reach Jong and let him know our intent."

The Sarge met up with Jong and Mallory and proposed that they board their plane and head south. Jong immediately called the pilot in command and told her of their plans. She indicated that he would file a flight plan and that the plane would be ready for departure in an hour. The Sarge then called Allen and invited him and Mike to join them on the trip. Both men declined because they didn't have access to their passports and other identification papers.

## CHAPTER TWENTY-FOUR

The flight to St. Thomas was uneventful. Asiram, being in good shape, probably minimized any discomfort issues. Mr. Christopher Carter personally picked the group up from the airport in one of their new transport vans.

At their resort, the group wasted little time in transforming into vacation mode. Both resorts had been totally transformed and represented the ultimate in design, luxury, and privacy on the island. Each room was appointed with the finest décor and gadgets that money could buy. The security had been increased ten-fold and had extended its reach around the island, targeting known criminals, and offering them alternatives to incarceration and disappearances.

Asiram asked Mr. Carter if he could prepare an enormous meal for the group. He told her that once word got out of their arrival, he asked his people to work additional hours to accommodate the group. Most of the members of the group weren't thinking about food but were more interested in enjoying the blue sky and the salty water they were looking at.

As the Sarge prepared to rest and enjoy his family and friends, his phone rang. Courtney said, "Please don't answer it."

He looked at her and said, "Honey, only Allen has this number. He keeps me abreast of who is tracking and trying to hurt us. I'm requesting your permission to answer the call."

Courtney nodded and walked away. When the Sarge answered the phone, Allen told him that the rumors about the

KGB were accurate and they were preparing a strategy to capture the 'idiot spy'. The Sarge told him that he wished them luck with that one, and for Allen to keep him abreast of any new developments as well as any information relating to his cousin. The Sarge once again extended an invitation to him and Mike to join them.

After hanging up the phone, the Sarge said to Courtney and Monica who had joined them, "If I can get them to middle America, then I can get them paperwork. Why didn't I think of this earlier? Have you guys seen Jong?"

Later, Courtney asked Monica, "Would you trust a son-of-a-bitch that ordered suicide vests to be put on your children?"

"Hell no! He would have to fly in from heaven with wings and shit on. Oh, sorry, hold on a minute." Monica yelled to the waiter, "Hey, we need two drinks over here, please."

Monica turned to Courtney and asked, "Do you take orders from other people? Did the Sarge and those guys take orders from other people? Sometimes you don't like what it is you're asked to do, but then you must consider the consequences. Yes, the consequences can be extremely difficult to swallow. Yet, if you've given up the world to survive and you can't trust the person who is in control, then I think you must consider all things that are thrown your way. Listen, I was there alongside you. I was there with people placing dynamite around us and not even making excuses. I say all of that to say this, if he has changed, then why can't we be accepting of his epiphany?"

"Have you had a drink already?" Courtney asked.

"I had two on the plane. Bloody Mary's with olives and celery. You didn't have a drink?"

"No, I didn't," Courtney replied.

"Oh, well. Oh, there's Ava. Shall we invite your husband's ex-lover over to join us?"

There was a long pause, Courtney turned colors, and said, "No, you didn't just go there. Are you fucking drunk to associate the two with me?"

Ava saw them and made a beeline to them and said, "It looks as if you guys are having an argument."

Courtney looked at Monica and then at Ava and said, "My friend asked me if I was going to invite my husband's ex-lover over for a cocktail."

Ava lowered her head and with a look of consternation asked, "What was your response?"

"I jumped her bones and didn't finish the conversation."

Monica yelled, "I tried to start some shit because my husband has a child and I couldn't give him that gift." Monica began to cry uncontrollably. Ava and Courtney hugged her, and Ava said, "Monica, that's no reason to attempt to hurt Courtney, whom you have known forever. It is also cruel that you would involve me. I knew Ben before any of this. The one thing we must be, is civil towards each other. There is a lot going on, women becoming pregnant, one about to have her child, mixed relationships from yesteryear, a one for all and all for one requirement for safety, and a son-of-a-bitch that wants us all dead. Monica, petty shit ain't going to work here or now."

Courtney looked at Ava with tears in her eyes. Ava walked over to her, hugged, and kissed her. She said, "It's those Bloody Mary's'. You know tomorrow she's going to feel like shit, and we'll have to support and forgive her 100 times. You are considered by me, as a true friend. Monica is a true friend. We sometimes do stupid and that is what friends are for—forgiveness. Let it go and damn, can I order a drink in this place?"

"I'm sorry and I didn't mean to piss people off. It sounded like the right thing to say at the time, but as I look back on our experiences, it was terrible, and I need to ask you guys to forgive my insensitivity. I just spoke out without thinking, a thing that will never happen again. I'm going to go to my room and read," Monica announced.

Ava said, "If you do that then it will prove that you wanted to start some shit between Courtney and me. Is that what you want to do Monica?"

"Oh, my goodness! Can you guys forgive me? Can we order drinks and forget about my stupidity?"

# # #

Allen called the Sarge back and said, "Mike and I are in danger. We left those phones that we used in an obvious place and within ten minutes, an entire army swooped down on them. We need to be extracted; can you help?"

"Give me ten minutes and let me see what I can do."

The Sarge in the meantime, gave Allen a number and said, "Call me back on this number, I have a scrambler on it."

The Sarge looked for Jong, but instead saw Mallory and asked him where was Jong? Mallory said, "He's in the water with his lady who is built like a brick shit house. Have you seen the body on that lady?"

"Mallory, you know I don't go around looking at my guy's girls. However, I happened to notice her from the window and damn, he hit the Powerball and Mega Millions at the same time. That body was designed by Fischer and sculptured by Leonardo. And she loves herself some Jong.

Damn, I might have to at least consider leaving my wife. I'm just kidding. I'm happy for him and the rest of the guys. I must admit, they have some trophies on their arms. All of the newly acquired ladies are drop-dead-gorgeous."

"I know exactly how you feel, but I would never leave my Monica for another," Mallory confessed.

"Hell, are you crazy? Courtney and she are the role models for all those others. They are the queen bees."

"I got off track. I need to have a conversation with you and Jong, asap."

Fifteen minutes later, a slightly inebriated Jong showed up and said, "I was working on my tan."

The Sarge said, "I have a problem and I need your input. Are you sober enough to do business, or shall I have someone else do your bidding?"

Jong looked at him and said, "No one can do my bidding because I am Mr. Amazing. What exactly is it that you want?"

"Mike and Allen are in trouble and people are trying to capture them. They can't come here because they don't have basic papers such as a driver's license or any real identification. If they can get to one of our planes in Maryland, they can fly to mid-America and get papers from our friends, and after that fly here."

"Okay, that's the extent of your request? Let me make a call or two and I will have this issue resolved in the next twenty minutes. Damn, I thought you wanted to talk to my girlfriend," Jong announced. The Sarge and Mallory displayed a devious smile.

#

The Sarge decided to call Clyde and make him aware of the incoming individuals and request that he secure the two men.

After talking with Clyde, he called Allen and said, "Get to Reagan National and you know the password. Go now and while you're in the air, we'll try to figure out what's best for everyone."

Allen hesitated, but did not ask the obvious question that was burning in his mind. He knew that the Sarge's people had a plane in Maryland and not Virginia. He asked the Sarge, "Is that where we can expect a ride?"

The Sarge replied, "Of course, you know where we hang out so why do you ask?"

Allen knew the Sarge had given him the necessary signal and told Mike that they needed to make their way to a private airport in Maryland. Mike looked at him and said, "The Sarge said Reagan. Last I checked, it was still in Virginia."

"Mike, do you trust me? Okay don't answer that question. I want you to cover your eyes and blindly follow me. Remember, you are as wanted by Diablo as I am. Trust me, and we can buy some time."

"It's not about trust, Allen. What I heard is different than where I would expect to go. Was Reagan a ruse? Listen, we're good and have little or no options. You talked to him so, therefore, I believe and trust him and, therefore, Allen, I blindly trust you. We both have been in the gutter too long and need to smell fresh air and watch civilization move on. I suggest we make a series of trips, by Uber, cabs, stolen vehicles, and finally Lyft. Whatever it takes, I just want out of here for a moment. I want to smell the roses and sleep in a clean bed, if only for a night."

Allen said to Mike, "Think about it. Why would they keep a plane in Virginia? That is too close to where Asiram's farm is. I know where they keep their planes and it ain't in Virginia. Do you have any cash on you?"

"I have a hundred-dollar bill in each shoe and that's it. How about you?"

"I have four bills, $100 each, two in each shoe. That should get us to the airport."

"If we successfully make the plane, we still don't have papers."

"I know that and I'm trusting in the Sarge to realize the same. He has become such a spy and is excellent at misdirection. Which brings me back to another issue, how the hell is Walter tracking us? At some point in time, you and I are going to have to submit to a strip search and magnetization. We just purchased those phones three days ago. Did you happen to call anyone?"

"The only person I called was Jacknovichic. He has left the clutches of the KGB and has made his way to Jerusalem."

"Why Jerusalem?"

"We both have a female friend who loves us but won't commit to either of us. She is helping him to travel to Turkey and then to Egypt where we have some common friends that will either betray him or get him safely to Cuba of all places. These routes have been prearranged with assistance along the way. Not a perfect plan but has worked for ages."

"Exactly what was your role under Walter?"

"I had two primary missions. One was to kill you. The other was to kill the senator."

"Okay, stop the 'BS'. What were your responsibility centers under Walter?"

"Apparently, you don't hear well. My first mission was to kill you and your entire family. My second mission was to assassinate the senator who is interested in the Carbon Factor."

"You had orders to kill me?"

"Allen, you sent your people to kill me twice in the tunnels."

"That's different. I didn't know if I could trust you and I was getting tired of looking over my shoulders. I called the hit off after you successfully killed my people by driving them to one of those tree companies and shredding them."

"I didn't want to make it so graphic, but they came to kill me, and I wanted to send a message to their handler, you. I knew it was you but realized that you and I had the same curse placed upon us."

"You shredded those guys like limbs off a tree."

"Yeah, and you've done worse. So, don't try to evaluate how sinister I am without looking in the mirror."

"Mike, we had a rude and obnoxious boss. Now, that same person is trying to kill us, so get on board, open your arms, and embrace me as I have embraced you. You are my family! My wife and kids act like I am dead until they need money. Screw them too. My only family is you and I hope that this is a reciprocal relationship."

"How do you know about their planes?" Mike inquired.

"He offered me an out long ago. He didn't know that you were on the hunted list at the time. I thought I would serve you up and disappear but decided against that selfish move," Allen responded.

"It's a good thing you decided on that path because I stood beside the Sarge and deleted a significant amount, of mercs," Mike amplified.

"Mike, are you obtuse or something? I was going to serve you up to Walter. Not Beckmire."

"Whatever. Just remember that I always have a third eye on your ass," Mike acknowledged.

When the two coconspirators arrived at the airport in Maryland, they were met by one of the pilots and escorted into the hangar where they were relieved of their side-arms and scanned. The pilot looked at Allen and said, "Sir, I'm going to need you to go in that room over there and relieve yourself of all of your clothes. Our scanner is showing that you have a cicada in you."

Allen inquired, "What the hell is a cicada?"

"It's a bug sir. A thing that emits a signal, a transmitter."

A surprised Allen walked into the room and disrobed. When he walked out of the little room he said, "This is so humiliating."

Mike looked at his private parts and said, "You don't need to mention that. We can see for ourselves."

As the pilot scanned him again, the alarm's noise level increased. As his body was scanned, it was apparent a transmitting device had been installed in his body in his shoulder area. After hearing the alarm, he said, "I'll be damned. I've been scratching that area for months. That son-of-a-bitch had his eyes on me all of the time." He looked at the pilot and asked, "So, what's next?"

The pilot answered, "This may sting, but hopefully, it will kill the signal." He then retrieved another device and placed it on the spot where the transmitter was installed.

"How on earth could they have put that in me without my knowing it?"

"Sir, there are hundreds of ways to install small devices in the body. It may have been strategically placed in your favorite shirt or jacket. It's dead now, but you might want to have it removed once we reach our destination."

Mike asked, "Where might that be?"

"Once we're airborne I will call Mr. Beckmire and you can have a long conversation with him about what he is doing and why. We are just your temporary transportation. We don't know the specifics of this matter."

## CHAPTER TWENTY-FIVE

When the man from the golden tower was elected President of the United States of America, a series of anomalies began to occur. It appeared that everyone he selected to head a cabinet post for a particular agency was the exact opposite of what and who one would expect in that office. Such is the case for his selection of Secretary for the Environmental Protection Agency (EPA). As a result of the off the cuff promises when campaigning for office, the President made assurances to miners who extracted carbon from the earth. China and Russia were securing coal, from wherever possible, and stockpiling it knowing that there was truth to the Carbon Factor.

Mother Russia continued to experiment with variations of the formula, but at each turn, the results were more destruction and loss of life. China on the other hand, explored the information it had on a virtual and theoretical framework, thereby experiencing no loss of life or destruction. It knew of the numerous attempts by the Russians to jump ahead of the pack without a precise formula and decided they would continue to develop virtual models as opposed to using actual experiments to test the theory.

The Americans followed the path of the Chinese and attempted to solve the problem by testing theoretical hypothesis. It was clear that the Carbon Factor was a very volatile composition and one not to guess about. Although several combinations of the process seemed containable, it was the variations in temperature, mixture, and containment time that created the uncontrollable environment. They didn't have the actual formula.

The new administration's primary goal was to bring jobs back to America, even though the newly elected family had manufacturing ties all around the globe, especially in China. The new president, although thought brilliant in some aspects of business, had no idea about the power and the effect of the Carbon Factor. As a part of his nepotistic administration, he assigned oversight to one of his sons. A fact that a great country would never forget or forgive. As he continued to dismiss daily intelligence briefings, America's arch enemies gained in knowledge and directed resources to understanding the by-products of carbon and how to contain them and, nuclearize them into horrific weapons. Yes, the American President kept his nose up his own anus as the major powers in the world, collected, tested, and attempted to create the world's most deadly dirty bomb. The Carbon Factor could be hidden in milk cartons with the capability of decimating small cities.

## Chapter Twenty-Six

The group enjoyed a spectacular dinner loaded with fancy champagne and other expensive delicacies. Mr. Christopher Carter interrupted the group to make an announcement.

He said, "I have to interrupt your festivities for just a moment, a moment that is particularly important to me and the staff here at the resort. When I first met you people, I thought you were a bunch of spoiled brats with too much money and time on your hands. Then, I met Mr. Mallory and his wife, Ms. Monica and briefly Mr. Jong. I was in a whole lot of trouble and didn't have a place to turn. God sent you people to me. He told me that you people were not angels, but you were good for mankind. I still can't explain my dreams, but I know I initially thought I was getting in bed with a bunch of carpetbaggers who did drugs.

"I called Mallory's bluff. He, his wife, Mr. Jong, and I, went to the bank that focused on stealing from people. Your group asked for my note and paid it off.

"I have been waiting for some incredible and undoable demand to be thrown at me. We made a deal, the place was gutted and reconstructed, I have a lifetime job and a new car. I can't keep people from booking the place for weeks and months at a time. We're booked and paid through 2025, every week of the year. In season and out of season the rates are the same. I pulled out my calculator and did some basic math and it looks as though me and my staff are going to earn a shit load of money. We've decided to take our funds and purchase a failing small hotel near the airport that has a wonderful beach and employ more of our people. I say all of this to say, I love you people. You have given this island new life by destroying the practices of those who would exploit simple minded people. We have developed a commerce/trade office to assist the island in attracting more businesses. We have corralled the crime issue, and never again will a pregnant woman be dragged on our beaches. This island thanks you, and I thank you and honor you as my partners."

There was a quiet in the room as well as tear filled eyes. Courtney elbowed the Sarge and he rose from his seat. He walked over to Mr. Carter and said, "When we first came here, we knew you were under a lot of stress. I asked two of my people to explore a relationship with you and they came back with what I considered a fair deal. By the way, do you think this deal is fair considering the alternatives? Okay, don't answer that now. You, me, and a few others will have a moment to talk. Listen, Mr. Carter, we try not to do bad deals. We knew the bank was about to take your property. We also knew that we could gut this place, rebuild it, let you manage it and control the operation. I looked at you and knew that you were an honest man. I trust everyone until they screw me and then I ask some of my friends to intervene on my behalf. Listen, I'm not going to spend our time here talking about trust. We trust you. If you need our help on other issues, then, talk to those you feel comfortable with. We love this place and hope you realize that when we want to come here, you might have to clear house. As a matter of fact, if we dislodge people from here, then I would like you to ascertain when they can come again for free—air, transport, room, food and booze!"

"Wow, Mr. Beckmire. Let me think about that and get back to you. In conclusion, I just want to say that in all the years I have been on this earth, I have never met a more honorable group of people than you guys and ladies. I mean, I think you people are angels performing charitable assistance for people who do business with bad people."

"Let's make a toast to our dear friend, Mr. Christopher Carter. May he continue to enrich our pockets with our fair share of the business. Mallory if you and Monica would entertain a conversation about the other place that he and his staff want to invest in, perhaps there is room for a few of our dollars as well. And, Mr. Carter, if there are other deals or people who are about to forfeit their life's work that we might be able to get involved with, then we would appreciate your looking out for future investments on our behalf."

#

In another place on earth, Mike and Allen were aboard one of the group's planes without a clear destination. After an hour in the air, the pilot called Jong, told him they were safely airborne, and the people were anxious to know where they were heading. Jong told him to hold on and he would find the Sarge.

The Sarge picked up the phone and asked, "Allen, how are you doing? Is Mike with you?"

Allen replied, "We're both here and are wondering where you are hijacking us to?"

"That is not an air friendly term to use; 'hijacking,' that is. Allen, put me on speaker. Anyway, you guys are going to middle America where a friend of mine will meet you at the airport, take you to our home there, and tomorrow to the local post office where you will obtain a passport and other different IDs. Actually, there will be two passports and two automotive operators' license, and I will instruct you on which ones to use when we extract you from places, until we terminate our common cancer. Do you have questions or problems with what we are about to do?"

"Sarge, we walk into a post office and we are dead meat. There are probably wanted posters for both of us," Allen announced.

"Trust me on this one. We have this under control and the guy who is going to issue the papers is a friend of ours as well as of the United States of America."

"Oh, I see. One of your weird friends, eh?"

"Allen, is this too overwhelming for you? You sound stressed."

"Beckmire, I don't like planes, and I usually have a panic attack when I'm on one, but I can't let this dude with me, see that."

"Okay guys. Listen, the bathroom is a combination head and shower. Clean up and the copilot has some approximate sized items for you to dress in. Sorry, it's not Armani or some other fancy designer. Get some rest, food, and drink which are also available at the ranch. Do me a favor, when you get there, don't go wandering around the ranch at night. The front and back porches of the guest house should be the limits of your exploration. Beyond those boundaries are some very unpredictable animals, as well as neighbors, who don't know you're there. Stay put, go to the post office in the morning, and from there straight to the airport with my man Clyde. The pilots will bring you to me. Allen, a specialist will meet you in the morning to remove the device from your shoulder and to check if there are any others. I want to meet with you guys in person so that we can plan our final assault on the devil. See you soon."

When the Sarge walked back into the room, Jong asked, "Is everything okay?"

"Yes. I believe so. I want to develop a world-wide plan to capture my cousin. I want to create false sightings with false rewards. I'm going to need your cousin working very closely with me. Is that a problem?"

"Sarge, it is never a problem between him and me. It is those foreigners who attempt to understand us and read between the lines and make judgements that create problems. We no have problem—it's called our culture."

"Jong, please forgive me if I overstepped my boundaries."

"Sarge, you no over-step anything. It's all good. It's like I never really understood all of the gibberish between John Lee and Jilkes, but everyone else knew they were shucking and jiving."

"Shucking and jiving, eh? Okay little brother. Keep me abreast of our two new friends."

The Sarge saw Courtney from afar in conversation with Monica and Ava and thought to himself, 'I need alone time with my woman'. He strolled up to the ladies, excused himself, and asked, "Courtney, might I have a word with you in private?"

Courtney acting surprised answered, "Absolutely! Is there something wrong?"

The Sarge positioned himself near her ear and whispered, "I want to make love to the only woman on earth I desire. I need you and I want you, so desperately. Can you break away from your friends and consider entertaining my wicked wishes?"

Courtney expressed sorrow to her associates for leaving their meeting and indicated that there was a matter that she needed to attend to.

As the Sarge and Courtney started walking away, she threw her right arm back and gave the peace sign. Ava said, "I'm going to kill Carlos if he doesn't attack me."

"Oh my God! Where is that husband of mine? Girl, I'm going to get my jones on. Catch you later," Monica acknowledged.

Monica walked up the stairs and from the end of the hall she saw two familiar faces, her husband and Mary Alice, who was scantily clad. As she got closer to her room, she saw a huge smile on her husband's face. Mary Alice was acting somewhat seductively, Monica perceived. As Monica's blood pressure and jealous antennae began to rise, Mallory turned around and saw Monica coming down the hallway. He gave no indication of alarm and kept laughing with Mary Alice. When Monica arrived, Mallory said, "Look at this moron." Monica looked in the room and found Jong dancing with earphones on to a Michael Jackson song. He was trying to imitate the King of Pop. It was beyond hilarious, but there was no denying it—Mallory was enthralled with Mary Alice's body and so was everyone else on the island. She had an amazingly sculptured form that would cause any woman to suspect that their man had cheating ideas on his mind. However, Mallory was a one-woman kind of dude. His eyes were fixated on Monica and there would be no other woman on earth who could seduce him.

After inspecting the hysterically, sterile environment, Mallory grabbed his wife and kissed her tenderly. He said, "Mary Alice, please excuse me. I must attend to my bride. She needs me to inject her with insulin."

"Oh, I'm sorry, I didn't know you had a sugar problem."

Monica said, "I'm lucky. I can get by with an injection once a month, sometimes I need it every week, and there are times more than one injection during a week. My husband attends to me and makes sure I get as many injections as needed. We will catch you later."

When they entered their room, Monica said, "I saw the way you were looking at that woman."

"Honey, I saw the way you looked at me. She has a fantastic body and she is my brother's lady. Don't go there and don't consider it. If you have doubts about my commitment, then we should discuss it. But don't go into the realm of bullshit. I love you more than life."

Monica looked at him and saw a person that was gentle and loving. She said, "I'm getting older and the women are getting younger and more beautiful. I love my man and I am a jealous woman. I love my man and I make no bones about it."

"Your man loves you as well. He also is not enticed by structure. He is enthralled with substance. No need for you, my love, to worry about me. I'm yours whether you want me or not." They began to kiss, and Monica broke out into laughter. She whispered, "I wonder if that child really believes that I have a sugar problem?"

"I bet you she does. Hopefully, Jong will explain to her what we old folks mean by insulin injection."

## CHAPTER TWENTY-SEVEN

The senator made a call from her private number to Beckmire. He was walking along the beach when the call came in but was afraid it would give away his location. He decided to walk back inside of the resort. He redialed the number and said, "Hi this is Ben Beckmire."

The senator said, "Good afternoon, Mr. Beckmire. Hope I haven't caught you at a bad moment."

"No, ma'am. How are you?" The two went on to express pleasantries. The senator asked him, "Have you seen today's New York Times?"

"I have not."

"Well, then let me give you a heads-up. Five Russian operatives were apprehended entering JFK Airport today with suitcases having false bottoms and carrying small firearms. I know you're wondering what this has to do with you, and so I'll tell you. Those men were sent here to capture the 'idiot spy'. They are of the belief that he has some additional information about the Carbon Factor and they surely need it. Now, in addition, our government is following seven other Russians who entered the country at various times during the week. We know they are on to you and I am offering you my help."

"Senator, unless I've been dreaming, your help has come in the form of people shooting guns at us, and an uncontrollable psychopath who is trying to kill us. This psychopath appears to have control over you. So, your kind of help is very suspicious, to say the least. The only way for this thing to work between you and me is that you give me intel on Walter, and once we have completely disposed of him, we will get you the final part of the formula. What you have is a placebo. Your brightest minds may eventually find the connections, but the costs could be significant."

"I have a better offer. You and your people come in from the cold, and I will offer you protection. You give us the formula and we will place Walter on the FBI's most Wanted List."

"Are you serious? They couldn't find a crackhead in their own basement. Look how they fouled up your election. Now, that is some real dumb mess you just said. Senator give me Walter or give us death in which you will never in a million years figure out the complex formula. No more tricks, or you will be our treat. Goodbye."

Courtney looked at her man and said, "That didn't go too well, did it?"

"As well as can be expected from a career politician. She can't control Walter and he has pictures of her doing some dastardly things."

"How do you know that?"

"Jong and I copied some materials that we retrieved from the ex-senators place. As we scanned the thumb-drive, we saw a familiar face during some sick sexual activities, if there is such a thing."

"Honey, are we going to live through this mess?"

The Sarge could see his woman's eyes swell up with tears and he moved to assure her that he would find a way out of this quagmire. He said, "I'm no miracle worker, but honey, I think we are closing in on my cousin. He realizes that he can't live in the 'W's' of the world anymore and that he must accept

Motel Five, or Six, as places of residency. He's too prissy to live like that for long. So, we're beginning to look in every sewer possible and have money spread out for rewards on his ass. Stay with me, baby. I need your strength to succeed. Without your faith, love, and strength, I do not think I could have made it this far. I need you and I love you so very much."

"I know, Ben. I'm crying because I would like to have another child, but I realize that I'm too old. I so very much wish I had met you earlier. We would have had a house full of children. My tears are about an old woman who wishes she had more time to live, love, and be happy. You, Ben Beckmire, fulfill my three 'H's—Healthy, Happy and Horny. It's that last one that I need you to attend to immediately."

# # #

Asiram so desperately wanted to go into the water, but Zanthius forbade her to do so. He talked about the risk of sand and other parasites entering their child's shrine. Suffice it to say, she was able to place her feet in the water and that was it. Zanthius said, "I think I would like a lot of children running around. What say you?"

"I say, I think I would like to take the son-of-a-bitch that wrecked my body and beat the living shit out of him. This ain't going so well, Romeo, so let it go. More children! Are you out of your 'd a m n mind'? I haven't had this one yet and this one has been a pain in my ass. Change the subject, Romeo, before we have a war here on the beach."

"Honey, you aren't happy being pregnant?"

"Zanthius, I am thrilled, but it is an all encumbering experience. Do you remember what I looked like when we met? Okay, ignore that one. Try this one. Am I still attractive to you, and do you still love me with all of this weight that I've grown into?"

Zanthius held her hand gently, walked around in front of her and got on his knees. He said, "Asiram, will you marry me again? I love you so much and you are so important to me. I know I'm new at this, but I assure you, I will become the best husband and father in the world. Insofar as your appearance goes, we can work on that."

"I knew you were going to screw it up. If you promise to work with me, I will forgive the last comment."

"You have my word. I will patiently work with you on your goals and objectives and I promise not to interject my own."

# # #

In middle America, Allen and Mike enjoyed the steam room, jacuzzi, sauna, and multi-jet showers. Mike said to Allen, "I haven't been this happy in a long time. A bath, a shower, steam, and sauna. Damn, that Beckmire knows how to live."

Allen acknowledged, "I once tried to kill that fucking guy and now, I'm enjoying his booze and hospitality. You know sometimes when you have that bad feeling about something, you need to follow your instincts. Well, I read about some of the things they did over in the Nam, and said to myself, 'are these people machines or extraterrestrials'? I mean their missions were one-way and they kept coming back, the 10 plus 2. I had convinced myself to leave these people alone, but the restaurant attack was completely screwed up by that old lady who happen to have a gun and thought that they were shooting at her. From that point on, this guy's machine grew and now it's awesome. I don't want to be on their bad side. That John Lee gutted Scottie from her bush to her brain and ate a part of her heart. No, I can't screw with these guys, they never seem to die. I have come to like, respect, and be obligated to these people. They have taken care of me, and mine, and provided for you as well. How can they just forget that my primary mission was to completely obliterate their existence?"

"I don't think they will ever forget that about you. You've heard the old expression, 'keep your enemies close', I think that's what they're doing with you rather than flat out cutting your head off! I'm just kidding. They are a great bunch of people, loyal to the core. You screw with one and you just bought yourself a package deal of badass people. They had no intention of getting involved in this until someone took a shot at Beckmire's son's mother, his wife and then the beast came out of his shell and has yet to return. I've worked with them. They have their shit together and they are a precise killing machine. I wouldn't want to create a problem between them and us and I, damn sure, hope you're not playing with a double-edge blade," Mike stated.

"Trust me, Mike, I'm an enemy who has been converted to a friend. I don't plan on having these people castrate and do other vile things to me. Nope, I'm on their team come hell or high water. As a matter of fact, I will die for their cause alongside them, if need be. My family abandoned me, those people took me in and provided for me and my children. I thought I was king only to find out my wife had been banging her guy, for years. He literally stole all my money and left her dumb ass broke. Anyway, I'm hungry. How about you?"

"Dude, you don't smell food cooking?"

"I don't have a sense of smell. Lost it in a hockey game."

#

Later as the men descended the steps, the smell of food was enormous. Mike turned a corner and looked at the table and asked, "Clyde, are you expecting more people?"

"No, not really. That's for you and the other fellow. Mr. Beckmire told me that you people had been living in dirty desolate places and that a bountiful meal would be perfect. Enjoy yourself, a couple of our neighbors will be patrolling the area. Try not to wander. This here land is unforgiving. If you care for a drink or two, the booze is kept in that cabinet over there. Remember, there is plenty of food, but don't overdo yourselves. You have my number if you need anything, and I will be here at 0900 hours to pick you up. Is that okay? By the way, if you feel naked, there are clean weapons under your pillows."

"Clyde, could you make it 1000 hours? I don't remember the last time I have had a full night's sleep and, in a bed," Allen recounted.

"I would prefer 0100 hours if that doesn't create a problem," Mike interjected.

Clyde looked at them both and said, "Sleep until you want to get up. I will have breakfast ready for you at 1100 hours and we can depart for the paperwork at 1230 hours. Is that a better scenario?"

Both men agreed and bid him a goodnight. Mike said to Allen, "That was a crazy ass plane we were on. It was loaded."

"I know. I hear they have a new jet they all can fit in and it can do transcontinental travel. Can't wait to see that one."

"Where the hell, did they get that kind of money? I hear they came into this game with a bankroll," Mike said.

"From morons like me who agreed to pay mercs on the spot after a successful encounter. The only thing is that the mercs couldn't best these guys on their worst days. Those guys are a well-oiled machine that you want to really think twice before coming up against them. That guy gutted Scottie from her snatch to her brain. Damn, that had to have been ugly," Allen responded.

Prior to their sitting down to eat, Beckmire called Allen and said, "My man told me that you guys are all settled in and are about to chow down. Is there anything you need from me?"

Allen said, "I, frankly, need to put some cash in two accounts for my children. Mike, do you need any cash, this is Beckmire on the phone?"

"I could use some spending cash to buy some clothes with tomorrow. Is that possible?"

"Allen, if I get you cash, would you like to handle the matter, or do you want us to do it? And how much are we talking about?"

"I need approximately $75k to place in my kids' accounts for school. If I had access to some cash, I could do it while I'm in town."

"In the morning, ask Clyde to call me and I can have him access the cash for you. Ask Mike how much does he need."

Mike responded that he only needed a couple of thousand and that he wasn't as greedy, or as needy, as Allen. Beckmire bid both men a good night and hung up the phone. Allen turned to Mike and asked, "Do you believe this guy? He's one of a kind and I doubt if I will ever meet another human being who is so concerned about others. He's like a saint."

"Now, this is Asiram's place, right?" Mike asked.

"I think so. This appears to be a guest house. Look at all the bedrooms and showers that are in this place. I guess the palatial spot down the hill is the main house. Which leads me to believe they had money prior to this adventure. I mean this guest house is new, but this ranch is not. It appears that there has been a lot of construction on this ranch, but at night it's hard to tell. You know what, I could give a shit. I'm thankful that the man didn't cut my balls off and found some utility for me. I am extremely thankful to Mr. Beckmire and will always have his back. I have seen what they do to people they don't like, and I'll be damn if I'm going to give them any reason to handle me in that fashion. You also fell out of sorts with our employer, Walter, and, therefore, he wants your balls hanging from the rafters as well. I have betrayed that son-of-a-bitch and he wants me as bad as he wants his cousin."

# # #

"This is the best meal I've ever had. I mean, I usually complain about food, but I'll be damned if I'm going to say anything about food that is so pure and tasty."

"Mike, how can food be pure?"

"When it is made by hands that have not been soiled."

Later, the two men watched as the moon and earth seemed to meet, and they drank Grand Marnier. Allen said, "That was a wonderful meal. This peace and serenity is so helpful to me. My mind has been in a state of flux because my environment has been full of people with both mental and physical issues, as well as individuals who have fought for this country, and are now living in alleys and sewers. That is some sick shit. We have enough to make a little difference and, when we see the Sarge, I would like to speak to him about us putting a program in place to help our veterans."

"I'm with you on that, Allen. Those guys fought in deserts and now they're living in sewers. Our country is in crisis and is out of balance. We just need to define the problem, ascertain specific issues, and put a long-term action plan in place. I mean you and I both have lived the high life. We can ascribe to helping our vets by demanding more and doing more public relations. The only problem with that is, we become targets. We've got to get Walter first and then think about this. Nothing can happen until we kill that bastard."

In the morning at 1100 hours, Clyde opened the door and yelled, "Come and get it."

The two men, both out of focus, came out of their rooms and Mike asked, "What happened to 0100 hours?"

"We're ranchers. At that hour, we're taking naps. Listen, I must get you to town, get you prepped, and get you legal identifications. Things must happen when we can make them happen. Here's the deal. You can eat hot food now or shower and have cold food later. Your decision but in 2.5 hours, a plane will be taking off from the airport, with or without you people."

The Sarge and Courtney completed a round-robin. For people in their age bracket, that thing called lovemaking was tumultuous and satisfying. After the initial flight to fantasy, the Sarge considered going to sleep. Courtney's insistence on a marathon session with her husband, created an 'I can do this mentality for the Sarge'. His equipment was polished well and his stamina was stimulated by the fact that the woman he was with was his one and only true love. He lifted Courtney off the floor and gently walked her to the wall and once again began to treat her need for passion as though it was a function of his existence. They kissed and sighed. He held her tightly and screamed that he loved her. Courtney passionately yelled, "Oh my goodness. I've been waiting for you to unleash the beast in you for a long time."

"Honey, this is my rendering of Picasso and my notions of da Vinci." Courtney and Ben Beckmire, together, smiled simultaneously as if they were John Glen blasting off into the heavens. The two banged together and hard against the wall until John Lee with Jilkes in tow, kicked in the door to the Sarge's room and saw the two lovers in their birthday suits. Jilkes said, "Sarge, we heard a commotion and, and, anyway, we thought our brother was in trouble. Damn, man, we're sorry." The two men backed out of the room with their heads bowed in humiliation.

Courtney said, "Oh my, I guess I have to now worry about those two being aware of my bounty!"

# # #

Later in the cocktail lounge, Jilkes said to John Lee, "You know he's going to kill us!"

"I was thinking we should take the plane and go back to the farmhouse and hide out. He, for sure, is going to want to have a talk with us. We done made a mistake. However, better safe than sorry, is the old saying," John Lee stated.

"I mean he was on task. Funny how you think that certain people don't do that kind of stuff. Our man was on task and was in complete control. Damn that was crazy and boy, she has some great looking equipment if I must say," Jilkes confessed.

"That be done what startled me, first. The sight of her in a different light will be worth the ass kicking we gonna get. I don't mean that in a disrespectful way, I just be saying that she be one good looking lady," John Lee declared.

As the group slowly began to swell in numbers, Courtney entered the lounge without the Sarge. She saw John Lee and Jilkes and looked away. John Lee nudged Jilkes and the two men sunk in their chairs. Courtney ordered a drink with an umbrella in it and walked over to the table where John Lee, Jilkes, Somara, and Yeshida were sitting. She said, "I need to have a quick word with you two gentlemen."

As they walked towards the door that leads to the beach, Courtney turned and said, "If I ever hear about your intrusion, I will find a way to poison you both. No, me jodas!"

The Sarge entered the lounge and saw Courtney with John Lee and Jilkes in tow. The men looked as if they had their butts kicked. Courtney walked over to the Sarge and planted a huge kiss on his lips, turned and looked at Jilkes and John Lee with one hand on her hip. The Sarge asked, "What did you say to my guys?"

"I told them if I ever hear about their intrusion, I will find a way to poison them."

"No, you didn't. Come on now, what did you really say to them?"

"Honey, I told you what I said. At some point, you should ask them and I'm sure they're going to confirm it."

"Honey, it was an honest mistake. Those are two of my best and they thought someone was getting the best of me. I'm glad they had the audacity to kick in our door and make sure that we were okay. Remember those fools that tried to kidnap Asiram?"

"Ben, I wasn't hard on them. I told them that if I hear about it then I would poison them. I didn't threaten them. I simply told them they would be poisoned."

The Sarge turned around and saw that Bernstein and Yvette were having a heated discussion. He slowly walked to the door and asked, "People, do we have a problem here?"

Bernstein said, "She is as stubborn as you are. I love her as much as I love you, but she wants to prematurely make an announcement about her being pregnant without scientific confirmation."

The Sarge said, "Sounds like the president." He then looked at his niece and inquired, "Did he select you as his mate? Did I sanction this gathering?" The Sarge then looked at Bernstein and said, "Did I not tell you not to pursue certain physical activities because she was in need of love and not lust?"

Yvette said, "Uncle, he played in the garden and we got blessed, I think."

"Sarge, that's the problem. She's not sure."

The Sarge looked at his niece and said, "He's your man. Make him feel royal by listening to him and honoring his wishes. A man will love a woman forever when she at least recognizes his worth and backs off assumptions she is not sure about. In this case, I go with him because you're not sure of anything."

Yvette looked at Bernstein and said, "The next time I'm tripping, walk away and come back to me later and ask me if I'm alright. I love you and I'm still dreaming about another life. Honey, please be patient with me. I'm trying to be a great wife and I so want to be a terrific mother to our children."

Bernstein hugged her and she realized he was crying. Yvette asked, "Why are you crying?"

"Come, take a walk with me," Bernstein requested."

The Sarge knew about Bernstein's issues and said to Courtney, "I need you to keep a tangential eye on those two. For some odd reason, Yvette thinks she's pregnant and she is somewhat over the edge. Just between you and me, Bernstein is from a family of men who have an extremely low level of testosterone and lack other ingredients to procreate. Please never mention that."

"Ben, that doesn't mean that he can't make a baby. It typically skips a generation, but I would have to know his family history. If someone goes into town, I would like them to purchase a lot of fertility kits."

"Honey, if she is pregnant, it is by her mate, Bernstein. Get someone to get you some kits. I mean we have so many rabbits in camp and rabbits procreate quickly."

The Sarge looked at Courtney and said, "By the way, that was incredible. The passion that engulfed our love making was something that we should always yearn for. I felt like Superman. I felt so vibrant and needed. It's amazing when you find yourself in a nontraditional environment. This is like when we first started dating. I mean we are always on guard and suspicious of our surroundings, but our passion is strong. We have had moments together before, but we never really abandoned ourselves to each other. We sometimes try to be too proper if you know what I mean. In that hotel and in that room, our past notions of passion came to the forefront and we put a hurting on that room until those two assholes kicked down the door." They both laughed and turned around and looked at Jilkes and John Lee. John Lee said, "Oh shit, they're both looking at us. Ladies, will you excuse us for a few minutes?"

The two men headed for the door and the Sarge bellowed out, "Hey, you guys heading for the door, I need to have a word with you."

Jilkes said to John Lee, "Don't let him get close to us. You remember how he suspended Jong from the floor, don't let him get that close to you."

As the three men headed out of the door, Jong said to Mallory, "Get Bernstein, Brown, McArthur, and Gladstone ready to intercede."

Mallory asked, "What the hell are you talking about?"

"There's going to be a fight. I know that look from the Sarge. He is about to take them guys on and win."

Mallory not knowing the circumstances signaled the designated people, but also told Chakes and Montomie to follow the group. When they were on the beach, the Sarge said, "You, assholes embarrassed my wife and she would like me to address the issue."

Jilkes said, "Sarge, before you go fucking crazy, let me say once again, when we walked by the room the noise level was like there was combat going on. How the hell were we to know that you and your wife were having a nuclear lovemaking session?"

The Sarge laughed and said, "Guys, I felt like I was twenty-two years old. I mean I showed my wife that I am still the man and she acknowledged it at the end. I just want to say, if you hadn't kicked down my door, I was probably going to have a fucking heart attack. She 'P' whipped me into a coma and you guys saved my life."

John Lee looked at him as he rolled up his linen shirt sleeve and said, "Why you be rolling up your shirt sleeve?"

"Because I'm hot. Why do you think?" The Sarge looked at all the people who had joined them in their private conversation and said, "Oh I see, you people thought that I was going to engage you in combat? Are you fucking crazy? You saved my old ass life. Listen, Courtney was embarrassed, but you guys lowered your heads and avoided eye contact. People! I love all of you, and the only person I wanted to kill was Mr. Amazing because he slapped me twice, but apparently for my own good.

"Listen, if you guys want to try me, then I won't resist. I just want to have a drink with my only friends and family. I don't know what's up with all of you being out here, but I just want to have a drink with you guys. That's all. I don't want to wrestle, argue, fight or be a part of the group that throws Jong's ass into the water."

When the group entered the lounge, Monica said to the Sarge, "Years ago, you, Courtney, Larry, Mallory, and I were having dinner, when a negative force and spirit appeared in the Italian Bistro, and we all dealt with it. Mallory and I would like to thank you, Courtney, and Larry for bringing us together and joining us into a family that is forever recruiting, expanding, and attempting to help people help themselves. That night was sad, but it made me realize how much my man, my husband, and my lover, loves me. Thank you, Ben Beckmire, and may God bless and keep us all."

Larry walked over to Sarge and said, "Big guy, we love you and surprisingly, your people are still here supporting you. What's the attraction?"

"I guess they love me as well, Son."

Asiram wallowed over to the Sarge, and said, "There is a lot of love for you in this room Daddy-in-Law, but the jury is still deliberating on a few of your cases."

Zanthius asked, "Darling, must you go there?"

"I'm just trying to bust his balls. He knows I would kill for him and anyone else in this group. I'm just wanting this motherhood stuff to start and this swelling to end and every time I look at my body, buddy, I want to make you my primary target."

"Asiram, I love you so much, it hurts me to think that you would harm me because you wanted to have my child and snag me."

"Let it go, Romeo. Let it go."

The Sarge intervened and said, "I need you people to listen closely to what I'm about to say. I have invited a person to this place who at one time attempted to kill us. I also invited a person who fought alongside us during one of our attacks. The one that tried to kill us is of concern to me and I'm sure he will be of concern to you. We had him in the barn and decided to spare his life for some information. He didn't know and I didn't know that my cousin was going to throw him under the bus and place a contract on him and his family.

"We as a group have been supporting his not so harmonious family for months. This person is a wealth of information and has provided us with critical information about impending attacks. Now, I know you people think I'm clairvoyant, I am not. It was intel from Allen that kept us safe and prepared. I don't expect you people to run up to him and show him love, but I do expect you to treat our guests with civility and kindness. He has saved us from the devil and has placed his own family in harm's way. We spared his life and he has saved ours on many occasions. Please be nice to our guests when they get here. Again, I don't expect you to love him, but I do expect you to respect his ability to find out things that could impact our safety that we don't have the faintest idea of how to uncover. Are there any questions?"

Asiram said, "Daddy-in-Law, the people coming here are they spies. Last I heard, you can't trust a spy."

"Daughter-in-Law, you are a spy and I trust you with my life and the lives of this entire group. Did you change, or do we still need to keep an eye on you?"

"Touché! I am married to your son. Allen is a snake who will do anything to live in luxury."

"Asiram, Allen and Mike have been living in sewers for the past five or six months. We've been giving them enough money to make sure they don't starve and to support Allen's family. Remember, Allen turned us on to a few of my cousin's stash houses and we negotiated a premium for that information."

"I don't want to pursue this much further, but who is the keeper of our money and the records?"

The Sarge looked to his left and said, "Mr. Amazing is our bookkeeper, accountant, controller, CFO, CPA, and auditor. He is it and has always been our man. Now, that we have more civilians, perhaps some of you might want to assist Mr. Amazing."

"Daddy-in-Law, you run a tight ship. Your people showed up from the hinder lands to protect my husband, his mother, my mother-in-law, and everyone else. I trust Jong, but in the real world, we need back-up for every function that has authority. If Mary Alice suddenly caps his ass, how will we know how to access our assets?"

The Sarge looked at Mallory and asked, "Do you have any input into this matter?"

Mallory was about to respond when Jong stood up and announced, "I have been purloining millions from you fools for a long time."

The room got quiet. John Lee quietly asked Jilkes, "What that purloining mean?"

Jilkes replied, "It means he's been stealing from us."

"Oh, that be a serious crime, right?" Jilkes looked at him and shook his head.

Jong looked around at the stunned faces and said, "What Ms. Asiram is saying, is what I've been trying to say to you for months, Sarge. Our assets have grown exponentially, and we have a shit load of cash on hand on any given day. You gave me complete authority to do whatever I think is in the best interest of the group and to handle all money matters. I've been doing this since we left the Nam. I buy and sell airplanes for millions of dollars. I buy this place with Mallory and Monica. We rebuild Virginia and mid-America, no one ever asks me about the money. I pay my cousin, a true conflict of interest, to protect us with technology in Virginia. I need someone to help me manage my crude bookkeeping."

Asiram asked, "Daddy-in-Law, I would like to go off on a tangent. Is that possible?"

"Go for it, but stay on the topic," the Sarge said.

"If I'm not mistaken, we should have a little less than a billion dollars from the captured funds from merc payments, from the government, proceeds from that LA drug deal that we thwarted, and a few other misguided moments. We have no liabilities. We are current on every financial aspect of our existence. My question is simple, where is all of this money?" Asiram inquired.

The Sarge looked at Jong, as Jong said, "No one told me this was an audit meeting. Give me ten minutes and I will attempt to address Ms. Asiram's question." As he turned to walk away, he said, "If you hear a gunshot, then you know you have been swindled." He smiled and walked away.

Brown said, "You know what happened to me and my stepfather? He tried to kill me for money. The one thing I know about every person that was with us in the Nam, is that money ain't ever been our issue. Ms. Asiram, no disrespect intended, but I'll bet you a million dollars that he comes back with a complete record."

Asiram said, "I'll bet you $2 million that he comes back with adequate information. You're missing my point. We have close to a billion dollars and no way to keep an accounting or structure for ensuring a satisfactory return on our investments. I would shoot my unborn baby if I didn't have faith in you people. I watched you people. I watched how you watch out for each other. I minimized the impact that post-Vietnam soldiers could play in the security of the 'idiot spy'. I watched you kick ass, over, and over again. I am a true believer that this only happens as a result of trust, love, and loyalty."

In the background a loud boom could be heard. After taking a defensive stance, the Sarge dropped to his knees and screamed at the top of his lungs, "I would kill you in hell if you just did stupid. We don't care about the money. We care about you."

People began to run towards the stairs. Mary Alice asked, "Did you hear that loud boom? What on earth was that?"

People continued to run towards the stairs. When they reached the floor Jong was staying on, they could see his room at the end of the hall and hear loud music. Mallory was first to reach the entrance to the room. He looked in the room and turned everyone else back. The scene was quite pathetic and without reason. Jong was on the floor in a compromising position, in a syncopated manner, and attempting to breakdance to Michael Jackson's *Thriller*. When people insisted upon gazing into the room, they saw Jong attempting to dance with a headset on and the volume turned up high.

The exploding sound that people heard was from the premature firing of a rocket. The entertainment for the night was fireworks.

Mallory went back into the lounge and looked at the Sarge who had a sad look on his face. The Sarge fell to his knees and said, "Damn, his soul. I'm going to kill his ass when I get to hell once again. I'm devastated."

"Sarge, why are you devastated and why are you going to kill him? He's in his room trying to breakdance to *Thriller*. I shook my head because it is so sad to see a grown man attempt to dance who apparently can't hear the damn beat."

"He's alive?"

"Sarge, that fool is up there trying to dance with the volume up loud and headsets on. What a scary sight!"

"Why did you have that sad look on your face when you walked into the room?"

"Because I saw one of our very own losing his mind. That fool has gone off the reservation and into town on a three-legged horse. I mean you must see it to believe it. I cleared everyone out and they should be here before he comes back."

Ten minutes later, Jong walked into the room and faced a group of smiling people. He said, "I guess I missed joke, or joke is me. Anyway, here are my rough notes of our assets. As of yesterday, we have $125 million in banks in New York. We have $250 million in banks and savings institutions in Washington, D. C. There is $150 million in Treasury notes tied to our non-profit. In middle-America, we have $50 million spread over co-ops and other farm related institutions. We also have $35 million in CDs and bank deposits there as well. We have $40 million spread over the island in various banks, but none in the bank that tried to steal from our local partners.

"In addition, we have $75million in the Bank of China, and $75 million in the Bank of Japan. We have in our stock portfolios with Smith Barney, Merrill Lynch, and Janney Montgomery Scott, approximately $85 million between the three institutions. We have several credit cards that are universal amongst us that have a total $10 million in available funds. We have four stashes of retrieved money that need to be laundered by my cousin. I think it will add another $40 million.

In clean cash, we have $32 million to play with and we have no liabilities. Our planes are paid for and our people are under contract until next June. We have a shit load of money. We purchased Facebook at an average price of $18.00 and we purchased 500,000 shares and made $49,500,000. We own Alibaba, GE, Charter Communications, Time Warner, Apple, Google, Amazon, Netflix, and a boat load of other companies. It's all tied to our corporation which distributes a check to each member of our group." He folded the pieces of paper and placed them in his pocket and ordered a drink. Jong looked at the Sarge and said, "Okay, that was all fiction. We don't have shit. I leveraged the money on bad investments and debts."

The room got quiet again and Jong yelled, "I need help with keeping this shit straight. We have cash everywhere. We have cash at Asiram's farmhouse, a truck load of cash at her ranch, and safety deposit boxes all over the Washington, D.C. area. I need help because I can't keep track of it by myself. We also need some rules. I spend what I want, on what I want, when I want, and who I want to spend it on. No one says a word. I engage my low-life cousin, and I pay him well, and send his kids to Harvard and other over-priced schools. I buy guns, ammo, booze, and food. I need help and I need it now because this group has expanded. We need to include them in our quarterly payouts. Every person that is here and has been here for over a year should be getting a stipend. Oh, I forgot about our personal accounts in those Swiss banks that have approximately $300 million or better."

Mallory yelled, "Enough. This is not a business meeting. This is our vacation."

"It's no vacation when people ask me questions about our assets. I no get the same vacation. Am I equal, or the workhorse with the brains for this group?"

"Whoa, horse. Asiram bet me $2 million that you would have this kind of data. Everyone here is a trusted soul. I must admit, some have earned more stripes than others, but our focus has been survival. In the interim we have come across legitimate ways to increase our assets. You are correct, my brother, this is not a business meeting, but I think we should schedule one and include a hierarchy that would have a President, Vice President, controller, secretary, treasurer, and legal counsel," Brown stated.

"Now, that is what I'm talking about. Don't abuse the little Asian guy, include some others to count beans, pennies, and millions of dollars," Jong admonished.

Asiram inquired, "So, Jong, you keep all of this on a couple pieces of paper?"

"Yes, because lately we've been moving a lot. I have it, as do the Sarge and Mallory, on disk as well, but I doubt if they have ever taken the time to look, understand and develop questions or strategies about our finances."

"I would like to volunteer to assist you in keeping our affairs in order, but I would also ask that Ava, Monica, Courtney, and Larry be a part of that group as well. I would also like to volunteer Rashida, Marisa, Yeshida, Somara, and Okema to assist us. This may seem cumbersome coming from a one-person show, but I think it makes sense. Jong, you make the decisions, we figure out what accounts things get paid from and Rashida and the others confirm and make it happen, thus creating checks and balances. They will also look for new charities to give some of this money to. I mean, come now, do we really need to have over a billion dollars in assets? Everyone needs a function, just like when we have to defend ourselves."

Mr. Carter knocked on the door and said, "I hate to interrupt, but it is dinner time and your meals are ready."

Monica said, "Before we go, just a thought. We all travel on one plane now. Let's have a meeting on the way back and decide the structure. I can provide the substance as well as rules of order. I think when we are here, we need to unwind, destress, make love and drink until we're silly, right, honey?"

Mallory looked at his wife and realized that for the first time in their relationship, she was getting beyond the misery of yesteryear. He smiled at her and said, "My wife is so smart. I love you, baby, and you're absolutely correct. Drink, unwind, make love and you said something else."

Asiram said, "Destress, that's the other one."

Zanthius said, "If I might get a word in. I sat back and listened to everything and everyone. My wife is correct, we all need a function, but more important is the fact that we are all a part of this adventure and we haven't lost a single soul. I personally thank God for my mother reaching out to me when I was on the verge of ending my life. I also thank my other mother and my Dad, who, I must admit, are a force to be reckoned with. This all started with me swallowing a capsule. I was informed that people from the Vietnam era were coming to help, I must admit, I was ready to surrender to the enemy. I've seen you guys in action and I'm glad I'm on this side of the fence. You people are damn good. I thank you for all of us."

The Sarge said, "People, Mr. Carter has told us it is dinner time. You know he doesn't like to serve cold food, so let's get in there and eat him out of house and home."

As the group headed towards the dining room, the Sarge grabbed Mallory and told him to secure Jong. The three men went into the dining room and participated in the blessing of the food. They immediately took leave after the blessing and went back into the lounge. The Sarge said, "I don't ever want you to joke about killing yourself. Even if we are penniless, you are my brother and I will always love you and will never turn my back on you. Don't joke about dying.

"On another note, you handled my daughter-in-law well. I realize she was simply curious, but when you went to your room, we heard a loud boom and we thought you had done the most incomprehensible act possible. Mallory told me you were trying to breakdance to *Thriller* and that no one on earth should have seen that. Our bond is beyond the faces on money. We have been to hell, kicked ass, and came back. Don't do that again."

"I won't do that again if you promise never to suspend me in the air with one hand by the neck."

"That didn't happen. You were hallucinating."

"Whatever, bully. I love you and I love you, Mallory. I would never take my life and I would never steal from my family, and I mean my only real family."

As the group began to eat, Jong's phone rang. It was the pilot who told him the wheels were up, with the two individuals on board. Jong relayed that information to the Sarge who asked him what was the expected arrival time? Jong told the Sarge they would probably lay over in Miami, take on fuel, and fly out first thing in the morning.

# # #

Mr. Carter eased over to the Sarge and said, "I know you guys have done a lot for my people down here, but I would like you to consider three other businesses that are about to be taken over by that bandit bank."

The Sarge jerked his head around and said, "I need you to talk to Monica and Mallory, if they find cause, they will bring it to me."

"Sorry to bother you," Mr. Carter snidely replied.

"The Sarge grabbed his arm forcefully and said, "You don't bother me. The issues on this island don't bother me. Your concern for others is what makes me happy. We are establishing a new structure. Talk to Monica and Mallory and if they don't like what you have to say, then come back to me. Don't get prissy on me. Okay?"

"Sarge, I would never get prissy with you. I just have a situation where people are going to forfeit their businesses to those carpetbaggers."

The Sarge forcefully slid his chair from the table and pointed to Mallory, Monica, Zanthius, and Jong. As the group assembled in the lounge, the Sarge said, "Asiram, I didn't point to you."

"Yeah, but you pointed to your grandchild's daddy, my husband, Courtney's son, Ava's son and I could go on and on."

"Okay, okay, I need you people to schedule an early morning meeting with Mr. Carter. Apparently, that bank is about to try to rip some people off tomorrow. Mr. Amazing, I need you and Monica to head this one. Is that okay?"

"Sarge, I'm on it and before I go to bed tonight, I will meet with Mr. Carter. Do you think I can engage Mary Alice in this one?"

"Hell, yeah. You two seem to do well as a team. Get the facts and share them with Monica and Mallory and they will in turn decide if we should consider this as a part of our expansion. Is that fair, people?"

Back in the dining room the Sarge said, "May I have your attention for a moment? You know sometimes we just overlook the deeds that people do and how they help us. I mean from day one, we have had support from everyone in this room and eventually from a person who tried to kill us. I know, you guys are wondering how can that be? Well, I believe in karma and lately I've been having dreams of my ancestor's homeland."

Zanthius stood up and yelled, "Pops, so have I."

The Sarge looked at him and said, "I know, Son. I once told you there are places and things in life that I don't know about or understand and they draw on my energy. I'm under the impression that something is wrong in the outback and I think it is related to my cousin. I may have to take one of the planes and head there. You can't come because Asiram is due any day now."

"Dad, I've been having dreams for the past few weeks. I told her earlier and she said that the hocus pocus was between you and your dad. I'm ready to go and we can leave her with Courtney and my mother."

"Son, parenthood is an incredible thing that you are embarking on. Plan to be there for the birth of your child. This is God's miracle happening before your very eyes."

"Pops, this thing is hitting me harder and harder each day. It's as though I'm in a maze, or a daze, or something. No clear visions, but multiple layers of disconcerting images that I don't understand."

"I'm going to talk to Mallory and Courtney and let them know that I, or rather we, are being called home for a mission. I suggest you talk to Asiram and attempt to convince her of the importance of this calling. It is strong between us and I didn't want to ask you or question you. It is a burning need that we must attend to."

After everyone was pretty much close to a state of inebriation, the Sarge had a talk with Courtney who essentially told him that she goes where her man goes or he don't go nowhere. Zanthius's conversation with Asiram pretty much followed the same lines. He attempted to reason with her about her current condition, but she insisted that if he goes, then she goes. What was more perplexing to the Sarge and Zanthius was the fact that the entire group stated they were going as well.

## CHAPTER TWENTY-EIGHT

At 0800 hours, a weary and hungover group of people boarded vans for their ride to the airport. The Sarge told Jong he wanted him to be close to him throughout this journey and for him to keep an eye out for and on Zanthius. Jong knew there were things and rituals he didn't understand from his own culture but saw the look of desperation on the Sarge's face and recalled the dreams and other nonscientific phenomena that occupied his brain.

At 0900 hours, a private jet touched its wheels down at the Cyril E. King International Airport in St. Thomas on the US Virgin Islands. The pilots told the backup pilots to prepare the plane for arrival. Allen said, "You two don't look or act like you know what you're doing back here."

"We're learning. She's the captain and I'm her copilot."

"Funny," Mike said as he star gazed at the female pilot from the rear, never having a chance to see her face.

"Sir, I assure you, those are the facts and depending upon our manifest, you might get a chance to have us fly you on another trip," the African American pilot stated.

When the plane pulled into the hangar and Allen and Mike walked down the steps, they saw the Sarge and waved to him. The Sarge along with Zanthius walked over to them and said, "You have a choice to make. We are all here because we have an emergency in Australia that we must attend to. You guys can stay here and enjoy the beach and the hospitality, but we are out of here in the next thirty to fifty minutes. You are welcome to come along."

Mike said, "Hell, I've never been there, I hear it's a wonderful place. I'm in. How about you Allen?"

"Damn, this is so sudden!"

The Sarge said, "Yes, I know; so is death! Listen, Allen, my people hate you because you tried to kill them. We're going to the land of mysticism and where they say the toilets run backwards. Me and my son have an issue there that we must attend to. I think and feel that you may, and can, be of assistance to us. This is not a holy mission, but spirituality does come into play. If you are without a soul, then the demons you will face may be more than your physical body can endure. Be it known that me and my people will be there to guide you."

"Damn, Sarge. What's this hocus pocus? That last paragraph scared the shit out of me. I have a soul, at least I'd like to think I do. I can't stay here alone, I guess I have no choice."

"Okay get your bags and get seat assignments from that little Asian guy over there."

Both men dropped their heads, and Allen said, "We travel lite and don't have time for bags and shit, we just change when we find something clean and keep moving. That's been our lifestyle."

"I'm sorry, guys. I know what you've been through. When we get to Sydney, I'm going to take you guys shopping for at least another pair of boots, thermal jeans, and a couple of body shirts."

When the two men stepped into the plane, Mike said, "Damn, look at this thing. This thing is brand new and it looks like each seat turns into a bed. Nice!"

Allen responded, "I'm still concerned about that hocus pocus the Sarge spoke of."

"Oh, don't pay him no mind. We both know there is no such thing as real magic and demons. Let's plan on getting drunk and sleeping for the entire trip."

The copilot came from out of the cockpit and said, "As a part of our preflight check, I have to ask if anyone is carrying any contraband? I need you people to check yourselves and make sure you have no weapons. Security, where we're heading, is extremely thorough. Hit your call button if you forgot to check your weapons."

There was initially the lone sound of 'bing' and then a plethora of 'bings'. Everyone on the plane was packing except Mike and Allen. Allen said, "Well, I'll be damned. Did you forget to tell them that we came in peace?"

Courtney called ahead and sent the spare crew members to the local hospital to pick up supplies, just in case Asiram started the delivery process during the trip. Everything that could and would be used in a hospital setting was to be made available on the plane. She had the pilots sterilize the back four seats by washing them down with Clorox and then again with alcohol. The four seats were covered with sterile sheets and disposable plastic was on the floor in the rear of the airplane.

Everything was in place she thought until the Captain came on the intercom and said, "Folks, we will be leaving momentarily. One of our pilots is on a mission and should be here within the next five to ten minutes with some materials that may be needed for this flight."

Jong got the look from the Sarge and walked up to the cockpit and said, "What's up? Why are we waiting on one of our pilots?"

"Apparently, there were some last-minute items needed in case Ms. Asiram decides to give birth in the air. This was all sanctioned by Dr. Beckmire. You know we don't work like this."

"I'm just checking. I guess she didn't tell her husband about the preparations. Keep me informed."

As Jong walked back to his seat, he pointed to Courtney. The Sarge asked, "Honey, did you send our people on a mission?"

"I did, Ben Beckmire. If your daughter-in-law decides to have that baby in midair, I wanted to at least have some rudimentary supplies for the delivery."

"That's my girl, always hedging her bets. In the future if you send our pilots away for anything, would you at least clear it with me or Jong? We have a protocol that has been severed. You know the deal with too many bosses."

Courtney looked at him and kissed him on the cheek. She got up and went back to Asiram and stared at her, probed, prodded, felt and evaluated her condition. Ava got up from her seat and said, "Okay, Courtney, what's your assessment. I mean we're still on the ground and we can take one of the other planes and fly her back to the states. It's your call, despite what Asiram thinks or says, she's not running this game. This game is being operated by the mothers-in-law, missy. Now tell me, any pain or concerns?"

"Just the aggravation that my mothers-in-law are causing me. Listen, I love you both and if I thought I was going to have this baby in flight, I wouldn't be on this plane for such a long ride."

Courtney said, "Anyway, we've taken the liberty to reserve the last four seats of the plane as our delivery room, just in case."

"Who is this 'we' you're talking about. Last I heard, you're the only doctor in this group?"

"See there, you think you know everything. Ava, is an apprentice and is studying hard to become a baby doctor."

Asiram looked at Zanthius who looked out of the window and began to sing. He placed his headset on and never stopped laughing.

Mr. Carter drove the pilot to the airport. When he got out of the car, Mr. Carter said, "You make sure that those people on that plane are safe. They are all wonderful human beings. Make sure that damn plane is alright to fly or I'm going to whip your ass in hell, young fellow." The pilot smiled and went to the plane without anyone in customs asking him any questions. The customs officials knew this group was righteous and that they played on both ends of the field— offense and defense.

When he arrived at the plane, he took the products on board and told the captain that he was going to do another visual inspection of the craft before they left the ground. His fellow alternate pilot said, "I'll join you."

The two men looked at the underbelly of the plane and inspected the tires, wheel wells, landing gear and every other aspect of a plane that insures a safe take-off and an even safer landing. Fifteen minutes later, they entered the cabin and told the captain that all looked well. She thanked them and told them to figure out breaks at five-hour intervals. She said, "I'm taking this bird off the ground and I'm landing this bird, so figure the schedule based on the fact that this is approximately a twenty-hour flight. You guys can rotate as copilots on takeoffs and landings if you like. We're going to go the easy route and take on fuel in San Diego. That will be our only stop until we land in Sydney. Prepare the cabin for departure."

# # #

Everyone flying into and out of St. Thomas, knows that the runway is short and there is no room for mistakes. As the captain throttled the jet and it vibrated violently in place, she released the breaks and it roared down the runway. It seemed instantaneous, from the roar to the take-off. It was up, up, and away. Allen said, "Damn, what kind of plane is this? This thing bolted down the runway and before you knew it, the nose was pointed towards the heavens."

The plane decelerated, the captain came on the intercom and gave them their itinerary and indicated that those serving them in the cabin were full-fledged pilots and were not embarrassed by the presentation of tips.

## CHAPTER TWENTY-NINE

In the galley, if you wanted a special meal, all you had to do was select which meal, push the appropriate heating button and push begin. The tray would eventually proceed down a shoot where condiments and desserts would be placed on the tray.

The Sarge went back to where Allen and Mike were sitting and asked, "Did you guys get some food?"

"No one invited us to eat," Allen said.

"Okay, the people who are serving us are pilots. Our food system is mechanized and has three buttons you need to push to complete your order. Now, if you guys are waiting for someone to serve you, then you might go hungry. No one is ever going to like or trust you if you don't mingle. Don't dwell on history. Focus on what lies ahead of us. Talk to them about what you want to do with those vets in the sewers and I assure you, they will be ready to help. Just don't sit back here like the enemy. Mike, you're not, but your buddy, well, he is hated by all, but he has the gift of gab. Entice these guys and gals to help you guys on that project. As a matter of fact, go to 3A & 3B and you will find my wife who is going to kick your ass first, but is interested in what you are trying to accomplish in the sewers."

"Sarge, I have a better idea. Is there a way I can speak over the intercom?" Allen inquired.

"Absolutely. I don't know how they do it, but you can do it from your seat. You put on the headset and hit some buttons and begin to talk. Mike, try to figure it out and let me know when you're ready. Great idea. Kill—sorry, speak to everyone at the same time," the Sarge stated.

After Mike figured out how the intercom system worked, he walked up to the Sarge and said, "I think he's ready to gain friends or be thrown off the plane, not sure which one is going to happen."

Mike showed the Sarge how to work the intercom system and the Sarge announced, "I need to have your attention for a moment. I know you people have seen strangers sitting midplane. The one that just walked back to his seat is Mike. You remember Mike, he fought alongside us on many occasions and was subsequently banished by his employer because he wouldn't follow his instructions to kill us.

"Now, the other guy, well, his name is Allen. Allen sent mercs to the farm to kill us on more than a few occasions. Yes, that other guy on the plane, his primary role was to assassinate us. He worked for my cousin and for the senator. Now, most of you know that we had Allen's ass in the barn back in Virginia and he realized at that point that we were not just a bunch of retired Vietnam vets. I think he learned to respect us then. Not sure, but anyway, that's Allen. He wants to make a few comments. Most of you know that this plane is a custom job with all kinds of special attributes, such as this intercom system. We also have weapons storage bins, a trash shoot that can compact and handle up to 400 pounds at one time and expel it into the air for immediate dissemination over a 40 mile radius. I say that to say this; Allen thought that he was being slick when he entered our plane with a lethal knife in his belt. It's up to you people to decide if we trash compact his ass or let him learn our ways."

"He saw all of you give up your weapons, but I'm going to show him one of the neat features of our plane. Everyone, stand-down." The Sarge got out of his seat and went back to Allen's row and said, "Look at those air nozzles. Those are two minimum caliber rounds armed because you have a weapon on you. Your choice, but if you attempt to move or retrieve the knife, you will be shot."

"Damn, Sarge. I didn't know what we were walking into. I thought a simple knife would at least let me cut straps."

"Chill out, my brother. All's good. I know that you're on our side. My people have not been privy to our conversations to realize that the information you provided me has saved our ass more times than they can imagine. Give them your honest feelings, and let's get over this mess."

Allen fumbled with the introduction and said, "If you believe in the wrong people for the wrong reasons, you can be convinced of anything. Think about that guy, Jim Jones! People can persuade you that other people are your enemy. After hearing it again and again, you begin to believe what you hear. I worked for some bad people. I was once your beloved Zanthius's boss. I have played many roles in this adventure and I am proud of none of them; Zanthius was expendable; I was expendable. Courtney, the Sarge, and Ava, were expendable. The only person who was not expendable was, Walter, the Sarge's cousin. I made a million mistakes but made one correct one. I gave up all that I had and joined a force to be reckoned with.

"I have been in contact with Ben Beckmire for many, many months. I have been living in sewers, not fancy hotels or flying around in amazing planes, but living in sewers with a lot of our real heroes. In those sewers, and Mike can attest to it, there are many of those who fought in our wars overseas.

Mike and I have drawn up a proposal but needs help to fortify our project. We have committed our own resources to the program, but if we are to spread nationally, we will need the support of influential people such as yourselves.

"Listen, we made a few million dollars on locating Walter's cash stashes. Prior to leaving the country, we found out where he has his main stash which is rumored to be worth a little less than a billion dollars. I'm no longer on the other side of the equation. I'm not trying to figure you out, hunt you down, or murder you. If I am to have a master in the future, it would be your leader, and not his cousin. His cousin is merciless, cruel, and endowed with a devious mind. He is sick with power, but surprisingly, has no ambition. He once must have had an open door to the US Treasury because he has stolen a lot of money and no one has asked about it.

"I am a valuable resource and Mr. Beckmire can attest to that. Back when I hunted you people, it was only business. Walter and the senator wanted you people beyond the notion of dead until they realized that they only had a portion of the Carbon Factor formula, a move that I thought was brilliant on your part. Listen, I don't want to preach, but I've turned the corner on this relationship, and Mr. Beckmire will agree to that. I have my ears and eyes in some very dark places that provide me with strategic information. I don't expect you to love me, but I would hope that you find some modicum of respect for what I bring to the table and let the history be just that. Thanks."

The Sarge came back on the intercom and said, "Allen, is being modest. Every attempt on us has been forecasted to me by he and Mike. Those attacks and number of attackers were provided to me by those two guys. I've forgiven the fact that he once tried to kill me, but I won't forget it. So, please try to be civil to him. This is going to be a long flight, so Mallory, perhaps you and Monica along with those who were suggested to assist Jong, could have a conversation with Allen and Mike about that Vets program they want to start once we finish with my cousin."

As the Sarge returned to his seat, he saw Courtney smiling and laughing uncontrollably. He asked, "Did I just make a fool of myself?"

"No, baby. I was thinking about how we were breaking records until your boys kicked the damn door in. That was some good love making, dude. I just want to let you know that my expectations for our sessions have just increased exponentially."

The Sarge sat down in the chair, smiled, and held her hand. He knew he had to get in better shape to attempt another he-man effort. He said to Courtney, "Honey, I'll be right back."

He walked down the aisle of the plane and hit Mallory on the shoulder and pointed to Jilkes and John Lee. As the men followed him into the sterile part of the plane, he said, "Guys, when we next put our feet on the ground, we are going to train as if we were just drafted into the military. We are old, but does that mean that we should be out of shape as well?"

Jilkes said, "John Lee and I were talking about the excess baggage that some of us were walking around with, Sarge. Yeah, I'm out of school on this one. We all need to do some serious training and get our shit together. Where we're heading, I can't imagine a better place to be challenged by the elements."

"Damn, I love you people. We never have to guess. We always know what's coming next. Love you."

John Lee said to Jilkes, "You know you just put the entire plane on notice—women and children are to be included in this here new effort. Something be going on that we don't know about, and I ain't about to ask."

"I think he realized he set a new standard for his bride. Remember what he said, 'we saved him from a heart attack'. Add the pieces together and you see where we come in."

"You be one smart colored fellow. How come you never ran for office?"

"Oh, I don't know. But I guess it's because I've been hanging out with some not so brilliant people of another persuasion."

"You mean, white people?" John Lee inquired.

"Damn, you're smart. Anyway, all of us have been so caught up with our companions that we've become a little lethargic. I mean, all the guys are just doing the minimum. We haven't thought about tomorrow for a long time. Love, peace, companionship, and lust. That's who we've become. A group of people who love to love and enjoy life. Besides that, the message I think that's being communicated is that we need to find his cousin and be done with it. This group enjoys life and helping people and making plans for tomorrow. The only thing or person that stands between us and our goals is the Sarge's cousin. Let's huddle with him and ask him to let us have a go at this. We might include Allen and Mike, but no one else, including our women. What say you?"

"You done flipped that switch again on me. You move from topic to topic without a comma. You make me sick, with your smartass self. I don't know what you be talking about," John Lee confessed.

"John Lee, I would like to get away from the group and personally hunt Walter down with the help of Mike and Allen. The question is whether you're in or out?" Jilkes said.

"Them there Asian ladies ain't going to go for that shit."

"John Lee, we have to become masters of our castles or serfs on the land that we should own."

"I don't be understanding a word you be saying."

"Listen, Country Bumpkin. This ain't about our women. This here stuff is about a greater cause and one that leads us to completion. You know me and you ain't never worried about being shot or killed. We always worried about each other. I think that you and I, along with Allen and Mike, can find Walter and end this drama. We are designed to help people and foster positive relationships. Walter is a beast, but he's the Sarge's family. He can't kill his own family. He needs us to intervene and do the deed for him without him sanctioning it or knowing about it. This scenario has been in my dreams for the past week."

John Lee looked at Jilkes and said, "You are so full of shit. You haven't been dreaming of anything except your new wife."

Jilkes turned away and hesitated for a moment and said, "Why are you challenging something that you yourself have been consumed with. You know damn well you have had the same visions. It's all going to be clarified once we get back to the Sarge's land of hocus pocus."

John Lee said nothing and started to walk back to his seat. Jilkes yelled at him and said, "Oh, so that's your response?"

"I got no response because there is something afoot here that is magical, and I don't be believing in magic. I need to speak to my woman."

"Can't you see? That's what we've been doing for a while now. We have been consulting with our ladies because they're pregnant and we are afraid of being killed. You've had the same damn dreams of being shot and dying and not killing Walter. Tell me the truth."

"Stop it. You be playing some freakish mess with my mind. I don't like where you be going with this here talk. I ain't ready for no coup."

"John Lee, I ain't either, but I be damned if I'm going to ignore a consistent dream, I've had for the past seven days. I'm telling you, we got to find Walter and we must do the honors for the Sarge. Rather, you must do the honors. I'm not into that gutting shit that you like. You go and talk to your lady and I will go and tell my lady what we must do. I'm going to take a quick nap. When I wake up, you and I will meet in the back for another round of discussions. This time, I think we should have Mallory, Mike, and Allen there."

The copilot came out of the cockpit and gently woke everyone up and made sure that their seatbelts were fastened, and tray tables were stowed. He later engaged the intercom and said, "We're going to pull the plane near a hangar. I have arranged for buses to pick you guys up and take you into the terminal. I would rather refuel with you guys off the plane. I'm assuming you'll have a total of forty minutes in the terminal."

Zanthius gently rubbed Asiram's belly and said to her, "Honey, we're about to make this run over the water. Do you expect to deliver within the next twelve, or so hours?"

Asiram smiled and confidently stated, "Actually, no, but I do expect to have this child in Australia within the next forty-eight to seventy-two hours, in the outback without a lot of clinical and sterile equipment."

"You are so silly. Why on earth do you think that's when it's going to happen?" Zanthius chided.

"You and your dad believe in that hocus pocus mess, I don't. I have learned to appreciate some things in the past few days, like the same dream that I keep having every night. It is peaceful and calm, but it is the same damn dream each night. I am surrounded by a bunch of people that I don't know who are scantily dressed and have markings or make-up on their faces. Courtney, Ava, Monica, and Marisa are nearby and are assisting in the delivery. That's all I can tell you right now. It's the same damn dream," Asiram recounted.

Zanthius looked at his wife, smiled and said, "I've been having the same dream, as well, but it is not about you delivering a baby. There is trouble afoot in the outback, and my dad and I, plus the guys are going to have to attend to it. Some tourist found gold in the area and speculators are doing dastardly things to the Aborigine people on land that is owned by them to get the gold. We will be in this part of the world for six days and then we will be on our final two quests—finding Walter and ending our connection to the Carbon Factor."

"Honey, you can't end your relationship to the Carbon Factor."

"Funny. As soon as we get back, we are going to turn the final part of the formula over to the senator and, therefore, end our involvement," Zanthius indicated.

While shaking her head, Asiram stated, "That won't end your involvement. I have also been thinking of Helga of late. If I know Helga, there are pieces of the formula spread all over the world. She was a complicated and thorough spy, and I don't believe that she would have just made the simple notations and clues we found and that would be the end of the trail. I've been waiting to express my sentiments on this to you, but every opportunity that presented itself, I guess it slipped my mind. Helga was an intricate woman, a tremendous spy, and a master at creating puzzles. I'm just saying, and I hope I'm wrong because that senator is going to be one mad human being. At some point in time, I would like to discuss this issue with you, your dad, and Mallory. I mean it's just a hypothesis, but I'll bet you a million bucks, you have more work to do to complete accessing that formula. That's my opinion."

As the plane began its descent into the San Diego International Airport the Air Traffic Controller directed it to runway 27R which is facing east. The copilot said, I know that landing strip, it's a dead end that is usually used to interdict drug traffic. He hit a button, and a camera system began to show ground activity. It was the equivalent of a satellite and could zoom in on the smallest items on the ground. The captain came on the intercom and said, "Mr. Beckmire and Mr. Jong, you are needed in the cockpit immediately."

As the two men entered the cockpit the captain said, "Look at the reception committee on the ground." Heavily armed men could be seen scurrying around on the runway near the hangar. The Sarge paused for a few seconds and hastily stated, "I don't like those metal fragments on the ground. Do you see them?"

"I see whatever you want me to see, Sir. Tell me what you want to do?"

"I want to get the hell out of here."

"Okay, back to your seats and buckle up and have everyone else buckle up tight because we're going to hit the ground and blast this bitch right back into the sky."

The captain approached the runway and confirmed it with the tower. As she began her approach, she told the copilot, "When I give you the word, I want you to yell into the mike that there are metal fragments on that runway."

The Sarge yelled into his intercom, "Make ready for a descent to the ground and then an immediate ascent into the sky."

The wheels were in place and locked, and all systems were a go for landing. Approximately two hundred feet from the ground the pilot looked at the copilot and said, "Now, would be a good time to raise the alarm."

He yelled, "There are metal fragments or something on the runway. Abort, Abort, Abort!"

From inside the plane, you could hear people screaming as the plane roughly hit the ground. The captain full throttled the engines and assigned the flaps for take-off and the plane performed above the standards of its specifications. It cleared the hangar with room to spare and appeared to point straight up into space.

At 20,000 feet in the air, the pilot reduced throttle and let gravity hold her in place for a few seconds. Jong said, "Now, that's a damn good pilot. Even if she's not Asian."

Courtney asked, "Did we have an emergency?"

"No, honey, we just had people waiting on us somehow. Excuse me, I need to see the captain."

The Sarge hit Jong on the shoulder and told him to follow him. The two men entered the cockpit and the captain said, "I could have handled that a lot less aggressively, but I wanted people to believe that we thought we were in danger because of metal fragments on the runway. We have already calculated our consumption of fuel, weather and range and have several areas to consider taking on fuel on our way to Australia. We believe in the 1/3rd fuel rule and we have enough fuel to reach our destination. Any deviation from the plan would create a problem, so therefore, we won't try to do that. There are several islands on the way where we can refuel. They had people all over the place there in San Diego. Someone is broadcasting on this plane. If I could be so bold and say, "Let me and my people figure this one out."

"Captain, I want my people to meet and greet you. Usually, it is Mr. Jong doing your bidding, but I want them to see what a woman, and a gorgeous one at that, can ultimately do."

As the captain assigned control of the plane to her copilot, Beckmire walked her out of the cabin and said, "People, this is my new best friend, and should be yours. That maneuver that was performed on the ground and then straight into space was orchestrated and delivered by this young lady, our pilot in command on this new aircraft. Give her a hand."

John Lee yelled, "I be done damn near messed my pants."

The captain said, "Almost and doing, are like night and day. We know what we're doing when we're up there in the front. We also expect that you know what you're doing when you are dealing with your issues. Together, if you handle your end on the ground, then we will handle our end in the air, and it is at that juncture that we can continue to forge a marvelous and continuous relationship."

The Sarge said, "Well stated. I just wanted you people to see who rules the skies."

Mike got out of his seat and walked towards the cockpit and Gladstone and Chakes jumped out of their seats and Chakes asked, "Cowboy, where do you think you're heading?"

"I just want to have a word with the pilot. I saw her from the rear on our other flight but didn't get a chance to see her face."

Chakes called out and said, "Jong, I need you to talk to our friend here. He was heading towards the cockpit."

Jong kissed Mary Alice and said, "He's been in the sewer too long. He just saw someone who might create a fanciful moment of existence for him. He's cool."

"Jong, on your rules and your rules alone, no one can enter the cockpit area."

Jong got out of his seat and said, "You're correct." He looked at Mike and said, "When it's her break, and if she is so willing, I will indicate to her that you would like to have a word with her. Can you give me a reason why I would say that on your behalf?"

"I just saw my future ex-wife and I want to screw up a relationship with her."

Jong looked at him and said, "Your future ex-wife? I no understand what you mean by that. That sounds crazy as all hell."

"Not to me, and I'll bet you the last $40 dollars that I have, she'll know exactly what that means."

"I'm going to give you a bump on that bet. I bet you a hundred to one that she doesn't have a clue about what you are referring to. Now, the rules have to be agreed upon before we approach her."

The mood on the plane was festive, which gave the crew an opportunity to walk through the plane and scan each passenger. As they walked down the aisle with their scanner, the units began to hum when they got to Allen, who was asleep. When Allen woke up, he found four people standing over him. He asked, "What the hell's going on?"

The copilot walked up to the cockpit and reported that a monitoring device was aboard the aircraft. After hearing the news, the captain made a forty-five degree turn towards the north to throw any tracking devices off. She instructed the copilot that he had control of the aircraft. She exited the cockpit and watched as the number of people standing around Allen grew. She pardoned her entry into the foray and said, "I need all nonessentials to go back to their seats now." She watched as people moved slowly back to their seats, all except Larry. She asked Larry if he heard her command and Larry responded by placing a finger over his lips. Larry then motioned for her to get the Sarge and then the two men invoked the street language learned when they eradicated the drug barons in Philadelphia. Larry said, "So, Allen, I'm going to have me a dirty martini, would you like one as well?"

Allen threw his hands in the air and said, "I would love to have one. Everyone else on this plane hates me, Larry, why are you being so kind?"

The copilot scanned Allen's body and pointed to his belt. Allen threw his head back and remembered that Walter had given him that belt for his birthday, four years ago. He thought to himself, "low life son-of-a-bitch". "That asshole has been tracking me from day one. Now, I know why those people showed up in the sewer and how he's been able to track Mike and me. They knew where I was at every turn."

Larry pointed to the Sarge and said, "Check out my new game. It's magnetized, but you have to throw it from an angle to make sure you know where it's going." He immediately placed the magnet on Allen's belt and the deal was sealed. The signal ceased to be emitted.

The captain thanked Larry and smiled at Mike. As she turned to walk away, Mike said, "I would really like to see the view from your vantage point, but I understand why there is so much reservation about people being in the cockpit, especially when the asshole next to me has been wired."

The captain asked, "Are you married or involved in a serious or nonserious relationship?"

"That's a personal question."

"So is seeing the view from my vantage point, personal. Now, sir, that is a perk that few ever get."

"I'm neither married nor in a committed relationship. I have been living in sewers and alleys. We've been hiding from a person who wants us dead. I guess that's not the kind of conversation that excites you, however, let me say this, I saw you and my heart began to beat faster. I stood up to come to you to profess my undying love for you, but I was intercepted by two big old guys. I would like to invite you to dinner, and I would like to attempt to explain what has happened in my life. Too much technology and too much visual stimulation. Damn, you're fine and my heart beats fast when I look at you. Just saying, and you don't have to believe me. This is crazy but give me a chance once we are on land to hopefully make a better impression.

"I saw you and things began to click. You and I have a lot to talk about. Just give me a chance. I'm absolutely crazy about what I've dreamt about, and how you showed up. Such a correlation and it's beyond denial that you're the woman in my dreams. As a matter of fact, she was in the shape of a bird and here we are on a damn plane. Please, don't think me crazy. Have dinner with me and let's see what happens after we discuss things."

The captain looked at him and said, "I can only have dinner in public, with the sanction of my bosses and with them close by for comfort."

"Done! Do you want to invite a priest in case you decide you want to marry me, or something like that?"

"We should have time to consider such things. Don't you think?"

As she entered the cockpit, she told the copilot to vector back to their original heading. He asked, "What's the big smile about?"

"Oh, nothing. Just had an amusing conversation with one of the passengers."

"I bet you I know which one."

"Well, it's easy to deduce who's who on this plane. We know all their mates and each time we land we pick up another individual. Have you noticed that as well?" The captain began to smile again, and the copilot said, "It's one of the two new guys who have never been on this plane before."

"You're so smart. No wonder you're the copilot of this bird. He's entertaining but he is a bit too loquacious for me. He wants to see things from my view, wants to have dinner, dreamt of a woman that looked like a bird, hence me flying, and asked if he should invite a priest along, as well."

"Why a priest? Is he planning to take communion or something?"

"No, that's just in case we decide to get married after dinner."

"Are you serious?"

"That is what that nut said, but I like his approach."

"Captain, it's only been a few months since you broke it off with that fool in New York. Need I remind you of the problems you created in my personal life?"

"You were once a lover who decided that he wanted more and eventually chose another. I didn't want a husband and children. I wanted to fly, fly, and fly. If a person was around when I returned, then so be it. We shared a wonderful relationship and one that I hope your wife will never find out about."

"Silly, girl, she knows all about us and I told her that you are sexy, brilliant, funny, and a perfect friend that would never return to yesteryear. I have said to her, if I were to cheat on her, it would be with you, but you and I both know that that ain't happening. I would never jeopardize my marriage. I love my wife and family more than life."

"Stop it! You're going to make me cry and perhaps feel sorry for myself. I'm an adventurer and you, my friend, are a wonderful husband and the only man I trust in this entire world. Does she know that all of my earthly shit is willed to you?"

"I tried to tell her about that, and she had one comment— I can't do anything about history, but if she comes into our future, I will kill the bitch." They both laughed and high-fived.

They landed in the Solomon Islands and took on fuel only. In less than an hour, they were on their way to the Northern Territory—Darwin.

CHAPTER THIRTY

In the Northern Territory and at the airport, the group was met by relatives of Ben Beckmire. They boarded two yellow buses the group had previously purchased on their last trip to Australia. Their guide, Waterbill, was a cousin of Beckmire's who told him the story of the gold find. He indicated to Ben and Zanthius that he was suspicious of the gold find, because since the beginning of time, the Aborigine had lived there and were quite cognizant of the precious metal. He said, "At the Marrara Swamp, it was rumored that gold was there by the bucket loads. News like that does not stay secret long. Before we knew it, the whites were here with their guns shooting and killing our people. The local constable had suggested to the tribal leaders that they sell the land and move further south. Every Aborigine knows that the inner lands are forbidding."

"Who do you suspect is the lead player in this action?" Zanthius asked.

"There is something on this land that developers want and need to expand their businesses. There is no gold here. We know where the gold is and can find it all over the place along with large diamonds. Crooked Abos attempt to steal and sell the secrets, but spirits protect us from fools and drunks. To your point, Zanthius, in my mind I think the constable is spearheading a group from the east who want full access to these lands."

"We're tired, but we have a lot of work to do while we're here. I don't want to wait until tomorrow. I want to see the land and those involved right now, but I also want to transfer some weapons from the plane to here," Beckmire said.

"No problem. All three of the people doing customs duty are your family members."

# # #

In the interim, Mike asked the captain if she was leaving her plane and she told him that it was important that the plane had eyes on it 24/7, especially in foreign lands. He said, "Perhaps I can stay here and help you watch the plane."

The captain said, "I think your expertise is going to be needed in the outback. Don't do stupid and don't fall for those scantily dressed indigenous women. Perhaps we can amuse each other with enticing promises when you return."

"I will be back for you and I will be pure of heart and mind."

The captain looked at him and asked, "Who talks like that? You seem to be a complex person, Mike. I will be here waiting to assess your pureness and cleanliness of mind."

The Sarge asked Mallory, "How do you want to assign this one?"

"I want you to take the slippery tongue Allen plus Mike with you, as well as John Lee, Jilkes, Zanthius, Chakes, and Montomie. What about weapons?" Mallory inquired.

"I don't plan on using any weapons. We are on a fact-finding mission until we find out who, in fact, is the mission. Don't you think that number of deployed men is a bit heavy? I mean eight guys go into a bar who are not from around here at the same time. What do you think is going to happen? Also, Mike and Allen don't know how we operate. Perhaps, we should keep them at the airport to provide extra security on the plane."

"Yeah, I see where you're going with that one. I thought you wanted to show them the other side of the equation—Australia? Is someone meeting us from here?"

"I certainly hope so. I texted a relative sometime last week. I hope he got it." The Sarge saw Allen and Mike and said, "Guys I'm going to need you to provide security on this beast of a plane. The captain and three of her crew usually do a twelve on and twelve off shift. You guys can cut it down to eight on and eight off. On your off hours, once we find out what we're up against, I'll have a driver pick you guys up and bring you into the outback. Can we count on you guys to be diligent?"

Allen asked, "So, at some point in time, we will be able to leave the airport, correct?"

"Absolutely, and if you want to walk around the little terminal then by all means schedule it with the captain. However, the captain is in charge of this detail and you guys must do what she says, or risk being left in an unfriendly area."

# # #

Once through customs the group assembled and was met by two faces that were familiar to Beckmire and Zanthius. The two men quietly greeted their guides and asked the group to follow them. The Sarge asked the guides the status of the situation there and the one guide shook his head and said, "We found the remains of six of our kinfolks on the side of the road with their throats slit."

"What do you mean by remains?" Zanthius asked.

"Mother nature must feed her flock, as well. They were eaten by the animals."

"Oh, I see." Zanthius responded. "Do you have any idea who is behind this?"

"We have ideas but can't get help from the local constable because we believe he's involved."

"They're killing people, and he hasn't performed a single investigation? Is that what you're saying." Zanthius inquired.

"He says, they have limited policing resources out here and it's difficult for him to investigate each little crime!"

Zanthius's eyes swelled and he said, "Perhaps if a white man was found devoured by animals with an obvious cutthroat, perhaps his tune would change."

Beckmire said, "Son, consider options, never announce them. I had that thought early on." Beckmire looked around and then asked, "Will Wajickee have an opportunity to enlighten me?"

"He is enlightening you, for I am him in another form. I know about your deployment scheme, but I want only you and Zanthius to accompany me while the others go and prepare for the birth of another King. Asiram will deliver the child consummated with you, Zanthius, here in the outback. It may seem strange to you, but we do this kind of thing all the time. Your wife will be assisted by Courtney and Ava but will deliver through the coaching of one of your distant relatives. I will be there as Wajickee to provide the notions of history as will be the Great Saltie. I must warn you Zanthius Beckmire De Lombardo that if you or Asiram's love and commitment to each other is not pure and sincere, the Great Saltie will devour this child immediately."

"Okay, let's pause for a moment. You can't play with my child's life based on making a judgement about our love and devotion. You are not God, so don't attempt to play him."

"Zanthius Beckmire De Lombardo, I advise a cautious temperament when responding to me. Perhaps I am God, and perhaps I am an unwavering God at that! Again, if this union is not pure then you will accept and witness the consequences. Also, soon, you and Asiram will be parents to another. The stork will call when Asiram is ready. Our bloodline is complex, pure, and the Beckmire Clan expands again and again. All that seems not to be, may be all there is to be. You, Zanthius, are a part of an intricate calling. I did not text you, or call, you, or your father. You two realized that there was a problem here in the outback and that those who are not of this earth, me, can't resolve it without decimating an entire group of people on this land."

Ben Beckmire, in an attempt to interrupt a dialogue that Zanthius could not conceivably win, responded, "Zanthius and I would like to request that all of the legends and deeds of those before us be considered in the birthing path of his child. We will not challenge the wisdom of our forefathers. I will just ask that they consider our plea for a safe and healthy delivery of another Beckmire. That is what we ask. Regardless of the outcome, Zanthius and I, will cleanse the area of those who would corrupt and kill our people."

Zanthius said, "I too plea as does my father that my child be born without issue in this great land. I will find and erase those who have ended the lives of our people for monetary gain. I will do so, along with our associates. The spirits of the dead, will make those deceased who killed our people for monetary gain. This I promise and assure the spirits. I will not falter in my mission and my father will escort me on this path of eliminating the enemies of the Aborigine people, not for the moment, but for an eternity. My child will share this vision or be a meal for the Great Saltie."

# # #

As the group began to drive along the coast, Mary Alice said, "I can't wait to swim in that water."

The driver said, "No, missy, you no want to swim in the water at this time of the year. The water is full of Cubozoa and other predators."

Mary Alice asked, "What on earth is a Cubozoa?"

"It be the 'box jellyfish'."

"Jellyfish, I'm not afraid of jellyfish."

"Missy, the box jellyfish has long stingers and if he hits you with one, you die within the hour. He is an unbelievably bad jellyfish. Not like those things in the United States."

"Anything else I should look out for?"

"Missy, there be small spiders that are very poisonous, all kinds of snakes and crocs. There also be all kinds of nice animals that don't kill."

# # #

Courtney said to Ava, "I guess I won't be going in the damn water anytime soon."

"That's two of us. Let me ask you a question? Do you believe in all this hocus pocus that Ben and now my son swear by?"

"Ava, I'm a damn doctor and the things that drive my profession are scientifically proven. I don't practice or believe in the things that my husband does, but I do believe that he believes that there are forces outside the realm of science. So, in essence, I encourage him to believe what he wants to because he knows that I must rely on science. Now, the last time we were here, I must admit, there was some pretty crazy shit going on. I'm sure you're aware that some of us have markings on our bodies that weren't there when we came here. So, you tell me. Do you believe in hocus pocus?"

"Courtney, it's all so mystical and to some degree, believable. Also, the notion of gigantic crocs, jellyfish that kill, spiders so small, but oh so deadly, and a shit load of snakes, this place gives me the heebie-jeebies. My dreams were so definitive and conclusive. I'm not sure what I believe in, but Carlos has been driving me crazy lately. He wakes up in the middle of the night screaming. I love him, but he is scaring me."

"What's bothering him? Have you asked him about his dreams?"

"He says, he keeps having the same dream repeatedly. There is an animal chasing me and when it catches me, it eats me."

"Ava, I'm going to mention that to Ben. If there is any place an animal could chase you and eat you, it's here in Australia. I will consult with Ben and ask him to speak with Carlos. Do you have a problem with that?"

"I need help Courtney. I am watching my man drift into a place that does not make sense to me and is greatly dividing us. I'm literally afraid to sleep with him."

# # #

When the group arrived near the coast, the drivers stopped the vehicles. Beckmire and Zanthius walked off with their two guides. Beckmire motioned to Mallory who stepped off the bus. The Sarge said, "I need Jilkes and John Lee to accompany us to the watering hole where we will find some of those responsible for the discontent and killing. No one else, just those two and Zanthius and I."

Mallory said, "Sarge, it appears to me that these people are playing for keeps. Do you want weapons?"

"Mallory, we can't show up with weapons. We're on a fact finding mission. No weapons."

"How about if we are nearby and just happened in on the place?"

"Mallory, this is not my operation. In this land, I follow orders without deviating from them. Keep our family safe and maintain control for you are our leader now."

#

It was midafternoon when Wajickee, in someone else's frame, entered a dusty and shabby looking place near the coast. When he walked into the place, the entire mood changed within the establishment. People focused their attention on him and wondered why this 'Abo', (disrespectful name for an Aborigine) would walk through the door. Wajickee meandered up to the bar and said, "I would like a pint, Mate. As soon as the barkeep approached him to tell him to get the hell out of the bar, Jilkes, John Lee, Zanthius, and the Sarge entered the establishment. John Lee walked up to the bar and said, "I need five pints of amber, Mate."

"Mate, this here place is private, and we don't serve strangers."

John Lee moved towards the entrance behind the bar and said, "You be serving us, or I be serving us with your piss ale."

Four rather large men emerged from their booth and said, "Abos can't eat or drink in this place. You people best be trying to find your piss ale somewhere else."

Beckmire asked, "Is that so? We be traveling to the swamps and don't want any trouble, just a few ambers and perhaps some info, and we will be out of here."

"Unless you darkies are as stupid as those who live around here, this place don't serve Abos no matter your color."

The Sarge said, "John Lee and Jilkes, address those fellows concerns and make them converts. In the meantime, we're going to teach the barkeep the ways of the bible."

John Lee walked over to the biggest guy and said, "Now, I like you because you be sounding like me when I talk. Now, I be saying this, and this be the last thing I be saying before we get into a fight. Now, we're some rough people who have killed thousands of people. We be a secret squad from Vietnam. Now, that I made that disclosure, when my boss man tells me to end your life, that is exactly what's going to happen. I will beat you to death while my non-Aborigine friend beats the shit out of those three guys. Your choice is simple--sit back and watch us work, give us the requested information, or join them in receiving an ass whupping that you will never forget. Simple choice, but that be what you need to decide."

The largest of the men said, "Are you poofters, (derogatory for homosexual), fucking crazy?"

That was the last question before Jilkes, the Sarge, and Zanthius got busy. John Lee, who held a person back to spread the word of their encounter said, "I warned you what was going to happen. Now, this is going to hurt."

After less than a two-minute fight, five Aussies laid knocked the hell out on the floor. The barkeep, his assistant, and the large Aussie were the only ones who were conscious.

The Sarge said, "I want to know who is the person or persons, who thinks it's okay to kill Aborigine people? I'm only going to ask that question once and from there, we start gutting people in this bar from their dicks to their brains. Who wants to go first?"

The barkeep said, "Listen here, mister, there be gold on this land and those darkies were offered a fair price." 'Wham'! That was the resonating sound of the Sarge slapping the man's face until it was disfigured and multi-colored. The Sarge said, "You will address the Aborigines properly or the next thing you will feel will be a knife opening your belly."

John Lee looked at the big guy and said, "I'm going to ask you a question and if you lie, that older gentleman will know it and, as such I, will be forced to hurt you really bad. I mean the kind of hurt that people die from."

John Lee unsheathed his blade and said, "This here knife has gutted people from their vaginas to their brains, has cut feet off, hands off, dicks off, ears off, and every other part of the body you can think of. Now, I know you be a big boy, but we be real bad people. Did you kill any of the natives? That be my question?"

The big guy replied, "I have been out here for three days. I'm an engineer and was just listening to these guys assure me that those people are selling the rights to their land, freely. I mean I was going to support them in the fight, but I didn't go to college to get the shit beat out of me like those fellows did. I'm just here to survey the land and not to pass judgement on the way things are done, according to my bosses."

"Just who be your bosses?"

"I mean, I ain't that high up where they give me direct orders. They send middlemen and secretaries to tell me what to do."

"Where do we find your bosses?"

"They mostly stay in Sydney and make deals. This isn't their cup of tea. They be city boys if you know what I mean. Now, if you wake that one up by the door, he's directly tied to them. And that barkeep ain't all that innocent. His ass is a game changer."

The barkeep exclaimed, "Why you two timing son-of-a-bitch your ass won't be around long when I tell them who gave them up!"

John Lee after receiving a wink from the Sarge, unsheathed his blade and slammed it into the barkeep's hand. Blood flew all over the place as the man screamed for mercy. The Sarge said, "You're going to tell us everything we need to know, or you will be walking around without hands, and when my boy gets mad, he starts neutering people."

The barkeep's screams woke up the rest of the guys on the floor. Zanthius retrieved the barkeep's shotgun from behind the bar and invited the men to join them. As the men staggered to the bar, they saw that huge blade standing freely in the wood, through a hand, and a menacing look from John Lee's eyes.

The Sarge said, "I want to know who is the piece of shit that murdered those Aborigine people."

Well, hell. There wasn't a need to threaten or stab anyone else because they all pointed to the barkeep. After calming the barkeep down, he began to give out names and addresses and confessed to several of the murders and implicated others. He exonerated the people in the bar but pointed to one of the men as being the person who delivers the orders.

Zanthius asked, "Why hasn't the law come down on you people?"

The barkeep answered, "Because he's a part of the scheme and has been promised a sizeable share of the profits."

"Is he responsible for killing the people?" Zanthius asked.

"His hands be dirty, if he had knowledge of what was going to happen and did nothing to stop it," the barkeep informed the group.

Wajickee said, "The Great Saltie is attending to him as we speak. He will not die, but he will be half of a man."

John Lee saw a roll of duct tape and retrieved it. He withdrew his knife from the barkeeps hand and wrapped it.

Wajickee said, "You have committed crimes against the Aborigine people and for that you must turn yourself into the local magistrate and confess your crimes and implicate everyone who had a hand in this devious ordeal. You may go against my wishes, but once you see the constable's condition, you will know that at any time we can reach out and touch you. And for your information, my friends, those here are indigenous to Australia, they have killed more people than you know, and if they come back here again, it will be to slay your families, and I do mean your entire families and bloodline. You people looking on, will also confess your knowledge of these crimes and make sure that everyone connected directly or indirectly is brought to justice."

John Lee looked at the barkeep's hand and said, "You got about three hours to get that thing attended to or the poison from my blade will kill you. If you don't do as the man says, and try to bring a force out here, then we will be back and teach you our art of war. There are some in hell who would quickly say that you don't want to see us pissed off."

The engineer said, "So, who do we talk to and make sure we be doing the right thing?"

"Your conscious will be your tell-tale, signs. If we come back this way again it will be on a killing mission—women, children, babies, and there will also be lots of decapitations and neutering."

## CHAPTER THIRTY-ONE

The information that flowed from those in the bar led to one person—Walter. Beckmire's cousin had staged the entire event to lure him and his merry band to the outback but lacked the resources to consummate the treachery of killing them. Walter attempted to hire men but lacked the physical cash to pay for his plan.

Beckmire surmised that his cousin knew he would come there first, thus leaving the women and children defenseless. Beckmire pulled out his cell phone and called Courtney. She answered the phone and said, "We had a little distraction, but we handled it."

"What does that mean?"

"Eight or ten men attempted to grab one of Larry's children but Ava, Monica, Marisa, and I, handled it."

"How did you handle it, honey?"

"Ben now don't get mad. Some of us are of the belief that we should not leave home without it."

"Okay, baby. What is it?"

"Those little .308's that were purchased. We neglected to check them on the plane and somehow realized that when we were stopped on the road. They came in handy! I hope you're not mad at us?"

"Where are you people now?"

"We're in a place that looks magical and serene and has a lot of your kinfolk hanging around with spears and other crude weapons."

"If I asked you to give your weapons to my guys, would that be a problem?"

"Ben Beckmire, this is my personal weapon. It's not for community use and besides, your guys got bows and arrows. They don't need our stash."

"We'll be there in an hour or so. Try to keep an eye on everyone. No wandering around without my family and friends. Okay?"

"Yes sir, Sergeant Beckmire."

When the Sarge and his crew reached the village, foodstuff was being provided to his group. He saw Mallory first and asked, "Did you know that your wife carried a weapon through customs?"

"I did not know that, but apparently, your family members who work in customs knew they were packing."

"They should have known. I mean everyone went through the scanners, right?"

"Sarge, this is your neck of the woods. I don't understand the animals, the language, the people, and most of all the continuous weird shit that happens here, you tell me. How could they miss weapons on, as far as I know, four of our women?"

"Don't ask me to explain because it just doesn't make sense to me. I wonder if the other ladies have weapons on them as well?"

"Why don't we quietly ask them?"

The two men began to ask all the ladies individually, if they had a pistol. The answer was unanimous, every woman had somehow been allowed to enter the country with a weapon. The Sarge walked over to where Somara, Yeshida, and Okema were and asked, "Are you people packing weapons and, if so, how did you manage to get them through customs?"

Okema replied, "That seems like a personal question, don't you think, Mr. Sergeant?"

"Okay, guys, just yes or no, do you guys have pistols in your possession?"

Yeshida said, "Mr. Sergeant sir, we will never leave home without them. They are like our lifeline if you know what I mean."

# # #

As the day began to transition into night, it was clear that a ceremony was about to begin and it would consume the Sarge, Courtney, Ava, Zanthius, and of course, Asiram. Wajickee appeared in his earthly form, approached Asiram and said, "It is time for you to give us another king who will do well by all people, but will pay particular attention to the Aborigine."

A feisty Asiram looked at Courtney, and said, "I need help with this one." She looked at Wajickee and said, "I'm not ready to have this baby, yet."

Wajickee looked at her and touched her stomach and said, "You be having another Beckmire in the next hour. These ladies will help prepare you and cleanse you."

"Just a damn minute, dude. I don't need anyone to help cleanse me and again, I'm not ready to have a baby. Don't you think I would know?"

Wajickee raised his hands into the air as Asiram screamed, "I think this baby wants to come out now."

Zanthius ran to her side and asked, "What happened? You said you weren't ready, and now you're ready? What happened?"

"I looked into the eyes of that demon and he raised his hands in the air and now I feel like this thing is about to happen." Asiram took a deep breath and that was the beginning of the end. Asiram entered a state of rest with the help of Wajickee who informed all that the baby would scream at midnight. He also assured Ben Beckmire that his nemesis had left the continent and was preparing for a confrontation in America.

For the balance of the night, the air was filled with sounds from the Didgeridoo and other indigenous creative instruments. Life, at this moment was spectacular, without threat and with a presence of calm engaging everyone's spirits. Zanthius and Asiram were in a comatose state and kept their eyes focused on each other. Zanthius drank a native drink, while Asiram drank a purified form of water that had been blessed by the gods and sanctioned by Wajickee. Wajickee knew that there was no way under any moon that these people would allow their first born to be sniffed by the Great Saltie. He lowered the tone of the sounds and said to Ben Beckmire, "Tell your son that the Great Saltie will view his child at the stroke of midnight and if the child is not pure then it will feast upon it."

"Is there another way to confirm this thing?"

"This is your forefather's way. There is no such thing as a substitution. Pure is as the sun sets and rises, the Great Saltie is the judge and jury, of who passes into the next life. I sense fire in her eyes, a final calm in his, and that boy that is within, is a firestorm of righteousness. In my estimation, he be a turning point for the wrongs that have been and continue to be placed upon the Aborigine people. I sense no harm, I sense no feast, but that child will give a scream that all who are unholy will hear and fear through eternity."

At 10:30 p.m., Asiram began to feel thunderous kicks in her abdomen. The movement continued until 11:00 p.m. Zanthius rubbed her stomach and attempted to keep her calm, but to no avail. She screamed at the top of her lungs, "If you ever do this to me again, I will murder you. The pain is monumental and continuous. Courtney, can't you give me a drug or shot. I need an epidural. This pain is off the charts."

Wajickee walked over to her and said, "My dear Asiram, you don't need any drugs to deliver this child. You need faith and focus, and all will be easy." He touched her forehead and she looked at him with a smile on her face. At 11:15 p.m. one would have thought that every animal in the nearby vicinity had begun to make their individual noises. Although sounding ominous and frightful, there was a calmness to it when combined with the music being played by the villagers.

At 11:40, as though the conductor had concluded the symphony, the bush became tranquil. The only night noises that could be heard would be that of Asiram beginning the birthing process.

Asiram's screams were mellow at first as if starting a sonata. They would begin to climb to a crescendo while grasping Zanthius's hand in a no release fashion. Shortly before 11:50, she bellowed forth a sound that surely could be heard throughout the Northern Territory. At 11:55 those same sounds, plus others, resonated probably all the way back to Sydney. The most horrific and amplified sound was made at 11:59.59 p.m., exactly, and it was not from Asiram. That sound was from the Great Saltie.

At precisely midnight, the screams of a baby could be heard. Its sounds were amplified by all the indigenous animals near and far and throughout all of Australia. Asiram and Zanthius were watching their son being held into the air by Wajickee who commanded Zanthius and Beckmire to follow him. As others began to follow, Wajickee thundered, "Do not follow, it is for certain that those who do, death will be your path."

At the water's edge, and as the moon reflected upon the water, there was a calmness. Wrapped in a blanket and placed beside the water's edge, lay Zanthius's son, and Ben Beckmire's grandson. Wajickee told the two men to close their eyes and keep them closed. He cautioned them to not gaze upon the Great Saltie.

Without warning, there was a thrashing in the water. Suddenly, something exceptionally large was making its way to shore. The only thing that could be heard were its deafening movements. It circled the baby and thrashed its tail violently. The baby continued to cry and the Great Saltie moved ever so violently in the baby's direction but veered off at the last moment. Zanthius and his father held hands firmly and continuously repeated the words, 'Do not gaze upon this scene'.

After several minutes of hearing the baby cry, Zanthius decided to take a look to make sure his child was okay, as did Ben Beckmire. They saw a colossal crocodile standing between an old Aborigine man and a newborn baby. As the old man bowed down to the earth, the Great Saltie began to back its way into the water. The Great Saltie knew that Ben and Zanthius, saw its image and acknowledged their gaze by rapidly closing both eyes as it backed into the water, disappearing quietly into the night. Wajickee stood up and approached the child and hoisted it into the air and screamed at the height of his lungs. He was joined in the annunciation by creatures small and large throughout the entirety of Australia.

As the three men walked back towards camp, Zanthius grabbed his father's arm and said, "You are a man that I respect, love and acknowledge as my father. I have a question? Did you see what I saw?"

"Son, I'm not sure what you saw, but I saw my great, great, great grandfather. His form was not what I would consider for the usual family portrait, but I will say that he acknowledged us both and allowed us to witness his presence, as well as sanctioned your child as a leader and ruler of the Aborigine people. Did you, in fact, see the power your son was gifted with?"

"Dad, I saw a big ass croc move around my child with the grace of a ballet dancer. I closed my eyes but opened them for a split second, despite Wajickee's warning. I saw that thing come out of the water and approach my son with its mouth open."

"Son, you also saw Wajickee hold your son high in the air and announce his being. This thing that you think you saw will not be acknowledged by me and, therefore, I suggest that you never speak of it in the future. Our future is in some way based upon our spirituality and acknowledgment of the fact that we're Aborigine."

When the three men entered camp with the baby held firmly and lovingly in Zanthius's arms, a happy sound was played on the didgeridoo. As the camp came alive to celebrate the birth of another Beckmire, the mood became festive. The members of the Beckmire group ate and drank things that they would not normally consider as food or drink, but nevertheless, were happy and inebriated.

As Asiram slowly began to focus and cuddle the life form that she had carried around in her stomach for nine months, she said, "You were a pain in my ass, but damn, I will do this again, and again, and again, because we need good people to balance the deeds of those who continually do bad."

Ben Beckmire walked over to Asiram and Courtney and said, "This is a wonderful moment for all and I'm glad that you didn't fight against the will of Wajickee."

"Daddy-in-Law, I didn't think I had the skill or the power to fight him. Your protector and provider is a wise man, and you can count on one thing moving forward, I will never doubt forces or things that I don't understand but are as apparent as night and day. I have seen some wicked shit in the past few hours and I believe that I'm a damn convert."

Zanthius said, "Honey, if only I could get you to use fewer curse words in the future."

"Sweetheart, oh my God, look at our child. He's big. If that's what you want, then just ask me. I love you with all my heart."

As the women doted over the new baby, Wajickee called for their attention. He unconditionally announced, "The parents, Asiram and Zanthius, have given me permission to pronounce, the name of their newborn son. I am proud to declare, that the child will be named after me! Just kidding, but what I'm not kidding about is that I want everyone to lineup and officially meet, Benjamin Beckmire De Lombardo."

Zanthius looked at Asiram and asked, "Did you tell him our proposed child's name?"

"I did no such thing. I thought you told him, and that it was another one of the rituals in the outback."

"Honey, I did not tell him anything and I don't remember being unconscious around him. I think I will ask him who told him the name?"

As Zanthius approached Wajickee, who said, "For gazing upon the Great Saltie you gave me the right to call out the child's name."

Zanthius started to deny the notion but decided there was nothing to be gained and everything to lose in this strange, but wonderful land. He said, "I just took a small peek."

"So did your father. His peek was expected. You see, your father is the real deal in that his blood line is considered royal."

Zanthius pressing the issue asked, "Wajickee, please tell me how you knew the chosen name of our son?"

"Zanthius, my boy, I am supposed to know all in the outback and that is why I'm allowed to be both man in body and a spirit. It is my function to know what people think. If not, then why be named a living spirit. Your thoughts, as well as Asiram's and everyone else's here, are things that I routinely decipher. Somewhere in your discussions with your wife, the two of you agreed on the name as a surprise to your father. I thought it was okay and decided to let the naming be a function of the two of you. I usually take the liberty of naming all Aborigine people. Enough with the nonsense about the name. Ask me the question that plagues your mind before I go on Walkabout."

"When I peeked, I saw the largest semiaquatic reptile that I have ever seen. What exactly was that thing walking around and thrashing the water near my son?"

"That was the Great Saltie, Zanthius. Prophecy says that your son will be your age before the Great Saltie shows up again. Prophecy also states that, the stork will visit you with much needed information and a surprise, my boy."

"I don't understand. Why will it reappear when my son is my age and how come no one has tried to capture or kill it? And what is the surprise that the stork will bring?"

"To capture it would be an impossible task and it is exceedingly difficult to kill a spirit. There are not many people who have seen the Great Saltie and there are none alive, save one who has witnessed his wrath. Attend to your family and new son, Zanthius. In time, all will be made clear to you and your father. I can't tell you all that the spirits may know or see. I am most certain on the stork; I will attempt to gain favor and find out for you," Wajickee announced.

## CHAPTER THIRTY-TWO

It was official, the senator's opponent, was the president-elect of the highest office in America, the Presidency of the United States of America. The world was in shock, the Russians had been accused of rigging the election, the senator was devastated, but maintained a significant amount of information and aspects of the formula for the Carbon Factor, a thing that the newly elected president had no idea about. It was obvious why the newly elected-president's alleged buddy, was not responding to the fact that the current administration just gave notice to a significant number of Russian Ambassadors to flee the country within the next seventy-two hours. The stakes on all sides of the water had just been raised.

Everyone was dumb struck that the election results were as they were, against reason. The initial polls had his opposition winning by a significant margin. The bully, the thin-skinned, egomaniac, and person who thought truly little of the female gender was the newly elected president even though his opponent won by over three-million popular votes.

In the opinion of most people, both finalists were flawed. With incorrect information being provided to the public at the final hour which included a new set of charges from the head of the FBI, it was no wonder the most popular candidate lost. The election and the preamble to it were a comedy of errors, the senator thought she had the election in the bag. Her opponent went to places where his strong minority of supporters lived in shacks, hated Blacks, Jews, Muslims,

Mexicans, and nearly everyone else that didn't live next door to their dumb asses.

Racially motivated attacks increased and seemly were ignored by the new administration. The new president-elect, empowered people in his administration who were tied to all kinds of hate groups. His cabinet was composed of billionaires and generals and his advisors were involved with hate groups. The president-elect also was a twitter freak and responded to those who did not like him or his decisions by negative tweets in the early hours of the morning.

The senator suspected that the Russians helped rig the election against her—but at what cost to her opponent. She felt that an alliance with the Russians, would parlay the knowledge of the Carbon Factor to her advantage. She knew that the Russians failed at least four times to replicate the formula. Her goal was to destabilize the incoming administration by having colleagues call for hearings on various aspects of his taxes, business dealings with various governments, and banks around the world, including Russia. In her less than rational mental condition, she swore she would sleep with the enemy to bring down the clown who was about to take office. In her mind, she knew this would be considered treason, but felt that this country deserved a better president. She had illusions of grandeur that one day she would still occupy the highest office.

The one problem with her plan was that she did not have the complete formula. She had her man-servant reach out to Walter, but to no avail. Walter was in hiding and had given up his high living to avoid detection. She sent Walter an S.O.S message to his email address under a disguised code name, one that he and only he would know. The second line of the message featured $$$.$$$.$$$. If Walter were alive and saw this message, he would certainly make contact. The senator decided to hedge her bet and attempted to contact the Sarge as well. She called on one of his throw-away phones that didn't get thrown away.

# # #

As the night began to turn into day and after a glorious celebration of the birth of a new Beckmire, the Sarge looked at his three phones and turned them on, one by one. He immediately saw the senator's area code and number. He went to Jong and said, "I think the senator is trying to contact me. Do you have any phones that can't be triangulated to locate our current position?"

"Sarge, I can call the phone at the farm and use the program to have it call the number that you want. It has a four-minute window at best before it begins to show that it's a relay."

The Sarge walked over to where Zanthius and Asiram were, and said, "I would feel so much better if you two stayed here for a while and let my grandchild get to know my relatives."

"Pops, what's the deal? If you're leaving, then we're leaving. Right, honey?"

"I promised not to swear much anymore, but Daddy-in-Law, have you lost your damn mind? We do well when we're all together. We can't be here and you there because that ain't good karma for us. You got a bunch of pregnant women and horny friends. You see what happened here in your world when those people tried to abduct one of Larry's twins. We don't need to be splintered; we need to stay as a unit. The baby will be good to fly in a few days and besides, we all need to take a break."

"Gee, people. I was just asking a question, but I did think it would be safe for you guys and the baby here."

"Pops, we can't roll like that. This group of misfits has survived because we have stayed the course together. Yeshida, Okema, and Somara are attached to your leadership team. Splitting us up will be a problem."

"Zanthius, I never said anything about Yeshida, Okema, and Somara."

"Pops, I don't know where that came from, that just rolled off my tongue."

"Damn, its truly spiritual. I was going to suggest that they stay here with you guys, as well."

"John Lee, Jilkes, and Brown aren't going to go for that, so forget about it. They would rather have their women in battle with them, feeding bullets into the clips and firing alongside them. Any casualties in our group is just what it is, a casualty. You don't have the power to separate families, especially considering the number of pregnant women who are in our group. Listen, Pops, we have killed a lot of people and have had few injuries. We haven't lost anyone, but the day is probably on the calendar that one of us, if not all of us, are going to catch terminating bullets. Everyone also feels that when that day comes, they want to be with the only real family they have. Sometimes, friendship is not thicker than blood. We would die for any of you. Is that right, baby?"

"I'm so proud of my baby's daddy. He just showed real leadership, character skills, and I agree with him a thousand percent. Just because we have babies, and some are pregnant, doesn't mean that we want to sit back in a shelter."

The Sarge walked over to his grandson and kissed him on his forehead. He looked at Asiram and kissed her on both cheeks and said, "I knew you were feisty. Don't ever change for him or me." He approached Zanthius and said, "It has not been the kind of relationship a father should have with a son. However, it has been the best damn time that I could experience with my son, who was just trying to escape from the depths of hell and survive with a new mindset. I love you, dude. Damn, I love you."

As the Sarge was about to walk away, Zanthius asked, "So, Pops, have you had a beer with Larry lately? I think it's about time. I don't want him assassinating my ass because you haven't given him any love lately."

The Sarge jerked around and said, "That's exactly where I'm heading. How the hell did you know that?"

"Dad, I'm thinking that in this place, we're just one."

#

A few minutes later, the Sarge saw Mallory, Monica, Courtney, Ava, and Juan. He yelled, "Honey, save a sober moment for me. I need to see Larry for a minute."

"I was going to suggest that."

The Sarge saw Marisa and asked her where her husband was? She told him he went for a walk. The Sarge did not want to raise the alarm but realized that in the outback, you don't go for walks at night by yourself.

He casually walked towards the water's edge and saw Larry sitting a bit too close to it. He asked, "Son, are you offering yourself to my ancestor?"

Larry turned around and said, "Who is your ancestor?"

"Oh, in this part of the world he's called the Great Saltie?"

"Oh, yeah. That's the giant saltwater croc that dispenses justice to those who have wronged the Aborigine people."

"Yes, that is who I'm talking about. Why are you sitting so close to the edge of the water?"

"Dad, I'm thinking about how we don't talk, have a beer, or do silly things together anymore."

"Yeah, I was thinking about that as well. You know your brother and his wife had a baby tonight and I guess I got caught up in that celebration and process."

"Dad, you've had a lot on your plate. And no, I'm not jealous of Zanthius. He's yours by blood and I'm yours by love. I just need you to recognize me by remembering the things we did together before all of this."

Larry began to cry and the Sarge sat down beside him and said, "You are my first born. Does it matter if I didn't biologically have you through natural channels? To me, it doesn't. I have a lot of people to concern myself with and the number keeps growing. I have had to divide my time and, therefore, I realize that I've not been a good father and/or friend to you. I also think that if you have an issue or you're feeling a certain way, you can say, 'hey, dad, let's have a beer'. Help me keep everyone in this group together and alive. I need you to do this for me and, in return, I'm going to summon two of my ancestors and let you decide for yourself who is crazy and who is not?"

"Come on Dad, I don't need anything except your guidance and love. I don't need no magical, t----r----i----c----k----s."

At the water's edge where Larry and Beckmire sat, the Great Saltie emerged from the water. The sound he made was ominous and could be heard throughout the Northern

Territory. Ben Beckmire grabbed Larry's arm and held him fast to the ground as the Great Saltie backed into the water.

Wajickee appeared in spirit form and motioned to Beckmire and Larry to leave. He looked at Larry and said, "His love for you is greater than genetics. You, my friend, were just sanctioned by a spirit."

## CHAPTER THIRTY-THREE

Less than two hours had passed since the senator sent out the S.O.S. message to Walter. Her private phone rang and when she answered it, he said, "That seems like a lot of money, especially, since I have been robbed by a family member. How the hell are you, Senator?"

"I'm fine and I hope you've given up this search for your cousin. I need him and his team alive, especially, since I lost the election that was hacked by Lucifer's cousin over in Russia. I want to make an alliance with him and share the Carbon Factor formula with him."

"Why would you want to do that?"

"It's called détente. I need you to stop trying to kill your cousin."

"Not sure about your intelligence information, Senator, but I've been on the run from him. I was in Australia and he showed up. I hired some people to end his existence and, as usual, he did them first. He is protected by old magic in my country and there is no way to get around it. As a matter of fact, if you sent a missile to his exact location over there, it would probably turn around and come back to the sender. You may not believe in magic Senator, but there are things in this world that have no explanation. And, insofar, as you wanting to make an alliance with the Russians, that is a huge mistake. That guy who is our President elect, will probably quit the job because he won't be able to deliver on his promises and his financial accounts will begin to dwindle significantly. I hear that Beckmire's group have additional parts of the formula and another entity has two additional aspects. If those numbers are correct in your email, then I will begin a very tactful search for the other entity and make sure it's credible. I would personally stay away from anything Russian for a while. Think about it. The Carbon Factor was developed by them and they kept the only copy of the formula in the same place they did experiments. Now, that says a lot about protecting your assets, doesn't it? I just think they're desperate because they have no economy and their leader is one of the richest men in the world. Go figure that one out. Anyway, I'm getting some dirty information out of Russia about another spy who has the complete formula for the Carbon Factor. In other words, the thing that so many people have died for, might just be a blank."

"Or the new thing that people are trying to sell might just be a fraud. Anyway, I'm placing my bet on the Beckmire document because I know they don't have a clue as to what it can do."

"Ah, Senator, you might be underestimating the skill set of the people involved. Do you think that someone could randomly separate aspects of a formula into four or more integral parts? I wonder what the odds, of doing that are. Anyway, the last group I will underestimate is Ben Beckmire's. What I used to consider impossible for a small band of old people, has been placed gently inside of a first edition book of knowledge. Don't fool with this guy and his people. They are formidable and determined. Negotiate or retreat. Don't attempt to do battle."

"Walter, I can't believe that you are sounding scared?"

"No, Senator! There is a difference. I now know my opponents and their abilities, as well as the fact that everything you see, you can't believe—magic, Senator, magic."

## CHAPTER THIRTY-FOUR

Three days later as the group prepared to break camp, Allen walked over to the Sarge and said, "I need your permission to cut my phone on and see if I can get a signal? It's important that we have updated intel before we fly and definitely prior to landing. I don't know about you, but I sense this could be our last hurrah."

The Sarge looked at Courtney and said, "Honey, you heard the man. This could be our end. Shall we go swimming or find some stretch of the beach and make passionate love? Your choice."

Courtney looked at Allen and said, "Have fun with my husband. He's such a nut."

Allen once again began to apologize to Beckmire for the breach in security by having a bug in his belt. He became monotonous in his rant professing undying love and loyalty to the group. The Sarge saw Mallory and Jong and beckoned them to join him. He then saw Chakes, Montomie, Gladstone, and Whitmore. They called out to Brown, Bernstein, John Lee, Jilkes, and McArthur. They were joined by Jong. They all walked to the water's edge and the Sarge said, "Allen, do you believe in spirits and huge animals?"

"Come on, Sarge. I'm just trying to tell you that I was not playing you and did not know that the damn belt was a signal. I know I tried to kill each one of you people, but we all know what happened with those efforts. I'm a team player now. If you want to kill me, then by all means, I only want to die by your hands, Ben Beckmire."

"Allen, do you think we're animals and we just kill for the sake of killing? You're one paranoid individual. We have had all kinds of spirits scan the very essence of your character. We didn't walk you down here to murder you or anything like that. I just want you guys to look at the footprints in the sand and never mention it to anyone."

Allen asked, "What footprints?"

The Sarge said, "The one you're standing in."

The Sarge said, "Listen up, I know my guys have heard about this a million times. They also thought I was completely crazy and in need of mental evaluations. I trust you, my friends, to witness the footprints of my ancestor. You may discuss this amongst yourselves, but never to anyone outside of this group."

John Lee asked, "So, how come your sons ain't here?"

"They had a face to face meeting with the Great Saltie."

"Both of them?" John Lee astutely asked.

"I did use the plural of the word, I thought," the Sarge said.

The men began to try to estimate the size of whatever made the imprints in the sand and decided that it was not safe to be near the water. The Sarge inquired, "Why don't you guys go for a swim?"

#

Later as the guys were still shaking their heads and trying to get over what their eyes had seen, John Lee said to Jilkes, "I be thinking that the Sarge done pulled some hocus pocus on us and planted them there feet prints himself."

Jilkes looked at him and asked, "Have you lost what little brain you have? We were in Vietnam and a few other places with that dude and we killed a shit load of people. Why would he go through such elaborate lengths to convince us that there is a monster in the outback? Come on, now. I don't believe in a lot of hocus pocus, but you got to admit, when it comes to the Sarge, we have seen some strange shit take place and his message has been consistent--this is a magical place. Look at the drawings on the cave walls, look at the strange animals, fruits, fish, and indigenous people. Look at the different colors of people and how about that blonde hair, blue eyed boy that was darker than coal? What about that little girl who was a redhead with green eyes and darker than a piece of coal, as well. This is a marvelous place if you have faith, and I don't want to cross paths with the demon side of this place, so I say, let it go Romeo. I don't want to discuss it because it scares me."

"That's exactly why I want to discuss it. That footprint is going to cause me to have some bad nightmares. I need to go and pray to the only God I know. This here demon is larger than the normal animal. I just want to go home and play with my pigs."

"Okay, John Lee. Get your shit together. We can't let the rest of the team know that we're scared of what we saw."

"Unless you be blind, they all want to get the hell out of here, and now," John Lee said.

# # #

Mike made a pass at the pilot, who suggested he not do that again. She told him that she was unaccustomed to kissing or having strangers attempt to kiss her so early in an undefined, relationship. He apologized and said, "You really don't get the gist of what's happening, do you? You have been in my head each day and night since I first saw you. I am of the belief that we are destined to be together."

"Oh, you mean until the next one comes along, and I become your ex-wife as articulated by you."

"Listen, I know I'm rushing things and I'm trying to convince you that I am your world, but believe me, I have never in my life felt this way about another human being. I confess to you that I have been in relationships and they have been all about sex. To tell the truth, I'm afraid of you, and all of this bravado is another side of me trying to avoid heartbreak. I know I came on to you like a hurricane, but I can only state that if you give me the time of day, I will give you a lifetime of happiness. Don't ask me how I'm going to do that? Something tells me you will be happier than any woman on this plane."

"Mike, I have work to do to make sure you have a safe flight. Ask Mr. Jong or the Sarge if you can have an empty seat since you're assigned a seat next to Allen. Tell him you want to have a conversation with the pilot of the plane when, and if, she takes a break."

An hour or so later and prior to boarding the plane, the Sarge asked Mallory to gather his guys. As the men assembled, the Sarge said, "In this land, there be demons that you can see. I can have Wajickee erase all that you saw and can't fathom. What say you?"

John Lee looked at each guy and replied, "I don't be knowing when real life had a story book ending. I'm afraid of what I saw, but I also be wanting to realize that there be a greater source and power of inspiration. I also be believing that there be other things to pray for, because it be seeming to me that everything that we do that is good, keeps us alive and together. I ain't no religious person, but I know what I saw and that there be enough for me to think about saying prayers for all of us each night before I go to bed."

Brown stepped into the center and said, "Everything is magical. I love my pregnant wife and I love you boys. You people know what happened to me because you rescued me from it. Me and my family will die for each one of you if it comes to that. I saw what I saw, and I would not want to see the thing that made those imprints. I pray that it protects us against a foe who is wicked and without conscious. I saw those footprints and I never want to see what wears those damn shoes."

Courtney and a few of the other women approached the area where the men were talking and the Sarge raised his fist in the air. Courtney said to Marisa, Monica, Ava, and Mary Alice, "Guys, this is not a good time to distract our men folk from their mission. My husband communicated a powerful sign to me and I'm going to respect the meaning of it. He needs time with his men, so let's go and get a drink before this damn plane takes off."

Wajickee summoned Beckmire and Zanthius and said, "By the time you come back here, the school and the hospital will be completed. Great doctors have been hired, equipment purchased, some that I don't understand the need for, and a lot of other things have been ordered that look like a waste of money. I alone, will travel east and confront the backers of the proposal and I will shape their thoughts or end their lives. Your future visits here will hopefully, be peaceful."

"A clear message has been sent and anyone who temps their fate and tries to hurt Aborigine people for their land will meet with a horrible death, along with his family. The one who is Mallory's wife reinforced the tenants of the land grant and added more protections for the Aborigine for the next 500 years, at which time I will rethink the land. Those easterners were concerned about gold and, truth be told, there are diamonds here the size of apples. On your next visit, I will give you a few of them to set up trusts and college funds for our people. We will cross the country and provide the same kind of hospitals and schools to all Aborigines in the outback. Thank you, my brothers, and I will see you on Walkabout."

# # #

Later as the crew began to prepare the cabin for departure, Ben Beckmire looked at Courtney and said, "The next time we come here, I promise you a night out on the town in Sydney. We'll start our day by having lunch at Manly Bay and go for dinner at this great restaurant that sells John Dory fish that is, oh so good, my love. Once this mess ends, we're going to travel and travel and then decide on where we want to live. I know you don't want to go back to our home in Philly."

"Sarge, I thought we had this discussion. I shot and killed a man there. I don't think that's the kind of memory I want to have thrown in my face day after day."

"I know, honey, I must say, you have been a strong member of this team. You have fired on people when necessary and you have saved lives according to your code. Just so that you know, we're going to have a meeting soon and once it's over, you'll be able to live anywhere you want."

"I don't want a whole lot of house. I like the idea of relocating where John Lee lives or just taking up residence in our hotel on the island."

"Now, that's a great thought. As chairman, there will always be a plane at my disposal, and we can go and come as we please."

"Ben, I just want a simple life with my man and a place where our kids can come and visit without a lot of drama. I don't want diamonds and pearls; I just want my man."

"Honey, speaking of diamonds, and this is not to be shared with anyone, Wajickee told me on my next visit he is going to give me a few diamonds that are bigger than apples."

"Ben, is that possible?"

"Honey, I don't know. I have no knowledge of the jewels. The purpose is to create scholarship endowments for our people and to build hospitals and schools in the outback, throughout Australia."

"Honey, I know a jeweler we can trust—Mr. Bassman."

"That's why I love you. You are always thinking ahead of me and solving my problems. Woman, do you love your husband, and is he a great guy?"

"I do love my husband, but I'm not filling his head with horseshit. Oh, by the way, Ava wants to use our resort to get married next month." With a look of an evil woman, Courtney asked, "Do you have a problem with that?"

"Why would I have a problem with that? She's not marrying me."

"You're right. However, I sometimes see the way you look at her and she looks at you. And don't tell me I'm seeing things or that I'm paranoid."

"Courtney, we had a child together that I didn't know about. I don't have a lot of respect for her because she hid that which is sacred from me; my son Zanthius. I will always love her, but I will never be in love with her. I'm in love with Dr.

Courtney Beckmire and there ain't no other person in this world for me."

"Are you sure, Ben Beckmire?"

"Are you crazy, Courtney? Where the hell, am I going to go and get the kind of loving you give me? Who is going to look after my old ass like you do? I don't know anyone and haven't got any Facebook friends who said that I was all that. I guess, I'm stuck with you."

Courtney punched him gently in the side. She saw her husband wince from the love tap and realized there was an issue that needed to be addressed. Without saying a word to her husband, she unbuckled her seatbelt and entered the cockpit. She said to the Captain, "I need you to abort this departure until I can check out the health of my husband. Something is not right."

The Captain immediately shut the engines down and instructed the ground crew that they had a medical emergency that needed to be attended to. As if by magic, when the plane door opened the first person that appeared was Wajickee who said, "It's gas, he'll be alright." He then whispered something in Courtney's ear and said, "He will sleep peacefully and without danger. Once you land in that pretentious place you call an island, have him sedated and get his rotten appendix taken out. He will sleep the entire flight and you, his lady, must not worry. He has arms around him wherever he is, which belong to the Great Saltie. Just so that you know, he has the weight of this entire group on his shoulders. He needs assistants, assign Zanthius and Larry."

On the runway, the Sarge stirred and asked, "Are we there yet?"

## CHAPTER THIRTY-FIVE

On the flight across the water, the movies featured were the new *Magnificent Seven* with Denzel and the new *Tarzan* movie. John Lee and Jilkes absolutely loved them. Their ladies weren't sure what was going on and kept interrupting the movie to ask questions.

Yeshida, Okema, and Somara began to move around the cabin and fully socialize with the other women. Everyone knew they were all connected, and as such, needed to be a little more familiar with each other. They also knew that the constant nature of conflict created harmony amongst them, but they still lacked understanding of the differences in culture and people.

Approximately three hours into the flight, Carlos stood up and yelled, "I want to marry Ava. If anyone has a problem with that then jump the hell off the plane."

Zanthius stood up and asked, "May I approach you in peace?"

"You may come forth."

"You make my mother happy. I know that you love her, but you have this dumb ass money thing that you're concerned with. Dude, she doesn't need money and never has. I don't need money and never will. What we do is as a family, and I as her only son state, I will proudly walk my mother down the aisle to engage in holy matrimony with you. I love you Carlos and Mom, I'll keep an eye on his ass." The plane erupted into loud screams and yells and Mallory engaged his intercom and exclaimed, "Another one bites the dust!"

The champagne was poured, and the group came alive. The Sarge who was almost comatose walked back to acknowledge the two and said, "Damn, I'm happy for you Carlos and for you Ava. We have not had an opportunity to speak freely about all that has impacted us, but I'm sure it will happen soon. Blessings upon you both."

Carlos asked, "So, Sarge, do we really have your blessing?"

"Carlos, I endorse it because I think it makes sense, but I have no sanctioning words to confirm it. You people are my family and as such we support your actions."

Courtney heard a baby crying and immediately left her seat. Asiram asked, "Why is he crying?"

"Asiram, he's crying because he's hungry and flying in a damn plane. Cover your breasts and let him feed upon the wonderful fluids from your body and soul."

"Courtney, I don't know a thing about what I'm supposed to do."

"Honey, you're lucky. You have so many people ready to assist you, that it's going to make you crazy. Those who are pregnant are going to watch you with a microscope to learn what to do. Those who have children are going to give you tips—good—bad—and indifferent. And some of us are going to envy you so much because we wish we could do what you're doing, all over again. Also, a few of them, missed this opportunity all together, so please be kind when Monica comes and wants to simply hold and love the child. It will be a true testament of your humanity. As a matter of fact, I can't think of a better couple than Mallory and Monica to be Godparents, can you?"

Asiram looked at Courtney and then her husband and said, "I thought that would be the role of you and your husband?"

"Honey, I'm your mother-in-law and my husband is your daddy-in-law. You can't compromise that position. It's clear, so forget about that math. Mallory and Monica, clean, pure, committed, and in tune with our mission. Let it be known to all that they are your choice, but again, if that's your decision."

# # #

As the plane began to descend into St. Thomas, the alternate pilots walked through the plane to make sure that everyone was prepared for landing. The captain engaged the intercom and reminded people not to attempt to enter the country with weapons. She pleaded for those with weapons to turn them in for safe keeping. Courtney and her crew handed over their weapons.

Once through customs, Mr. Christopher Carter and the driver met the group with the new luxury-liner bus. Courtney whispered to him that they needed to go to the hospital immediately because the Sarge needed to have an appendectomy. Jong hurriedly got everyone onto the bus and told the driver to take off. As the bus was about to leave, John Lee screamed, "Stop this damn bus! Where be Jilkes and his lady?" Everyone looked around and they were not on the bus. John Lee said, "Open the door. Larry, Chakes, and Mallory come with me."

As the men headed back towards the terminal, John Lee could see Jilkes and his bride waving their hands frantically. John Lee said, "I'm going to buy me a collar for that boy."

When they entered the bus, Jong said, "I'm going to develop an accounting system so that this thing no happen again. We are a lot of people and I can't keep track of each little and big farts."

# # #

At the hospital, Courtney said, "I've registered him under an alias, so he doesn't show up on any data bases. You people should head to the compound and enjoy yourselves. I'll keep you informed about his progress."

Larry said, "Mom, that's not how this is going to go down. These guys are not going to leave you and him here alone." He looked at Mallory and asked, "So, how do you want to play this one?"

"Thanks, Larry. I need Chakes, McArthur, Gladstone and Montomie to hang around here along with you, Larry. Is that a problem?"

Larry asked, "Why would that be a problem?"

"These guys will follow my orders. I didn't know if you had plans for later."

Jilkes said, "Corporal, I don't like this situation. We don't do well when we split up even when we think it's safe. I prefer to make arrangements with the hospital and try to bed-down here tonight. I mean, we don't know how this thing is going to go. It might be able to be done robotically, and that would cut down on his recuperation time. Courtney, what's your opinion?"

"I'm waiting for the doctors to get back to me after they run more tests. However, I don't think it's necessary for all of you to stay here at the hospital."

"Mrs. Beckmire, you're right about that, but I can assure you one thing, we are not splitting our resources and we are not leaving this hospital without the Sarge. What say you?" Jilkes inquired of the group.

There was a loud roar and Jong said, "Let me see what tribe that Asian nurse is from. I might be related to her. You never know."

Ten minutes later, Jong walked back to the reception area and said, "Mr. Amazing has done it again. I told her that we could fund that addition that was dreamed about in a drawing on the wall. She looked at me and made a guttural remark about my ancestors which made me realize that she was from China. I made a similar remark about her ancestors and she realized where I was from. After a lot of how you got here and do you like it here, I asked her what did the different colors on the drawing represent? She told me it was a dream. I told her we never liked to be separated and if she could accommodate all of us today or until our friend is able to travel to our resort then we would make a substantial contribution to that dream. You know Chinese people, when you offer a donation, they want to know how much. I told her that we were the owners of the newest resort on the island and she perked up and asked, would you like food and water to be included? I told her that space was all we needed but would appreciate the convenience of having bottled water nearby."

"Wow, brother, you are Mr. Amazing. So, Mr. Carter, do you think you can cater meals for us and the hospital staff? I don't want to burden them with our needs. I want us to be invisible people. I don't want them to hear or see us. Is that clear?" Mallory asserted.

When the Chinese lady saw Mr. Carter, she walked over to him and asked, "Is that dung, just dung or is he for real?"

"They own the majority portion of my newly constructed resort. You and your husband should come for dinner sometime and, of course, as our guest."

"I judged the book by the cover. I should have at least opened it before I insulted his ancestors."

"I'm sure he insulted yours too, so treat it as a wash."

In another part of the hospital, the Sarge was being evaluated, scanned, poked, and had tubes inserted into his arm. He asked Courtney, "What happened to me?"

"Wajickee told me to take you to the hospital and get that rotten appendix removed. We just landed an hour or so ago and came straight here."

"How did he know I was sick?"

"Listen, dude, do you want me to believe in magic or not? I don't know, but he told me that you would sleep the entire trip and to immediately take you to the hospital, which I did."

As Mallory and Jong selected people to protect the area where the Sarge was, Jong walked over to Mallory and said, "I have seen that man before and I don't think he's a friend."

"Are you sure?"

"I am damn sure. I never forget a face."

Mallory caught the eye of Jilkes who alerted John Lee and pointed to the man sitting in the corner. Mallory placed his hands together as if they were in cuffs. John Lee walked nonchalantly towards the hallway with Jilkes following him. They swooped down upon the guy and subdued him. Jong walked over and asked, "Who are you and what are you doing here? How did you know we were here?"

The guy looking a bit perplexed replied, "I know you people. I removed a bullet from one of you and you bought us a new x-ray machine. Let me up. You people have a ranch in my hometown that's owned by that mysterious woman named Asiram. Am I correct?"

"Who are you and what are you doing here?"

"My wife and I are here on vacation. She apparently neglected to pack her meds and didn't tell me. We got here last night and began to have a wonderful time when she collapsed in my arms on the dance floor. She is diabetic and has high blood pressure. She left her meds at home. We are on our first vacation in fifteen years."

"Why are you here? Did one of you take another bullet?"

"Nothing as sexy as that, but one of us has something wrong with his intestines," Jilkes said.

"Oh, that's my specialty. Who's looking at him?"

"I don't know. That's your specialty?"

"Why with you people must I always repeat myself? I'm not licensed to practice in the islands, so don't go getting any ideas?"

Jong asked, "Can you oversee the procedure?"

"I guess I could, from a teaching perspective, but guys, I have my own issues."

Jong inquired, "Is there a way we can help?"

"I don't think so. They have her stabilized, but don't have the necessary drugs and/or a pipeline here on the island to get her drugs and won't be able to get her medication until tomorrow night."

Jong walked over to Mallory and had a conversation. He returned to the doctor and said, "You oversee the operation on our man, and I will have our pilot pick up the prescriptions for your wife and have it here in less than four hours. I call that, quid pro quo."

"Mister, don't play with me."

"Mister don't play with us. You specialize in what ails our friend? If so, then you look over the shoulders of the operating doctors and we get the drugs here in less than four hours. We have a plane in Miami that is ready to go. Your choice."

The guy jumped up and ran to the front desk, spoke with the Chinese nurse, and told her the situation. She gave him a prescription pad and he wrote down what he needed. She in turn called it in to a pharmacy nearest to the Miami airport and was able to fill the prescriptions. His wife also needed a booster shot that was not available at the pharmacy because of the cost. However, a pharmacy in Fort Lauderdale had a patient, who was in Europe, who had an ample supply of the medicine and a pen was available in the pharmacy refrigerator.

Like clockwork, the wheels of good people were placed in motion and things began to come together. The attending physician in St. Thomas didn't have a clue as to how to treat the Sarge. While the Sarge's system began to poison itself because of the ruptured appendices, Dr. Hopkins walked into the office where the resident physician was and said, "You're about to be threatened by the most interesting bandits that I have ever met. Do not resist, just do as they say and we all will live through this ordeal. Oh, and by the way, the patient's wife is a doctor, as well. Now, I'm not going to tell you how to conduct the operation, I will show you where and when to cut. Make a call to the front desk and have the Chinese nurse assist us. I know you have a good anesthesiologist on duty. By the way, what is your name?"

"I'm Dr. Campbell, Bruce Campbell."

As Dr. Campbell was about to respond about the anesthesiologist, the Chinese nurse entered the room and said,

"I've emailed your wife's prescriptions to pharmacies near the airports. And I found the booster pen in Ft. Lauderdale."

"Nurse Chen, we have another emergency. Please change into your scrubs and scrub down for an emergency surgery." He looked at Courtney and Dr. Hopkins and said, "Let me show you where you can scrub and change."

John Lee looked at him and said, "We be coming to where you have to do all that scrubbing. No offense, but we don't be knowing you all that well."

# # #

One hour and forty-five minutes later, the doctors, a dazed John Lee, and a sick Jilkes exited the operating room, after the successful removal of a rancid and putrid aspect of the Sarge's body. Dr. Hopkins said, "Nurse Chen and Doctors, you guys were phenomenal in there. You help me make the right cuts. You clamped the right arteries. You did everything right and you helped a good human being and his wife. I can only say that I liked what I saw and I'm sure he's going to be fine and be able to get out of here in the next twenty-four hours. Good work people."

When Dr. Hopkins walked out of the operating room, a nurse walked up to him and said, "A private jet left the mainland and will be at our airport in the next hour and fifteen minutes with all of the requisite prescriptions."

Dr. Hopkins walked over to Courtney and said, "Two things, great work in there, and who the hell are you people?"

"Doc, it's a long story. When my husband stabilizes, I will tell you a story about people who help people help themselves and have an affinity for doing what is right in this world, even if they have to eliminate slime on occasion."

John Lee and Jilkes were in a corner talking and Jilkes asked, "Did you see the way they just cut him open? I mean that was some crazy stuff. I'm so glad they are so smart, know the human body and know how to work on it. That was amazing."

John Lee said, "I be needing to tell you something, my woman is having a hard time with this pregnancy thing. It's causing her a lot of discomfort."

"I can't believe you said that. Yeshida is sick almost every morning. I think we need to talk to Courtney about them. Maybe they're not doing something they should be doing."

Courtney remained in the recovery room with Ben Beckmire. Her alone time with her husband was interrupted by the likes of Jilkes and John Lee. Jilkes said, "We know you have a lot on your plate, but he and I are having issues with our women. They're always sick and throwing up. Is there something you can do to help them?"

"Oh, my God. Guys, they're probably switching up on their diets and not digesting all the things that the babies need. Listen, once I get the big guy settled, I will hold court with all the pregnant women and examine them personally. I'm sorry, as you know, there is always a lot going on with this team."

# # #

Later that night, as Zanthius and Asiram attempted to sleep in shifts, his phone rang and Asiram answered it. She said, "Hello—hello—hello? Who is this?"

There was quiet on the other end of the phone, but she could discern that someone was breathing on the other end. She finally hung up the phone. She looked at a sleeping

Zanthius and started to knock the shit out of him because she thought it was one of his old lovers trying to make contact. She relented from that action when she remembered he had recently discarded his last cell phone, like they all had, and had acquired a new number.

Twenty minutes later, the phone rang again. However, this time a whimpering sound could be heard in the background. Asiram could not discern if it were real whimpering or the sound of music in the background. Once again, the phone was disconnected.

# # #

Allen and Mike were taken to the resort instead of the hospital. Captain Carla was being cautioned by an ex-lover to be strong and not to bite the new fruit too early. She looked at her copilot and asked, "Well, how the hell do I look? You keep thinking I'm going off to meet the parents, I am just going to dinner with Mike, the silver tongue rogue who is, oh so, charming."

"Captain, you look fantastic and it would be my pleasure to escort you downstairs to meet your date."

As the two started out of her room, Carla looked at her friend and said, "I was always yours." She kissed him on his mouth and headed for the door. Her copilot pulled her back into his arms and she turned her head away from an awaiting kiss. She said, "We can't have it both ways. I love you, but you moved on, and so must I."

At the base of the steps, Mike was patiently waiting with a single rose behind his back. Darrell the copilot said, "I am placing my Captain and my friend in your hands. Don't make me have a conversation about what happened, with you'."

Mike looked at Carla and said, "You look spectacular and thanks, Sir, she is in good hands; hands that were sanctioned by the spirits in Australia. Give me a time she must be back, and she will be here five minutes early."

Darrell responded, "You're two consenting adults. No timetable, but remember she is scheduled to be on standby tomorrow afternoon for a flight, if, in fact, there is a need."

Carla said, "Thanks, Darrell." She looked at the silver tongue rogue in front of her and said, "So, Mike where are you taking me for dinner?"

"We're going to have dinner on the beach and watch the sun set, and the moon rise. Seriously, I have a lot to say to you. I saw things on the continent that didn't make sense to me until I looked at who was in front of me. I just want you to listen to me in earnest and decide what you want from that point. I'm not trying to seduce you, but I must say, you are one beautiful lady. I just need you to listen to me for a few minutes and then you can challenge me."

Mr. Carter met the duo at the door and told them that he had arranged for a special, magical table by the water. He also gave them suggestions for their meals and indicated that the lobster on the menu was freshly caught within the last two hours. Mike asked him if they could have a few moments together before considering drinks and food and was granted a fifteen-minute window to enjoy the view, sounds and each other.

Carla and Mike looked at the table by the water with a canopy, candles burning, and just enough breeze to keep the biting critters away. As the moon cast its shadow upon the water and the small but steady tide continued its ebb and flow, Carla asked, "Did you put this all together for the awesome ambiance?"

"I could say I did, but Mr. Carter knows how difficult it is to impress a woman and he read my mind. It sincerely looks magical and I hope you're happy with the presentation. I'm not good in this venue, I'm more of the knock it down and let someone else reconstruct it type, if you know what I mean." Mike paused for a moment and then looked at Carla and said, "Let me explain who I am and what I'm trying to accomplish. To say that I don't want to enjoy wonderful pleasures with you would be a total lie. You are an amazing woman with great skills and a body that is incredible and desirous. Yes, I want every inch of you from your toes to your head, but most of all I want your brain and a commitment. I don't know what happened to me in the outback but my dreams were always about birds, planes and a beautiful woman."

"Mike, I'm a little thirsty. Do you think you can order me some water or something?"

"I'm sorry. I just had to say those words to you, and I neglected to check on your needs." He summoned the waiter and asked for two bottles of water. Carla looked at him and asked, "Mike, I would like to order a bottle of champagne? However, it's been a long time since I've been able to have a drink and listen to someone profess so much nonsense, so I might just have to switch to Scotch."

Mike smiled and answered, "You may have whatever you like. I just want you to listen to me."

"So, Mike, I'm a pilot for a group of people that I admire. Not sure what you did to find yourself in their royal company. Let me say this, I don't have time for bullshit. I don't have time for games. You can't seduce me. I don't have a desire to sleep with you."

"You don't understand me. I'm advocating a lifelong commitment to you. I'm afraid to plan that far ahead with you because you seem to doubt everything I say. You think that I just want to bed you and forget you. Something happened to me in the outback. I can't explain it to you, but I ask that you look at me as a serious suitor and someone you can trust. I'm no fraud but I have been involved and surrounded by people of question. I saw you and admired you. I saw you from the rear and I really admired you. I looked into your eyes and realized that your glowing beacon was summoning me. I had some incredible dreams in Australia, and as I decipher them, they were all about you, and me. I can't deny what I saw or how I feel. I know our first interaction may have seemed flippant, but it was because I didn't know how to respond to someone like you."

"What on earth does that mean, someone like me?"

"Listen, you're the captain of a new aircraft, not to mention the fact that you handled that thing on the West Coast superbly with that touch down and shoot for the moon trick you did."

"Oh, you noticed that move?"

"Not only did I notice it, I, was under the impression that it was going to be my last moments on earth. You have a lot of skills. I have a degree in business. You fly a complicated machine, and I worked for a crook. You see where I'm going with this? I thought I was working for a governmental agency and it turned out to be a place that if you're caught, you're on your own and no one knows you. I felt that it was highly unlikely that you would bite into my news feed, so therefore, I gave you the information that first came to my mind— bullshit. I'm beyond that now and I want you to know the only thing that I want from you is understanding and the beginning stages of trust. I can wait on everything else until hell freezes over but those two things are at the epicenter of what's important to me."

"Oh, my, here comes our champagne! Do you always talk so much? In my world, I like to breathe, reflect, and breathe some more. All that matters is not all that is important at that moment. There are things around us that are as important as those things we try to express. Mike, I like you without a bunch of qualifications. I would be a fool to say something stupid like I'm not interested in you physically for that is the first thing as humans we see. I will say that I'm not emotionally tied to you in a way that would lead me to a physical encounter yet, but I will not dismiss it from a list of things that I may want from you later, but I will not act on it until I am confident that this is no passing fancy."

The two toasted the evening, the view, and each other. Carla said, "I will admit, your approach is stunning and refreshing. I even heard you refer to me as your future ex-wife. What is that supposed to mean?"

"That's when I first saw you and reflected upon your looks and not the person. If asked today, I would not have that same response."

"Mike, I think you're a scoundrel, but I believe there is hope to transform you into a wonderful, and perhaps, a useful human being. Let's lighten the subject and enjoy the view and the champagne. I would like to make a toast. Here's to you and me in the same cockpit, as captain and copilot. That's the dream I had while in the outback."

Mike stared at Carla for almost thirty seconds and finally announced, "Did you know that I have my pilot's license for twin engines, but not for jets?"

"Mike, is this more 'BS'? I thought we covered the range and tolerance for that?"

"Carla, I am a licensed pilot who is qualified on twin engine aircraft. And that my wonderful and beautiful lady is no bullshit."

# # #

On another part of the island, Beckmire woke up and asked his lovely wife, "Honey, can you fix me a cup of coffee?"

She looked at him and said, "Darling, oh darling, oh my special love, you are in a hospital recovery room. We performed an operation on you to remove some very nasty and ruptured aspects of your appendix. You're going to be alright, but you're going to have to rest for the next four to six days, my beast of a husband."

"How did this happen and who caused it?"

"Honey, you're still under the influence of some powerful drugs. I just need you to sleep and tell me when you feel pain. Don't try to think or do anything. Just tell me when something hurts, baby."

"Damn I love my wife. I think you are the only person who cares about me."

"Well, Mr. Beckmire. There are two big handsome men standing in the foreground who refused to leave your side, including when you were in the operating room. So, I don't think I would say that if I were you."

"Let them identify themselves."

Jilkes said, "John Lee, this might be a good time to slap his ass like Jong did. As a matter of fact, call Jong and let him come in here and slap the Sarge again."

Courtney said, "Okay guys, there will be no slapping of my husband today or tomorrow or for the next five days. He is in my care and I will shoot the person, or persons, who try to slap him and then I will operate on their asses to try to save them. Pass the word. Ben Beckmire is off limits."

## CHAPTER THIRTY-SIX

Mike and Carla spent the entire night talking on the beach and questioning different propositions, proposals, and attempting to define their notions of relationships. However, they weren't the only people spending an enormous amount of time on the beach.

Approximately 150 yards away from where Mike and Carla were sharing a spectacular morning, two silhouettes lingered on the beach, and made their journey to the resort. From afar, it appeared as if they were lovers. In the midst, of what appeared to be passion that turned into a struggle, a third person appeared. It was Allen. As he comfortably kissed each woman, a fourth person entered in their sanctum. Within seconds, although the kissing continued, the slicing and stabbing began. Mike casually looked down the beach and saw what looked like an assault occurring. He jumped up and instructed Carla to alert Mr. Carter.

By the time he got to where the confrontation had occurred, he found the body of his associate, Allen, cut, sliced, stabbed, and dead. One of the assassins attempted to escape in a tender that had been lingering around the shore.

Carla ran into the lobby and yelled, "Mike needs help on the beach. Someone is being attacked and he needs help."

Mr. Carter hit an alarm button, and spotlights from every aspect of the resort's property lit up and the cabinet that held the weapons stash was unlocked. The resort's security drove their four-wheelers down the beach. What became obvious was there was a body on the beach, and a man attempting to escape but couldn't because the engine to the tender had succumbed to water in the carburetor. One of the security personnel detained the man in the launch who had blood all over him and the other security guard caught up with the three women who were attempting to flee.

Mr. Carter called Mallory and told him about what happened and that those responsible were in custody, and that it did not happen on the resort's property. Mallory asked, "Who was the victim?" When he was told it was Allen, his head fell, and he shed tears. He said, "The Sarge is not going to be pleased about this. Where are the people responsible for this?"

"They are being transported here as we speak," Mr. Carter said.

"Do you have a place where they can be held until I get a couple of people out there to interview them before you call the police. We need to delay any police action by thirty minutes. Do you feel comfortable doing that, Mr. Carter?"

"We can place them in the safe room we built. I sent a van for your guys as soon as I got the call from your captain. It was the little lady that came in screaming that Mike needed assistance on the beach. I can attempt to preserve the scene and the people, but please hurry. I'm trying to protect our name, although it did not happen on our property, it happened to one of our guests."

"I'll have four or five people there as soon as possible."

Mallory, Jilkes, John Lee, Brown, Bernstein, and McArthur entered the van and each man was presented with a box that contained a .308 and two clips. John Lee said, "These here guns definitely be for women, but they be good for this mission as well."

#

Once at the resort, the team was met by Mike, Carla, and Mr. Carter. Jilkes said, "Mallory, I'm not sure what we're walking into, why don't you leave Brown and Bernstein here at the resort to keep a look out."

Mallory looked at the two men and asked, "Do you have an issue with that?"

"It might make sense to leave Mac here as well and take Mike. Mr. Carter is going to have to report the crime and there are going to be lots of questions to deal with," Brown said.

The men got into the mule and drove to where Allen's body lay. When they arrived, everyone noticed the viciousness of the attack. It appeared that passion was the motive based upon the way his face was slashed and stabbed repeatedly. It also appeared that more than one person took part in the attack. He had back wounds from a different kind of knife and some facial wounds were from a serrated blade while other facial wounds appeared to have been inflicted by a razor.

Jilkes looked at Allen's shoes and noticed that they had different heels on them. As he looked closer, he saw that the right heel of the shoe was newly constructed. As he examined it, he discovered how a spy, namely Allen, attempts to stay a spy, by concealing information on a flash disk in the sole of his shoe. Jilkes removed it in a clandestine fashion.

The guards placed a tarp over his body and radioed Mr. Carter to call the police. Mallory and the crew went back to the hotel and asked Mr. Carter where the suspects were being held. He directed them to the room, and Mallory extracted the lone male from the group. He said, "That was our friend. Why did you maliciously slash and stab him? Where did you get that picture of him?"

"Man, who you be? I no be answering your questions. You fucking Yankees think you own the world but not this here island, man. This island belongs to the people and when you hurt one of us, you hurt all of us."

John Lee pulled out his knife and said, "Now, this here be a knife. I be going to ask you a question and if you don't answer it truthfully, I be cutting a finger off. Now, you don't be knowing me or my friends, but we ain't no boy scouts. I will gut you from your dick to your brain and I'm pretty damn good at that. Now, this here be my question? Do you work for Walter or is this some personal shit?"

"Man, who the fuck be Walter? That man out there, on his way to hell, hired my baby sister, raped her repeatedly, and when him finished with her, him gave her to his men to continue the abuse. Him name be Allen. He once was a big shot up there in DC, with fancy cars, and drivers, and monogram shirts. My baby sister was found face down in Haines Point with her throat cut and a $2 bill stuffed in her mouth. Him be the man that did that. He came here and I saw the devil myself at the airport. I asked my other sisters to dress the part to lure that son-of-a-bitch to the beach. We all done killed his ass. We all cut him man, slashed his ass and sent him on his overdue journey to hell man."

John Lee asked, "You be telling me the truth?"

"Man, I don't know you, but I know that devil laying on the beach."

Mallory yelled, "Mr. Carter, did you make that call?"

Mr. Carter was stalling and trying to find a way out of this mess. He said, "I'm in the process of dialing now." Even though he did not make a call.

"Hold off on that call. This here is one for the books and we ain't got a dog in this fight. John Lee, you and Jilkes go and corroborate his story."

"How the hell do I do what that big word says?"

"Big Country, it means cross check and see if we can detect the truth of his story by what the women say," Jilkes said.

"Oh, I knew that," John Lee announced.

# # #

When they entered the room where the women were being held, Jilkes looked at the oldest looking woman and noticed she had a lot of blood on her. He asked, "Are you bleeding?"

"Who be you, man? I have nothing to say. We did what we did and no questions necessary."

"That guy out there said you people tried to rob the Yankee."

"Man don't be doing that television shit on us. We not that dumb," the elderly lady asserted.

"You're not that smart either. You can't kill people and try to rob them," Jilkes stated.

"You're right man. The thing we tried to steal from him was him life, and I think we done did that. Him bleed an awful lot so I'm hoping him bleed to death," the elderly lady confessed.

"Why you do this kind of thing to that man?" Jilkes asked.

"Why you be asking and who you be?"

"I'm part owner of the resort here and I'm trying to figure out how to help you murdering ass women. Stop playing games and answer the damn questions. Why did you kill him?" Jilkes adamantly demanded.

"Him raped and killed my daughter, their sister."

John Lee looked at Jilkes and said, "I be needing to talk to you outside."

The two men huddled with Mallory and decided it was a local matter but one that they wanted to slant. John Lee walked back to the brother and asked, "What be the purpose of the tender out there?"

"I was going to take his ass out to sea and feed him to the fish."

After moments of cogitation, Mallory finally said, "Mr. Carter, we don't want to be a part of any of this. Legally, it did not happen on our property and we can prove that. However, our obligation is to call the police and let them ferret this matter out."

Mr. Carter said, "Mr. Mallory, I know everyone on this island including those women in custody. The older woman is my ex-wife, the girls are my daughters, and that man is my son. I delayed the call purposefully, to give you time to at least ask relevant questions, and I knew you would. Whoever your friend is out there on the beach, he was not a good person. I saw the pictures of how he and his friends violated my child. This is a murder and it should be investigated by the police. I can make the call, but I know in my heart it would be the wrong thing to do."

Mallory looked at him and said, "We can't be complicit in this matter." He looked at his guys and signaled for them to meet him on the terrace. He said, to them, "What a cluster fuck. Any ideas as to how we avoid compromising ourselves in this matter?"

John Lee replied, "I be liking an alternative to that expensive justice system. Just like when that woman killed my favorite pig and hung my woman from my banister, I needed my own justice system. I think them people out there deserve the same right. We be doing this kind of stuff often. How the hell can we be trying to judge them people for killing that scarecrow of a man, Allen? I think that be the same asshole that tried to kill us."

Jilkes said, "I'm with Big Country. I don't know 'sh', and didn't see, 'it'."

Mike was about to say something when he was cut off by Brown who said, "Guys, you know how I feel, and I shouldn't have to express it. How about you my little Jewish friend?"

"We all knew he was bad soup. It didn't happen on our property, but close by, and we know the circumstances. I guess it's like me watching that guy beat the shit out of Yvette. After a moment or so, you don't give a shit about anything except righting the wrong before your eyes."

Mallory looked at McArthur and asked, "What's your take on what we should do?"

"Hell, I'm with the guys and they said it just like I read it. Hands off and assist where we can."

"Mac, what does that mean?"

"Mallory, I'm with the group. You do one of mine like that and I will hunt you all the way to Mars. That could have been any one of our sisters. I suggest we clean them up and let them do their thing, but we take pictures for our archive in case one of them can't sleep at night. We need to put the fear of God in them. John Lee, I think we should take the tip of the brother's finger off to remind them to be quiet about this event," MacArthur announced.

"You know I follow orders, but I be saying, this one don't feel good to me. I be wanting to let them clean up their own shit and we ain't got a lot of time to consider this because the sun is going to hit the front in less than an hour," John Lee reminded them.

Jilkes said, "Okay, all of us don't need to be in the middle of this shit. Leave me with my fruity friend, and he and I, will be the only people who interact with them. The way we're heading, we are going to involve almost half of our team in this mess and that ain't good. Mallory, if you agree, then I suggest that you and the rest of the guys, head out and provide protection for our leader. I don't like none of this shit, but think about it, half of us are out here and the other half is in town. I don't like this because we don't do well when we are split up."

"Brown and Bernstein give Jilkes and John Lee your weapons and your clips," Mallory stated.

# # #

John Lee and Jilkes went into the room where the brother was being held and John Lee said, "This is going to hurt." He sliced the tip of the man's baby finger off. The man yelled and Jilkes said, "You need to shut the hell up and listen." The man was about to say something when Jilkes slapped him almost unconscious. He said, "We're going to take pictures of everyone here. If you ever try to involve us in this mess, then we will send photos and blood samples of you and your family to the police. Here's the deal, we don't leave things undone. My boss wanted us to conclude the situation and have all of you floating in the sea. You, my friend, lost the tip of your finger. If we can't reach an agreement that all of you will keep quiet, then I will go in that other room and hack your family to death. And then I will assist you in blowing your fucking head off! Are we clear so far?"

He attempted to answer when Jilkes placed a hand over his mouth and said, "This is not our fish fry. That guy was an associate and a person who provided us with lifesaving information. If our leader feels differently about this situation when he is apprised of it, then we will seek you out and conclude your lives. However, in the interim, I suggest that you have your family clean up. You need to fix that tender and take his body out to sea. There is a lot of blood on the beach. Have the ladies get some chickens or something, light a fire, and act as if they're practicing voodoo or some shit. If you people don't sell it, then we will have to go to work on you, and that would be a shame, because we all feel sorry for what happened to your sibling. You screw this up and, we lay the a-bomb on you and your family. It will not be personal; it will just be the kind of business that we are paid millions of dollars to take care of. Are we clear?"

"Man, who be you?"

"Man, that's the wrong fucking question. You my friend have forty-five minutes or so to get that piece of tender of yours working, get the body off the beach, and get his personal belongings such as cell phone, rings, wallets, and other identifiers back to me. We are not going to wait at the property edge for you to figure shit out. You need to give me everything that is on him within the next fifteen minutes. Load him into your tender, meet us at the property threshold, give us all that is his, and take a long boat ride. I suggest that you take something to weigh him down. Take those bags over there to wrap your fingertip in. Don't leave any DNA on him!"

# # #

One hour later, a small fire was burning where the body was removed and the heads of four chickens were placed around the fire to cover the four corners. The locals knew not to disturb the ritual and beckoned foreigners to stay away from the ritual site.

John Lee and Jilkes extracted something personal from each person involved in the murder of Allen. Jilkes said, "I think we have enough incriminating evidence as well as their confessions, to convince anyone they are responsible for the murder and we did not participate in this activity. I'm going to leave all that we have with Mr. Carter and let him deal with any fallout. We were never here and if you try to involve us; well, that's another toothache that you don't want to experience. We are feeling generous and hope that you people do the right thing. Clean up your act and never discuss this with anyone, including yourselves."

As the men were preparing to leave, Mr. Carter said, "I just don't know what to say about you people. You do the unexpected, help those who make bad decisions make it right, both personally and financially and yet, never pass judgement. I thank you for all of us. The people in there don't know how to thank you because they think it's a ploy. I know better. I thought the notion of us doing business together with the resort was a ruse until we entered that bank and I almost had a heart attack. I don't know who you people are, but I thank God for your presence and benevolence on this tiny island."

# # #

Jilkes and John Lee met up with Mallory and the others and headed back to the hospital where they were camped out. Mallory asked, "So, what was your resolution?"

"We took evidence of blood and hair samples from their anatomies, pictures, and verbal confessions and turned them over to Mr. Carter. I told him we expected him to handle any fallout from this."

Jilkes felt his pocket and said, "I also took this little baby from the sole of Allen's shoe. Sorry, Big Country, didn't have time to tell you because the guard was about to discover what I did," Jilkes stated.

"Did you get a chance to review it?"

"Really, John Lee? I've been with your dumb white ass since we left the hospital. Anyway, I saw the difference in the shoe heels and thought I was James Bond for a moment. Moreover, my fingerprints are not on the sole of his shoe if that is what you are thinking. I used a rubber glove. We can come back to this, is there any update of the Sarge's condition?" Jilkes asked.

"We just got here. Monica said Courtney wants her man to sleep without any interruptions. Let's get Jong to open this thing up and see what's on it," Mallory said.

After being summoned, Jong appeared with his laptop and headsets on his ears singing in a loud and obtrusive manner. John Lee stopped him in his tracks and asked, "What kind of mind fucking music you be listening to? We be in a hospital, moron!"

"I'm just trying to stay relevant for my woman, my friend. We dig a different kind of scene."

Jilkes inquired, "Are you doing drugs or something?"

"Come on now. You people know I don't be doing no damn drugs. I'm simply happy with life and my new lady who has missed two months of her cycle."

"Damn, seems like we got some baby making people amongst us. Take a look at this drive and let me know what you think. Not sure you know, but Allen was murdered near our resort," Jilkes announced.

"Are you shitting me? Who iced him?" Jong inquired.

"A bunch of locals, who are all related to Mr. Carter. It appears Allen had a strong hand in the abuse and demise of a family member, was recognized by a sibling, and the pieces were put in place to terminate him."

"Who knew he was here?" Jong asked.

"He apparently was spotted at the airport by an immediate family member, who confirmed his presence. If in fact what they say he did to their family member is true, then may the fish feed upon his putrid body."

Mallory said, "I'm not sure of our exposure and until the Sarge is coherent, I'm going to need everyone on full alert and this ain't no drill, people."

## CHAPTER THIRTY-SEVEN

The Asian nurse aroused the group at 0700 hours and said, "Mr. Beckmire is awake, resting, and hungry. I told him that all of you people were here in the hospital and he asked me, 'why didn't I send you home'. I told him that Mr. Jong is persuasive and promised a sizeable contribution to the 'dream wing of the hospital', if we accommodated him. He wants to speak to a Mr. Mallory and to that person with the platinum tongue, Mr. Jong. I will allow you people five minutes with him and no more. Do not discuss subjects that will cause stress or continuous worry. Do not excite Mr. Beckmire. Am I perfectly clear? And Mr. Jong, you are like your ancestors, unless you keep your word about the 'dream wing'."

"What might my ancestors be if I don't keep my word?"

"They be serpents and snakes, slime and bowel products, dogs and cats mixed and forever out of harmony."

"That represents a family from hell. Take it back, you witch, or I will summon your mother who was bred from the dung of a cow, and the urine of a horse, and the pollen from a bee. All of Asia knows what that produces."

"A thousand apologies, Mr. Jong. I did not know that you stayed in touch with the other side of the world. I rescind my comments and I know that you are, and they are, people of their word. A thousand apologies."

As Mallory and Jong entered the Sarge's room, Courtney said, "Keep it short, sweet and to the point. You got two minutes."

Mallory, knowing how precise she can be when it comes to her man said, "Sarge, last night, Allen was murdered by locals who are related to Mr. Carter, who were seeking vengeance for the death of a sibling. He was sadistically slain. Mr. Carter's younger daughter worked for Allen in DC. They alleged that he raped her and then allowed his men to use her as well, before they murdered her. She was found on Haines Point with a $2 bill stuffed in her mouth. The locals knew it was him and they slashed, stabbed and cut him into hell."

"I knew someone was going to die. I am glad it was he they killed, as opposed to one of us. These next few weeks are going to cause a tremendous strain in our relationships, and our sanctity is going to be challenged. We are going to need divine intervention because a mountain of issues are going to beset us. All who are pregnant will not deliver in the natural order of that event. Some of us who are friends will challenge that relationship by mortal combat. I have seen things and events and I worry about our resolve as a group. So many have joined us that we know little about, except that people have shared both carnal and emotional attractions since the inception."

"Sarge, what the hell are you talking about?"

"My dreams have been about the unnatural and I have tried to piece them together in relationship with this current group. I have seen John Lee pull his knife on Jilkes. I have seen Brown point a weapon at Bernstein; I have seen you, Jong, slap Monica; I have seen you Mallory seducing Mary Alice, and Ava stabbing me to death. There is something out of balance and we must figure it out. Perhaps the demise of Allen will give me clarity in the next few days, but I need everyone to be on guard against stupidity. For some odd reason, I keep remembering a quote by Sam Elliot, the actor, who said, 'when you're dead, you don't know you're dead and all of the pain is felt by others. The same thing happens when you're Stupid!"

Mallory looked at Jong and then at the Sarge and said, "He's fine and our time is up. Let's go and enjoy a Bloody Mary. I need one after last night."

As the two men were about to leave the room, Beckmire said, "Watch for signs of discontent and immediately intervene. Until a ceremony is conducted, and I don't know for what, we are going to witness events and character changes that will test our faith in each other."

Mallory looked at the Sarge and said, "We have already tested our character and faith. Get behind who we are or disband this group before we begin to fight and kill each other."

The Sarge said, "This is what we must do or face self-destruction. I will not wait until I slap his wife, or John Lee pulls his knife on Jilkes, or Bernstein or Brown pull guns. This must end in reality and not in folk lore. These are my dreams and I must check them and their source by demonstrating your concerted belief in each of us."

A few moments later, the Sarge sat up in his bed and asked, "What are you people doing in my bedroom?"

"Ah, in case you haven't noticed, you're in a hospital."

"Who gives a shit? Is this still my room?"

Mallory looked at Jong and said, "I guess the dog is back. Shall we leave?"

The Sarge looked at the two men and asked, "Did Allen have any information of value on him before his demise?"

"Allen had a thumb-drive and I haven't had time to check it out. Mallory tell him the story of the family," Jong said.

"Sarge, it is alleged Allen hired a young lady, raped her, and then turned her over to his henchmen who killed her with drugs. She was found with a $2-dollar bill stuffed in her mouth. Her brother, who apparently works at the airport, saw him disembark from our plane and when he was certain it was him; he engaged his mother and sisters to seduce him, knowing his propensity towards women of color. He was slashed, stabbed, mutilated, and bled to death on a beach near the resort. After hearing the story, we collectively made the decision to allow the family to clean up their mess, with the proviso that we have evidence and took pictures of the entire event for future use if, in fact, we are ever pulled into their scheme. Sarge, he violated that little girl and then his men dumped her body across the river from the airport in DC. Sarge, what I must tell you, once again, is that they are all a part of Mr. Carter's family. The deceased, was his youngest daughter."

"Are we sure it was Allen?"

"The brother had a picture of Allen and it was no mistaking that it was him. I think we're covered on this one and the brother, as we speak, is out in the middle of the water dumping his body with weights on it for the fish to feed upon him."

"Did we search his body for any additional information?"

"Sarge, we were lucky to notice the sole of his shoes and realize that he had a false heel. It was a bloody mess, I mean he was stabbed by the brother, slashed with a razor by the mother and cut deeply by the sisters. They butterflied his ass, in other words."

The Sarge called for Jong.

"No, Sarge, you need your rest," Courtney said.

"Honey, if there was ever a time, I needed you to be invisible, it's now. I need to know if we are in danger and the information Jong has could assist me in determining that. I promise you, ten minutes, and lights are out. Please, honey, I might be hurt but I'm still responsible for a lot of lives, including yours, my love."

Jong inserted the thumb drive into his computer but wasn't able to access the files because he needed for a password. He said to the Sarge, "I need a password and it's going to take some time to figure this one out. Why don't I come back when I've cracked it?"

"No need to go away. Just type in Walterasshole.1."

Jong typed in 'Walterasshole.1.' and was amazed that the system allowed him to access it. He yelled, "No way. Did you guess that or did Allen give you his password?"

"In passing one day he murmured 'Walterasshole.1.', and it kind of stuck with me. I had no prior information it just came to me that I heard him say that phrase under his breath one day. I guess I'm lucky to listen to the small things in life."

As the men scanned the title of the files, one caught the Sarge's eye. He asked, "Why would the devil have a file called 'Hail Mary'? Open that one and let's see what it includes."

The file contained a payment ledger and amounts paid to senators, congressmen, their aides, and family members. Of particular note, Allen made payments directly to the senator who failed to become the president. A cursory view of her name indicated in the past two years, payments in excess of $8 million dollars were made to her.

Jong asked, "How could he make these payments for your cousin, and yet be the target of his wrath? I think this thumb drive is more likely the reason he wanted him dead than anything to do with us. I mean, look at the names on here, they are all high-ranking members of our government. What a nasty shame."

"Jong, pack your things and go play with your woman. My man needs his rest. Take Mallory and the rest of the people with you. Good day, gentlemen."

The pack had barely left the room when the Sarge entered a deep sleep and continued his dream state. Notions of intergroup discourse seemed to subside, and his visions were of peace, tranquility and lots of babies being born. Courtney looked out of the hospital window and thought what a great life she and her comrades shared, compared to the poverty just miles away from the hospital. She knew the picture on the wall of the wing they wanted to build would be the first of many projects the group would undertake on the island, and most of it would be funded by the revenue from both resorts and the various other investments the group had made on the island.

## CHAPTER THIRTY-EIGHT

Exactly four days later, Ben Beckmire was frolicking in the water with his slimmed down and extremely beautiful wife. Courtney dropped a significant amount of weight simply sitting by his bedside and worrying about her man. The Sarge pretty much waded in the water and let the natural healing power of the saltwater help cure his body.

Benjamin Beckmire De Lombardo was extremely attached to his mother's breasts for obvious reasons. Zanthius was a new and doting father. He was handing out cigars and receiving accolades from members of the group and made his mother one happy lady. Ava De Lombardo who was soon to be married to Carlos and was a happy grandmother. She and Asiram became close and discussed the difficulties of being a good mother and not smothering the child, like she once did with Zanthius, in terms of socialization. She said to Asiram, "If there is one thing I have learned during this adventure, is you never know who is going to help you, and from what strata in life they may come from. This is the greatest group; no, I don't mean that. This is the greatest family I have ever had the privilege of being associated with. Everything is about the person next to you or across the table from you and little is about the individual unless it is about his or her contribution to the family. This is simply amazing. No hierarchy, just people knowing there is no wrong decision when it comes to protecting each other."

Asiram looked at Ava and said, "I have never heard you talk about you and rarely do you confide in me about Zanthius. Perhaps this is a good opportunity for us to speak freely and honestly about what we expect from each other in relationship to the baby. I mean one day I would like to come to Valencia for months at a time and have you come to wherever we are living for an equal amount of time. I used to think that you and Courtney, didn't think I was sophisticated enough to be with Zanthius. I responded to those thoughts by swearing and doing things that were not lady like."

"Don't you think we knew what you were doing? Are you nuts? Do you think Courtney and I reached this moderate age by being blind and stupid?"

"I'm glad we're having this talk because it's important to me that you have a strong relationship with your grandson from the beginning. You know I hated your son for doing this terrible thing to my body, but I have to confess, I want to have some more little beings."

"Girl you are talking up my alley now. If I may be so bold, I would like to see you have at least one more. If the second one is not a little flower, then I would like for you to have another. If that one is not a flower, then I would like to say a special prayer and make your fourth and last one a girl. Now, ain't that some crazy shit. I'm literally having a conversation with you about the number of children you should have. I would love to see a female come out of your essence. I think secretly, you probably wanted a princess yourself. Come on now, tell the truth."

"Frankly, Ava, I didn't care what it was, I just wanted it out and over." The two women laughed and hugged. Asiram said, "You're right, I did want a little girl."

# # #

Ben Beckmire was sitting on the beach soaking up the rays when he saw Mr. Carter. He called out to him and confided, "I guess we had a turn of bad luck a few nights ago, didn't we? From what I was told, he did some pretty despicable things to a family member of yours. Mr. Carter, do you think it warranted death?"

"Mr. Beckmire, I was not the judge in that case, but I reverse the question and ask you, if it was one of your family members, what would your response be?"

"Good point, Sir. What concerns me is the mechanics of the event and where it happened in relationship to our property and to, unofficially, one of our guests. We can't stay in business and achieve the kind of successes we are mounting if this kind of thing happens near us again. You know, if we add that a pregnant woman was dragged off the beach, you have a recipe for a disaster; financially. Listen, I'm not really concerned about the monetary aspect of those two events, I'm concerned that it could happen to my wife or my daughter or my grandbabies. You see where I'm going with this. Although the deeds are horrific, I need you, Mr. Jong, along with Mr. Mallory and his wife to devise a new security plan. I do not want to close off the property and enclose it with a gate. However, if it will save lives and keep our people safe, then I'm willing to do this."

"Mr. Beckmire, you can't close off a beach and put a fence up where your property begins and ends. That just ain't natural. I mean I know you people think that you can do whatever the hell you want, but there are limits, even for you people."

The Sarge looked at Mr. Carter with a scowl on his face and said, "Perhaps I disrespected you with my previous comments, but I personally would never slap the hand that pulled my ass out of the fire from a bunch of thieving bankers, and then gave ownership rights to this property, an annual salary, a new vehicle, erased all debt and ensured a job for life. Seems to me if I'm sounding a little arrogant, you should be able to tell me my shortcomings in a more professional manner than to accuse me and my people of being something we don't see ourselves as, modern day Robin Hoods? Yes, and without unreal expectations."

"Mr. Beckmire, I should be slapped and fired. That didn't come out how I intended, but maybe how I meant it. I don't do well expressing myself sometimes, but I said what I wanted to say, but in the wrong manner."

"Chris, first of all, let's dispense with the 'Mr.' shit. I don't want puppets and my people don't do well being pulled by strings. We have a leadership group, but each man has the ability to obligate us and to engage us in all kinds of deeds. We are not your usual Robin Hoods, but we are respectful and dedicated to helping people help themselves. This business relationship has worked out well and I thought it was to your advantage as well as ours. Am I correct?"

"Mr. Beckmire, sorry, Ben, I have the best damn deal on the entire island. I own a portion of this property, I get paid a salary regardless of occupancy, I get a portion of the sales, I get bonuses, and everything else. However, I'm having some health issues and I can't afford to get the treatment that I need."

"So, Chris, you get pissed at me? Why didn't you come to me and say, 'dude, I have some health issues and I need $X'?"

"Ben, we made a deal and it is the best deal that I could have made. My problem is I need to visit the Mayo Clinic in Minnesota, and I'll need to be there for a couple of weeks. I don't have a backup system in place for the operation of the resort."

"Oh my, I see what you mean. Chris, we are partners and you are a part of our family. Let me summon Mallory and Monica and see how we handle this thing. It will not be a problem and, as a matter of fact, you can use one of our planes to get you there and bring you back home. Look, there's Jong on the beach with his lady, can you ask him to excuse himself for a minute and speak with me about an emergency?"

# # #

When Jong arrived, the Sarge said, "I need Mallory and Monica, we have a critical situation that we must attend to immediately."

When all the requested members arrived where the Sarge was sitting, he said, "Guys and gal, we have an emergency. I had a conversation with Chris and found out that he has a medical situation that must be attended to in Minnesota. The problem is, he will be gone for two weeks, if not more, and there is no back up management to run the resort, unless we placed the responsibility on Mr. Carter's neighbor and another one of our partners."

Mr. Carter said, "I don't be liking that at all. My neighbor is lazy but was a victim like me. Listen, we're coming into high season and every room has been paid for in advance including the overflow that we send to his place down the beach. However, I must say that some of his upgrades supersede ours."

"Okay, Chris, I'm trying to figure out how to cover the place," Ben Beckmire said.

"Ben, after looking at my calendar and that of my husband, I don't see any pressing issues that are going to require me or him to travel to the states in the next few weeks or even the next month. Do you have something to do in the states that can't wait another month or so? Can't we deal with everyone we need to from here? We can triangulate phone calls. Can't we all heal, including you my master, and enjoy the saltwater?" Monica inquired.

"Monica, you make a compelling argument and one that I think needs to be decided by the group and since it's your suggestion, counselor, can you make the arrangements for tonight to discuss the matter?"

"Excellent idea my wonderful leader. Your wish is my command."

As the group disbanded, Chris asked, "You did hear me when I said every room was paid for in advance?"

"I'm going to need you at the meeting whenever she sets up the dinner. I have two other questions, for you. Can you get the mother, brother and the sisters who were involved in the Allen issue to meet with me prior to dinner? My second request is, can you get a vehicle and take me and two of my guys up the road to those adjoining properties? I would like to have a conversation with the owners. Where we are on the island reminds me of a cul-de-sac in a high-end neighborhood. The only difference is here when you drive in, the first two properties are 'dives' and then the neighborhood improves dramatically. Chris, do you know if they were a part of that crooked bank's plan to expand their presence? I mean, why wouldn't you focus on the two properties that complete the cul-de-sac and not the ones you see when you first come into it? Do you know those people?"

"I do, but I don't get your cul-de-sac question."

"From the air, it is obvious where we are situated. I noticed how the property is shaped and how there is a natural divide that ends with a huge rock formation."

Chris said, "I guess I just tried to hold on to my property and the fool next door did the same thing. If I'm not mistaken, those two have to have full payment made by Friday or they're going to be evicted."

"This Friday?" Ben asked.

"I'm almost sure, because one of them is being divorced and the wife is spreading rumors around town that she is going to get paid really big in a matter of days."

"I'm going to go up and take a shower and will meet you in the lobby in twenty minutes. Don't be late," Beckmire indicated.

# # #

As the group assembled in the lobby, Mallory walked over to the Sarge and said, "This is highly unlike you to commit to a meeting without input?"

"Man, we be in the islands."

"Tell that to Allen."

The Sarge looked at Mallory and asked, "Can you get me a second van with Chakes, Montomie, Brown, Bernstein, and McArthur riding in it?"

"Give me ten minutes to check on the status of each man. I will give you the okay sign at that point."

Fifteen minutes later, Jong walked up to the Sarge and Chris and said, "We're all outside waiting on you two to complete your séance. We're ready when you people are."

As the group drove up the scenic coastline road, Jilkes said to John Lee, "I think that I could open a business down here and run it as a sole proprietorship."

John Lee asked, "What that word be meaning?"

"Ah, it was intended to mean that I could see myself and my business partner opening a place down here and operating it, just the two of us."

"Who that be your business partner?"

"Don't make me kick your country ass. Who else has been closely by my side in life and death situations? Don't make me put the hammer on your head again."

The group pulled into the parking lot of the first property in the cul-de-sac and exited the vehicles. Mr. Carter walked through the doors first and as he approached the bar, the owner slammed a sawed-off shotgun on the bar that went off. The group took defensive positions in the rear, sides, and front of the place. The owner yelled, "That was an accident! This is a friendly bar and restaurant. That was an accident!"

Chakes and Montomie hit the back door while Jilkes and John Lee entered the front of the bar and took up separate defensive positions. Mr. Carter said to Jilkes, "He reloaded his weapon and is prepared to do battle. Mr. Beckmire, can you please step forward and show him this is not a hostile encounter?"

Ben Beckmire walked slowly into the bar and Jilkes said to the owner, "If you move a fucking muscle, I will blow your head off."

The Sarge motioned for him to stand-down. He walked to the bar with his hands held high and said, "I would really like a Bloody Mary with olives and celery. Will that request get me shot or can I put my hands down?"

"That blast was an accident that scared us more than it scared you guys. Let me say a few things to move this discussion forward or backwards. We were prepared to kill you people on sight," the owner said.

The Sarge said, "Wow, and we came here to discuss a business proposition that would benefit us all. Truly, that shotgun blast scared the shit out of me. I really need that drink."

As the tension reduced and the notion of a potential relationship increased, the owner said, "My friend, who owns that other property, is in my kitchen with a shotgun. Let me go and fetch him."

The Sarge said, "He has already been fetched by my men. Can you guys leave the damn weapons alone, and can we talk about a situation we want to present to you that will save your family farms and lives? Why were you people ready to shoot us? Did we do something along the way to offend you? Did someone tell you a story that's not true?"

"We heard from the bank that you people are drug dealers and are attempting to increase your domain here on the island. We know that you paid off the loans for those two properties and that you placed guns to our neighbors heads to complete the arrangement."

Jong said, "That statement holds no notion of the truth. We do not need this headache. We have other issues that concern us. You listen to the bank that owns your ass and is probably foreclosing on you as we speak. You no have customers and you don't have quality food to eat as I look at that kitchen. This is a low class joint."

# # #

Twenty-five-minutes later, everyone came out of the unsanitary place with smiles on their faces. A new relationship and building plan had been briefly discussed and a new local leader had been agreed upon—Chris Carter.

Essentially, each place would be demolished, and a new building would be built in its place and they would have a similar relationship as Mr. Carter. Each owner realized they were about to lose their property to the bank and considered this new opportunity to own their properties outright, a tremendous gain for them.

# # #

The owners of the properties that were facing foreclosure, arrived in town and at the bank with, Mallory, Monica, Jong, and Mr. Carter. The bank manager turned his head to see who was coming in and when he saw who it was, he shook his head violently. Jong walked to a service representative and said, "We want to settle the loans that these two gentlemen, Mr. Wilson and Mr. Smith, have with this bank. We feel, and they feel, that your services are not in their best interest since you are more interested in of taking their properties. Please printout the outstanding balances for both properties including all fees. I also need you to tell your manager that our lawyers are going to file a suit against him and this bank for slander, in the amount of $75 million dollars. This will happen within the next few days and will be filed against your national bank in New York. We are sure they're not going to want to hear that they are in the middle of another investigation. I hope you have an alternative career."

CHAPTER THIRTY-NINE

At Mr. Carter's resort, the new partners met with the team and hashed out the details. Monica told them they were days away from forfeiting their properties to the bank. She told the owners, "I, as well as the group, are offended you would spread offensive information about us being drug-dealers. That is so far from the truth and almost caused us to walk away from this deal. Now, our group paid off your loans and we are willing to invest in your businesses, but at a cost. We will demolish the current buildings and put in place three crews from the island to work around the clock to rebuild your structures once you meet with the architect and agree upon what we're proposing. What we propose may not meet with your expectations. Just be prepared to offer an alternative.

"We will move roughly $3 million into the local bank and Mr. Carter will be our signatory, as he currently is. However, some of us ladies love to decorate and will make the intermediate appointments of the rooms and the facilities. Please offer them your support. It would make all of your lives stress free. Again, please try to keep us all happy. As you can imagine, we are extremely important to this relationship.

"We need you to think large and about huge profits. I will craft the deal for your review and approval. It will not be written in legalese, but straight forward English. You will become an employee of ours with a guaranteed salary, benefits, part-ownership status, a retirement package, new vehicles that will hopefully shuttle the rich and famous in and out of your palatial resorts, and you will maintain enough ownership in our joint property so that you are able to buy us out at any moment, for a fair price. There is only one thing I must say to you, Mr. Mallory, is my husband, and if there is any suspicion of a hustle, he will personally place a bullet in your fucking head. Are there any questions? Oh, and by the way, you're expected at dinner at 7 p.m. at Mr. Carter's place."

# # #

When Jong got back to his room, Mary Alice was sitting in a corner crying her eyes out. He threw himself down on the floor and said, "I beg you to forgive me for whatever I have done that offends you. My love supersedes any expressions from my land and I just want to make your journey, a happy one."

"I am happy. I am crying because I think I'm pregnant."

Jong stood up, and suddenly hit the floor, headfirst. Mary Alice went out on their balcony and yelled for help. McArthur and Chakes got there first with Gladstone, Montomie, and Whitmore following at a close second. As the men entered the room, Mary Alice said, "I told him I think I'm pregnant and he stood up and then hit the floor, headfirst."

Whitmore said, "I think I probably would have the same reaction. He'll be alright except for that bump on his forehead. Congratulations." He proceeded to hug Mary Alice, as did the rest of the group.

A blurry Jong woke up and asked, "Which one of you pirates hit me?"

Whitmore grabbed him and said, "I didn't know you still had it in you?"

Jong responded, "Had what in me?"

"The ability to impregnate a woman."

Jong started to say something and fell headfirst onto the floor again.

Whitmore summoned Courtney and explained the situation to her. After she arrived, she examined him, and said, "I guess he didn't know he had it in him."

"That's the same damn thing I said!" Whitmore exclaimed.

#

Much later during the cocktail hour, the Sarge looked around the room and was astonished by the number of pregnant women in the room. He gently grabbed Courtney by the arm and asked, "Honey, will you walk with me for just a few moments?"

When Ben Beckmire and Courtney reached the threshold of the door that leads to the beach, he said, "Courtney, everybody in that damn room is pregnant. Is that correct, or am I hallucinating?"

"Ben Beckmire, you are not hallucinating. I took stock the other day and realized that all the women are big and eating a lot of food out of their culture. Those Asian girls are eating fried chicken and collards and black eye peas, mixed. Listen, Samora, Yeshida, Okema and Mary Alice are pregnant, I think. I also think that Bernstein laid a seed. Not sure, but damn near."

"I have to address the group at dinner. Should I make mention of that fact?"

"Honey, this is when you ask your wife to make a few comments and act as if you have no clue whatsoever. The funny thing is when we were in Australia, I dreamt that all the women were having children, including me. You know, that was a nightmare, because I am, and you are, too damn old to be making babies. I should rephrase that and say, you are too old. I might set a new record but if you fathered a child it would truly be a miracle."

"Whatever. I'm not interested in being a new father at this age."

Courtney looked at him and walked back into the dining area. The Sarge walked in, with a sense of guilt and a stupid look on his face. In front of the entire group and away from prying ears, he looked at Courtney, dropped to his knees and began to whisper, "That was so insensitive of me. I beg you to forgive me and allow me to make it up to you."

"I don't need diamonds or gold. How are you going to make it up to me?" Courtney inquired.

"In any way you desire," Ben Beckmire acknowledged.

Courtney looked around the room at the people looking at them and said, "I suggest you stop minimizing me and allow me and the other women to enjoy our dreams; whatever they may be!"

"Honey, you're in your--sorry, whatever." Ben Beckmire looked at the inquisitive group and murmured, "You surely don't want to become a new mother!"

"Ben Beckmire, once again, you keep trying to tell me what I want to do. I say to you, you shouldn't have taken some of the women to the outback. I have seen a glow and a wisdom that you men have ignored." She leaned over and whispered in his ear, "Even Monica is out of sorts. Don't you dare mention that to Mallory."

Beckmire said, "I'm done with this conversation. I will not say any more about this. Perhaps this is all a dream. You try to figure it out and I will as well."

After rising from his knees, the Sarge said, "Sometimes I say the most obtuse things to my wonderful bride. That exhibition in the corner was a testament of my love for my wife and also, my lack of concern about what people think, and I don't care if anyone is wondering if I am weak because I was on my knees, pleading with my wife!"

#

After a cathartic moment and plea for forgiveness, the Sarge said, "I would like to acknowledge our two new partners. Even though they almost shot us earlier today, they realized that they were in a bad way with that bank that gives good banks, a bad name. For those of you who don't know, we have partnered with two individuals who were about to forfeit their properties to that same thieving and conniving bank that had a controlling interest in Mr. Carter's place. My crew knows what we do and how we do it. For you newcomers, we try to help people help themselves and sometimes we throw away a shit load of money trying to do that. Mr. Carter, are you making money since the resort has been rebuilt and reappointed?"

Mr. Carter looked around the room and said, "We're booked two years out from now and everyone has prepaid to be here."

Beckmire looked at the two new partners and said, "I don't know what you signed on to, but I will let our lawyer, Monica, explain what we are about."

Monica approached where Beckmire was standing in a very meek fashion and said, "Our two new partners were about to kill anyone who walked into their establishments that they didn't know. They took aim at our people. Yes, those guys had guns on our men folk. However, they had the wrong people in their sights. Our people were there to offer them an opportunity. You know sometimes wisdom supersedes all other things. We, without the demise of any of our comrades, were able to convince them to lower their weapons and engage in a conversation beneficial to everyone. We are located in a cul-de-sac in the midst of two poorly operated and dilapidated establishments. You two guys will own your properties, but we will have the majority stake in that proposition."

Monica paused before continuing, "As you know, we help people help themselves, we don't rob people of their possessions and, as a matter of fact, we came here for a vacation and found out that you guys were in the process of being screwed in a very precarious orifice without the application of Vaseline. We are not the enemy. Our leaders are compassionate and we attempt to facilitate the local needs.

"The problem is that sometimes that causes ill-will. Let me speak for our organization and say very clearly; you try to screw us, and we will bring the snow upon you, even beyond our graves. We provide each person that we do business with an insurance policy, to protect our interest. Your notes have been paid off, you have the titles, and you will have said titles amended to include our foundation as part owners, with the appropriate and agreed upon percentages. This is a good deal for you and one that we don't really need. We didn't need to do a deal with Mr. Carter, but it would have been a shame to watch him get rear ended without recourse. Welcome to our family. I will let you know when we have the architect on board and when everything can start to happen. Just be mindful, we will probably use three shifts so things are going to move in a hurry. Don't worry, have a talk with Mr. Carter and he will tell you how we work."

# # #

Jong walked over to the Sarge and asked, "Can we take a walk along the beach? I promise not to assassinate you. If you like, please ask Jilkes, Mallory, and John Lee to accompany us."

"This must be a high-level discussion we're about to have. What's the nature of it and why do you carry that computer everywhere?"

"We have internet connections at our luxury resort and, therefore, I never know when my fearless leader is going to ask me for some crazy ass information. Better to be prepared, is what I say."

As the men began to assemble and walk down the beach, the Sarge said, "I feel like one of those characters in the Godfather who is about to get whacked. If someone wants to take over this outfit, I will quietly go into hiding and never seek revenge."

John Lee looked at the Sarge and said, "Why you be saying shit like that? I will kill anyone who thinks like that."

"Whoa, John Lee. I'm just kidding."

"Well, ain't no need to be kidding about one of us trying to whack you. We be loving you and Ms. Courtney."

"Okay, I see he ain't going to leave this alone so let's move on," the Sarge said.

"This is as good a place as any to discuss this matter," Jong said. "Guys, I went through most of the files on that flash drive that Allen had in his shoe. Sarge, there is some disturbing news on it relative to your son. As you know, Allen and Helga were lovers, and Zanthius played in the flower bed as well. Apparently, her death was staged because there are transmissions from her after her alleged death, unless she is writing from the other world."

"Jong, I don't need to know who was screwing whom. What is it that involves Zanthius?"

Jong replied, "Sarge, I'm not sure about any of this. I'm trying to analyze what's on the flash drive. At some point, during his communications with Helga, Allen alludes to the fact that she was the best lover he ever had and he wanted to renew their relationship. Helga indicated that she didn't trust him or his two pet dogs. I'm thinking she was talking about Ariel and that Shari woman, at which point Allen states, 'How about your new young lover, my new hire? I have heard from a variety of sources that you screwed him in Switzerland. Now, I know you don't want to hear about all this screwing mess, but she goes on to say, 'What a big ass mistake, I sure hope I bleed soon.''

"Jong, what the hell are you talking about?" the Sarge asked.

Jilkes interrupted and said, "It sounds to me like the woman who saved his ass and got him out of Europe is the same woman we thought was killed in Europe. Apparently, she has risen from the dead, and is pregnant at the same time. Is that a fair assessment of the situation, Jong?"

"Hot diggy damn! Jilkes, you be the best translator on earth. That woman rose from the dead and delivered a baby boy, and it ain't Allen's. Allen earlier asked her, 'what's your intent?' In a later transmission, she told him she was beyond trying to decide, and therefore, she was going to be a mother for as long as she could before they found her. She added that she felt that was going to be soon. Allen goes on to call the other woman Katyiena, a treacherous wench, who played a role in faking Helga's death. He also states that she was supposed to disappear but has since been seen in the hands of the KGB. He said she was given millions to disappear and reconstruct her facial features."

Ben Beckmire looked long and hard at the people surrounding him and said to Jong, "Your movie, go and get the star."

As Jong was heading back to the hotel, Mallory said, "It makes perfect sense in terms of timing. Asiram just gave birth and he probably had sex with them around the same time. What's the issue? To me, Ben Beckmire, you just found out surreptitiously, that you have another grandchild. Boy, Zanthius is some kind of prolific."

"Stop, it, Mallory. Not funny. Not funny at all."

As the group continued to speculate about the relationship and everything else relative to Helga, Zanthius and Jong showed up. Zanthius asked, "So, Dad, what's up?"

Ben Beckmire said, "Son, sit down in the sand and watch the ebb and flow of the water for a minute. I want you to relax and calm yourself, completely."

Zanthius sat and conjured up all kinds of scenarios as to why he was there. He even envisioned that the group had elected him to replace his father. What a dreamer!

Ben Beckmire said, "I'm not sure if you are aware or not, but we found a thumb drive in the heel of Allen's shoe. Now, Son, there is some serious contentions in that unit about things that will have a helluva impact on your life. I'm not sure that I can recount all that has been presented to me, so I'm going to let Jong give you the gist of what's on the drive."

Jong looked at Zanthius and said, "The woman Helga may not be dead. She was pregnant and had a baby, and that baby is yours. Her death was staged. This is the information that I'm gleaming from the disk."

Beckmire yelled, "Damn, Jong! How about a couple of maybes in that proposition?"

Zanthius sat there and gazed into the water, remembered what Wajickee had said about the stork and another Beckmire, and said, "Hold that thought, I'm going for a swim."

Zanthius dove into the crystal blue water and began to swim away from shore. Jong said, "There is also a not so happy message about the Carbon Factor, as well. The last one was recorded apparently not long ago, and it was from a friend of Allen's in Russia. The message states that the final aspect to the Carbon Factor formula is in her possession. It also states that it is rumored that someone called the 'idiot spy' has enough of the pieces of the formula so they at least should know how to connect all the dots by now. The rest of the stuff on the drive is cryptic and relates to potential places where he has money stashed. Now, one other discombobulated message spoke of a monastery. And of all places, in Valencia. At the end of that message, it states that there, the 'idiot spy' will find a bundle of joy."

The Sarge said, "I can only hope that it was Allen's intent to share some of this information with me prior to his demise. Okay, here comes Tarzan. I hope he has developed a strategy for telling Asiram. I don't want to be on the same planet when that goes down."

As Zanthius approached the group, he said, "At this point in time it's all conjecture. While in the outback, I dreamed that Wajickee told me that a stork would be visiting me soon. I thought he was talking about my Ben, but it turns out that he was alluding to another baby being born from my seeds."

"Son, you may think that this is an unproven mathematical or scientific theory, however, you will find a bundle of joy in a monastery in Valencia according to the last message deciphered."

"Asiram is going to kill me."

"I think we all know that's going to happen. The question is whether you want to run away, or face it like a man," Beckmire asked.

"Dad, I have more courage and character than that. I'm your son and from what I've seen, running is not an option. I will invite her to a quiet dinner on the beach and tell her all that I know and hope that she doesn't shoot my ass."

"Son, I must say your life is full of adventure. If I were to question your past, I wouldn't be surprised if you were like a 'Johnnie on the Spot' with the ladies and more reflective of a Chameleon. Not to make light of the situation, I also must thank you for getting into trouble and bringing the best friends that a man could ever have back together again for one last hurrah. So, we kind of owe you. Also, we all have gained untold wealth because of our adventures. The funny thing is, I don't think it's over. I see a lot more drama coming our way because one of Allen's messages indicates you and Helga are the only ones that have the final aspects of the formula for the Carbon Factor. In other words, you may have the formula but you are overlooking something. If that premise is correct, it's probably very ordinary and you're not placing enough credence to think out of the box."

"Dad, Larry has sole possession of the final part of the formula, not me."

"Wrong again, Son. According to the message, you have the final aspect. More importantly, with or without Asiram's permission or understanding of the events, there is the potential of another Beckmire, my grandson, who will not live in a monastery. I will talk to Ava and Courtney, and they will figure this one out. All you must do is come clean with Asiram. Look at all the women in this group. You don't think another baby will be well cared for?"

"Dad, please give me the luxury of having a conversation with my wife before you spread the notion. Will you allow me that courtesy?"

"Zanthius, my boy, I will allow you to do whatever you need to do. Just be mindful that me and mine have our own minds when it comes to certain things."

"Jong, I need you to continue to decipher the information on that disk, including where he has funds stashed so we can incorporate them into our accounts and set up scholarship funds for his girls. I'm not sure he wants to leave his wife with a lot of money because she has found a new gigolo. I guess we'll see how long the love lasts once the money runs out, and then maybe we can endow her as well."

"Damn, we do good work," Jong stated.

## CHAPTER FORTY

Asiram arranged for Ava and Courtney to watch the baby. None of the ladies had any idea what Asiram would be confronted with. Asiram jokingly said, "I hope that *conjeo* is not going to try to seduce me. I need more time before we play that game again and I'm going to make sure we have a family planning kit in front of us first." The women laughed and Ava said, "I'm sure you have other attributes to sustain your man during this hand off and penis out period." Once again, there was loud laughter from the two ladies. Courtney said, "I have some medicated lip gloss if you would like some." The three broke into hysterics.

As Asiram was escorted onto the beach by Mr. Carter, he said, "God is in the air tonight. He may want to wash some souls clean with his teardrops. Not to worry, I will keep an eye out for you."

Approximately thirty feet away from the table, Mr. Carter gently released his hand from Asiram's arm, and it appeared for the next thirty or so feet, Asiram Beckmire De Lombardo was floating on air. Within ten feet of their table, a tearful Zanthius Beckmire De Lombardo fell to his knees and lowered his head almost to the sand. Asiram said, "My love, your troubles are my troubles and my troubles are yours." She fell to her knees and raised her husband's head until it was eye level with hers. Asiram said, "Those are not tears of joy, but they should be. Our child is God's gift to our family and friends. There is nothing that is going to shake or deter me from loving you, Zanthius Beckmire De Lombardo, no matter your sins."

Zanthius looked deep into Asiram's eyes and said, "Helga is not dead, she had a little boy, it is alleged that he is mine, and he is in an orphanage in Spain."

Asiram's smile left her face. She stood up and yelled, "Hell no! That bitch done did it again. She ain't dead; she rose from the dead and was impregnated by my husband. I hate that bitch! I can guarantee you one thing--my mission is to find her ass and make her dead, dead, and dead some more."

Zanthius was about to say something, when Asiram in a protective manner, said, "Honey, please, get off your knees. It makes you look weak, and weak you are not. I had some horrible visions and dreams in the outback, and I'll be damned if that wasn't one of them. I received a message about three months ago, that simply stated, 'bundle of joy'. I thought it was about one of our group. I also realized that Allen, may the fish enjoy his ass, shared a relationship with Helga. I say all of that to say, I am going to tell your mother and Courtney. I'm also going to tell Jong that we need one of the G550s to fly to Spain. I'm guessing that is where the child is, right?"

Zanthius looked at Asiram and said, "Stop playing games. Did my father intercede on my behalf? Did he tell you about the cryptic messages from Wajickee and/or the information from Allen that alluded to the fact that Helga delivered a baby and he's in an orphanage in Valencia?"

"Damn, I thought it was Barcelona. Anyway, I'm taking our child and going to look for your other child, Rabbit!"

"Why are you calling me 'Rabbit'?"

"Because they are, other than cockroaches, the only other species that I know that procreates faster than you, my darling. I love you, and we weren't married at the time. We all made adult decisions. The outcome is just 'beautiful' as the newly elected person in the USA would say."

"Asiram, stop the bullshit. Tell me your real feelings."

"I don't like the position that your actions place me in, but I am your new wife, and this union occurred prior to my meeting you and you seducing me. In that light, I find compassion and benevolence, as well as the ability to want to keep you from telling a story, that is not true in order to hide the facts."

"I will never lie to you my wife, but I will bend the truth on small issues to maintain the peace. I don't know the status of Helga, but I wonder why she would callously place a child she birthed in a monastery."

Asiram thought for a second before saying, "Honey, I think her staged event was flawed, and the Russian government knew she had proprietary information that could eliminate any future failures and deaths associated with their attempts to cultivate the Carbon Factor. She is a traitor to them and needs to be found. Therefore, all Russian assets are probably focused on the truth of her existence or death. She is a defector and they want her for so many reasons. I believe her actions are all that were available to her—she's on the run.

"If in fact the stories about her are real, and not a fabrication to lure you out into the open, then we must assume they think that you know something or have other aspects of the formula that will finalize their development of the Carbon Factor. In any event, there are a lot of assumptions that we must deal with. Insofar as the notion of Zanthius's number two is concerned, we must first confirm certain rumors about Helga. We can't go blindly into what could be a trap. I know that at the very least, Walter would assume if a child were involved that we are much too morale to leave it in a monastery."

Zanthius agreed, "First of all, we need to speak to my father, and if I know him, he is not going to divide his team and besides, my Mom will get a chance to check on her properties and figure out where in Valencia the child might be. I'll have to ask Jong to scan that disk again and see if the name of the child is included. Let's go and see my father and get his take on what we should do."

"Honey, I want to have dinner first. I took the liberty of ordering for both of us when you asked me out to dinner. Mr. Carter had fresh lamb chops flown in from the mainland and I am chomping at the bit for some."

# # #

During dinner, the Sarge and Courtney strolled along the beach and stopped where Asiram and Zanthius were dining. He asked, "Are we good?"

Zanthius replied, "We're better than good."

"I mean did you two have the needed conversation?"

"Daddy-in-Law, we did, and I want to use that little plane to fly to Spain with both of my mothers-in-law. Is that going to be a problem?"

"Of course not. What I would prefer you do first is to have the rabbit present his case to the team."

"Why are you calling him a rabbit? That's the same thing I called him."

"I mean if the information is correct, then he would have to be related to the, Leporidae, the scientific name for rabbit. Come now, two children who apparently were born days apart? That's called overtime! Anyway, I don't like the notion of dividing our resources. Don't worry *conjeo*, I'll present it to the guys and get their approval."

"Mr. Beckmire, you know I'm doing this with or without you, don't you?"

Courtney said, "Ben, you know I have to stick with my daughter-in-law on this one and I'm sure Ava, Somara, Yeshida, Okema, Mary Alice, Marisa, Yvette, Monica, Rashida, and everybody else are going to side with her. And besides, it might be good for Ava and Zanthius to visit their home."

"This is tantamount to blackmail. That is not how a group, or a society operates. You are going to congregate with all the females and then rally them against the men and if we say no, then we will feel your wrath in a more profound manner. Is that what you're basically saying?"

"Honey, I think you hit the head with a nail—ouch!"

"I just want to be sure before I spread the word that there was a shadow meeting of people of another gender who are threatening to withhold certain earthly endeavors if the other gender does not assist them in locating the alleged child of my extremely prolific son. Is this information correct?"

"Daddy-in-Law, I knew you would find a way to book this trip. The withholding of certain privileges will certainly get most people's attention. You are the best daddy-in-law in the whole world."

"You bribe me and then throw accolades at me? What a hustle. Enjoy your dinner."

# # #

Ben said to Courtney, "I haven't seen a lot of my daughter lately, have you?"

"I was thinking about that this morning. I haven't seen Juan either. I wonder if they killed each other," they laughed.

Ben said, "Everyone is an adult with adult needs. I think our little lady would be offended if we started poking around in her business at this point. I would hate to have to kill Juan if he has hurt my baby. I love where we are because I could feed him to the fish."

Courtney looked at him and said, "Not funny. Allen turned out to be a good person, after all of his mean-spirited events."

"Yes, he did, but I cannot forget, or forgive the number of times he engaged people to kill us. Somehow, I liked him, but I kept both eyes on his ass."

As they continued to walk along the beach, Beckmire saw Chris and told Courtney that he needed to have word with him. He approached Chris and asked, "When are you due in Minnesota?"

"I have an appointment three weeks from Tuesday. Why do you ask?"

"We are probably going to leave here in the next day or so for Spain to try to locate a monastery that might be holding a baby--one of our own."

"Oh, I see. If I had to guess, I would pick Zanthius as the father. He reminds me of a *conjeo*."

Ben broke into laughter that was pretty much uncontrollable.

Chris inquired, "What's so funny?"

"That is exactly what I called him, and his wife had called him, prior to me calling him that. And now here you are calling him a rabbit, he wouldn't believe me if I told him. Anyway, the people who attended to Allen, do they have any other skills?"

Chris said, "The mother is a helluva cook, one of the sisters is a certified CPA, the other is in college and the brother has a degree in business from the University of Florida."

"Oh my, such talent. Is the brother a person who can be trusted?"

"The entire family is trustworthy. What was done to their sister and my daughter was despicable, and there was no arrest. The sister, unknowingly to the person who raped her, took a photo of him. From what I heard, he came back later that night and tried to violate her in another manner. She was apparently drugged, and after the man in the picture had his way with her, he allowed four members of his protection squad to do whatever they wanted to her. They kept feeding her drugs and forcing injections until she over-dosed. They took her to Haines Point and placed a bill in her mouth and dropped her off where the statue 'Hand that's rising from the ground', used to be."

"Chris, would there be a problem if you hired your son and his mother?"

"Oh no, Ben. They are very respectable people. However, you can't hurt people because you are powerful and think you can get away with it. Your friend got what was coming to him. The problem may be he wasn't sentenced by a court of law."

"Chris, he was not my friend. Just so that you know, he is responsible for the deaths of over 200 men and women. He sent them to our farm to kill us. He was not a friend, never has been and never would be. He tried to kill me. I converted him when his boss turned on him and put a contract on his ass. Not a friend of mine. Anyway, my point is precise, is the brother, sorry Chris, is your son a person who you could train, mentor, and show the ropes?"

Chris's eyes watered up and he started to cry. Beckmire asked, "What is it about that question that brings you to tears?"

"Man, you no understand the relationships on this here island. I trust everyone including those fools who tried to kidnap Ms. Asiram. Truth be told, I would have assisted or committed the crime against your friend. Sorry, I mean against your guest, Allen. For the person he killed was remarkably close to me--she was my youngest daughter."

Beckmire looked at him and his eyes filled with water. At every juncture, he wanted to say something. However, the words would not come out. Beckmire finally manifested a few sounds that were unintelligible. He cleared his throat and said, "Can you summon them here now?"

Chris pulled out his phone and made a call. It would be a while before anyone showed up, but he knew they would be there.

Courtney walked over to her husband and asked, "Honey, what's wrong?"

"All is good, I will tell you later, but for now, I need to have a few more moments of privacy with Chris. Chris, will you walk on the beach with me?"

"Of course, Ben."

As the two men walked along the beach, Beckmire asked, "Did you have any input into the demise of my guest?"

"Mr. Beckmire, I did not know what was happening and when I found out about it, the die had been cast and the man was dead." Chris looked at Ben and inquired, "What if I did have a hand in that mess, what would be your reaction?"

"Chris, let me tell you a story. This group gathered because someone tried to kill my son that I didn't know I had, his mother, my wife and me. I called my friends and told them about my problem and since then, we have been kicking butts all over the world. Let me make it crystal clear to you. We don't do drugs or anything that could be classified as such. What we do is right the wrong that people like the guy who is now fish bait, tried to do. He enslaved people. We liberate people.

"There was no need for us to develop a business relationship with you. It happened because we accidently found out that you were about to forfeit your life's work and we realized that the place was in a state of disrepair. It was in horrible shape, but it offered us an epic view of the water and a calming foundation for reflection. In other words, it made us feel at ease and safe." Ben was about to say something else when he saw a figure approaching him rapidly. He turned to Chris and said, "I got this. Stay behind me."

Courtney walked into view and yelled, "Hey, stop in your damn tracks or I will blow your head off."

Chris yelled, "Stop! Everyone stop! That's my son!"

Jilkes and John Lee appeared from out of the shadows and Jilkes said, "We had his ass covered from the start."

Courtney asked, "What were you going to do? Throw sand at him?"

Jilkes said, "Ms. Courtney, you ought to know we don't roll like that." He flashed his weapon and so did John Lee.

John Lee inquired, "Where you be getting that thing from?"

"I have friends in high places," she said.

John Lee said to the stranger, "We don't be knowing you, and therefore, I be needing to search you. If you resist, that there black guy will shoot you in the ass. Do we be having an accord?"

"My dad called me and that is why I'm here."

398 c. benjamin lattimore

"Who be your dad?" John Lee asked. The man looked at him and then said, Mr. Carter." John Lee and Jilkes in harmony said to each other, "Oh yeah, the missing fingertip."

"My mother and sister are on their way here as well. Please don't pull weapons on them. Dad, what is this about?"

"Son, I want you to meet the devils that you said I sold out to, as opposed to having the bank take, steal, and leave me without a penny."

"Dad, I said that then because I was grieving for my sister. I saw the person in the picture she sent me, and I lost all focus on reality. I am planning to turn myself in to the police tomorrow to alleviate any problems for mom and my sisters."

Beckmire said, "Whoa, wait a minute. There is no need to be doing anything like that. I called you here to meet you. I'm not a judge and I sure as hell don't want to hear about a guest who went fishing at night and fell overboard. I called this meeting to ascertain and understand your skill set. Your dad needs to have a procedure done on the mainland and I just wanted to know if you can run the resort until he recuperates? I don't know anything about anything else. Can you help at the resort is all I want to know?"

"Dad, who are these people?" the young man asked.

"They are my partners and they want to know if you can operate this business while I go for treatment in Minnesota?"

"Why can't I come with you?"

"Trust me and trust my judgement. My partners have an engagement in Spain that they must attend to. It might take them a while to figure out where the individual is that they are looking for. Therefore, they don't want to take the chance of the resort being without leadership. You're an educated man and perhaps smarter than I am. I know about your dreams of acting and singing, but by now, Son, you have learned that there are obstacles to success in those trades. I'm paid a huge salary and I will direct that to you if you successfully operate the resort while I'm in Minnesota. Son, you don't have many options. It's called plug and play. You will play because they have video of my family slashing, stabbing, and cutting a guest. You will show up here tomorrow at 7 a.m. to begin a new life that may require you to kiss some ass. When your mom and one of your sisters arrive, I will assign tasks to them as well. You did what I wanted to do, but you didn't include me. You hung your mother and sisters out to dry and now I'm trying to find a way to rewash them. Not many options available."

## CHAPTER FORTY-ONE

Jong continued to analyze the flash drive that was in the heel of Allen's shoe. The only word that consistently was used when speaking about options for Helga's child was the word 'route'. Later that morning, Jong saw Zanthius, Asiram, and the baby in the restaurant. He walked over and started making gestures. Asiram indicated that the baby was asleep.

Jong said, "Okay, but I need to have a word with Zanthius." The two men walked away from the table and Jong said, "I've look at that disk many times and no names stick out. The word 'route' was used several times and it no make sense to me where it's used."

Zanthius thought about what Jong had said and thanked him. As he rejoined Asiram, he said, "I'll be damned." He yelled for Jong. When Jong reappeared, he left the table again and said, "Jong, can you show me where Allen and Helga used that word?"

Jong opened his Apple laptop and selected the file. Zanthius saw the several notations using the word 'route' that did not make sense to Jong. He looked at the entire passage and yelled, "Route is significant. It is the Route of the Monasteries of Valencia. If I'm not mistaken, it is the directions to the Five Monasteries in Valencia. If, in fact, that is the case, I must figure out which one is where my son is being cared for! I need to speak to my mother and see if she knows anyone who can get us access and information. Jong, you are all they say you are. You are, both Mr. Amazing and the Master of Tenacity. I thank you so very much for your dedication to helping me figure this one out."

At the table, Zanthius told Asiram what he and Jong had discovered, and he wanted to confirm certain aspects of the monasteries with his mother. Asiram said, "I hope I can handle two little rambunctious boys. Will you help me, Zanthius?"

"Asiram, Venus de Milo could summon me, and I would have to tell her that I love my wife so much that I would prefer death rather than be involved with another woman. Insofar as helping you, I plan on being a full-time father with house duties to share. You are my life and my soul. And after you accepted and decided to lead the charge into this unknown territory, I will exponentially serve us to make sure that our house is always in order. You are my heartbeat. Never forget that."

Rashida, LaGina, and Juan entered the restaurant and Zanthius asked, "Rashida, where have you been?"

"This little rabbit has been trying to prove a point! He wants to marry me and have more children. He thinks sex is the way to make all of that happen. Rumor has it that there may be another one for you guys to take care of. Is that true?"

"We are trying to put the pieces together to see if, in fact, that is true."

"Asiram, are you good with that?"

"Rashida, after all that we have been through, I'm pretty much good with anything that keeps us together. When I say us, I mean this entire network of strange and diverse people."

Rashida walked over to Asiram and whispered in her ear, "Now, I can honestly say I love you and mean it. Those words mean so much to me because they remind me of when the Sarge and Courtney took a gamble on two wayward kids; me and Larry and welcomed us into their home without any rules other than to respect the home and the occupants. Now, Girl I got your six and if Zanthius makes a left turn, I'll be there to make his ass go right. Just kidding, my brother. What a perfect scenario. If this story is true and I'm sure it is, because we don't do fantasy, that takes the burden off you to have more children."

"Rashida, I want a little flower, like LaGina."

#

Ava and Courtney entered the restaurant and saw Zanthius, Rashida, Juan, LaGina, Asiram and the baby, and headed straight for them. Zanthius said, "Mom and mother, we need to figure out some new titles. Courtney, my mother has earned the title of mom. What would you like me to call you?"

"Zanthius, what would you like to call me?"

"I would like to think about it and decide at another time. More importantly, mothers, I think I have a beginning clue as to where, if in fact the story is true, my alleged child is, at least in the general vicinity. Mom, or rather mothers, thanks to Jong looking carefully at every word, I believe that the child is in the 'Route of the Monasteries in Valencia'. This may present a slight problem because there are five connected Monasteries in Valencia. Has anyone seen my father?"

Courtney said, "Look behind you, he's outside having a conversation with Jong and Gladstone. If I had to make a bet, he is setting the stage for us to leave."

# # #

Beckmire walked into the restaurant and headed into the kitchen where he was confronted by a woman he did not know or had not seen on the property. As he approached her, she said, "You must be the eyes behind this group?"

"No ma'am, I be the eyes in front of this group. Who might you be?"

"My ex-husband is Mr. Carter, and he demanded that I be here to begin my training. I told him that he no longer determined what I did, but he assured me that it was either I do this, or you show certain officers a video."

"That is not true because I don't know what happened. Insofar as I'm concerned, my guest fell off the boat while fishing at night. My name is Ben Beckmire. What is your name?"

"Man, you know my name, why you want to start off playing games?"

Chris Carter came into the kitchen and said, "Woman, you will follow the script, or you will play solitary in prison. This is my boss and he no know your damn name. Stop acting like you control something. You no control a damn thing, and if you don't want to see the video that puts you, your son and your daughters under the prison, then I suggest you keep your damn mouth shut."

"Chris, you are part owner and manager of this place. If this lady is going to be that disrespectful to one your guests, then I suggest you place her somewhere out of the reach and eyesight of the guests."

"Beckmire, this woman is a good woman, but with a hard head. I will spend time explaining the relationships and then she will join the team, I promise you. She has no options."

# # #

When Beckmire entered the restaurant, Zanthius yelled, "Pops, come here for a moment, please."

"What's up? Hi, honey. What's up, Son?"

"I think we have narrowed the possible location of my alleged child and it's Valencia, Spain. You and my mother apparently met there and had lunch at the McDonald's. Asiram gave you no options yesterday, but I'm taking a different approach than my wife. We need to go to Spain, and we need to go soon. We have three jets for the group. Can we use the 550 to make the trip?"

The Sarge looked at all who were in front of him and said, "You people know I don't like separating my resources. How about we all take a trip to Spain and try to sort this thing out? First, I find the story to be incredulous, but the rabbit is the rabbit. We will need all our resources there to protect each other. Listen, I want to have a meal. The plane is being prepared and the pilot is putting in an alternative route just in case we are being set up. I know you unconventional types take advantage of us by the book types."

After the Sarge started to walk away, Zanthius turned to his mother who was busy holding her new grandson, and said, "Mom, the Monasteries in Valencia, why are they termed, Route of the Monasteries?"

"Son, you should know that. It's because they are connected somewhat. Any good Catholic from Spain should know that, especially people from the Valencia area."

Ava paused for a moment and realized the nature of the question. She then said, "Oh my God! Oh, my God! She placed the child in our back yard. How could she have known, and why would she choose Valencia? More confusing, is which Monastery out of the five did she select?"

"So, Mom, you think this might be correct? I mean why would anyone go that far to fabricate a relationship and create a destination for a child? This thing, or adventure, has grown from protect our immediate family to now searching for a child that may or may not exist. I'm perplexed about the options as well as the validity. Not sure about this one but I know I must have my father with us to succeed," Zanthius responded.

"Zanthius, your dad, my daddy-in-law, is critical to all we do. I would never recommend we do this kind of action alone, and that is why I have enlisted the services of all my ladies to withhold from giving certain pleasures until we have been there and done that, in Spain. I would suggest that you make it a high priority on your father's list. Oh, and by the way, remind him that his wife is in on this deal as well."

"Honey, we already went through this thing. Everyone is on board."

"No harm in reinforcing the notion. Ratify it and confirm a lift off time and date, my love, and then all will be good."

# # #

Mallory went to the Sarge and asked, "Why is this Spain thing so big? We already said we were going to do this, but why are they acting like we're not? We realize they hold us in their grip because of what they have between their legs— neither brains nor brawn, nevertheless an important tool. I said to my wife and partner that all would be good. As I approached the subject of sex, she said to me, 'until a plane that I am on is on its way to Spain, there will be no roll over and help yourself."

"WTF?" The one I'm married to said, "I know all of the issues and if you fail in this mission, you and your boys will understand the power of women united."

"She said that to you?" Mallory inquired.

"She not only threatened me but told me to occupy another room until that plane is in the air and pointed towards Spain," Beckmire confirmed.

Courtney was noticeably clear as she waltzed into the room, and said, "There is a rebellion in progress, and I think that Spain thing had better happen soon. We have a Beckmire in an orphanage, and that is not where Beckmire's reside. You have 24 hours or we're out of here on our own."

"Honey, please don't do ultimatums. Anything could occur that might change the nature of this event. Let me work through the issues. Also, realize that I'm on your side no matter if it be stupid or crazy. I love my wife and there is nothing I wouldn't do for her. I just ask her, and her rabid partners, to allow me to secure one scene before we start filming the next scene."

Courtney looked at Ben and said, "It's that silver/gold tongue that got me into a lifelong commitment with you. Now, that I'm in it, I need you to simply say that when my wife gives me a command or a suggestion, I'm on it without any discussion. Let me hear you say that honey."

Mallory said, "I have to leave, I can't bear to hear my leader humble himself to his wife in front of me." At the precise moment Mallory was leaving, Jong appeared at their door. Courtney saw Jong, and said, "We're busy. Can the matter that led you to our door, wait?"

"Everything I know can wait. I came to tell the Sarge that I know that the child has the final portion of the Carbon Factor formula and that we should leave immediately for Spain."

"The Sarge is ready to leave. Ain't you, Sarge?"

"Jong, spread the word. We are out of here in two hours. Let the process begin."

Ben Beckmire looked at Courtney and said, "Baby, you don't have to threaten me. Any rational proposition on your part motivates me to action. However, I realize that sometimes it is nice to forge a bond, present a proposition, and demand a consequence. Listen, they're all important to me but there is only one woman who can mandate a reaction from me, and that is you. Honey, I'm yours and you're mine. No need for games! Just say what you want, and I will make it happen. Do you think that I want my grandson in a monastery? Get real honey; we're on the same page. I guess the women sometimes wind you up because they know that you control the trigger— me. I love you, Courtney, and this was going to happen anyway. I just have to take care of a few things while we're here, and then we are bound for that magical place in Spain."

"Ben Beckmire, you say that with a smile. I would hate to perform open heart surgery on your ass."

"Me too, baby. Me too!"

the end

also in the 'idiot spy' series